Pink Sand and Parasites

A fictitious account of events leading up to
one of the darkest days in the history of Bermuda.

Also by the author:
Java Jaunt, published by Amazon in 2012.

4

Dedicated to the ladies in my life, especially Elaine, for her enthusiastic support and providing the drawings – and to the people of Bermuda.

Chapter One

August, 1972

The piercing screech of a metal bucket scraping on the stone-tiled floor set my teeth on edge, causing me to start and swing round. Dripping sweat parted company with the end of my nose and arched through the humid air. Just inside the doorway, leaning heavily on the end of a mop-stale and peering up at me, was the tiny figure of a woman, her head covered in a brightly coloured turban. She was wearing a buttoned floral dress, which reached almost to the floor, not quite covering her bare feet. A man's tie, knotted around her waist, completed the ensemble.

"*Hi,*" she drawled grinning, "*I'm Dilly, your next-door neighbour,*" her voice pleasantly husky, with a faint West Indian lilt. "*I figured you folks could use some help cleaning the place up a bit.*" She grasped the pole with both hands and leaned even more heavily, a huge pair of brown eyes smiled out of an evenly featured, coffee-coloured face. Long dangling earrings, each featuring a colourful parrot reached halfway down her cheeks.

"*Hello,*" I stuttered, thrusting out a damp hand. She looked at it but her hands never left the mop. Awkwardly I let my arm drop, slightly offended.

"*If you move, I'll start with this floor,*" she announced, standing upright for the first time. "*I'll mop the kitchen.*" Even upright, this child-woman barely reached my chest.

"*But why would you want to help?*" I asked rather stupidly, "*or did Mrs Harding ask you?*" She laughed, a chesty, infectious, satisfying sound.

"*You must be English.*" It was a statement not a question. "*I figured it was the best way of getting to know who's living next door, without peering from behind the curtain,*" she chuckled and grasping the handle of the bucket, lifted it into the stone sink and turned on the tap. Water dribbled out, spluttering like a sick child. "*Best not drink this,*" she called out over her shoulder. "*It hasn't rained lately and no-one has lived here for some time.*" I didn't grasp the significance but I didn't say anything, I was jet-lagged and more than a little overwhelmed by the day's events. The slow progress of filling the bucket obviously caused my unsolicited helper some frustration for she suddenly hissed, "*Man... you'd better call the water company and get yourself a load of water.*" When the bucket was half full, she turned off the tap, gripped the handle with both hands and prepared to hoist it over the edge of the sink.

I stepped forward: "*Let me!*" I said, reaching towards her.

8

"No I can manage," she moved between the sink and me, stood on tiptoes and lifted it clear, slopping a few drops on the floor and down the front of her dress. We have a stubborn and independent lady here, I thought and discovered later what an understatement this was and what a profound effect this stubborn and independent lady would have on my life.

My new boss appeared suddenly through the front door: *"I've turned the electricity on, I'll show... Oh you have a helper."* As recognition dawned I thought I saw her expression harden.

Barely lifting her eyes from the wet patch of floor, Dilly nodded and continued mopping. *"No one lived here for a while, things get dusty."*

"Well, that's very kind!" I thought my boss sounded too enthusiastic. She turned to me, *"Come, I'll show you where the electrical switches are."* I followed her outside and round the back of the tiny single-storied house Fastened on the wall, with a minimum of protection was a large fuse box and half a dozen switches. She explained the function of each switch and I grunted understanding, I'd been awake for almost twenty hours, almost ten of which had been spent sitting on a plane or in airports, to say I wasn't really compos mentis was an understatement. Mrs Harding sensed my weariness: *"I'm leaving now, I suggest you get some sleep, I'll be back tomorrow morning about ten to show you the school and the nearest grocery store."* She looked at my long trousers - *"and the shop where you can buy some shorts! There's beer, water, sandwiches and fruit in the fridge, that should keep you going."* She smiled, as I

9

thanked her profusely for collecting me from the airport and being so kind. She walked purposefully towards her small car chattering about how I would soon get used to the heat and humidity. I leapt ahead and opened the door. All the windows were down, and brightly coloured files were scattered on the back seat. As she started the car she turned, looked me in the eye and hissed: *"Such cheek, the place was cleaned last week. I'd encourage that woman to leave but be diplomatic – it's never wise to upset these people."* I nodded, unsure of what she meant. The engine coughed into life and she pulled out into the lane, I watched as she disappeared into the distance, leaving a trail of white exhaust fumes drifting hypnotically beneath the tunnel of pink oleanders and palm trees. Flopping against a tree, conscious of the rivulets of sweat running down my body, I contemplated the building, which was to be my new home. The freshly white-painted walls and massive roof tiles, constructed of local limestone, relentlessly reflected the early afternoon sun. The simple structure stood on its own, in the lee of a clump of whispering pines. I discovered later that they were called Casuarinas and tens of thousands had been planted to replace the native Bermuda Cedar that had succumbed to disease in the 1940's. Some twenty yards to the right stood a double-fronted bungalow, painted a very pale shade of blue, surrounded by a low hibiscus hedge that sprouted saucer-sized salmon coloured flowers. On the far side of the house, providing deep shade was a huge tree, the like of which I had never seen before. Even now in the middle of summer it had a scattering of red flowers fluttering like exotic birds amid the branches. I presumed this house was where my mysterious maid lived, for it was some hundred yards to the nearest house, away to the left, separated by a dip filled with brambles. Rising up from this dip were two magnificent Royal Palm trees standing sentinel, while the whole area around the house was covered in short, scorched grass.

I was awoken from my surveying by a shout from the helper now standing in the front doorway. *"Can I make you some tea?"*

"Yes, that would be great," I ambled towards her. *"Is that your house?"* I nodded towards the blue bungalow.

"Yes, that's were I live." In the kitchen she had laid out two cups and saucers and one plate, almost covered by a huge piece of carrot-cake. I lowered myself wearily onto a chair while she busied herself pouring water into a china pot. *"Mon, you look bushed. How far you come today?"* I explained I had flown from London to New York, sat about at JFK for three hours and then caught the flight here. Before I could say more I caught sight of a movement at the doorway - the huge round eyes of a child peered round the jamb. As I watched, another pair of eyes peering out of a smaller face edged into view. I couldn't help but grin at their mischievous expressions.

Dilly sensed my gaze and without turning round called out: *"If it's who I think it is, come in and say good afternoon nicely."* After a great deal of giggling and pushing the smallest child dashed in and threw her arms around Dilly's legs. Two others followed and also wrapped themselves round their mother. Four pairs of eyes pierced my sagging body. *"Let me go and stand up so I can*

11

introduce you to our new English neighbour." The two older girls disentangled themselves and stood self-consciously. *"This is Pearl, she's the oldest."* Dilly gently pushed her towards me.

"Hello Pearl, pleased to meet you." Following her mother's snub, I just smiled but Pearl thrust out her hand. I hurriedly grasped the tiny fingers. *"How old are you?"* I asked.

"Ten last month, 23rd to be exact; what's your name?"

"Cross, Jack Cross."

"Good to meet you Mr Cross, you've got a nice smile," she said politely.

I was introduced to eight-year-old Renee and five year old Vernee before their mother sent them packing to play outside.

In the aftermath of the whirlwind it was suddenly quiet. *"Great girls,"* I said sipping the tea.

Dilly nodded. *"Eat your cake,"* she ordered, *"I made it fresh today."* She resumed mopping, humming softly to herself, in between bouts of relentless questioning. After about an hour or so Dilly left and I unpacked. I'd only brought two modestly sized suitcases and everything easily fitted into the bedroom cupboards. Kicking off my shoes, I flopped on the bed and gazed through the wide-open window at the bright blue sky. The last I heard was the sea breeze gently conversing with the Casuarinas and the distant shouts of children before drifting off into a fitful sleep.

About midnight I woke and padded off to the fridge for a beer. It was pitch black and pleasantly cool. Propped

12

back on the bed I could just make out the silhouette of the Royal Palms against an amazingly clear, starlit sky. I mulled over the day's events, cursing the fact I was wide-awake when all respectable people were asleep.

*

The decision to apply for the teaching job in Bermuda had not been given the level of rational thought, which I usually brought to my decision-making. I had been through the most painful and distressing time in my life and needed to get away to save my sanity. A drunken driver had criminally snatched my darling wife, of two years, away from me. The procession of events marched vividly through my head, yet again. Jilly had been teaching an evening class that dark, wet December night and was walking to the bus stop just at the precise moment an otherwise respectable businessman, fell asleep at the wheel, having *over-indulged* at the office party. His words muttered at the court case. His car had mounted the pavement and totally devastated my life - that sounds selfish but poor Jilly knew nothing, she was killed instantly.

The aftermath was an indistinct fog, the policeman at the door, the hospital morgue, the sobbing in-laws, the heart-wrenching funeral and later the court case - all the events now merged into one agonising blur. When it was all over and the numbness was beginning to abate, I decided that putting distance between the situation might ease the pain and lift my dejected spirits. Browsing the *Times Educational Supplement* in the staffroom one Friday, a general advertisement for teachers to work in Bermuda caught my attention. I read it several times and went off to the library to find out where the hell Bermuda was. No it wasn't in the West Indies, where my limited Geography had supposed. It was in fact one thousand miles north of the Bahamas and eight hundred miles from Cape Hatteras, North Carolina. In fact, not much over an hour's flying time from New York. I had written a half-hearted letter of application, been interviewed at the Bermuda tourist office in London and a week later offered a job. I wrote a letter of acceptance without much thought – I just had this urge to do something different in a totally new environment. Well, from first impressions it certainly seemed different: the wall of heat and humidity that hit me as I left the plane, officials in tailored shorts and knee-length socks with jackets and ties, the vivid turquoise sea and glorious white sands - it was different. I coined the adjective *kodachromatic* driving from the airport, for at first glimpse, it appeared a photographers' paradise, everything was saturated in vivid colours.

*

The moment I left the British Airways' VC10 and strolled across the tarmac the humidity turned me to instant jelly. My unsuitable clothes stuck to my body like a wetsuit. The terminal building was even worse despite huge fans idly rotating the foetid air and the queue to have one's papers checked moved at a pace to match the heat. Eventually my papers were stamped and somewhat grudgingly, I thought, the officials allowed me in to share their island paradise.

Outside the terminal most of my fellow passengers were being calmly transferred into taxis, the contrast with JFK or Heathrow could not have been greater. There were smiles and laughter and gentleness. The Headmistress of the school, Mrs Harding, had written to say she would meet me and so, while waiting, I wandered away from the main entrance seeking a glimpse of the sea but didn't get very far when she arrived; a tall, slender woman in her early fifties, with near blonde hair set in tight curls. She had a natural smile and I immediately took a liking to her. She invited me to come and meet Maurice and headed for the parking area. Maurice turned out to be a battered Morris Minor convertible, with the roof up. *"The sun is too hot at this time of day"* she explained.

The airport is situated at the extreme end of the Bermuda archipelago built mostly on reclaimed land. The school, Mrs Harding told me, was right at the other end some twenty miles away. This first journey was a revelation. For a start the maximum speed allowed was twenty miles an hour and so it was a wonderful ambling trip. We drove along narrow well-kept roads, edged by a bewildering array of colourful plants and trees and sometimes so close to the sea I could feel and taste the salty spray. There were picturesque bridges, pastel coloured houses, tiny coves, white sands, grand looking hotels, modest holiday cottages, and boats of every description. And the smells, my nose was filled with the heavy fragrances of frangipani, oleander and scents I did not recognise – I was entranced. At one point the road took us through the middle of a golf course with warning signs to watch out for flying golf-balls! Throughout the trip, Evelyn, as Mrs Harding insisted on being called, kept up a running commentary about her island home and the names of the places we passed: Castle Harbour, Long Bird Bridge, Blue Hole, Willingham Bay, Harrington Sound,

Devils Hole, John Smith's Bay, Spittal Pond. We stopped above Horseshoe Bay, Bermuda's largest beach and again I marvelled at the colours, the endless horizon, the cotton wool clouds, white surf on the distant reefs and savoured the strong, warm onshore breeze carrying with it yet another barrage of unfamiliar scents. I couldn't wait to explore - and sample that unreal sea.

Twenty minutes later we were in Long Bay Lane and driving down the colourful tunnel formed by the pink oleanders. Halfway down, Evelyn drove off the road and bumped onto the grass. *"Well there it is,"* she said, *"your new home. I'm sure you'll like it."* She switched off the engine and for a moment there wasn't a sound except for pollen-seeking bees and a distant Kiskadee.

"Well," I said to myself, *"You wanted something out of the ordinary, looks like you might have found it!"*

*

I woke with a painful start, immediately wide-awake through some sixth sense. The bed was close to the window, which I had left wide open, protected only by a thin wire mesh fly-screen. I glimpsed a male black face no more three feet away from my own, which caused my heart to thump, though he instantly disappeared. I leapt out of bed and quickly checked my belongings; my wallet, watch and camera were still on the chest where I had left them. Whoever he was, he hadn't been inside, I felt sure. I threw on some clothes and rushed outside, it was just light with a faint glow in the eastern sky from the rising sun, still well below the horizon. I quickly circled the building but there was no sign of anyone. Despite my anger at the intrusion I was aware that the early morning air was wonderfully fresh and cool. The land at the back of the bungalow, under the Casuarinas, was higher than the surrounding area and I scrambled up for a better view. Some hundred yards away were another couple of cottages but no one in sight anywhere. I walked out to the lane and wandered fifty yards or so in each direction. Nothing. As I was up and wide-awake I decided to go and explore. I grabbed an apple from the fridge, shut the windows and let myself out, carefully locking the door behind me. Once in the lane, I turned left and strolled under the oleanders. I came to a house with a row of dramatic Bird of Paradise plants edging the property and determined to return later with my camera. Further on a couple of upturned boats resembling sleeping snails lay in a garden beneath a *Boats Repaired* sign. I'd read that nowhere in Bermuda is it possible to be more than a mile away from the sea - so where was it? I stood and listened again. Absolutely no sound except for the occasional raucous cry of the *Bermuda cockerel*, the yellow fronted Kiskadee. The land away to my right rose quite steeply and I found a lane which headed upwards. I passed by a couple of half built houses, surprised to see they would both have huge cellars. Near the top of the hill the lane petered out into a footpath by which time I could hear waves gently striking the shore. I wasn't really prepared for the view as I crested the hill and stood arms akimbo for what seemed an age, soaking up the scene before me: an unspoiled rocky coast with the shimmering sea as golden as the early morning sky. Far from shore the silhouette of a small boat and a man fishing. A pair of White-Tailed Tropicbirds or Longtails, as the

17

Bermudians call them, fluttered along the low cliff, I knew they were Longtails because I had read about these harbingers of spring in a guidebook that I had picked up at JFK airport. I scrambled down to the water's edge, found a flat rock and settled down to gaze and enjoy the apple. I was only a couple of bites into the apple when barely three of four yards from me, a swimmer emerged from behind a rocky outcrop. A floppy white hat masked the face and the breaststroke motion was leisurely in keeping with the early morning calm. A female voice bubbled across the intervening water. *"You startled me, I don't usually see anyone at this time of the morning!"* She turned towards me and after a few strokes scrambled ashore. She was not wearing a swimsuit but a baggy tee shirt and equally voluminous khaki shorts. I rose, as she thrust out a hand, while removing her hat with the other. *"Miles-Smith, Laura. You must be Mr Cross."*

"How an earth do you know that?" I blustered, as she carefully chose a suitable rock and lowered herself gingerly to sit alongside me.

She laughed, *"Ah, the bush telegraph is pretty efficient in this part of the world."* She looked at me uncomfortably hard and then gazed out to sea: *"I've lived here over fifty years and I never tire of this view. Every morning it's different. The sea a different colour, the cloud formations, the movement of the sea..."* she sighed, *"We are blessed."* She rested her chin on her drawn-up knees.

"It is fabulous," I agreed. *"Really fabulous. Do you swim regularly?"*

"Every single day, all year round, and about this time before most people are up - unless the sea is too rough. Which means, all told, I probably miss a couple of months each year. I have no wish to risk my life fighting the ocean."

Were you born here Mrs Miles-Smith?" I questioned, taking in the youthful figure and shock of grey hair held back with a flowing blue ribbon.

"It's Miss - and call me Laura, the rest is such a mouthful. Yes, I was born here, fifty-seven years ago last week actually. My father was sent here by the British government, some five years before that but he's dead now. God rest his soul. I was educated here," she continued in her crisp upper-crust accent, with a hint of something not quite British. *"Left the island for university in Ottawa, then back again and never left since - accept for the odd holiday of course. You have to get off the island occasionally or you get rock-fever. So they say. Does make you appreciate the place more, if you leave now and then."* She chatted on about this and that, putting names to many of the plants that surrounded us, as well as the occasional fleeting bird. *"Do I assume from our meeting, you are an early-bird? If not you should be, it's the best time of the day;"* again the piercing gaze.

"Well, yes and no," I explained. *" I was awoken by a man outside my window, I think he may have been trying to get in. I woke with a real start."*

"Did you get a good look at him?" she asked.

"Not really, he was black and exceptionally tall, it wasn't really light," I replied.

"Oh don't worry, that would be Jimmy, he's harmless enough. He lives with his father, a boat-builder, quite close to you, a bit simple but always curious," she was trying to sound reassuring. *"He's actually quite a talented carpenter."* She slapped her knees, clambered to her feet and exclaimed: *"I must go, as much as I am enjoying our early morning chat. Must tidy up you know, before the cleaning girl comes. Silly isn't it but we all do it. Don't like the cleaning girl to think I'm untidy!"* She giggled like a schoolgirl.

I rose too. *"Yes, I should get back,"* I said.

"Come with me and I'll show you where I live, then you'll know where to come when I invite you for drinks. Do you play Bridge?"

"No, I'm afraid I have never played Bridge," I answered.

"Never mind," she continued striding off towards the lane, *"we'll soon teach you."* I was not sure what I thought about this invitation; I had always associated Bridge with snobby upper class Brits - which was not a group I wished to be associated with. We had only walked five or six paces when she opened a high wooden door set in a thick hibiscus hedge. A carved nameplate high on the door spelled out *Plymtree Cottage*; she caught my gaze, and before I could ask said: *"The place in Devon where my father came from... well here we are."*

I glanced down the short path that led to a low bungalow swamped by colourful climbers and shrubs. A mewing tabby cat stalked towards us its tail completely vertical like a radio antenna. *"The bell's on the gate post, I usually keep the door locked. I won't ask you in because the girl will be here in a moment. I will organise drinks in a week or so and introduce you to some of the locals."* I thanked her and she wrung my hand again and disappeared behind the door, her muffled voice cheerily greeting the cat.

I set off down the narrow path towards my new home thinking of what an unusual character I had just met. Very warm and friendly, like someone straight out of a colonial history book - and in her youth obviously quite a stunner. By now the sun was well up and despite walking under the heavy shadow of the trees, the temperature was rising. All thoughts of my early morning intruder dispelled from my mind, as I looked forward to what the day had to offer.

*

Maurice's squeaking hooter alerted me to the fact that my guide had arrived. I had been ready promptly at ten o'clock but when Mrs Harding didn't come I settled outside on the porch, seated in an old wooden chair and read more of the guidebook. It was now 10.45; time I was to learn was flexible and could vary according to the weather and situation.

The first port of call was a small shopping plaza comprising of a large supermarket, a drug store and a tiny menswear shop. Evelyn led me to the latter, where I was reluctantly fitted out with three pairs of knee length Bermuda shorts of varying hues and three pairs of matching knee length socks. I had tried to argue that I only needed one pair of shorts, until persuaded by Evelyn, that with one pair in the wash and one pair waiting to be ironed, three pairs were a minimum. She reminded me of my mother!

The elderly white Bermudian gentleman who was apparently taking unnatural pleasure in measuring my inside-leg, nodded in agreement.

We left the air-conditioned comfort of the small shop and climbed back into the car. *"We'll do the Piggly Wiggly supermarket last"* Evelyn announced, *"Otherwise everything will cook."* In less than two minutes we were driving under huge Casuarinas and onto the asphalt playground of the school. *"As you can see, it will take you less than ten minutes to walk to school. Long Bay Lane is at the end of the school field."*

"That's great," I responded, excited and anxious to see more.

The school comprised of two parts, an older sprawling single story building with green shutters, while in one corner stood a new, rectangular two-storey block. I was puzzled at the sight of two workmen on the roof of the old building adding fresh paint with long-handled rollers. Evelyn caught my gaze, *"The roof is painted every summer because it is our water catchment area."* She went on to explain that every house has an underground tank and rainwater is collected from the roof. This explained that what I had seen earlier in the day were not cellars being built but in fact very large water tanks. *"One learns to be very frugal with water,"* lectured Evelyn, *"Like when showering, one wets oneself, turn off the water, soap up - and wash it off. Same with the toilet – only flush when necessary. You can buy water, of course, but only as a last resort. Managing on what God provides becomes a challenge and having to buy water means you have failed!"* We moved around the outside of the building and I noticed with great satisfaction the spacious field, almost the size of three soccer pitches. I was shown the airy hall, which doubled as a gymnasium, a well-stocked, musty-smelling library and a minimally equipped science laboratory. Back in Evelyn's neat but sparsely furnished office we discussed my role. Although I had been teaching Mathematics and Physical Education for almost ten years, she wanted me to teach all subjects to a class of twelve year olds – and take responsibility for the P.E. programme throughout the school. After a long discussion about how this was to be achieved she led me to the new block and up to my classroom on the top floor where she left me to check the resources, while she returned to the office promising to take me to lunch in an hour's time.

I hauled up the blinds, gasped and took in the view. How could anyone concentrate sufficiently to teach or learn in such a room? There were large windows on three sides, one overlooked the roof of the old building, the other the neighbouring pastel coloured houses and gardens, while through the third was a distant view of the sea dotted with small sailing boats. It was just too bright with all the blinds up and I experimented until I didn't continually squint. There was no air-conditioning in the school and so I also needed to throw open some windows. This done, I stood in front of the chalkboard and viewed my classroom. Twelve double desks, a couple of cupboards, a number of empty bookshelves and several large cardboard boxes piled in the corner. My gaze returned to the sea. How Jilly would have loved this. I folded my arms gripping my chest, thinking of the time we visited the Peloponnese in Greece, where we spent two weeks in a secluded village luxuriating in the sun and sea. But if anything, this was even more special. Unbidden, a tear ran down my cheek and dripped off the end of my chin to join the moisture on my sweat-soaked shirt. '*Oh Jilly*,' I choked, '*why did you agree to fill in for the sick teacher that miserable fatal night?*' Getting a grip on my emotions I heaved one of the boxes on to a desk and began sorting.

I felt that I had hardly made a start of checking the materials when Evelyn called and said we must go shopping and get some lunch. I closed the windows, dropped the rest of the blinds and sped down the steps, my spirits lifted by the bright room, at the quality of the resources and the thought of soon being back with children again. Even Evelyn noticed the spring in my step and commented.

The Piggly Wiggly supermarket was a revelation. Firstly it was heavily air-conditioned, such that many of the workers wore cardigans over their white overalls. And the products were mostly American and unfamiliar. I watched, as Evelyn filled the trolley with exotic sounding items including Pepperidge Farm soup; Betty Crocker Pudding and Hellmann's Real Mayonnaise. At the tills polite but giggling teenagers packed the purchases into brown-paper bags. I noticed they were all black, while most of the cashiers were of Portuguese origin. I commented about this once we were outside coping with the heat that seared up from the tarmac. Evelyn replied that it was probable the girls on the tills were related to the Portuguese owner. After quickly filling my fridge with our purchases we chugged off again in the faithful Maurice.

Ten minutes down the main road from my house we turned up a narrow lane and through a banana plantation. Evelyn informed me we would be lunching at the Pompano Cottage Colony. When I asked for the definition of a cottage colony, she explained that it was basically a number of holiday cottages set in lovely grounds with a central restaurant and pool area. We emerged from under the bananas trees on top of a cliff with a panoramic view of the ocean. I was fascinated by the contrasting sandy-bottomed clear water close to shore and the vivid change to turquoise further out, where the seabed plunged downwards. Even through this darker turquoise, almost black reefs were clearly visible. I stood entranced not knowing that this area would be one I would get to know well.

Evelyn interrupted my musings and led me up steps and onto a delightful terrace where she introduced me to the manager, obviously a friend. He turned out to be German and shook my hand warmly. *"Heinz's son will be in your class,"* she murmured, giving me a very straight look. If anything the terrace gave an even broader panorama than the one I had been admiring, Heinz guided us to a table shaded by a huge fluttering umbrella at the edge of the terrace with a splendid view over the ocean; the hypnotic sound of the gentle swell, though far below, clearly audible.

Lunch was a buffet with every imaginable delicacy. We loaded our plates while the Maître d'hôtel guided our choice every step of the way. It was apparent Evelyn was a popular and well-known visitor. To appease Evelyn I chose

25

to drink mineral water, after she had clearly stated drinking wine or in fact any alcohol during the day was not recommended and something she never dreamed of doing. After a second helping followed by an assortment of wonderful deserts we sank into our comfortable seats and did our best to drain a constantly replenished coffeepot, magically refilled several times before we even had to time to ask. The afternoon lazily drifted away and I was grateful for the opportunity to rest and catch my breath after several hectic days.

Chapter Two
September, 1972

The next few days flew by as I prepared for school, explored the local area and gradually organised my life. I only caught sight of Dilly once but when I did she invited me to her house the following Saturday night, saying that some people were coming round for drinks and a barbecue. I thanked her and asked what I could bring. *"Nothing. Come about seven,"* she had shouted, as she disappeared back into her house.

I spent most of Saturday morning on the small beach at the end of the lane where I lived. The sea was lusciously warm and the small bay totally calm, protected from the swell by a long promontory and the shallow reef. At one end of the beach was a mangrove swamp, an official sign indicating that it was a Nature Reserve; across the bay, in the other direction, was a cottage colony that I later discovered was called Cambridge Beaches. It had taken me exactly five minutes to walk to this spot from my home – I felt totally spoiled. A couple of days earlier I had bought a mask and snorkel from the supermarket but never having used one before, practised in the shallow water for some time before venturing further out. The seabed was covered with grass

27

but there were only a few tiddlers to be seen, until suddenly I came face to face with a small grazing turtle that took one look at me and fled. I nearly choked with excitement, as I foolishly sucked seawater down the snorkel tube.

When the sun reached high overhead and its fierce heat sapped all strength, I packed up and strolled back down the lane to recuperate under the Casuarinas. I found an old deckchair at the back of the house that, despite its looks, managed to bear my weight and so under the great tree I sweated, read, dozed and sweated some more.

Later, under the spluttering excuse for a shower I became aware of a great deal of noise and laughter emanating from the general direction of Dilly's house. Several cars were pulled up onto the grass or parked along the road. The air was filled with cheerful shouts. After some deliberation I decided against shorts and pulled on a pair of long pants, donned a flowery shirt, ran a hand through my crew-cut hair and headed for next door.

As I rounded the corner of the house Pearl, Dilly's eldest, ran up to me and buried her hand into mine. She had been lying in wait. She peered up at me with her mother's wide brown eyes. *"Mr Cross, you're late,"* she scolded.

"I'm sorry Miss Pearl, did I keep you waiting," I squeezed her hand.

"Are you going to teach at the white school Mr Cross?" she asked inquisitively.

"Yes, it's white" I replied unthinking. Pearl gave me a quizzical look.

"Do I have to call you Mar. Cross, Mr Cross?" She appealed.

"No – Jack's all right," I laughed.

"Good - come and meet my Dad." She dragged me across the grass towards the barbecue. A huge man with a bushy moustache was laying chicken legs across the grill; sweat dripping from every protrusion of his face, as if he had just stepped out of the shower. Excitedly Pearl appealed to her father to stop what he was doing and meet the new neighbour.

"Man you nag worse than your mother," he snarled in mock anger, mopped his hands on the apron that he wore round his waist, turned and thrust out a huge calloused hand. *"Glad to meet you Mr Cross, I'm Karl, welcome to Bermuda, I've heard a lot about you, mainly from Pearl here."* At this Pearl let go my hand and wrapped herself around her father, gazing adoringly up at his face. *"Mind my pinny girl, it's all greasy, you'll spoil that nice clean frock."* She let him go and threw a light punch at his ribs and skipped away. *"Man oh man, I don't envy the guy that ends up with her when she's growed up."* He guffawed, his voice unusually deep with a wonderful West Indian melodic lilt. *"Let me just get these little beauties cooking and I'll get you a beer and introduce you around."* He busied himself for a few moments with obvious expertise born of years of experience, then wiped his hands, removed his apron and pushed me towards the backdoor.

The large living room was sparsely lit and crowded with laughing faces. Reggae boomed away in the background, all conversation was at shouting level. A beer was thrust into my hand and Karl chatted. He told me he was a carpenter and had been born in Barbados, he came to

29

Bermuda when he was eighteen and had never been back. After a few minutes he introduced me to the nearest person. *"Eggy take care of our new neighbour, I have dinner to cook,"* he slapped me on the shoulder and pushed his way outside again.

Eggy introduced himself as Egbert Foley; he was a short man with a slight paunch visibly wobbling under his Hawaiian shirt. Peering at me over the top of a pair of large sunglasses, wedged halfway down his nose, he thrust a tatty business card into my hand, while telling me he was the best tourist guide on the island. He also claimed to be the most knowledgeable botanist, geographer, geologist and ornithologist to be found on these fair isles. Egbert was not the most modest person I have ever met but with his smiling eyes and wicked wit he was great company. He introduced me to some of the other guests, I was confused for, like him, they all seemed to be taxi drivers; I collected more business cards. Each boasted of their skill in providing the tourist with all the information they needed to know. It was clear from their enthusiasm, they were all in the right job.

As I moved around the room being passed on from guest to guest like a relay baton, I suddenly became aware that I was the only white person in the room. For a moment I felt uncomfortable, this was a new experience. I didn't understand why I had this feeling, for I was being made so welcome, everyone was unbelievably kind to this stranger in their midst. To be in the company of black people was out of my experience; even in my classes in England I had only once taught a black child. I suddenly remembered how upset he had been when his classmates would not believe that he was English and how I had had to calm him down and lecture the other boys. He had been tearful, saying that although his father was born in Dominica, he himself had been born in England and this made him English. In retrospect I probably had not been very convincing when explaining this to his peers.

I felt a hand on my shoulder; it was Karl enquiring if people were taking care of me. Having assured him I was being well looked after he introduced me to a tall, handsome man about my own age and moved on.

We exchanged greetings and introductions. *"It seems everyone I have met tonight is a taxi-driver."* I said.

The man, who had said to call him Just, looked round and nodded. *"There are quite a few taxi-drivers here but there are plenty in my line of business too."* In answer to my question he told me he was a Maître d'hôtel at a local cottage colony. He nodded towards a group in the corner and said they all worked at the new Southampton Princess Hotel. Before slipping away, he too handed me a business card and said to call him any time when I needed a table in the restaurant.

I emptied my beer can and went in search of a refill. As I eased my way through the throng it suddenly struck me that the room seemed to be filled with men, with conversation revolving around cricket, soccer and local politics. No different in fact from the last party I attended in England, except noisier. My perambulations had taken me close to the door into the kitchen where I could see another party was going on. So this was where the ladies were, if anything, there was even more laughter and joking but the

31

sound was at a higher pitch. Dilly was closing the door of a huge refrigerator when she spotted me and beckoned me towards her. I eased my way across the kitchen, the ladies stepping back to let me through, like some dignitary, though, I'm sure, it was just to give themselves room for a clearer look at the intruder. I reached Dilly's side and she grabbed my hand and held it up and shouted, *"Ladies, this is Jack Cross my new neighbour."* Introductions completed she returned to filling an array of bowls with salads on the huge table. It was apparent that Dilly had lots of help in the kitchen, each lady cheerfully busy; this was obviously a joint effort. In the next few minutes I was kissed on the cheek, or hugged, or had my hand formally shaken, asked if I was married and generally grilled. Whereas the men were more interested in telling me about themselves and their aspirations, the ladies seemed more interested in finding out about me. Some of the remarks were a little blunt and I grew embarrassed at which someone even screamed, *'Oh look he's blushing.'* With a broad smile on her face, Dilly called out for the ladies to behave themselves. Grasping my empty beer can I escaped back to the safety of the men's lounge.

Later that night, after a wonderful supper, the front room throbbed as the reggae was turned up and couples danced. I wasn't a spectator for long as a procession of ladies pulled me on to the floor and forced me to follow their wild gyrations. I noticed Pearl dancing with her father, a far away look in her eyes as she concentrated on the special movements she had either seen on television or invented. As Bob Marley's voice ebbed away my latest partner nodded her thanks and spun round several times on her toes, as she searched for another victim. I laughed at her antics, turned and found myself captured yet again. This time it was Dilly. Musically the mood had changed to a gentler beat. Silently and weightlessly she took the lead totally absorbed by the hypnotic rhythm. In my arms she seemed even more petite than I remembered and was still barefooted.

"*Great party*" I murmured into her hair. She tilted her head and gazed into my eyes but gave no indication she had heard or understood what I had said. She lowered her gaze and pressed against me as we swayed, making little progress on the crowded floor.

The spell was suddenly broken by a loud rasping shout: "*Yella woman, where are you yella woman – we're all out of beer.*" Dilly let go my hand, turned and equally loudly responded, "*Then it must be time for you to go home Baldy my friend.*" I was shocked at this blatant reference to Dilly's light coloured skin but she was obviously used to it and took it in her stride, giving as much verbal abuse as she got, as she headed for the kitchen.

About three in the morning I fell into bed having thoroughly enjoyed myself. I had been well fed and *watered* and had discovered so much more about my Bermudian hosts. If the people I had met tonight were typical of Bermudians in general, then I was indeed fortunate because the warmth, humour and kindness was overwhelming. An unexpected result of the party was that whenever I was out and a taxi passed by, inevitably the driver would toot the horn and wave. I was recognised, even if I didn't know who was making contact. It was a gesture that helped me feel comfortable and at home.

At school, the new academic year began with a formal assembly in the gymnasium. The students sat in neat rows on the polished wooden floor, the girls in white blouses and grey skirts and the boys in white shirts and grey shorts. The teachers were seated down each side of the gym and I noted with pleasure the quiet banter between some of the teachers and the children seated at their feet, both obviously pleased to see each other after the long summer break.

Mrs Harding stood at the front and when everyone was settled she clapped her hands and all eyes turned to her. You could have heard a pin drop. This was not something I was used to. She went on to welcome everyone, told a humorous anecdote about her summer travels and then asked me stand, as she introduced me to the children and my new colleagues. It appeared I was the only new teacher this term. She asked if I would tell the children something about myself. As I launched into a story about my last school, my eyes ran along the rows of scrubbed white faces. White faces – I suddenly remembered the question little Pearl had asked. I found myself stumbling over my story and cursed my naivety. I peered again at the expectant faces, out of the two hundred or so children sitting there, I spotted only two black faces. I glanced at my colleagues, they were all white too. I was indeed teaching at *the white school*.

Introductions over, Mrs Harding asked the children to stand and nodded to the young lady seated at the piano. She started to play and the children burst into the British National Anthem, *God Save the Queen*, with great gusto. I could hardly contain my amazement – and then my embarrassment, as they sang verses to which I did not know the words.

When the last note had died away, Mrs Harding congratulated the children on their singing, wished them a happy day and directed the first row to leave.

The first few days were such a revelation, in so many ways. I got to know my class and established clear discipline boundaries, which they typically tried to push, as all kids do with a new teacher. But compared to my last school, discipline was not an issue and we soon settled into an amicable working regime.

I was surprised at the make up of my class, they were all eleven or twelve years old but then a common factor blurred. One boy told me that his father worked on Wall Street in New York and that he commuted; he came home Friday evening and left again Monday morning; another that his father was a Captain at the US naval base. There was another boy whose father who was a Petty Officer at the British Naval Dockyard. A Canadian boy told me that his father was a radio engineer at the Canadian naval base. Then there was the German boy, whose father was manager of the Cottage Colony. But at the other end of the scale was a painfully thin, shifty eyed boy who told me his father collected bottles. When I looked puzzled he replied that he dived for them, they were collectors' items. Another boy laughed and said he didn't have a father but his mother was responsible for emptying lots of bottles, which amused everyone. Then there was Graham. Graham was one of the two black Bermudians I'd spotted in the Hall. His father, he told me, had been drowned at sea and he lived with his grandfather, it soon became apparent that Graham was the class lawyer and the most articulate and popular student in the class. Then there were the girls, all nine of them, each appearing so sophisticated and mature in comparison to the naïve, rough and ready boys, whom they tended to ignore. Typically, the girls were smarter too and harder working, each eager to please. I soon discovered that there was a wide variation of ability in the class and I soon had four separate levels operating. This meant extra hours of preparation and some after-school coaching but well worth the effort.

Gradually, as well as getting to know my students, I got to know my new colleagues, there were sixteen of us, plus Mrs Harding and a part-time secretary. One Saturday evening soon after attending my neighbour's party, Evelyn invited the staff for cocktails. Most of the teaching staff was female but husbands or partners had also been invited. I couldn't help but compare the evening with my neighbour's earlier party. At Mrs Harding's soiree the men, including me, were dressed in colourful Bermuda shorts, worn with long socks and blazers. Conversation was polite and measured, Mozart gently playing in the background – no reggae booming ghetto-blasting here.

It was apparent that all my colleagues had been living in Bermuda for many years and outside of school all had their own lives to lead. While they had all been pleasant enough and tried to make me feel welcome and part of the team – so far it had all felt a little superficial. This evening at Evelyn's did little to dispel this feeling. Sipping a rum punch I wandered round the room examining the pictures on the walls and the books on the many shelves. There were several photographs of Evelyn with a tall, bronzed man I took to be Mr Harding. Although she was referred to as Mrs

Harding, I didn't know if she was widowed or divorced. I was peering at one particular picture of the pair of them standing on the open deck of a fishing boat with a huge Marlin or some such ocean-going monster hanging behind them. Judging from Evelyn's appearance it didn't appear to have been taken so long ago.

"My late husband, Marlborough!" I hadn't been aware of Evelyn's approach. She sighed, *"It was only a week after that photograph was taken - he went,"* she paused and took another breath, *"he went missing at sea, presumed drowned."*

"I'm so sorry, I'd no idea, no one said anything – when did it happen?" I was surprised none of my new colleagues had mentioned this fact to me.

"It was almost a year ago, last October. They didn't find his body or his boat. We'd only been married for about a year." There was an awkward pause. *" I understand that you too have been touched by tragedy?"*

"Yes, my wife was killed in a road accident," I murmured," *I know how you must feel."*

She smiled and squeezed my arm. *"And now there's poor Mr Duckett. Such wickedness!"* Evelyn shook her head in disbelief. I didn't know what she meant, nor who Mr Duckett might be. Evelyn read my expression. *"You didn't hear that the police commissioner, George Duckett, was shot and killed last night outside his home."* I had not heard this piece of news and I was shocked. How could such violence be perpetrated in such idyllic surroundings? Skilfully Evelyn moved the conversation on and towards more cheerful topics, saying we would return to discuss our mutual losses at another time.

The only other guest, besides me, without a partner appeared to be the black-haired young lady who had played the piano at the first assembly. I hadn't seen her around school since and so moved across the room to where she was pouring Bacardi into her glass. *"Are you drinking that neat?"* I asked *"or can I get you some coke?"*

She gave me a very straight, slightly glazed look and asked for coca cola. I obliged topping up her glass, apologising that I did not know her name. She moved away from the drinks table and apart from the other guests. I followed. *"I'm Eloise Shaw, otherwise known as Ellie. You're Jack aren't you."*

"Yes, Jack Cross, I saw you on the first day and haven't seen you since. Where've you been hiding?"

She shrugged, *"I'm just the part time music teacher. I breeze in, teach a few lessons and breeze out again. Like a piece of flotsam tossed on the ocean of life. No, no that's not a very good metaphor; I'm mixing the tide with the wind. Well I guess you understand what I'm trying to say. I'm peripatetic, some would even say peri-pathetic"* She raised her glass in a mock toast."

"I thought the children sing extremely well." I said ignoring the negative overtones.

"They do sing well. And they like to sing. You'll have to excuse me I'm slightly tipsy," she emptied her glass at one go as if to emphasise the fact. *"Would you get me another?"* I took her glass and returned to the table and filled it with ice and coke leaving out the Bacardi. She was

leaning against the wall when I returned: *"Are you trying to get me sober Mr Cross? I saw you omit the most important ingredient."* I apologised for the oversight and suggested that some food might help. *"I'm not eating Mr Cross, only drinking,"* she muttered.

"I'm sure that's not true, you look very fit." She did indeed have a very shapely, athletic build. I then noticed she was wearing trousers while all the other females were in more formal evening frocks.

"What I mean is that tonight I am not eating, only drinking – and this drink needs some rum." She thrust the glass at me. I took it and suggested we found somewhere to sit. I was concerned that she would slide further down the wall and end up sitting on the floor. Noticing a chaise-longe empty I took her elbow and guided her towards it. She sat heavily, an inane grin spreading across her face. *"I haven't felt like this for some time Mr Cross – I like it."* She flopped back against the cushions and closed her eyes. I was at a bit of loss and so went in search of some bread and cheese. When I returned she was sitting up, elbows on her knees but looking distinctly green. *"I need some air before I throw up'* she gurgled. I helped her to her feet grasped her forearm and walked quickly towards the door. There were a few steely stares from a couple of our colleagues but generally our exit went unnoticed. Outside I sat her on the wooden steps leading down to the garden where she breathed deeply trying to clear her head. I tried to make conversation but she wasn't interested and it wasn't long before she leaned over the side of the steps and vomited. I gave her my handkerchief and fetched a glass of water from the kitchen.

She sipped for a moment or two and then murmured: "*I feel like death, would you do me a favour and take me home. I've got a car parked round the corner.*" I agreed and said I would first go and say goodbye to Mrs Harding.

"*Okay*," snapped Eloise " *but don't tell that good for nothing bitch I'm the reason you're leaving.*" I was startled at the vehemence but returned inside, found Evelyn, thanked her profusely and made my excuses for leaving. She saw me to the front door and as soon as it had closed I made my way to the back of the house to find Eloise.

She struggled to her feet but then found she could hardly stand and so I half carried her out into the road to her small green Volkswagen Beetle parked under the oleanders. She leaned precariously against the bonnet and searched her handbag for the keys. Eventually I took the bag, riffled around, found them and unlocked the doors. Having settled her into the passenger seat, I squeezed behind the wheel and turned the key. "*Okay Miss Eloise, I need some directions, where do you live?*" I had to repeat my question several times before I got an answer and some basic directions. She had a small house quite close to the ferry stop at Cavello Bay that I had used a few times when going into Hamilton. Upon our arrival, once again we went through the female ritual of the handbag search and again it was necessary for me to take the bag and find the key. I helped her through the door and propped her against the wall, while searching for lights. There was a gentle thump, as she slipped to the floor. It was clear she was in no position to help herself and having established that she lived on her own, I carried her into a bedroom and laid her down. I removed her shoes, found a bowl from the kitchen and put it at the side of the bed. It struck me as I gazed down at her helpless, prostrate form, that Eloise was in fact a very attractive young lady, if you chose to ignore her unusually ashen complexion.

I wandered back into her living room, a little unsure whether it was safe to leave her in her present condition. I didn't want her choking on her own vomit. I glanced at my watch; it was just before midnight, and decided to wait a while to see if she improved. The room was sparsely but comfortably furnished and dominated by a large, black upright piano, complete with elaborate candelabra. There were candles everywhere, some in proper holders but most in bottles of every hue and shape. There was a sagging, overfilled bookcase and other books and maps scattered around on chairs and tables. Above an ancient fireplace was a long, wooden mantelpiece decorated with several photographs in old Bermuda cedar frames. A huge stuffed Barracuda in a frame hung above the door leading into her bedroom. I wondered momentarily if this were significant, I'd read that Barracudas were voracious creatures.

My eyes were drawn to a black and white photograph showing a man and a girl standing on the deck of a boat. I picked it up and held it under a lamp. They were both holding fishing rods and smiling broadly. I peered at the man, who despite having a broad-brimmed hat pulled down over his eyes had familiar features. As I stared it dawned that this was the second time I had seen a photograph of this man tonight. I felt sure it was Marlborough Harding. My attention turned to the girl, could it be Eloise? I guessed she would be about twenty-five now, the girl in the picture looked about ten. I was undecided but curious and examined the other photographs. Except for one they were all quite recent and showed Eloise with different people. The exception was another black and white photograph, a professional portrait of an attractive middle-aged woman I supposed to be Eloise's mother.

Having exhausted the photographs I turned my attention to an untidy pile of books and maps on a coffee table. The maps were in fact charts showing reefs away to the north and west of Bermuda, there were three different ones. The books all dealt with various aspects of diving and as I flicked through I wondered about Eloise's vicious outburst against Mrs Harding. A soft groan from the bedroom brought me to my feet and I peered in. Eloise was up on one elbow looking at me out of one eye. *"Oh God. I'm sorry,"* she muttered, *"what time is it?"*

"Almost one o'clock," I replied.

"Thanks for bringing me home, not that I remember much about it. Why did you stay?" she asked.

"I just wanted to be sure you would be okay," I replied.

"I'm fine," she said swinging her feet over the side of the bed. *"I'll take a shower and then I'll be fine."* She didn't look fine and I didn't envy her the hangover she would have tomorrow. She looked up: *"Really - thanks, I don't usually get in this state, well not this bad. Take my car and leave it in the school car park. Put the key under the floor mat. I'll collect it some time later."*

After satisfying myself she would indeed be okay, I let myself out and drove up and over the hill towards the school, confident that Eloise would survive. I left the car as instructed and walked down the pitch-black lane towards my home, the arching oleanders blocking out the starlight. The only sounds accompanying my march were the loud and incessant chorus of tree frogs. My musing on the evening's events was interrupted by the sound of a car behind me. The lane was narrow and instinctively I stepped off the road masked from the headlights by a tree. The car stopped outside my home and the engine was turned off. The door opened and I recognised Dilly's voice. I heard her say *'Goodnight Eggy'* and realised it was Eggy Foley's taxi. She closed the car door quietly and waited until the car drove away. As she walked down the path towards the door, I called her name in a loud whisper. *"Jack is that you? Man you made me jump. What are you doing walking about at this time of the morning?"* she hissed.

"I could ask you the same thing – but I'm a gentleman," I laughed quietly.

"What do you mean by that – I've been working Jack Cross."

"Working until two in the morning?" I queried.

"Yes working – and tonight I'm home early, so there!" she continued, still whispering: *"I need a nightcap, will you join me?*

I agreed, asking for a ginger ale, I'd had enough alcohol for one night. She responded that she didn't drink when she was at work and so she needed a Bacardi to make her sleep. She disappeared indoors and moments later we were seated on her porch sipping our drinks. She had warned me that we were sitting outside the girls' bedroom and needed to keep our voices down. During the next fifteen minutes I was amazed to discover that my neighbour Dilly was a dancer who worked from nine o'clock until two o'clock, six nights a week during the summer months and three nights a week out of season. She was part of a group, she told me, that rushed from hotel to hotel to perform for the guests. There were fifteen of them in the group and so together with their equipment they needed a fleet of taxis to ship them around and ensure the very tight schedule was kept. I now understood why there were so many taxi drivers at her party; they were obviously key members of the operation.

"How an earth do you manage to combine this with running a family?" I asked. She chuckled and explained that she was usually in bed by three o'clock, up at six to give Karl his breakfast and get the girls ready for school. By nine o'clock she was usually back in bed for three hours and then did the washing, cleaning and shopping before the girls and Karl came home.

After emptying her glass Dilly climbed to her feet. *"I must go or I shan't get my three hours sleep,"* she said yawning. *"You must come and see the show sometime, one Saturday night would be best."*

"I'd love to, I really would," I answered enthusiastically.

"Okay we'll talk about it another time. Goodnight." She disappeared indoors and I strolled home suitably amazed. It wasn't surprising that after such an eventful evening, leaving so much to think about, I had trouble sleeping.

The following days evaporated, as every waking moment seemed to be filled with school affairs. I organised a soccer team and played a few friendly games against neighbouring schools. The boys were so keen that the one evening per week for training was not enough for them and they pleaded for more. I was happy to oblige. It also became a matter of routine that once training was over, we would all jog down to Long Bay to swim. After about fifteen minutes I would round up the boys and we would stroll back to school, the kids skipping around me full of questions and stories of how we would become Bermuda football champions and take on Manchester United.

After the first few matches, I realised that I actually had a pretty good team. Graham Simmons, the big black boy from my class, was the star centre-half and was an inspiration to the others to perform beyond their natural talents. Most of the schools we played against were much larger, with more students competing for a place in the team. They each had a full-time physical education teacher who, without exception, would be British and well qualified. Through the soccer games my circle of friends gradually grew and I occasionally met with some of these teachers for a chat and a beer.

The first time after Evelyn's party that my class had a Music lesson, I walked with them to the assembly hall, which served as the music room. I was interested to see Eloise again and discover if she had recovered. She was seated at the piano, hammering out a sea shanty while her class sang with great gusto, Eloise's melodic voice soaring high above the children's. As the song ended she spun round on her stool, loudly clapping the children and calling: *"Fantastic, lets do the chorus again – and remember sing, don't shout."*

Peering round the door I was treated to another chorus. After further praise from Eloise, the excited children crowded round her before she ushered them towards the door to make their way reluctantly back to their classrooms. It was then she saw me, blushed and averted her eyes to my class, inviting them to enter and sit on the floor.

"Does this class sing as well as the previous one?" I asked, noticing that Graham and two other boys had disappeared into a storeroom, to return with a box full of instruments and two guitars.

"Thank you Graham," said Eloise before answering my question. *"Differently I would say, we have a few boys who say their voices are breaking and this is why they are growlers. Sounds a weak excuse to me."* She glared in mock anger at the group. *"Stay and listen and make up your own mind."* She still had not looked me in the eye.

"Sorry I have to see Mrs Harding, perhaps next time," I replied. Eloise organised the distribution of the instruments while Graham and another boy drew up chairs and tuned the guitars. As I left and wandered down the corridor towards the office, the strains of a very slow, ponderous version of Bob Marley's *Hey Woman Don't Cry* caused me to grin. Obviously work on this song was in its early stages.

I got into the habit of taking my class to Music each time but found having a proper conversation with Eloise impossible. On one occasion I awkwardly asked if she would be around after school to discuss my class's progress but she replied that she had to dash to teach Music at the neighbouring Boaz Island School. I hesitated to ask the question what she was doing after that - and the moment was gone. I questioned myself afterwards why I even thought of wanting to see Eloise again. I felt suddenly guilty and unfaithful to Jill's memory. It was strange sensation, leaving me empty and confused.

*

The shrill ringing of the telephone woke me about seven o'clock one Saturday morning. It was Don Jeffers one of the sports' teachers I had met. *"We need a fourth man for tennis this morning at 9 o'clock, how are you fixed?"* He sounded much too cheerful for this hour of the day.

I feigned wakefulness: *"Great, yes I'd like that. Where?"* I asked.

"Carlton Beach Hotel, we've booked a court for two hours. Then later on we're going fishing on Charlie's boat – do you fancy that?"

"Yes that would be great." I meant it - this would be a new and exciting experience.

"Okay- you don't have to bring anything, the beer's already cooling and Charlie will have the bait organised. See you at nine." He hung up and I dived under the shower.

I took the bus to South Shore and strolled down the Yucca edged drive towards the Carlton Beach Hotel and along to the courts. The others were already there and knocking up. I was really thrilled to be playing tennis again. I had played a great deal as a teenager, occasionally at university but never since. Jill was not sporty and the opportunity to play never seemed to arise. Don was the best player in our group, with the rest of us about the same level. Don was a huge chap, about six feet two inches and built like a front-row forward but with very quick reactions. It made for some very competitive games and a vigorous work out. The guys were good company and through conversation I found out more about their schools and island life. Don had lived in Bermuda for five years, the other two, Charlie and Alan for three years. I also learned that Alan had a live-in Canadian girl friend that worked at the hotel – hence the ease of booking a court. The other two said they didn't have regular girl friends and after hearing about Jill said they would soon have me fixed up, despite my telling them repeatedly I wasn't ready to get fixed up.

When the two hours were up, we reluctantly handed over the court to the young American couple who had waited patiently until we finished the set. Then at Alan's suggestion we made our way up onto a terrace where guests sheltered from the blistering sun under huge, floral umbrellas. Alan was on first name terms with the joking Barbadian waiter, who soon supplied us with icy cold beers. It was an idyllic spot, perched above the rocks with uninterrupted views out to sea. Not for the first time in recent weeks I felt utterly privileged.

Conversation revolved around the tennis, the planned fishing trip and ideas for organising a game of golf at the recently-opened Southampton Princess Hotel's nine-hole course. I had never played golf but none of them saw this as a problem. Don reassured me that I seemed to have a good eye but advised that I brought a good supply of balls, as their were plenty of water hazards.

Charlie asked what we thought the motive was for the recent shooting of the police commissioner and the wounding of his daughter. Various suggestions were put forward. Don was thoughtful and then quietly said that a friend of his was a policeman and on duty that night. It appeared George Duckett was drying dishes in the kitchen of his home in Devonshire when he heard a noise outside and when he went out to investigate he was shot from close range in the back. The daughter rushed into the kitchen and was hit by a shot fired through the window, though luckily she was not badly hurt. Mrs Duckett tried to phone the police but the line was dead. In the end she drove to the police headquarters, about a mile away, to get help. Don confided that the police had rounded up known criminals and members of a subversive group but didn't keep them locked up for long. We were all staring at Don as we listened intently to his inside information.

"Well, who is responsible?" demanded Alan, *"and who's next?"*

"Could be someone upset by the way the police have been closing in on the drug barons," said Don *"Or from the group of Black Berets that want independence for Bermuda. Or criminals looking for revenge. There are plenty of Bermudians with a motive. And my source tells me the nearer you get to the top – the more that corruption is the way of life. Anyone could have brought in a hitman!"*

"Could even be the IRA I suppose," said Alan over the lip of his glass.

I had not contributed to this conversation; I was genuinely shocked and still not convinced that this island paradise was like a Chicago suburb.

The depressing tone of our conversation was abruptly halted by the sound of high heels clicking loudly on the flagstones, causing each of us to turn towards the source. A stunningly good-looking girl dressed in a dark blue matching skirt and jacket was heading in our direction. *"Why wasn't I born a man?"* she called out. *"Tennis and boozing while I'm working my socks off."* It was Alan's live-in girl friend and I'm sure we all felt a tinge of jealously, as she wrapped her arms round his neck and chewed his ear.

"Put me down," yelled Alan, *"I'm all sweaty."*

"I need the salt," she hissed in mock lust.

"Jack, this hussy is Mildred. Mildred say Hi to Jack Cross, he's new to Bermuda."

We shook hands, as her laughing eyes peered deep into mine, she said: *"Well I wish you good luck Jack Cross, you're in with a bad crowd."*

She turned her attention to Alan: *"So you're deserting me and going off fishing tonight. What time shall I pick you up?"* Alan looked at the others. After much banter, it was agreed that Mildred would bring her car to the dock at nine o'clock. Mildred ruffled Alan's hair and announced that she had to get back to work. She bid us farewell with a wink and shimmied back towards the building, four pairs of male eyes glued to her shapely, undulating hips. She must have known because as she reached the door she glanced over her shoulder and gave an exasperated toss of her head.

"God... you're a lucky dog!" sighed Charlie. We all agreed.

*

Charlie's boat was moored in Ely's Harbour, it was about eighteen feet long, with a small open cabin providing enough shade for two people. Its wooden construction had been lovingly painted; white hull and pale yellow superstructure. *"Odd name for a boat,"* I said perplexed; *"Next Best Thing?"* Charlie laughed. *"Next Best to What:"* I persisted.

"My girl friend," chuckled Charlie reluctantly – and we all laughed and pulled his leg.

After filling the gas tank and a spare can, Charlie and Don checked everything was in its place and then Charlie slowly steered towards a gap leading to the open sea. The harbour was truly beautiful; as I looked back I could see Somerset Bridge, reportedly equipped with the smallest drawbridge in the world, just wide enough to take the mast of a sailing boat. Above, the oleanders gleamed pink on Scaur Hill, an old fort which looked both easterly over the Great Sound towards Hamilton and out to the west where we were headed. I trailed my fingers in the water, wallowing in the scenic splendour. A can of icy beer was thrust in my hand and the joy was complete.

We rounded Wreck Hill and followed the Southampton parish coast, the channel marked by the occasional orange buoy. Charlie opened up the throttle and the noise of the powerful outboard engine drowned out any conversation. I picked out the Pompano where Evelyn Harding had taken me for lunch and marvelled at the rugged cliffs topped by pastel houses surrounded by Casuarinas, a few surviving Cedars and multi-coloured shrubs of oleander and hibiscus. A pair of Longtails played tag over the waves and children could be seen playing in the shallows.

The short chop of the ocean gradually gave way to a gentle rolling motion indicating that Charlie had cleared the reefs and was heading out into deeper water. Don already had a line trailing behind the boat a look of optimism on his square face.

When the land was little more than a smudge on the horizon, Charlie suddenly cut the engine and threw a sea anchor overboard. The silence was palpable. The boat gently bobbed in the swell as the other three busied themselves fixing pieces of squid onto hooks.

"Why this particular place," I asked Charlie.

"We are over a deep reef which is usually a good spot," he replied.

"How an earth do you know, we're over a reef?" I asked, peering down but seeing nothing.

"Just a case of lining up a few landmarks. Sandys' church spire, Wreck Hill, the lighthouse...you know." I didn't. He threw me a piece of squid and a length of line. *"Let's hope you have beginner's luck."*

Charlie only had his line in the water a couple of minutes when he was busy hauling in a catch. *"Damn Bream,"* he hissed. He chopped it up and threw it back. *"Let's see if that will bring in the big boys."* Over the next hour or so I sank several beers and caught a few small yellowtails, which I was assured would be great on the barbecue.

52

It was starting to get dusk when Don pulled in his line to find everything gone, literally – the hook, line and sinker had mysteriously disappeared without him knowing. I peered down into the water wondering what kind of razor-toothed monster had sliced through his line. An involuntary shudder went through me and the small boat suddenly seemed very vulnerable in this huge expanse of ocean and so far from shore.

Some time later Charlie let out a shout and heaved on his line. He ordered the rest of us to take in our lines, as he stood precariously in the middle, allowing his catch to swim round the boat, while with each circuit he gradually pulled his victim closer. After almost ten minutes he was seated on one side with the catch just out of sight below the boat.

"What do you think it is?" I asked. *"Tuna? Barracuda?"*

"It's a shark," said Don quietly. *"Charlie let me bring it in. You know I have always wanted to try."*

"No it's too dangerous," hissed Charlie, still gently pulling in the line.

"Come on, I have to try sometime. You hold the line and I'll come behind you and grab it." Reluctantly Charlie agreed, so Don staggered across the boat and positioned himself behind Charlie. *"You bring it to the surface,"* said Don, *"and I'll bring my hand up behind him grab his head and lift him over the side. Alan, you have the hammer ready."* The sweat was gathering on Don's brow, his face screwed up into a determined scowl.

"Are you sure about this?" Charlie looked at Don. *"We don't want any mistakes. Once you grab the head -*

don't let go. When it's body is in the boat rest its head on the gunwales." He looked at Alan. *"Then hit it – hard, no messing. Keep you feet well out of the way."* He looked at me. *"Jack you get in the bow to give us more room."* Somewhat bemused at the thought of hauling a shark over the side, I didn't need telling twice. Charlie looked again at Don *"Are you quite sure?"*

"I'm sure. I've watched you do it enough times." Don spat on his hands and wiped them on his shorts. *"Okay,"* he said, *"if you are sitting comfortably, we will begin."* Charlie gently reeled in his line until the dark shape was lying peacefully just under the water.

"Bugger me it's a monster," said Don, the sweat now dripping off the end of his nose in a continuous stream

"No - usual size," contradicted Charlie calmly.

"I'll never be able to lift it over the side," objected Don. *" It's too heavy."*

"It's okay, it's under four feet. I'm bringing his head up. Come on my beauty. Up you come," he whispered. *"Okay Don. Get ready… "GRAB!"*

As Don's hand touched its head the Shark went into over-drive, lashing its tail, soaking Don and pulling the line out of Charlie's hand. Charlie cursed jamming a foot on the reel lying in the bottom of the boat as Don fell flailing backwards. Alan and I killed ourselves laughing at the pandemonium; it was like a farcical scene from an early Charlie Chaplin movie.

After restoring order, Charlie repeated the performance of gradually hauling the shark closer to the boat for a second try. This time Don managed a good grip on the shark's head and whisked the flailing creature into the boat, its tail pounding the floor, as he forced its head against the gunwales, screaming for Alan to hit the thing before he lost his grip. Beating the thing to death with a hammer seemed a tawdry way to end the life of this majestic creature. But philistines that we were, we all celebrated its capture with another beer from the cool box. *"Shark steaks all round tonight,"* yelled Don victoriously waving his beer can in the air.

Back at the dock I learned how to gut and clean fish in front of Mildred and a crowd of small boys, who offered advice and laughed at my efforts to fillet the small yellowtails. It was about ten o'clock when we reached Alan's house. The three of us lounged around in his garden as Alan barbecued our catch. I learned that Alan and Mildred's tiny one bedroomed wooden cottage was in the grounds of an estate owned by a wealthy businessman. In return for keeping the grass cut and looking after the main house when he was away, Alan and Mildred lived rent-free. There were no near neighbours so they could make as much noise as they liked without fear of repercussions. This was just as well for we all laughed a great deal, as we went over the techniques for catching monster sharks and how these could be improved. Sliced up on the grill the monster did not seem the same creature whose lashing tail and lethal teeth had caused the adrenaline to flow in such bucketfuls. After we had eaten our fill of the catch, Mildred produced a Pavlova she had made, the beers flowed and night drifted away.

Riding home in a taxi during the early hours, I determined there were two things I needed to complete the enjoyment of my new island home - a pair of wheels and a boat.

Chapter Three

October, 1972

"What are you doing for the half-term holiday?"
Evelyn Harding asked me one day early in October. I hadn't
even given it a thought. I had been so busy organising my
life it had not registered that the following week would be a
holiday. I admitted this fact to her and she seemed pleased at
my total involvement with school and island life. *"Many
people use the opportunity to go to New York to Christmas
shop,"* she informed me. *"But you will have missed out on
the cheap flights."*

*"Well I don't think I'm ready for New York yet. Too
much to do and see here."* I responded.

"Remember," she continued. *"If you plan to visit
England next summer, book your flights soon or they too will
be gone."* I thanked her but felt unwillingly to look that far
ahead. That evening I thought about the coming week's

holiday. I had recently purchased a second-hand motorbike, so getting around the island would not be a problem. I loved riding the bike and enjoyed the feeling of freedom it brought. I would use the week's holiday to explore all twenty square miles of my new home and perhaps do some research into boat ownership. I had also received a formal invitation from Laura Miles Smith, for drinks and light supper during the holiday and had responded, equally as formally, to say I would be delighted to attend.

During the week leading up to the holiday I bumped into Eloise in the corridor as she rushed away from a music lesson; as it was lunchtime, I was on my way outside. *"Are you off to Boaz Island School?"* I enquired.

"No I'm not needed today" she replied. *"They have something on. In-service training or something."*

"I'm just going outside for some fresh air and a sandwich. Will you join me?" I looked into her face, she seemed more relaxed then usual.

"Sure" she replied, enthusiastically and we headed for a bench under a large Poinciana tree at the edge of the field. The children were not out yet, they ate their sandwiches under another huge tree outside the hall and under supervision. There were a few vast billowing cumulus clouds playing hide and seek with the sun. Eloise gasped, as she flopped on to the bench, *"My it's humid,"* she murmured. *"It's hurricane season you know?"* I agreed with her, though for me, a newcomer, it seemed hot and humid all the time. *"You have that pleasure to come - hurricanes I mean."* We chatted on about this and that and I felt myself drawn to her. She had a pleasant voice, easy on

the ear, soft with a slight Bermudian lilt. By now I could distinguish between a true Bermudian accent and one from further south, from the Caribbean. She was articulate and good-looking in a dark sultry way. Today her hair was piled on top of her head and held in place with a bright blue ribbon. She caught me staring at her but didn't look away. I coughed somewhat embarrassed but held her gaze.

"*You look very fit, do you play any sport?*" I asked, offering her one of my sandwiches.

She shook her head and took an apple from her bag. "*I play hockey most Sundays in the season and the occasional game of squash – and swim quite lot, of course.*" She went on to explain the details and ended up suggesting I joined the men's' section of the hockey club. I had not played hockey before and told her I thought it a lethal game, having watched a school pal loose all his front teeth from an over enthusiastic back swing during a boys versus girls school game. She laughed and said I must be soft. Conversation flowed easily and the moments passed until the children poured out from the picnic-tables under the tree. Most raced on to the field while a few others headed for the shade of the trees around the edge of the field but it wasn't long before we were surrounded and the target of questions and stories. After handling the barrage for a while, Eloise stood and said she must go. I wandered with her towards the car park.

"*Perhaps we could have a meal one night?*" I ventured "*or go out for a drink. Perhaps in the holiday. Are you around?*" I hoped the nervousness I felt didn't show in my voice.

"Yes that would be nice. And no, I am not going anywhere during the holiday. Call me." With wave she was gone and I was 1 left with a young audience giving me knowing looks.

*

The first day of the holiday I spent swimming and reading on the beach at Long Bay. There were a few children playing in the waves but on the whole it was pretty quiet. There wasn't a cloud in the sky and I was grateful that I had remembered to take a large umbrella, which I propped in the sand to provide some shade. A few sunfish sailing boats lazily drifted by, barely enough wind to fill their tiny sails. Returning from a vigorous and lengthy swim I settled down with my Len Deighton, marvelling at his attention to detail. I had always fancied myself as a writer but since arriving in Bermuda had hardly put pen to paper. An exercise book set aside for the purpose contained nothing more than a few scribbled first impressions and a draft of poem about the sea that I had composed after riding my newly acquired bike along the South Shore. But it was rubbish and I knew it.

An hour or so later a tiny figure skidded along the sand and threw herself down alongside me in a great imitation of a baseball player diving for first base. It was Renee, Dilly's middle child. She gazed at me wide eyed but except for an initial giggle said not a word. She wriggled in the sand and made herself comfortable.

Moments later Pearl came into view holding little Vernee's hand. *"Hi Mr Cross, Jack"* she called out.

"Hey girl - you can't call Mr Cross - Jack," objected Renee, *"he's a grown up. And a teacher,"* she added as an afterthought.

"Yes I can so, he said it was all right. Isn't that right Jack?"

I nodded, *"Yes, I don't mind."* I said, winking at Renee.

She looked at me sternly, *"It's not right,"* she said, climbing to her feet before turning and sprinting into the sea.

"Do you want to see me do a back flip?" asked Pearl in a matter of fact voice. I agreed, a little surprised at the offer. Pearl let go her sister's hand and gracefully leaned backwards until her hands touched the floor and with the lightest of kicks her long legs flowed gently over her head and she was back on her feet. I congratulated her, envying her suppleness. *"That's not it"* she said, *"I'm warming up. "*

" Oh sorry," I responded equally seriously. *"It's very important to warm up."* Little Vernee wandered off to the water's edge already bored by her big sister's antics. After a couple of cartwheels and handstands she pronounced herself ready and insisted I sit up to watch the performance. Taking a big breath she rose athletically upon her toes, sped along the sand and almost faster than the eye could follow launched herself into an arching cartwheel before snapping into a flic-flac followed by a back somersault. I was amazed and spontaneously clapped at the display of agility. She walked towards me and bowed deeply.

"Who taught you how to do that?" I asked.

"My Momma," she said *"well… and Mr Jeffers at school."*

"I know Mr Jeffers," I said.

"I know you do," she replied. *"Most people at school don't like him but I do."*

"Why don't they like him?" I asked puzzled.

"Cos he's white, the only white teacher at our school," she said seriously.

"Does it bother you that he's the only white teacher?" I asked, puzzled.

"Nope, Mum says it's not the colour of your skin that matters but what the person is like underneath." She was eyeing her little sister sitting at the water's edge.

"Your mother's very wise," I responded, a little surprised at this information. *"I know that Mr Jeffers loves teaching at your school, he's always telling me what great students and friendly teachers there are,"* I said.

Pearl was drawing in the sand with a long elegant finger, a brightly painted fingernail displaying evidence that she had been experimenting with her mother's nail varnish. *"Well,"* she paused *"it's okay on the surface but underneath people think as we children are black we should have black teachers."*

"I don't see that it matters what colour the teacher is," I said quietly *"but I do think it's a shame that you don't have any white students. Your school and mine should be all mixed up."*

"No that's no good - white kids are different," she said.

"Why different?" I was puzzled.

They think themselves better than us." Pearl continued.

You really think so?"

"Yes"

"I have one black boy in my class and he's the most popular boy in the class. Everybody likes him. And he gets on well with everyone else," I said.

"Oh, you mean Graham Simons. Nobody at my school likes him because he goes to your school. They think he's stuck up and he thinks he's white."

"Oh Pearl?" I was growing exasperated and had to remind myself she was only ten years old. But out of the mouths of babes and sucklings…?

"Don't you have any white friends?" I enquired. *"Surely at least one."*

"Nope, all my friends are from my school," she replied.

Pearl's words really bothered me. How could a new generation be growing up with the same old prejudices that had marred relationships during the past? I remembered the warm and welcoming people I had met at Dilly's party. Surely they didn't feel the same way underneath all their friendliness? But then there was the question of the police commissioner's death; was his death due to issues regarding race or drugs? I'd read in the local paper, *The Royal Gazette*, a few weeks' back, that the inquiry was no further on and that Scotland Yard detectives from London had been flown in and a reward of $25,000 offered for information leading to the capture of the assassin or assassins. I was beginning to wonder exactly what was going on beneath the exotic and tranquil surface of my newly adopted home.

The girls and I all went for a swim before making our way slowly down the lane towards home, enjoying the thick shade provided by the overhanging oleander branches. The three girls held hands and after a while Pearl buried her hand into mine and looked up into my face. *"I didn't hurt your feelings with what I said?"* she whispered earnestly. I looked down at her beautiful black face, aware she had her father's dark colouring rather than her mother's coffee complexion.

"No I'm not hurt but a little sad." I replied.

She squeezed my hand and again in whisper said: *"I like you Mr Jack, don't be sad."* I thought of what her father had said about his daughter at the barbecue, she would certainly be a handful for some future boyfriend. *"My teacher said that this was Mark Twain's favourite walk."* Pearl pronounced loudly.

"Really," I said, *"Long Bay Lane his favourite walk? What do you know? Well I read that Mark Twain said to his friends: You can go to heaven if you wish. I'd rather stay in Bermuda!"*

"Who's Mark Twain?" asked Renee.

"A writer" replied Pearl. *"He wrote Huckleberry Finn."*

"What's it about?" persisted Renee and as our unlikely foursome strolled silently hand in hand, down Mark Twain's favourite walk, in dappled sunlight, Pearl entertained us with a lively synopsis of the famous tale.

Once back home the girls wandered off into their house while I settled with a book in a hammock that I had strung up between two Casuarina trees. I wondered whether or not to call Eloise, which made me think of my dead Jill. It was a year and a half since she was killed, was that a decent enough time, I asked myself, to be thinking of fixing a date? I mentally flicked through our relationship, which probably only lasted for just over two and a half years. I met Jill at the school where we worked and we went out together for about six months before she proposed that we got married. We had joked about it not even being leap year. But that's the way she was: always wanting to be in charge. It hadn't all been plain sailing, her controlling personality had often led to conflict to which her reaction was to stalk off and refuse to speak. Later, after what she considered to be an appropriate amount of time, she would resume relations as if nothing had happened - and it was rare that either of us would apologise. In retrospect, I realised that this aspect of our relationship had always bothered me. I knew that I was basically a softy who wanted a wife who whole-heartedly returned the love I gave to her. The confrontations, almost always, over something I considered insignificant, were a blemish on our relationship. But like so many memories, it's the good ones that usually stick. During my musings, a red-breasted cardinal had landed above my head and was gazing down at me, as we watched each other I decided against calling Eloise. Before I could even get started again on my book I saw Pearl and Dilly heading towards me. I struggled upright and swung my legs over the side. After exchanging greetings Dilly said: *"I believe my girls have been bothering you, when you are supposed to be on holiday."* I assured her it had not been a problem and that I had enjoyed their company. Dilly turned to Pearl and speaking quite firmly told her she should be sure to give me some peace. She then instructed her to go and look after her sisters. She turned to me: *"Sorry too if Pearl has been speaking out of turn."*

"Did she tell you what we had been talking about?" I asked.

"Yes, she did. She was worried because she thought she had upset you," continued Dilly

"She didn't upset me." I replied. *"I just felt so naive. I had no idea race and colour was still such an issue - especially for one so young."*

"Well it's complicated and some people benefit by continuing this way of thinking; while others use it as an excuse. You know - it gives some people a political power base, while others say their colour stops them making progress with their career," she sighed heavily.

"Is there still real prejudice here? You know over getting jobs and such?" I asked.

"Yes I suppose, in some cases. But even in your country I hear some people only get good jobs if they went to the right school or come from a certain class. I guess it's not so different. You can't generalise. The main problem is that it's not so long since we blacks all had to sit at the back of the bus and the back of the church. We were second-class citizens! It's not surprising we still have chips on our shoulders - and it'll take a long time till they go," as she spoke, she was watching her children.

"Oh Dilly," I sighed, *"this island is absolutely idyllic. It's so beautiful, and from what I see, no one is really poor; no one goes hungry. There's work for those that want to work - if people can't get along here, there is no*

hope for the rest of the world... and where does the murder of the police commissioner fit into all of this?

Dilly looked as if she was about to say something but she stopped herself and silently contemplated her bare feet.

I continued: *"I think having racially segregated schools doesn't help. It just emphasises the two races instead of working to integrate. Pearl says she doesn't have any white friends and probably most of the kids in my class don't have any black friends. Having integrated schools would be a great way to start."*

"I agree," replied Dilly. *"I hear government is already planning to make some schools bigger and close others and force integration. After all people have free choice where to send their kids but most folk still send their kids to the school they went to."*

"Well I hope the government gets a move on," I retorted.

"Okay," said Dilly firmly, *" Having got that off your chest and put the Island to right, let's talk about really important things. Like how about coming to watch our show on Saturday night at the Southampton Princess? It's that new hotel that dominates the skyline just off South Shore Road, it only opened in August - what do you say?"*

*

"So pleased you could come Mr Cross - Gin and Tonic or a beer?" Laura Miles Smith welcomed me onto the terrace in front of her small bungalow; she looked quite stunning in a voluminous floral dress, which swept the floor as she moved. I asked for a beer and was directed towards an ice-filled cool box standing under a table. There were

about a dozen or so guests standing around. She took my hand, held it up high and shouted:

"*Everyone, everyone this is Jack Cross, a new edition at the local school. Malcolm, introduce Mr Cross around.*" It was command not a request.

Malcolm was a short, paunchy, grey-haired man who informed me he was a retired civil servant – *Tax Department* he had said proudly, looking around, as if for plaudits. He lived in Warwick, on South Shore Road and knew Laura through the weekly Bridge sessions. Like the other men present he was dressed in his knee-length Bermuda shorts, with a shirt and tie and blazer. I had agonised over what to wear earlier that evening and fortunately had guessed right and so was similarly attired. However, I did not match Malcolm's sartorial elegance, for he was wearing a sky-blue blazer, maroon shorts and matching sky blue socks. He invited me to follow him and introduced me to the other guests. Small knots gathered round us, eager to find out more about the stranger in their midst.

I have always been interested in people and much more comfortable asking questions about their lives, rather than discussing my own limited experiences. I soon discovered that I was a real outsider, these were all Bermudians, white Bermudians, proud of their history and their achievements and although very careful in what they said, obviously very concerned the way the black majority was taking over government and some of the businesses, which had, historically, been the preserve of white Bermudians. There was talk of the retirement of the Lord Martonmere, the current Queen's representative and the appointment of a new Governor, named Sharples; while theories concerning the death of the police commissioner figured prominently in the conversations. I contributed little to these discussions; as a newcomer it would have been impertinent. But I listened carefully, fascinated how, as an outsider, I seemed to be able to move comfortably between the racial groups. I couldn't help thinking of little Pearl's statement that *White's are different.* This group certainly was and I wondered about their offspring. Another reason for my sense of being an outsider was because I must have been twenty years younger than anyone else in the room. As the evening wore on I found myself increasingly the target of the ladies, both individually and in pairs. The conversation inevitably began with an invitation to join them for Bridge. I had given up saying that I had never played Bridge because that had not deterred them but instead used the argument of pressure of work, and lies about squash and hockey training. A particularly amorous lady of fifty something, who had earlier whispered that I should call her Madge, invited me to join her on a well-cushioned, comfortable looking cane sofa. As soon as we were settled she ran her hand over my naked knee and purred: *"Tell me, Mr Cross – how many ladies are there in your life? What do you really do in your spare time?"* She emphasised the really in an intimate, conspiratorial tone. Conversation was really difficult for she had obviously had a surfeit of G and T's and everything she said had a double-entendre. Her hand was back on my knee when we were both cast into shadow; the owner being a massively built, broad-shouldered man, with a huge face and florid complexion.

"So Madge, I see you have cornered poor Mr Cross." He laughed, a deep, rumbling sound.

"Nothing of the sort, we were resting our poor tired feet, weren't we Mr Cross?" She gave me a knowing look. *"Have you met my husband Wilberforce – Wilberforce Marshall?"*

We both stood and as Madge wandered away, Wilberforce wrung my hand and exchanged pleasantries. He invited me to sit and gently eased his massive bulk next to me. *"So you're a teacher. A noble profession. Thought about it myself once – but then came to my senses,"* he chuckled amused at the thought. Conversation flowed easily, he told me he had managed a financial company for many years and later had opened his own business. Although he was retired, he still spent two or three days each week supervising the company's activities. I asked him what kept him busy on the other days? His face lit up and he enthusiastically told me of his passion for boating and all about his pride and joy, a sailing boat called *Crazy Dream*.

I listened as he recounted tales of cruises to the Turks and Caicos, and to mainland America; of mountainous seas, which his *Crazy Dream* had taken in her stride; and days of idle pottering around the Bermudas. *"Don't go far these days and not very often – got a heart problem but just love being on the sea,"* he sighed.

I sympathised and explained that I had been thinking of buying a boat, not particularly to go anywhere but just to be out on the sea, for the peace and solitude it provided - and a spot of fishing.

"What sort of boat are you looking for? A motor cruiser or a sailing boat?" he asked. I explained I had a budget of two thousand dollars and how I intended to trawl round the boatyards to see what one can buy for that amount. He talked of the need to have any such purchase checked by an expert before parting with any money and said he knew someone who would be glad to help. Suddenly a thought struck him, he looked me square on, with a questioning expression on his wind and sun ravaged face: *"Have you ever done any sailing?"*

"Only in a small dinghy, nothing bigger," I replied.

"Principles are the same;" he grunted. Again he peered at me as if trying to make up his mind, then looked away at the knots of guests still idly gossiping. He stared at me again, arresting my eyes with an intense gaze. *"Would you like to learn how to sail my boat? It might help you make up your mind what sort you want."* He looked into his glass. *"I hate to see it lying at anchor, little used."* I was a little stunned by this offer and slow to respond. *"Come and have a look at it before making up you mind. It's moored at Foot of the Lane. You know, near Hamilton, just as you round the bend from here going into town. Past the island where Johnny Barnes stands. What do you say? I could meet you there tomorrow morning about eleven o'clock."*

I knew exactly where he meant his boat was moored and had seen the amazing man, named Johnny Barnes, who stood each day at the traffic island greeting everyone, he was a living legend. I thanked Mr Marshall for his kind offer and agreed to meet the next morning.

71

Soon after ten o'clock I thanked Laura for a pleasant evening and along with several others bid her farewell. As my fellow guests tumbled into their cars I fumbled my way down an unlit path leading down to Long Bay Lane, tired but happy.

*

The next morning I was up early and busied myself with household chores while it was cool. Later I cut the grass before showering and riding off towards Hamilton and my appointment with Wilberforce Marshall. I was in good time and so turned off Middle Road to take the Harbour Road that followed the coast. I loved the view across the Great Sound towards the capital of Hamilton, the pastel-coloured skyline topped by the cathedral tower. Across the water there was a cruise liner tied up on Front Street, it looked like Cunard's Franconia. I thought it quite amazing that such huge vessels could moor right against the quay, in the centre of town, allowing passengers the convenience of a luxury downtown hotel within easy walking distance of the shops.

Reaching the appointed place I parked my motorbike on the grass and walked over to the harbour wall. It was a very sheltered and picturesque spot where dozens of boats of different shapes and sizes were moored. I wondered which one was Wilberforce's boat but they were all too far away to read names. Before I had chance to consider my next move there was a shout and Wilberforce came into view. There was no mistaking his huge frame. He beckoned me towards him, as he turned and walked towards a parked car. Reaching him he turned and shook my hand warmly before asking me to pick up a box of gear in the boot of his car, while he carried a couple of oars and a large bag. At the water's edge, chained and padlocked to a ring set in concrete, was a small fibreglass boat, just big enough for the two of us. I turned it over and pushed it into the water. Once aboard he handed me an oar and we began paddling between the smaller boats moored close to shore. As we cleared a gleaming white cruiser Wilberforce puffed: *"Straight on, straight ahead."* I gasped; there she lay, *Crazy Dream*, pretty as a picture, perched as serenely as a princess on a turquoise carpet; with White's Island and The Great Sound in the distance behind her. She was single-masted schooner some thirty or forty feet long, I calculated.

"Wow Mr Marshall, she's a beauty. What wonderful lines!" I spluttered inarticulately.

Wilberforce grunted in reply, he had obviously found the short row rather strenuous. *"Please,"* he puffed, *"call me Wilber, everyone does. At the stern there are steps"* he wheezed. He had stopped paddling and was just using his oar to steer while I dug in deep. The boat had a swimming platform at the stern with steps leading up to the deck. Grabbing the handrail I made the boat fast before climbing out on to the small platform, taking the box and bag, before holding out a hand to help Wilber Marshall aboard.

The next couple of hours just flew by as Wilber showed me round his pride and joy and explained what everything did and how everything worked. There was a well-fitted galley and two cabins both fitted with two bunks and clever storage cupboards everywhere. On deck it all seemed so complicated and I marvelled at the thought of him sailing the boat single-handed.

"You'll soon get the hang of it," he kept saying and *"if it all becomes too much you can always resort to the engine."* After running through all the basics again, he asked if I was ready for my first lesson, to which I readily agreed. Wilber started the engine and I was despatched to untie the mooring ropes. First he gently reversed away from the mooring before nosing *Crazy Dream* out between obstacles of boats and buoys. Once we were well clear of the land I was instructed to raise the jib sail and then was given the responsibility of the wheel. Wilber stood at my shoulder, offering advice as we motored past the anchored cruise ship, which was the *Franconia*, as I had suspected. We skirted several small islands and sailed out into the centre of the Great Sound where Wilber switched off the engine. The adrenaline was flowing and I quickly got the feel of the wind and found the boat surprisingly easy to handle. Wilber directed me to tack to and fro a few times before he said I should put up the main sail. Even though there was not much wind, the sail soon filled and the speed picked up. All the time we were sailing Wilber was offering advice and teaching me the rudiments of this ancient skill. I was thrilled to pieces and thoroughly enjoying myself. At some stage he disappeared, only to return a few moments later with two cans of beer and a plate of sandwiches. He showed me how to set up the self-steering device, which I watched with suspicion while gratefully sinking the Heineken.

It was growing dusk by the time we had securely moored *Crazy Dream* and had returned to Wilber's car. We sat inside where he showed me a set of charts, explaining that it was necessary for me to learn where the major inshore reefs lay and the deep passages that ran between them. When it became too dark to see them clearly, he pushed them into my lap and told me to study them at home. When he discovered that I was on holiday he asked if I wanted another lesson the next day - I leapt at the chance and so we parted promising to meet at nine the next morning.

The ride home along Harbour Road was a dream and I kept glancing sideways at the Great Sound and where, just a few hours earlier, I had unbelievably been skipper of an ocean-going yacht. I was still pumped and the adrenaline was still flowing thick and fast when I reached home. I grabbed a beer and dived under the shower singing loudly my impression of Rod Stewart: 'We are sailing, we are sailing.' My musicality was interrupted by the insistent tone of the telephone. I grabbed a towel and rushed. *"Jack Cross,"* I said.

"Hi Jack Cross, you've been elusive today." It was Eloise.

"Well it's a long story but I've been out sailing," I blustered, remembering I had said I would call her.

"Does that mean you are too tired for some sporting action?" she asked, sounding slightly disappointed.

"Not at all," I responded, *"quite the opposite, I'm all fired up. What did you have in mind?"*

"Well, I was down at Dockyard today visiting the wife of a naval officer I know. She mentioned that there is a squash court there that only seems to get used when there's a

75

Royal Navy ship in dock... and she gave me a key," she explained.

"Great idea... but," I groaned, *"I don't have a racquet."*

"No problem, she loaned me two racquets and a couple of balls. We're all set to go. Why don't you come to my place on your bike when you're ready and we'll go from there? What do you think?" she asked.

"I think that's a great idea," I enthused. I looked at my watch, it was just after six o'clock. *"Have you eaten?"*

"No, I thought we could come back here afterwards and I could cook pasta or something. Not much sense stuffing ourselves beforehand," she replied.

"You're a star. I'll be with you in thirty minutes," I laughed. I hung up the receiver, skipped a few nautical steps and continued crooning *'Sailing'* where I had left off, what a great way to end a perfect day, I thought.

*

"Tell me about the Dockyard," I said to Eloise, as she drove over Watford Bridge. *"What goes on there? I heard rumours that it is likely to close."*

"Well it stopped being a proper dockyard back in 1951, put hundreds of people out of work," she replied, *"I know because my grandfather worked there. It's been the headquarters for the West Indies fleet since then, with just two ships. But you're right there are rumours of closure again. Certainly it's nowhere as busy as when I was a child. There's only a handful of sailors here now. As to what do they do? Service navy ships passing by, routine maintenance and stuff I suppose. Well, what else"* she continued. *" If I*

remember my local history lessons, there has been a British naval dockyard here since the seventeen hundreds, can't remember the exact date, sometime when the British were fighting the French in Canada. Umm what else? It's located on Ireland Island – and the squash court is behind the old Officers' Mess."

It was pitch black as we drove across Boaz Island and across Grey's Bridge onto Ireland Island. Eloise was concentrating, for the road was narrow, not that we had met a single vehicle in the last ten minutes. I had taken my bike out to Dockyard once and had wandered among the derelict buildings. The kids in my class often talked about their trips there and how you had to watch out for giant centipedes that could bite your arm off. It had been like a fisherman's tale with Colin, the shifty eyed boy, telling us he lived on Ireland Island and he knew. He had seen them. He had stretched his arms wide. The others objected to his exaggerations and gradually the arms came in and we eventually established that they were about six to nine inches long and did indeed have a painful bite. I had seen these creatures in Greece and could well believe that they could be found among the debris littering the floors in many of the ancient buildings.

We found the old officers mess, sadly almost a ruin and parked outside. Eloise had brought a flashlight and she led the way behind the Mess and along a short path to the door of another building. We knew it was right for over the door written in black paint on the white wall were the words *Squash Court*. I held the torch and Eloise struggled with the key. After a little gentle persuasion she succeeded in turning the lock and threw open the door and went in search of the

77

lights. We were pleasantly surprised with the interior. It was clean and freshly painted and the composite floor was excellent. Eloise was already in a tracksuit and she started knocking up while I found the small changing room.

"I can't remember if you said you have played before or not," she called out, slapping the ball vigorously off the side-wall.

"Only a couple of times, just enough to learn the rules and the basic strokes," I admitted, rattling the base plate with my first hit. It wasn't long before I had acquired the knack and was able to give Eloise a decent game. She stripped off her tracksuit and with each game we became more and more saturated. At the end of the third game, which she won again but only just, she called time and said she had brought a drink in her bag. I went to fetch it from the changing room. When I returned she was leaning against the wall breathing heavily. *"You were kidding me,"* she gasped, her chest heaving, beads of sweat dripping from the end of her chin. *"You can't be that good after only playing a couple of times."* I too leaned against the wall and looked down at her. She was so wet; she might as well have been naked for her tee shirt clung tightly, revealing every delicious curve, her nipples hard and erect. I tore my eyes away and took a gulp of the coke she offered. After a couple of minutes she pushed herself away from the wall and stood on the T of the court. *"Okay one more game and then you can carry me home,"* she said.

"More likely you will have to carry me home." I retorted planting a sly slice into the back corner. The last game proved to be the longest game of the evening, as each

of us chased every shot determined to outdo the other. This was some competitive lady I decided. Hurling herself for one of my drop shots Eloise's feet suddenly slid from under her and she fell awkwardly. The floor was wet from our exertions and she had lost her grip. She sat up quickly but did not attempt to stand. I rushed towards her anxiously demanding to know if she was all right.

"I don't think I did my ankle any good," she gasped, as I bent to undo her lace and gently eased off her sneaker and sock.

"Stay there, I'll get a wet cloth." I searched the changing room in vain and eventually stripped off my shirt and ran it under a cold tap. I wrapped it round her ankle hoping that it might help reduce any swelling. She sat looking at me as I ministered to her foot. I glanced up, her hair was stuck to her head, her faced gleamed with sweat and drips glistened on her ear lobes and chin. Despite this, I thought she was the most beautiful and desirable woman I had ever seen. For a moment I remained motionless on my knees and then without thinking I eased slowly towards her, awkwardly enveloping her in my arms nestling my face against her slippery neck before sliding round to her wide and equally hungry lips. Moments later her arms were above her head as I struggled to remove her sodden shirt. Free of the obstruction I pulled her to me again both of us oblivious of the sweat and its unromantic scent. I gently laid her against the cold floor feverishly running my tongue over her face and breasts. I lapped her nipple and she gasped and cried out, as if in pain. Eventually she pushed me away and I

watched spellbound as she fought to remove her shorts clinging like a second skin.

"Oh damn," she swore, *"don't just sit there, help me."* I moved closer and pulled while she eased the sodden material over her hips. Once she had freed herself of her clothes she turned her attention to my shorts and we fell into each other's arms grunting, laughing and finally sobbing under the searingly, brilliant lights.

After what seemed like hours, Eloise sat up and looked at my prostrate form. *"I wonder if that's the first time anyone has made love on the Royal Navy's squash court?"* she said. I opened my eyes and looked at her.

"You really are gorgeous," I said. *"And no, I don't suppose it's the first time,"* I rolled on to an elbow to get a better look. Eloise eased towards me and kissed me hard and long. I pulled her into my arms and we lay there exhausted.

Slowly, as if doped by some mysterious drug we eventually dressed, packed up and made our way back to the car. Eloise leaning on my arm to ease the weight on her ankle. *"Do you think that would have happened if I hadn't twisted my ankle,"* she murmured in my ear as she hopped along.

"Of course," I whispered back, *"I knew it would happen the first time I saw you."*

"You're right," she agreed, *"me too."*

I drove back to her cottage, windows wide-open, tree-frogs serenading us, while concentrating on keeping the Beetle on the narrow road. Once inside her home, she cautiously tested her weight on her ankle and insisted she was all right and no serious damage had been done.

"Let's save water," she said suggestively, *"and shower together."* Standing in the narrow bath taking turns to get under the feeble spray was very precarious. Taking turns to soap each other added to the danger, while the mounting excitement of caressing and exploring each other's bodies made the exercise totally life-threatening. I climbed out first and held out a towel. Daintily she moved towards me and I wrapped it round her before sweeping her into my arms and carrying her to the bedroom. We were better prepared this time and in less of a hurry, which heightened the sensation and ecstasy of the moment. An overwhelming sense of satisfaction and completeness swept over me – a feeling I had not experienced before.

Some time later Eloise busied herself in her tiny kitchen preparing a pasta dish, while I struggled with an unfamiliar bottle-opener. Suddenly she turned towards me tears pouring down her cheeks. *"Whatever's the matter?"* I said, rushing towards her throwing an arm protectively around her waist. *"Is it your ankle... something, I said – or did? I'm sorry..."*

"Shut up stupid, of course it is nothing you said or did," the tears continued to flow. *"It's the onions!"* Without a word, I flipped her round crushing her to my chest.

*

Dead on nine o'clock I was at the appointed place eager to get started on my second sailing lesson. I had told Eloise about my day with Wilberforce Marshall and she told me she had never met him but knew he was a well-known businessman and his wife an active member of various Bermuda charity groups. Today Wilber had brought a proper hamper basket, as well as various bits and pieces for the yacht, which meant two trips in the tiny rowing boat. Task completed, I began unfastening *Crazy Dream* from its mooring, Wilber started the engine and then insisted I took the wheel and guide the boat through the many obstacles towards the Great Sound. He then insisted that I circle round one of the small islands and return to the mooring for the experience of controlling the vessel in a tight situation. He stood at the bow calling directions, a gaff in his hand. I couldn't help thinking that despite his age he looked an impressive figure in his mariner's cap. It took me two attempts before I got close enough for him to hook the buoy from the sea. We repeated this exercise two more times until he was satisfied that I could competently handle the boat We then motored out past the Hamilton harbour with its towering cruise ship moored to Front Street, between the islands of Saltus and Dyer, following what Wilber called Two Rock Passage. He went on to tell me that the shape of the Bermuda islands are often described as a fish hook, with the Great Sound being the partly enclosed hook portion. Almost in the centre of the Great Sound is a group of islands, some private and residential, others the public were allowed to visit. He instructed me to raise the sails, turned off the motor and we tacked our way across the Sound towards Cavello Bay where Eloise lived. Once again it was a perfect day, with quite a strong breeze so that filling the sails was not a problem. Having tacked a few times into the wind, Wilber told me to go about and practise running with the wind behind and then how to perform a controlled jibe. I was glad that I had learned the rudiments of sailing as a pimply teenager, years ago on a cold, grey, English reservoir - and more recently had swotted up on the terminology from a book borrowed from Somerset library.

Later in the morning I noticed the *Franconia* easing her way out of Hamilton and through Two Rock Passage beginning her return voyage to New York. During the summer this was a popular weekly cruise. Wilber told me there would be a Bermudian pilot on board until the ship had cleared the reefs lying away to the north. We were sailing close to the peninsula housing the American Naval Air Station, as the giant ship rounded Spanish Point and gradually disappeared along the North Shore. Wilber directed me to sail towards the Dockyard some two miles distant. The wind was blowing straight out of the west and I managed to draw close to the Dockyard on one long tack. As we drew nearer Wilber advised me to lower the main sail, until I had more experience, and switch on the engine. Gingerly I edged *Crazy Dream* toward the main pier until I was close enough for Wilber to call a passing workman to catch the rope and make it secure. I switched off the engine and sighed with relief before leaping ashore to make the rope fast at the rear. Once completed, I gazed around the Dockyard area looking for the squash court but eventually decided we were too far away. Back on board Wilber called me to join him in the galley. He unpacked the hamper and within a few minutes we were sitting in the cockpit tucking into a delicious lunch. *"You're a natural,"* said Wilber between mouthfuls. *"I can't believe that you haven't sailed before."*

"I love it," I enthused. *"I just love the sensation and the challenge of harnessing the wind."* It was true, I didn't yet feel in total control and the adrenaline flowed continuously. I reminded myself that the conditions had been almost perfect on both days. It would be totally different sailing in rough seas and gale force winds. *"I'm really grateful Wilber for giving me this opportunity to sail. It's really very kind of you."* I looked at him propped comfortably against a fat cushion drinking from a can of orange juice.

"Rubbish," he retorted, *"haven't you worked out yet that I'm being selfish?"* He emptied his can. *"With my dickey ticker I'm in no state to sail on my own. You can see how strenuous it is. I'm making use of you!"* He laughed. *"Once I'm satisfied you can handle the boat in all conditions you are welcome to borrow it any time you like - on condition you take me out occasionally."*

"It's a deal," I grinned, *"if this is being used, I love it!"* I looked around the boat imagining sailing out to sea with Eloise as crew. The sun was unforgiving and I shifted into a corner to find some shade, Wilber seemed not to notice, his cap pulled down over his eyes against the glare.

"That's a fine old building," I said waving my beer in the direction of the shore. Wilber followed my gaze; *"Yes, built by the British navy as a storehouse back in 1857. Known as the Clock tower, of course."* He referred to the fact the building had twin towers, the southern one housing a large clock. *"The northerly tower is a bell tower, it was used to summon the men to work. You should go and have a closer look one day, if you're interested in such things.*

Madge and I climbed up once, years ago. The bell was inscribed 'Haste When I Call' and the name of a navy captain who was in charge at the time. There's also a tide indicator on the tower, which is pretty unusual." He opened another can of orange juice.

"Yes I am interested in local history, I'll have to go explore one day," I replied. *"I hear that one of the buildings here is a prison?"*

"Oh that's Casemates, away to the left. Used to accommodate the sailors when the place was busy. Seems to house mainly drug addicts and dealers these days. Yes," he mused, *"the Dockyard used to employ well over a thousand people at one time. Many of the skilled craftsmen on the Island did an apprenticeship here. Sadly most of the place closed down in the fifties, left a great gap."* He looked at me, *"well if you've finished let's get going and have a look at the North Shore."*

As we parted at the end of the day he had asked if I would be free to sail the boat on Sunday morning. I had agreed and he told me to be at the quay at ten o'clock. Madge and some friends would be joining him. He took my phone number and said he would call if the plans had to be changed because of the weather.

Later, cycling home along Harbour Road, refreshed by a cooling breeze but feeling pretty tired after a day in the sun and the wind, I counted my blessings. I felt fortunate to have met Wilber Marshall. He was such a thoroughly nice guy. Easy going, generous. *"Jeepers,"* I thought, *"I've fallen on my feet,"* even if, as he said, he was using me.

It was completely dark when I arrived home, although still only six o'clock and the shrill noise of the tree frogs filled the humid air. I gathered a can of beer from the fridge, kicked off my sandals and collapsed on the bed. My instinct was to reach for the telephone and call Eloise and share the pleasure of the day. But I didn't. For some reason on and off during the whole day I had been haunted by the memory of Jill. I was swept by guilt each time I thought of last night's lovemaking and the intense emotions that Eloise had stirred. Every time I thought of Eloise, a hazy figure of Jill would appear in the background and an icy shiver would run down my spine, as I lay propped against the pillow my emotions were totally confused and ambivalent. I was almost euphoric after the day's sailing; I was certainly euphoric that Eloise had come into my life but somehow I was angry with myself for letting primeval instincts desecrate Jill's memory. I emptied the can and with eyes closed, gave myself a good talking to. I was being stupid. Jill and I had loved each other, neither of us were perfect, the relationship was not perfect, there was no knowing whether it would have lasted into old age; the indications were there that it would not. But her violent death had left a deep scar and an intense sensation that I needed to treasure her memory. I was struck with a strong feeling that by shutting out that memory when with Eloise, I was somehow being unfaithful to her. Unthinkingly I reached out for the phone and held it against my chest, Jill was gone, I needed to move on. But as the mental battle waged on, weariness took over and eventually I succumbed to neither of the women but to the enveloping arms of Morpheus.

The next morning I awoke early. I grabbed some breakfast, stuffed a towel, swimming gear, camera and a map into a rucksack before jumping on my bike and heading off on a voyage of discovery. It was a perfect morning, not a cloud in the sky and the roads relatively quiet. I had determined that the first stop would be Gibbs Hill Lighthouse. Having parked my bike at the foot of the graceful Victorian lighthouse, I paid the admission fee and clambered to the top of the 117 feet high tower. The view from the highest point on the island was fantastic and I busied myself taking photographs in every direction. I decided the view towards Hamilton was the most spectacular with the myriad of tiny islands shimmering like jewels in the Great Sound. I was amazed by the thousands of white painted roofs, each reflecting the early morning sun, like sequins set on a green gown. Eventually, satisfied I had exhausted the photographic opportunities, I leaned on the rail and slowly digested the fabulous landscape. I felt a poem coming on and took a small notebook from my camera bag and scribbled down a few phrases for future use. And then the arguments I had battled with the previous night returned. I leaned further over the rail and focussed on the rocky ground far below. There is no logic, I kept telling myself. There is no logic in trying to pretend Jill is still alive. It is useless to think that any moment she will climb up those last few steps and join me on this precarious ledge. There is no logic …a solitary tear dripped from the end of my nose and fell, probably to evaporate before reaching the ground. A taxi drew up and a group of people spilled out, their voices drifting upwards and breaking my reverie.

87

From Gibbs Hill I biked into town, waving at Johnny Barnes, the eccentric old gentleman standing at The Foot of The Lane, the entrance to Hamilton. I'd heard that he was there every day waving to the travellers, wishing them a good day. Somehow this simple act symbolised the Bermuda I was growing to love. I parked my bike underneath a Poinciana tree on Front Street, strangely empty now that the cruise ship had sailed away. I hoisted the rucksack on my shoulder and wandered along the Front Street shops, each filled with beautiful objects tempting visiting tourists to part with their hard-earned dollars. Later I wandered to the back of town and found myself in Court Street. Except for a couple of sleeping dogs, it was deserted and seemed little different from the other back streets and yet it had a reputation - one that suggested it was not wise for white folk to linger. I found that hard to believe, trying to remember which of the tennis partners had advised about steering clear. Nearby I stopped at a small café and sat outside sipping a long cold Sprite through a straw. I tried to engage the old black lady who served me into conversation but although she was pleasant enough she wouldn't be drawn. I paid my dues and wandered on, taking in the City Hall and the ancient Perot post office before reclaiming my bike. From Hamilton I rode out to Spanish Point, a spit of land facing out towards Dockyard and sat on the rocks watching a group of children playing in the azure blue water. Before long the temptation proved too great and I was in there with them enjoying the cooling surf. Afterwards I stretched out in the shade of a giant Royal Palm – and battled to keep both Eloise and Jill out of my thoughts. It was a losing battle and again I was bombarded with a sense of guilt. Disgusted at my inability to clear my head I sat up and cursed. *'Right'*, I said, almost aloud. *'Sorry Eloise, it's too soon!'* Clambering to my feet I determined that as soon as I was home, I would telephone and explain.

Chapter 4

November, 1972

I wandered aimlessly about the living room of my tiny bungalow for some time, dressed in nothing more than a towel, trying to sum up the courage to call Eloise and rehearsing what I would say. When I eventually decided I'd got the words sorted out in my head and called – there was no reply. At half hour intervals, for the next two hours, I tried again but she was obviously out. It then struck home that I knew so little about her. I had no idea who her friends were, assuming she had friends and we had never talked about family. She had mentioned playing squash regularly in Hamilton but the hockey was only on Sunday afternoons. I had absolutely no idea what else she did with her time. Flopping in a chair I tried reading the *Royal Gazette* but found myself absorbed with the question of where she was and whom she was with. For some unknown reason it annoyed me she wasn't home to take my call. I fetched a beer from the fridge and flopped again and folded the paper over to concentrate on the crossword.

A problem with mites turns Jean endlessly green. What a stupid clue! I doodled with my pencil. *A problem with mites....* lice....louse... lousy. Endless Jean....jea.. turning green - j e a l o u s y. Huh, how apt I admitted to myself, the feelings gnawing at my inside were awfully akin to jealousy. And yet, I was about to tell Eloise I had no intention of seeing her again. I started to reassess the situation and once again the old arguments invaded my brain and brought an end to the logical thought needed to solve the crossword. I was so screwed up. Was there a rulebook somewhere for such situations? What was a reasonable period of time between the cruel ending of one relationship and being able to successfully start another. Would it be fair to start a new relationship when it seemed there was the danger of ruining someone else's life with the paranoia of the past?

At some time I must have dropped off to sleep, the emotional and mental energy expended on how to deal with this relationship, combined with a windswept day in the sun knocked me out. A crick in the neck at some time in the early hours eventually woke me and I stumbled into bed.

Sometime around ten o'clock the next morning I tried Eloise's number again but she didn't pick up. I thought about riding round to her home but in the end decided against that idea, changed into my swimming gear and sloppy T-shirt then towel in hand, jogged off to the beach. After completing a long and strenuous swim I wandered along the coast to a jetty where two lads rented out the Sunfish sailboats. They didn't hear me approach, the younger one was lying flat out on the ground in the shade of a wall, arm flung across his eyes, his partner sitting on a step, feet dangling in the water, quietly whistling. As I drew near I could see that he had been dropping crumbs in the water attracting a small shoal of tiny but colourful *Sergeant Majors*. I called quietly, hoping not to wake his sleeping buddy. Recognition flashed across his even black features. *"Ah, Mr Jack, a great day for sailing, just the right amount of breeze,"* he said with a cheeky grin.

"How do you know my name," I asked.

"My kid brother plays in one of your soccer teams," he explained. *"He likes you man, even if you are white."* His face split in two as he grinned, showing a perfect set of gleaming white teeth. I ignored the final comment and soon established who his brother was. I settled down alongside him on the step, the sudden movement frightening the *Sergeant Majors* down into the depths. He told me his name was Joel and his partner, his cousin, was Raymond. I asked him where he lived, which secondary school he had attended and whether he had another job. He was full of stories and questions about England, Manchester United and his hero Clyde Best. I hadn't realised Clyde Best, the popular West Ham player was a Bermudian but my newfound friend soon filled me on his career and local family connections. I learned that Joel was on commission for renting out the boats but there were not many tourists about at this time of year and so he helped milk the cows at a nearby farm, both early in the morning and again in the late afternoon. The fact there

were cows on the hill close to Long Bay took me by surprise and he offered to show me sometime, if I was interested. After spending some time amiably chatting I asked whether it was possible to hire a Sunfish and, as I had no money, whether I could pay him later. *"No problem,"* he had replied pulling one of the boats close to the jetty for me to scramble on board.

Remembering my childhood sailing lessons, it wasn't long before I was tacking across Long Bay and close to the Cambridge Beaches Cottage Colony nestled so perfectly under a forest of slender palms. The fabulously turquoise sea was reasonably calm so I decided to tack in the other direction out towards Daniel's' Island. I was really enjoying myself and as there was a constant breeze I tried taking the small boat to its limit until, mistiming an oncoming wave and with the sail pulled as tight as it would go, my arrogance was suddenly shattered and without warning I was plunged into the sea. Fortunately I had the presence of mind to keep hold of the sheet and because the boat was little more than a surf board I was soon back on board and proceeding more carefully and at a more leisurely speed. There was a glass-bottomed boat anchored over the coral sea gardens close to Daniel's Island, with a few tourists snorkelling round the old wreck which, I had been told, was resting on the shallow bottom. I thought to myself that while sailing this Sunfish was great fun, there was not the same feeling of power and exhilaration that I experienced at the helm of *Crazy Dream*.

Drawing near to Daniel's Island I was suddenly aware of strong currents running counter to the tide and my progress was suddenly arrested. It was strange, the sails were filled with wind but I was going nowhere. Deciding discretion was, as they say, the better part of valour, I very carefully jibed and made my back towards the jetty. As I drew near Joel dived into the water and with a few powerful strokes came up alongside the boat, grabbed the rope and towed me in. Raymond was now awake and came to help. We sat together chatting for a while afterwards, until pangs of hunger forced me to thank them with promises of returning later to pay my dues.

"*No problem man,*" drawled Joel, "*you ain't going nowhere!*"

*

Saturday morning, Dilly knocked and called my name before putting her head round the door. I was hanging a picture on the living room wall that I'd bought the day before. It was an Alfred Birdsey print of Hamilton Harbour and Albuoy's Point, quite close to where *Crazy Dream* was moored.

"*Hey man, you been painting?*" asked Dilly padding silently to the middle of the room on bare feet. I sighed aloud and gave up trying to get it level and left the picture hanging lop-sided.

"*Dilly, it shows you know nothing about me, the only thing I can paint is walls and ceilings. I'm really good with a roller.*" Dilly glided in front of me and my senses caught a waft of some exotic perfume. She grasped the picture, gently manoeuvring the frame until it was level.

"*You just need a little patience man,*" she breathed standing back, squinting with one eye. Satisfied it was level she turned her gaze on me. "*Okay for tonight? You still on for the big night out?"* She shimmied round me, one eye still on the picture.

"You mean the Southampton Princess and your show, I certainly am. What time? Where and when?" I was genuinely looking forward to the night out

"Okay, we've only got two shows tonight," she said fixing me with those liquid brown eyes, her tone business-like. *"Not so many tourists about, so Elbow Beach is off. You come with me in the taxi at seven o'clock. You can look around and get yourself a drink. I'll be busy. Your table is booked for eight o'clock in the main dining room and the show starts at nine o'clock and runs for an hour. When it's over we move on to Cambridge Beaches for a show that starts at midnight. But you can get a taxi home from the Princess when you're ready. How does that sound?"*

"Fantastic," I replied, *"I'm really grateful Dilly. By the way what do you think I should wear? I guess I need to be smart."*

"Wear your best Bermudas and blazer with a tie. They won't let you in without a tie," she commanded.

"Momma are you there?" It was Pearl calling from outside. *"I'm here honey,"* Dilly replied. *"I'm coming now."* Pearl appeared round the door and greeted me.

"Momma that Renee is being real nasty. She won't do what I say. You gotta come and give her a good talking to." Pearl's face was screwed up in annoyance. *"Okay girl. I'm coming,"* said Dilly reassuringly, arm around her daughter's shoulder. She glanced at me raising her eyebrows making for the door. *"You be ready at seven o'clock, you hear me?"*

95

The day slipped by filled with household chores, washing, ironing cutting the grass. I tried calling Eloise but again without success and I had given up trying to think where she might be, though in one rash moment I did think of phoning the hospital. By a quarter to seven I was showered, shaved and dressed in my salmon coloured Bermuda shorts with matching socks, white shirt and college tie, the dark blue blazer over my arm. I felt a bit of a Wally and wondered what my old friends back home would have thought about my outfit but knew such gear was de-rigueur and I would just blend in. I heard a car draw up and the sound of a horn and made my way out. It was a taxi and Eggy Foley was just getting out. He saw me approaching and his face lit up. *"Hey Jack! How goes it man?"* pumping my hand and slapping my shoulder. I was amazed he remembered my name. *"Just got to go inside a moment"*. He was carrying a package. At that moment Dilly appeared at the door in jeans and T-shirt carrying a large case. She greeted Eggy and I noticed he was holding the package behind his back, out of her sight. *"Must just say Hi to my old friend Karl."* He slipped passed her and into the darkness of the hallway. I took the case from Dilly and moved towards the taxi.

"My ain't you the bees' knees!" said Dilly with a straight face.

"You think I'll do Ms. Dilly?" I responded jiggling my hips.

"Hmm, nice legs!" still a straight face. I ignored her, put the case in the boot and helped Dilly into the back seat of the car.

"Don't the girls get to see you off?" I asked.

"Not today, they are staying overnight at my sisters. They like that, she spoils them." Eggy reappeared whistling, as I got into the front seat.

The drive to the Southampton Princess passed quickly, while Eggy amused us with constant tales of the more eccentric customers he had ferried around that day. He dropped us at the main entrance and two liveried doormen leapt forward to open the doors. Their faces lit up when they saw Dilly and they almost fought for the privilege of carrying her case. With a shout of *"See you later,"* Eggy eased away to join the queue of taxis waiting to pick up guests heading for other destinations. The interior of the hotel was truly sumptuous and as I stood and gazed around, Dilly took my arm. The man with the case had disappeared. She walked me further inside and down a wide corridor to the main dining room. At the door she introduced me to the Maître d', called William, resplendent in his dinner jacket.

"Okay Jack," said Dilly, *"When the time comes you find William here and he will take you to the table. Have a great time. I need to go, see you later."* As she turned to leave, I was aware of the same perfume lingering in the air. William and I watched, as ballerina-like she floated down the corridor, a diminutive figure, with an amazingly upright posture. William spoke: *"That's some lady,"* he coughed and our eyes met. *"Mr Jack, you come and see me about ten minutes before eight and I'll get you seated."* I thanked him and wandered away. After some fifteen minutes I found myself in a beautiful bar affording views across the Great Sound. I ordered a beer and settled down for that favourite

of pastimes – people-watching. Judging by the accents, the majority of the guests were American; almost without exception looking tanned and well-heeled.

At ten minutes to eight I slowly made my way to find William. The dining room had already filled up and there was a lively hubbub of noise and laughter. I spotted William busy helping guests find seats. After some minutes he returned to the door, acknowledged my presence and asked me to follow. When he reached a table for two, in prime position, right up against the stage, he pulled out a chair. The table was beautifully laid and fresh hibiscus flowers floated in a glass bowl, a candle flickering in its centre. *"Enjoy your evening sir,"* he said before speeding off to assist another diner. At the back of the low stage was a white grand piano and an elderly black gentlemen in a white suit leisurely playing popular tunes, apparently oblivious of the people now filling the room. Suddenly aware of movement across the table I glanced up, it was William pulling out the chair opposite. A young, slim, black woman in a sequinned mini dress eased out from behind him, saw me and froze. Her hair was piled on top of her head, emphasising her long neck, against which huge dangling earrings glinted. *"There must be some mistake!"* she said.

"No mistake Mam," replied William. *"This is Miss Dilly's table."* By now I was on my feet trying to introduce myself. She ignored my outstretched hand, avoided looking at me and uncomfortably eased herself into the chair, where she busied herself finding a suitable place on the floor for her handbag.

"*I'm sorry, I didn't catch you name,*" I said. "*Are you a friend of Dilly's?*" She visibly struggled to regain her composure.

"*Yes, yes I'm a friend of Dilly's. My name's Marsha.*" She threw a fleeting glance in my direction, which I caught and held on to. She was stunning. "*How do you know Dilly?*" she asked, fiddling with the cutlery.

"*I'm her next door neighbour. I only arrived in August, in Bermuda that is, Dilly has been very kind to me.*" She nodded but didn't reply. "*What about you, how do you know Dilly?*"

"*Oh we just met, I've known her about a year.*" She was still rearranging the cutlery and clearly ill at ease.

"*Marsha, do you mind if I ask you something?*" I questioned. "*Were you expecting someone else?*"

"*No,*" she shook her head. "*No, no I thought I would be on my own.*"

"*So did I,*" I laughed. "*Dilly gave no indication that anyone else was coming.*"

"*Dilly's idea of a joke, I suppose,*" she said quietly. I thought she added *but not funny*, but I couldn't be sure and chose to ignore it.

"*Well, we're here so let's enjoy the occasion,*" I said encouragingly. "*What would you like to drink?*" She asked for wine and in double quick time I was testing a bottle of *Nuit Saint George*. Conversation was stunted, she only answered in monosyllables or nodded or shook her head. It was hard work; she clearly had no interest in getting to know anything about me. She hadn't asked a single question except the one about knowing Dilly. But I wouldn't give up,

I liked a challenge – and she was a striking dinner companion, even if she wouldn't speak! As the sommelier poured, I hoped the wine would loosen her tongue. A waiter appeared at her elbow resplendent in his uniform and asked if we wished to help ourselves from the carvery or order a la carte. She asked for the menu, muttering under her breath that she didn't want to fight with the tourists at the carvery. I thought I'd better do the same. The waiter stood patiently while she studied the menu, asking the occasional question. Eventually she gave her order, her French accent almost perfect. I gave mine, my French less than perfect. I raised my glass: *"Here's to a pleasant evening,"* I toasted *"And good health."* Nothing. No response, though she lifted the glass to her lips and sipped. *"You appear to speak good French,"* I began. *"Have you ever visited France."*

She nodded her head. *"I studied in Paris for year."* She said somewhat reluctantly.

I persisted: *"What did you study...French?"* I asked. She nodded. *" Did you enjoy your time there?"* I continued.

"It was okay." She responded quietly, her eyes glued to the pianist.

"What do you do for a living, do you have a job?" I began to wonder how long I could keep this up.

"I'm a lawyer," she responded, still in a monotone. I hid my surprise and let the silence swirl over us and looked again at the elderly gentleman, in a world of his own, eyes on the ceiling, fingers flitting from one George Gershwin melody to another. I glanced back at my silent companion. She was staring at the pianist too, looking thoroughly bored. I suddenly felt sorry for her and wondered what personal

trauma she was trying to deal with. *"Look,"* I said deliberately. *"Why don't I ask if they can find me another table and leave you to your thoughts. It's obvious you are finding the situation embarrassing."*

She started and looked around. *"Seems pretty busy to me. I don't think they would find you another table. Saturday nights are usually a full house."* She sounded resigned.

This was not the response I had been looking for and felt my hackles rising, her attitude was downright rude. *"Is it me or the unexpected situation that's upsetting you?"* I said bluntly. *"I don't remember saying anything to cause you offence."* The arrival of the entrée stopped me in my tracks. Except for a mutual *Bon Appetite* we ate in silence. Later, while we waited for the main course to arrive I topped up her glass thinking to myself that she was not drinking fast enough to loosen up. *"Have you met Dilly's daughters?"* I asked. She nodded. *"Great kids."* I continued. *"Pearl is a very smart girl. We've had some pretty intellectual discussions... particularly about the problems of race."* I stared at her, as I said this but there wasn't a flicker. *"I think it's a shame the schools aren't more integrated."*

"Black and white cultures are different," she pronounced, *"separate schools are more appropriate."*

"That's utter rubbish," I retorted. *"How can people live cheek by jowl on this tiny island and not share a similar culture. It's 1972 not 1872, it's time to forget about skin colour and move on."*

"You don't know anything," she retorted hotly.

"What kind of law do you practise?" I asked, a suspicious thought creeping into my mind..

"Among other things, helping poor oppressed black people get justice," she almost snarled. I'd obviously found a nerve but I couldn't help but smile.

"At least we're talking," I said quietly. *"I'm sure Dilly would want us to be enjoying ourselves. Eating in silence in such great surroundings is not much fun. I admit I was trying to provoke you into saying something. I'm new to the island. I've never really known any black people. In the part of England where I was brought up and in the area where I worked I just never came across black people, oppressed or not. And here, here all I see are happy smiling black faces, if they're oppressed they don't show it,"* I proclaimed.

"Of course they don't show it. Throughout their history they have smiled and sung. It's their way of dealing with hardship and injustice." The main course arrived interrupting her argument and we both commented how delicious it looked and how wonderfully the meal was presented. I picked up the bottle and topped up Marsha's glass again, perhaps this magical brew was having the desired effect.

During the last outburst, it suddenly occurred to me that the lilt in Marsha's voice was different. *"You're not from Bermuda are you Marsha?"* I questioned.

She shook her head and waited until she had finished chewing. *"No - I'm from Jamaica, I've been here a year longer than you."*

102

I asked if she had completed her law degree in her home country but she had shaken her head and told me she went to university in Miami. By the time we had finished desert she was in full swing arguing her case, like the lawyer she was, for the way Whites manipulated Blacks not just in Bermuda but also throughout the world. I had tried several counter arguments but she wiped them out, as if I was in the dock of some southern courtroom. During the heated discussion several men had brought a set of drums onto the stage and rigged up some microphones. The waiters were whizzing around as fast as they could go, most of them clearing up the debris from dinner, others refilling glasses. After asking Marsha what she thought, I ordered another bottle of wine and quickly filled her glass. A huge man in a floral shirt walked out to the microphone and welcomed everyone. He told several jokes and asked people to cheer as he went through a list of countries of their origin. Eventually, satisfied that he had warmed everyone up, he asked for a big hand for the Princess's own band and seven brightly attired men took their places and immediately burst into well-known calypso songs. After about ten minutes the master of ceremonies returned, thanked the band and called for a loud welcome for the *Bermuda Islanders*. To loud applause Dilly's group came skipping onto the stage, whooping noisily, guitars strumming madly and the drummer beating the skins unmercifully. Without any further introduction they launched into an exciting show of singing, dancing, fire-eating, juggling and tumbling. It was a wonderfully colourful sight, the men all in brightly coloured shirts, the girls dressed like peasants in vivid long dresses, split to the waist. Dilly stood beating a tambourine, slightly at the side, watching carefully and, I thought, seemingly masterminding the operation. I was pleased to see that the Calypso beat – and\or the red wine, had Marsha swaying and had put a broad smile on her face. I was suddenly aware of what unusually long eyelashes she had, while there was a glistening hint of perspiration in that no-man's land between nostrils and the carmine- painted upper lip. She caught me staring and I turned away slightly embarrassed. The mood suddenly changed and three men with guitars stood together and harmoniously sang a couple of well-known spirituals. While this was going on Dilly and another girl set up a couple of limbo poles and placed a bar across. As the singing stopped the limbo music started and a couple of the girls shimmied their way under the bar. The bar was moved lower and lower and when it was at a seemingly impossible height, Dilly, a candlestick in each hand began shuffling towards us. As her head drew near to the bar she placed one of the candlesticks on her forehead and continued, arms outstretched, to work her way under the bar. Her hair was trailing on the floor behind her, the back of her head almost touching the floor. As she cleared the bar, grabbing the candlestick at the last moment, a huge cheer broke out and she gave a wide and expansive bow. The music dropped and the leader announced that they wanted some members from the audience to try their skill. Even before he had finished talking Dilly was dragging Marsha and me reluctantly onto the floor. Marsha kicked off her impossibly high-heeled sandals and with great style, eased under the bar, I followed somewhat less elegantly. There were about another ten people on the stage and as each successfully ducked under, Dilly and her partner lowered the bar and the number of people involved decreased. Before long only Marsha, two other women and I were left. The music was hypnotic and Marsha was swaying continuously to the beat. It was my turn but I knew before I started that it would be beyond me. Barefooted I shuffled forward, my feet were under the bar, which was close to my chest but then came that moment when, to a great groan from the crowd, I fell backwards in a heap. As I scrambled to my feet Dilly pushed me to one side with instructions to wait. The two ladies tried, failed and returned to their seat, which just left Marsha. Playing to the crowd, her mini skirt up round her hips, clearly displaying a crimson pair of knickers to everyone on the front row, Marsha shimmied expertly under the bar. Dilly caught her arm and raised it high, as Marsha used her other hand to push down her skirt and restore some sense of decorum. One of the other girls ran up with a couple of packages, Dilly presented one to Marsha and the other to me. Talk about a put up job, I thought, but my face was wreathed in smiles. As we returned to our seats the group burst into a lively finale before leaving to huge applause with the diners on their feet clapping in unison to the calypso beat. The show had certainly got everyone going, the band returned and diners tumbled onto the floor to dance. The noise level had soared and I had to shout to make myself heard.

"*Shall we dance?*" I mouthed. She shook her head but I could tell the solid beat had tapped into some basic instinct, early memory, call it what you like but her fingers were drumming on the table, her head gently swaying to the beat. *"Come on I said, you know you want to,"* I was on my feet holding out a hand. Ignoring my hand, for the second time that evening, she slowly got to her feet and followed me to the dance floor. It was a crush, with space only available to shuffle and sway. I tried to take her hand but she kept her arms by her side, content with her with own company. A gap suddenly opened up, I grabbed her and swung her round, she was unbelievably light on her feet but immediately she used the momentum to swing out of my arms and into a routine of her own. Despite the enormous heels she moved gracefully, athletically and a small circle of space grew around her as people moved back to watch. Her eyes were almost closed, she was totally absorbed by the music. I swayed on the edge of the circle as intrigued as the rest, by her sensual movements. Gradually the open space closed again and I used the opportunity to take her right hand in my left and slide my arm round her waist. I felt her stiffen and the fluid movement dried up.

"I need a drink," she shouted in my ear, pulling out of my arms and easing her way off the dance floor. When we reached the table, she poured herself a glass of water and I excused my self and headed off to find a toilet. Out in the corridor I looked for a sign, without success so wondered away in the opposite direction from the foyer. Somehow or other I found myself at the back of the kitchens and passed a room with a glass panel set in the door. I glanced in and was surprised to see a crowd of uniformed employees seated or leaning against tables listening to Dilly. I couldn't hear what she was saying but she speaking forcefully, her face knotted

106

in seriousness, her hands waving expressively to make her point. I was intrigued and strained to hear what she was saying. Suddenly the door was flung open and a huge uniformed figure filled the doorway demanding to know if he could help. I muttered that I was looking for the toilet. He stepped out into the corridor and politely but firmly pointed back the way I had just come. A few moments later, washing my hands and peering into the mirror, I pondered upon what I had just seen. What had Dilly been saying? And why were those around her hanging on her every word? I was truly puzzled. Re-entering the dining room I was hit by a wall of hot, stale air, which wasn't surprising considering how many people were packed in. The dance floor was still awash with dancers, some concentrating seriously on their steps, others slightly the worse for alcohol, spinning almost out of control laughing and giggling.

I was relieved to find Marsha still at our table and before sitting leaned over and asked if she would like to go out onto the terrace for some air. She nodded, so I picked up the bottle of wine and our glasses and followed her.

Outside she perched on a low parapet overlooking the South Shore while I filled our glasses and handed one to her, we both commented at the refreshing, cool air.

"You're a great dancer Marsha," I said honestly. *"And a real expert at the limbo."* It was too dark to see her expression, as she looked out to sea. *"What was your prize, mine was a bottle of Whiskey?"*

"Prize, oh, um… perfume I think, I didn't look properly," she replied.

"Have you seen Dilly's show before?" I asked, desperately trying to make contact.

"No, tonight was the first time. It was very good, I enjoyed it."

"I thought it was great," I enthused *"in fact I've enjoyed the whole evening – who wouldn't with such great entertainment, wonderful food and such a beautiful companion."* For a fleeting second she glanced in my direction before returning her gaze to the darkness of the ocean, where only a line of distant breaking surf was visible and much too far away to hear. She had one deliciously long leg thrown over the other, as she perched, her foot jigging slowly to the distant beat. I could only really see her in silhouette and although the huge earrings glinted, her black face melted into the night. *"Would you like me to top up your glass?"* I picked up the bottle and moved closer.

"No, no thanks. What time is it, I should be going?" She emptied her drink. I looked at the luminous figures on my watch.

"It's only eleven-thirty," I replied, "and tomorrow is Sunday."

"I have briefs to read, I'm in court on Monday morning." She hadn't moved.

"Marsha, I really have enjoyed this evening but I have this very strong feeling that you have found it a strain and my company has, for some reason or other, caused you distress. You've been really cold towards me and conversation has been pretty one-sided. You don't know who I am, you don't even seem to care. I doubt if you have

108

even remembered my name. Don't you think I'm due some kind of explanation?"

"Your name is Jack," she hissed, glancing in my direction. *"You live next door to Dilly. And tonight is the longest time in my life I have ever spent, socially, with a white man. And yes, it's been a strain."* She was on her feet.

"Perhaps with practice you could get used to it, and it wouldn't be such a strain," I suggested. She didn't answer but thrust out a hand, shook mine firmly and thanked me for my company and before I could reply stalked elegantly back into the dining room. I followed, her swaying hips, accentuated by the tight mini skirt, as she went through the dining room and disappeared into the corridor – and I supposed out of my life. I sighed, went back to the table, ordered a beer and watched the crazy visitors enjoy themselves, while I sat and quietly felt sorry for myself.

*

I was up early Sunday morning and by eight o'clock was cycling into Hamilton. It was a fabulous morning and the roads were quiet. I stopped along Harbour Road just for the pleasure of drinking in the wondrous view of the sparkling Great Sound, the buildings of the city apparently piled up on each other in the distance, the sentinel islands and the multi-coloured sails of the few early birds. A couple of Longtails glided by on silent wings remaining parallel with the coast, their elongated tails trailing kite-like, their vivid whiteness contrasting sharply with the cloudless azure sky.

At Foot of the Lane, I locked up my bike and walked down to the water's edge. Wilber had beaten me to it and I could see him paddling gently between the anchored boats, which cast deep shadows in the early morning sun. I realised he was going away from me and so I settled on the grass under a tall palm tree to wait.

About fifteen minutes later he came back into view, saw me, rested on his oars and waved his cap. It was still a few minutes before he was within hailing range. *"The car's open, can you bring everything that's in the trunk, the hamper and the beer,"* he called out breathlessly. By the time he had reached the shore I had the items on the small jetty. He was puffing hard although he had only been rowing very gently.

"Sorry if I'm late," I apologised.

"No you're not late, I came early, had a few jobs to do aboard first."

We loaded the stuff into the small boat and rowed away. Once everything was stowed, I started *Crazy Dream's* engine and we set off slaloming our way to Albuoy's Point, a quay and park area, close to Front Street, where we were to pick up Wilber's wife Madge and his visitors. Wilber really looked the part, standing at the bow, rope in his hand steadying himself by leaning against a stay. He was dressed in his usual sailing outfit of baggy shorts, voluminous check shirt and with his navy-blue captains' cap pulled down over his eyes. As we drew near to the pickup point I could see a knot of people waiting. The closer we got, the busier I was concentrating on making a good impression by managing to get *Crazy Dream* safely alongside the stone dock without scraping the paint. Wilber threw the rope ashore and one of the group held it while the others, one by one, stepped

110

aboard grasping Wilber's hand and acknowledging his boisterous welcome. Madge came straight up to me, immediately rubbing her hand up and down my arm. She gazed up into my face announcing how pleased she was to see me and how very glad she was that I had been going sailing with Wilber. *"You have no idea how it raises his spirits,"* she whispered conspiratorially. *"Lewis, come and meet Jack,"* she called out to a short, black, overweight, moustachioed man. Lewis Lane waddled awkwardly towards me dressed in red and white striped Breton style shirt, white shorts and sailing shoes; an unlit cheroot clamped tightly between his teeth and baseball cap pulled tightly down over his eyes, which were hidden behind expensive looking sunglasses. Our introductions were interrupted by the last man stepping athletically aboard and Wilber shouting for me to get us on our way. I gunned the motor in reverse and gently moved away from the dock before aiming the bows for the open water of the Great Sound.

As we left the last of the moored boats behind, I was able to take stock of the visitors. They had their backs to me joking with Wilber, who was laughing loudly. His eyes caught mine and he stopped mid-sentence. *"Darren, Colin that's my new friend Jack at the helm."*

The two men turned round, one raised his arm in a mock salute: *"Hi Captain Jack, I'm Darren Davies,"* the shorter man called in a broad American accent. I guessed he was about fifty, looked very fit and was wearing expensive looking leisure gear, his white shirt contrasting starkly with his jet black face, dominated by a huge squashed nose. Colin

111

was also black; he was a mountain of a man bursting out of his ill-fitting pale blue Tee-shirt, his arms bulkier than my thighs. He didn't speak, just gave a deep nod, his lips tightly drawn but with his dark, reflective glasses and shaved head he looked a real thug. I had caught a glimpse of a black woman in the group but because of manoeuvring the boat it was only a glimpse and now she was not in sight. Madge wasn't on deck either so I presumed the pair was below. A few minutes later Wilber made his way to towards me and said it was time to put up the sail, he would steer the boat. He shouted, warning everyone what was to happen and I set to, raising the main sail and the jib. As the wind filled the sails Wilber switched off the engine and the deep throbbing stopped to be replaced only by the whispering sound of the wind and the slapping waves. With Wilber at the helm I introduced myself properly to Darren and Colin, the latter deliberately, I'm sure, setting out to crush my hand in his massive grip. Before we got past the pleasantries Madge called my name from inside the cabin. I made my way down, ducking into the galley area.

"*Jack can you take these drinks outside,*" she said, pushing a heavily loaded tray into my hands "*Oh, I don't suppose you've met Marsha yet have you?*" I stiffened, another Marsha, I thought or the same one – surely not! My mouth fell open as I looked over Madge's shoulder - it was my companion from last night. She looked me hard in the eyes and was gently shaking her head. I stammered probably open-mouthed, puzzled and trying to read her mouthed message. "*Yes,*" said Madge, smiling wickedly, "*she does take your breath away doesn't she.*" She turned her head to

112

look at Marsha whose expression of concern slipped instantly into a welcoming smile, something I had not had the pleasure of observing the previous night. I wallowed in it, thinking of what might have been.

"*Stop that Madge*," laughed Marsha.

I balanced the tray on a step and put out a hand: "*No I don't think I've had the pleasure.*" This time my hand was grasped firmly and with a warm smile of gratitude. I took the tray outside followed by the two ladies, where they distributed the drinks to the men.

Madge and Marsha had changed into bikinis and as Madge joined her husband at the wheel, a huge fruity Planter's Punch for herself and a pint glass of orange juice for Wilber; Marsha took a towel and stretched out on the foredeck. Davies and Lane had settled themselves amid cushions close to the wheel, near enough to speak comfortably with Wilber. It was then apparent that Colin was a minder for one of the two visitors, he was sitting apart, his giant fingers masking the drink in his hand, an expression of sheer boredom and unease painted across his massive scowling face. We were now in the middle of the Sound and Wilber was skirting round the marker buoys, which a fleet of dinghies were racing round. I made my way towards Marsha and sat on the deck, my knees up under my chin, a glass of Punch resting on one knee. I glanced down at her well-oiled, muscled body glistening in the sun. Because of her large, dark glasses I couldn't tell if she was aware that I was beside her or not.

For a few moments I sipped my drink. "*So reading briefs today are we?*" She didn't reply. "*So which one is the boyfriend?"* I asked in a low voice looking beyond her towards Spanish Point.

She started. *"None of them,"* she whispered, *"but thanks."*

"Then why the secrecy. Why didn't you want Madge to know," I questioned.

"It has nothing to do with Madge, I didn't want my boss to know we had met before," she whispered, turning on her side and sipping her drink.

"Which one is your boss?" I persisted.

"Lewis Lane," she replied, looking in his direction.

"Is he a lawyer too?" I asked, my eyes lifted to the top of the mast checking the wind direction.

"No he's an American businessman, spends his time between here and Florida. I look after his legal affairs here." I still couldn't see her eyes but noticed the huge dangling earrings of last night had been replaced by tiny diamond studs.

"Who's Darren Davies?" I asked, curious about Wilber's guests.

"Darren Davis, I don't know. Never met him before, I think he's just a friend of Mr Lane's," she was sucking a piece of ice from her drink.

"And the bruiser, who does he take care of?" I asked.

"You mean Colin." She grinned. *"Colin looks after Mr Lane. I guess his official job description is chauffeur."*

"And you expect me to believe that Mr Lane, your boss, is not your boyfriend as well?" I knew I was being unduly provocative.

114

"Why do you think that," she hissed.

"Why else wouldn't you want him to know that we'd met before?" I asked.

She looked hard at me over the top of her drink and I wished she would remove her glasses so that I could see her eyes. *"Think what you like,"* she snarled and lay back down, conversation on the matter clearly closed.

I looked across at Wilber, he was still laughing, Madge clinging to his arm, as they shared a joke with their two guests. The guy Colin had his feet up on the bench seat, head at an awkward angle apparently fast asleep. I looked down again at Marsha taking in the scarlet lipstick and purple painted toenails. What a shame, I thought to myself, that this gorgeous creature doesn't have a personality to match her beauty. I tried to reopen peace negotiations: *"Had you met the Marshall's before today?"* I asked

"Yes, a couple of times. My boss had some business with Mr Marshall and we had dinner. Another time I went to their house with Lewis. How come you're such friends and sailing his boat?" I explained the situation of how we had met and how Wilber had offered to teach me to sail in return for helping out. *"I didn't know he had a heart problem,"* she murmured, almost to herself.

"Apparently he went to the States to see specialists and they decided there was nothing they could do. He just has to take it easy and not physically overdo things," I explained, repeating what he had told me earlier at Laura Miles-Smith's home.

"Poor Wilber Marshall," she responded sounding concerned. *"Do you think we will get the chance to swim today?"* She asked, changing the subject.

"I'm sure that can be arranged, though I don't think the other visitors will be interested," I answered. At that moment Wilber called out to me and said that he needed to tack, would I give a hand? I joined him, undid the cleats and reset the sail. Wilber then asked me to take over the helm and to take the boat towards Dockyard and then he led the two men and Madge down the steps and into the salon. I noticed Marsha, up on her elbow watching them go. Madge came back outside almost immediately with a towel, made her way to where Marsha was lying and settled herself down besides her, where, although I couldn't hear, she asked Marsha to spread sun cream on her back. For some time I was left to my own thoughts, as I steered *Crazy Dream* on a long tack across the Sound towards the open sea.

As we drew nearer to Dockyard, Wilber came up the steps. *"Jack, you can go about now and take us back through Two Rock Passage, I've nearly finished, I'll be back out in a few minutes."* I nodded and then explained that Marsha had asked about the chance for a swim.

"No problem," he replied, *"swing west of Hawkins Island and I'll come out and show you where we can stop for a swim."* He disappeared back inside and I called out to the ladies to keep their heads down, as I swung the boat gently into the wind and onto a bearing taking us towards the US Naval Air Station.

Some ten minutes later Wilber appeared again and came to stand next to me. He advised me to steer the boat closer to the group of islands clustered centrally in the Sound. He called out their names, Pearl Island, Hawkins, Alpha. As we passed the latter he switched on the engine and told me to lower the main sail. This disturbed the ladies who had no choice but to come and join us in the cockpit. Wilber then steered the boat very slowly through a narrow passage and into a sheltered lagoon, hemmed in by three islands. I threw out an anchor and as soon as it held, Marsha was over the side, hitting the water like an arrow. Madge climbed more daintily down the rear steps before launching out in a ladylike breaststroke; head and recently permed hair held well clear of the water.

"*Anyone else,*" called out Wilber. The male visitors shook their heads.

"*Go on Jack,*" he encouraged. Fortunately I had thought to wear brief swim trunks under my shorts, so I stripped off and leapt over the side. As I came to the surface shaking water from my face Marsha shouted: "*Five only for style, wouldn't you say Madge?*"

"*I only have him down for three,*" replied Madge. Ignoring the banter I dived down again. It was quite shallow and the bottom completely sandy, there was only about two feet of water under the keel. I swam round the boat under the water and surprised Marsha by coming up alongside her, splashing water over her head as I did so. She squealed and pushed me under.

"*Now then children,*" called out Madge, "*be nice to each other.*" She made her way to the steps and climbed back up into the boat. Marsha did a lap of the yacht and also climbed out, thanking Wilber for finding such a great place

117

to swim. I had been lying on my back guiltily watching Marsha's shapely figure, as she athletically heaved herself up and into the boat. I was just about to follow suit when Madge called everyone's attention to a turtle that had come gasping to the surface not ten yards from where I was. I dived under the water and swam in its direction and was rewarded with a good look at his mottled shell before it put on speed and easily outpaced me. I raced to the surface mimicking the turtle coming up for air, to a round of applause. A couple of strokes took me back to the steps and I clambered back aboard.

Madge and Marsha quickly dried themselves before disappearing into the galley, to reappear some time later with plates loaded with chicken salad; while Wilber busied himself de-corking a bottle of Moet Chandon champagne. Once everyone had eaten their fill, plates cleared and the glasses emptied, I heaved up the anchor and Wilber delicately manoeuvred *Crazy Dream* through the narrow straits and back out into Two Rock Passage. He decided he would use the motor for the rest of the trip home and so I busied myself putting away the sails. Marsha and Madge sat together on the foredeck enjoying the late afternoon sun deep in conversation and then, before we reached the dock at Albuoy's Point, went below to change into their shorts and T-shirts. I really wanted to speak to Marsha again before she left but there wasn't a chance and in a trice all the guests were gone and Wilber was guiding his precious yacht towards its mooring point, while Madge busied herself clearing up in the galley. It took three trips backwards and forwards in the small rowing boat to take first Madge and then all the bits and pieces to Wilber's car. Madge waited inside while Wilber and I completed the final chore, pulling a cover over the cockpit and threading up the securing laces. As he climbed in beside Madge he shook my hand and thanked me profusely for helping out. I, in turn, thanked the pair of them for inviting me, telling them how much I had enjoyed the opportunity to be with them and on the water again. Madge insisted I went round to her side of the car where she pulled my head down to the window and placed a wet kiss directly on my lips: "*Thank you so much*," she purred, "*See you soon*,"

*

By seven-thirty the next morning I was back at school and busy finding the materials I needed for the morning lessons. I was glad to be back in the familiar routine, despite having had an adventurous week's holiday. The day passed quickly, the children also appeared pleased to be back in school and were full of tales of their week's activities. Evelyn organised a short assembly at the beginning of the day to welcome everyone back but there was no Eloise and no singing. I wasn't really surprised, as Monday was not a regular day for her to be in school.

It was quite late when I eventually made my way home, I had spent time preparing lessons for the rest of the week and mounting some of the children's artwork. I strolled across the school field and decided to walk along the West Side for a glimpse of the sea. Along this narrow lane there were only a couple of places where there was a clear view of the sea due to ocean-side houses owning the land right down to high-tide level. At one of the gaps I stopped

119

and perched on top of an uncomfortable piece of ancient coral stone. The sea was like a millpond but the air seemed hazy; on the horizon there were amazing, brilliant white mountains of cumulus clouds changing shape even as I watched. It was unbelievably humid. I strolled on, deciding to make my way up to Sandys' parish church, named for Saint James. At the gate I stood for a moment gazing at the beautifully proportioned, whitewashed building, with its elegant spire before walking down the long driveway flanked with whitewashed tombs, stopping occasionally to read the inscriptions. I wandered round the back of the church for a new and different perspective of the west side coast and sat on a low wall. By now the sun was low in the sky and distant clouds gradually took on an orange glow, and then grew redder as each second passed. When the sun dropped into the sea and abruptly disappeared I took one last glance at the now purple clouds and walked quickly towards home, already imagining a long, cold, pre-dinner beer.

That evening I wrote a long letter to my ex in-laws explaining my need to get away from England with all its painful memories and trying to describe my new life in Bermuda. As I pondered over the wording it occurred to me that this was the first time I had ever written to them. It was such a difficult letter to write but they had always been kind and supportive and James, Jill's father, had often quietly told me to count to ten when he had witnessed Jill being particularly obstreperous. *Just like her mother*, he would mutter. They were of course devastated by the loss of their only daughter and the last time I saw them seemed to have suddenly become very old. I read and reread what I had written and eventually satisfied, licked and sealed the envelope and determined that this would be the first and last letter I would write to them. A first step in the separation process I thought.

Of course writing the letter meant I stirred up all the old memories and when I fell into bed the whole tragic episode reverberated round my head and I tossed and turned unable to sleep. Eventually cursing my inability to switch off - I turned on the bedside lamp and scrabbled around seeking something to read. I'd finished the Deighton; Le Carre's *A Small Town in Germany* lay unstarted, this wasn't the right moment I thought. Ted Hughes *Crow* was not for this hour of the night; which left the well-thumbed *Shropshire Lad,* given to me by my parents for my seventeenth birthday and that was never far from my reach. I flicked through, not really concentrating, until one particular verse caught my attention:

Along the field as we came by

A year ago, my love and I

The aspen over stile and stone

Was talking to itself alone.

"Oh who are these that kiss and pass?"

A country lover and his lass;

Two lovers looking both to wed;

And time shall put them both to bed,

But she shall lie with earth above,

And he beside another love."

"*Oh Shit!*" I sighed, slamming the book shut and letting it fall to the floor.

*

The children had just left the classroom for the morning break and were clattering noisily down the stairs, I leaned over the banister and shouted irritably for them to walk and keep the noise down. It was unbelievably humid again and every pore oozed sweat. As I peered down I was suddenly aware of a face looking up at me, it was Eloise coming up the stairs.

"*Hi*," I said a little uncertainly. "*Where are you off to?*"

"*I'm coming to see you*," she replied. I backed into my classroom and she followed, closing the door behind her.

"*I owe you an apology*," she started. I was puzzled but said nothing. "*I said I would call you - and I tried but you didn't answer and then I unexpectedly had to fly to the States. I only got back last night.*"

"*I wondered where you were, I tried to call you several times.*" I said.

"*I'm sorry, I was looking forward to spending more time with you but I had this phone call and I had to get on the first flight I could find.*" Momentarily she reached out a hand and gripped my arm. I didn't respond. "*Did you find things to do?*" I explained about the exploring and sailing but for some reason didn't mention the night out at the Princess Hotel. "*Will you come to supper tonight?*" she said brightly, trying to catch my eyes. I was avoiding looking straight at her in case she could read my thoughts.

I was in turmoil and after what seemed an overlong dramatic pause, blurted out: "*Eloise, I'm sorry but I'm not ready for this. It's too soon after Jill's death. I'm pretty screwed up and...*" I paused unable to find the right words:

122

"I guess, I guess I just need time. I like you very much, very much. But somehow it seems wrong. Like I'm being unfaithful to her memory. I'm sorry... Damn... I'm not making a very good job of this." I looked out of the window, wiping the perspiration from my brow with my arm. *"I really thought that after a year I could move on but every time I think about you I'm wracked with guilt."* I looked down at her slightly forlorn face. *"Eloise I'm sorry, can I take a rain check on that invitation?"* She coughed, clearing her throat, then came and stood alongside me at the window for a moment, where I was staring into the distance - and then silently, without a word, she quietly opened the door and was gone. I felt so empty and slumped on a desk my eyes unfocussed on the floor unsure whether I felt sorry for myself - or plain stupid. However, my melancholy didn't last long, it couldn't, as my students came bursting into the room and I was bombarded with questions.

At the end of the day it was soccer practice and running up and down the field with the kids helped lift my spirits and clear my head. It's hard to stay miserable when you're around kids, they are just too demanding, full of questions and jokes and joie de vivre. As training came to an end, we followed the usual routine and jogged off to the beach and launched ourselves into the sea for fifteen minutes before jogging back to change. After chasing everyone out, I stood at the gate as they all cheerily made their way home, politely wishing me a nice evening. By the time I left the building the breeze had picked up, blowing dead banana leaves noisily across the playground, the sky was an ominous mixture of grey and black and it wasn't just night coming on.

Later that evening just as I was thinking about bed, there was an enormous clap of thunder and moments later rain lashed the windows and I rushed to fasten the shutters. The storm continued until the early hours, by which time I was asleep and ignorant of its fury.

*

Before I left for school the following morning Wilber telephoned, he told me that a hurricane was forecast to be passing close by the islands within the next couple of days and would I help to ensure *Crazy Dream* was safely moored. I agreed to meet him as soon as I could get away from school.

I arrived at the appointed time and we paddled out to the boat, armed with extra rope and a length of chain. He had obviously carried out this operation many times before and knew exactly what needed to be done. Between us we replaced the mooring rope with the chain and added another mooring rope as a precaution. Wilber said that he was fortunate that this corner of the harbour was pretty sheltered and rarely was any substantial damage caused to the yachts moored there. As we busily did what we could to ensure *Crazy Dream* would come to no harm I noticed several other boat owners busy checking moorings. When all was secure Wilber suggested we went for a drink and we drove along Front Street where he parked and we strolled up Queen's Street to the *Horse and Buggy* for a beer and orange juice. Wilber was obviously known to the barman who asked after his wife and joked about the imminent hurricane.

"*Tell me about hurricanes,*" I said, once we were comfortably seated by a window, looking out over the street. "*What do you do, shut yourselves indoors?*"

"*Well,*" began Wilber, "*it's usually just a big blow and the biggest danger is getting hit by something blown off a roof, falling tree and the like. Best shut the shutters and stay inside. Depends how bad it is. Obviously the storm whips up the sea and great waves roll ahead of the hurricane, so you know it's on its way.*" He laughed, emptied his glass and called for another. "*The houses are built to stand the storms, especially the old ones with stone roofs. We've had a few good blows during my lifetime but nothing as bad as in 1926, I think it was. One royal navy ship capsized and sank somewhere off South Shore and a couple of other navy ships were blown loose up at Dockyard. Luckily most hurricanes roll by without creating too much damage. It helps being only twenty square miles sometimes. So tell me how you're getting on with the new job.*" I told him about what I was doing and how much I was enjoying the kids. Later I asked Wilber if he had been born in Bermuda and he told me his family went back to 1740, according to his brother who had worked out that an early ancestor had emigrated to Bermuda from Scotland at that time. After some fifteen minutes Wilber hauled himself to his feet and announced that he must be getting back and we wound our way back to his car. He dropped me back at the Foot of the Lane so that I could pick up my bike and with a cheery wave he pulled out into the traffic heading towards his home in Smiths parish, the opposite direction to where I was going.

I decided to ride back to Somerset via the South Shore, rather than my usual route along Harbour Road, I wanted to look at the open sea for any sign of the forecast hurricane. I stopped above the Carlton Beach Hotel, where I played tennis, and watched the waves hammering into the distant rocks. I continued to Church Bay and pulled onto the small car park, left my bike and walked out to the cliff's edge. Although still high above the sea I could plainly hear the roar and taste the fine spray that filled the air. Further out waves were crashing on the exposed reefs and a heavy mist hid the horizon. Except for the temperature, I thought, and the humidity, which you could almost cut with a knife, this bit of coast could easily have been deepest Cornwall.

It was dark by the time I got home but I determined I must go and thank Dilly for last Saturday night, I was feeling guilty that it was already Tuesday and I hadn't expressed my gratitude. The back door was open so I called out as I knocked and the middle daughter, Renee came running. *"Hello Mr Cross,"* she said, her face lighting up and then turning round called *"Momma it's Mr Cross."* Dilly appeared, wiping her hands on a towel, and I decided, looking rather stressed. Renee disappeared back inside where I could hear a television cartoon in progress.

"Hi Dilly," I said, *"I just wanted to thank you for last Saturday night. The show was fantastic - and the meal wonderful."*

Dilly smiled, *"I'm glad you enjoyed yourself,"* she said.

"I really did but I must owe you some money, William the Maître d', wouldn't accept anything, he said you'd taken care of everything." I continued.

"It's okay," explained Dilly. *"It was all above board, the hotel allows me to take a couple of guests once a month. Don't worry they keep check, they're not that generous."*

"Are you sure? Well, thanks anyway, it was really great." I said gratefully.

"How did you get on with Marsha?" Dilly said with a sly look from underneath her long lashes.

"Has she spoken to you since that evening?" I asked keeping a straight face.

"No, she hasn't called. Why do you ask?" said Dilly

"I just wondered. She seemed very surprised to see me there." I added.

"So?" Dilly was now smiling broadly.

"So, if she had called I wondered if she might have told you how she felt about it." I went on.

"No, she hasn't called. Do you think she had a good time?" asked Dilly.

"I don't know, that's why I'm asking you. She enjoyed the show, enjoyed winning the limbo competition but it's possible that's where her enjoyment ended." I said.

What are you trying to say Jack? That she didn't enjoy your company?" Dilly scowled.

"Well, yes, no. She basically said she wasn't in the habit of socialising with white men." I explained.

"God damn the woman," Dilly hissed. *"She lives like a damn nun and she's so damn bigoted. I thought*

127

spending some time with a nice guy like you might help ease her prejudice. I despair!"

"So you were plotting Miss Dilly!" I said, looking stern.

"I was trying to help the woman move out of the nineteen sixties and into the seventies," she said.

"You're a marvel Dilly Simons, you should get a medal for community relations." I joked.

"They don't give medals for failure," she added. *"I'm going to call that woman and give her a piece of my mind."*

"Careful what you say Dilly. Don't spoil my chances, even if they are only zero." I grinned and changed the subject, *"Are you out working tonight?"*

"No I'm not working but I have to go down to the Cambridge Beaches hotel." Then as an afterthought she added, *"Why don't you come as well? We could go on your bike - it would save me bothering Eggy."*

*

About nine o'clock Dilly came and tapped on the door, she was wearing jeans and a long-sleeved blouse, her hair was wrapped in a brightly coloured turban. After getting her settled we wobbled off down Long Bay Lane towards Cambridge Beaches, Dilly's arms loosely round my waist. I had never taken anyone on the pillion before and so had to concentrate hard, an added complication being the solid blackness that my meagre headlamp barely managed to penetrate. I was slightly relieved that we arrived at the main entrance without mishap and Dilly showed me where to leave the bike. We then made our way inside the foyer where a couple of receptionists leapt to their feet and greeted Dilly like a long lost friend. I was introduced and then she led me to a bar, again the waiters gathered round, the pleasure of seeing her clear on their open faces. We settled in a couple of very comfortable armchairs and drinks arrived.

"In a few minutes I have some business to attend to," she said peering straight into my eyes. *"You can wander round, though being dark there's not much to see. But over there they have newspapers and magazines. Have another drink, they won't charge you, it's my treat."* After a few moments Dilly finished her drink and eased herself out of the chair. *"I'll be about twenty minutes, no more than half an hour, I promise,"* she said and walked purposefully towards a door over which was a sign pointing to the Dining Room. I took her advice and picked up a Herald Tribune and a copy of Time Magazine and settled down to read.

After about fifteen minutes a smartly dressed young waiter came by and asked if I needed another drink, I ordered a Heineken and asked where the toilets were. He pointed towards the door Dilly had gone through and told me how to find them. I rose and made my way through the door. A long carpeted corridor stretched before me and I wandered slowly down the corridor admiring the paintings and wonderful flower displays. I passed the dining room, empty except for a few stragglers and beyond were the toilets. Afterwards, I wandered a little further down the corridor. Double doors at the end led out onto a terrace and an exotically lit but deserted swimming pool. I walked round the edge of the pool and as I was about to re-enter the corridor saw Dilly through a window of an adjacent room. I strolled over and saw, once again, she was at the front of the room addressing about twenty or more uniformed hotel staff. I tried to hear what she was saying but the noise of the sea behind me, together with a rattling air-conditioner nearby, drowned out any possibility. I looked at the audience, as on the earlier occasion they were hanging on her every word, their faces etched in concern. I made my way back inside, grateful for the air-conditioned atmosphere. Back in the bar I settled down behind the *Tribune* and tried to work out what Dilly was up to.

It wasn't long before I heard her flop into the chair alongside me apologising if she had been a long time. I reassured her that I had been quite happy relaxing with the daily newspaper, the first one I had seen since I left England. The handsome young waiter appeared and Dilly ordered herself a Rum and Coke, checking if I needed another beer.

"*Would it be rude to ask, but what you have been doing?*" I asked. "*I saw you talking to some people, as I walked down to the pool area.*" She thought for while, not saying anything, sipping her drink.

"*This isn't the time or the place,*" she replied quietly. I didn't pursue the matter and we talked about other things. About ten o'clock she slapped my bare knee and asked me to take her home. With loud and cheery farewells we made our way out and were soon wobbling down the pitch-black lane. It wasn't long before we were back, I switched off the engine and we coasted to the rear of my bungalow. It was windier now and the palms were swaying and rattling noisily, like shingle washing on the beach. "*Is it too late ask you to join me for a coffee,*" I asked.

"*Sounds good*," she replied and followed me inside. I put the kettle on and Dilly settled herself into one of my two chairs. "*Pretty sparsely furnished, your home*," she said looking round. I was standing at the door of the kitchen waiting for the kettle to boil.

"*You're being polite*," I replied, "*bare, I'd say, but as you can see, I do have good taste - I think they call the style minimalism!*" She glanced up at my Birdsey print and grunted. The kettle whistled and I returned to the kitchen. For a while we chatted idly and then I commented that I hadn't set eyes on Karl, her husband, since the party.

"*Oh, he's gone early, back when it's dark, watches TV, sleeps a lot.*" She said quietly. Her hands were wrapped round the mug, holding it close to her lips.

"*Does he ever go with you when you're performing?*" I asked.

"*Nope, he stays and looks after the kids*," she frowned and looked at the floor.

"*Does he ever go fishing?*" I asked, making conversation, rather than really wanting to know what the man did with himself.

"*He used to*," replied Dilly "*before*," she stopped herself and took a swig of her coffee.

"*Before what?*" I asked.

"*Doesn't matter*," she replied.

"*I'm sorry*," I said quickly, "*I wasn't meaning to be nosey*".

"*It's okay, it's okay. I keep telling myself I'm over it but*," she paused, "*I guess I put it to the back of my head and try to get on with life but it's never far away from my*

131

thoughts." She was talking to herself rather than to me, as she emptied her coffee. "*I've had three rum and cokes tonight and I'm talking too much. Just ignore me*"

I regretted starting this conversation, didn't know what to say - so said nothing but gazed down at her finely chiselled face, seemingly even smaller with the turban wrapped tightly round her head. As I watched, a tear squeezed over an eyelid and raced down her cheek. She made no attempt to wipe it away. I was surprised, she struck me as being a real tough character, emotions always well under control, not one to give way to tears. Suddenly she slapped her knee and hissed angrily:

"*I could have forgiven him for fucking that good for nothin' bitch but not for what he did to me.*" More tears were slithering down her face. I found her a tissue. She wiped her eyes and blew her nose hard.

"*I'm sorry Dilly. I didn't mean to start something.*" I stammered.

"*You didn't start anything. He did... and now he's made it ten times worse.*"

I asked myself if this was the same strong woman I had seen addressing the employees at the hotel an hour or so earlier. Her face was screwed up into a scowl, head shaking with anger, her arms wrapped round her knees, now pulled up to her chest.

"*I need to tell someone,*" she said, staring at me intensely. "*It has to be a secret, please not a word to anyone. I trust you Jack. Talking it through might help me sort it out and help me decide what to do.*"

I was apprehensive now, not wishing to get involved in Dilly's private life. She cleared her throat and in a low monotone, tense with emotion, began to tell me the reason for her anger. *"Karl went to the Bahamas with his skittles team a couple of years ago,"* she began. *"He was only away a week. He said he got drunk, fell into bed with some diseased whore, then came back and messed up my life."* She was in control again now, speaking calmly, looking everywhere but at me. *"I got so sick, I thought I was dying. I had so much pain. Then the doctors decided I'd got some sexually transmitted disease,"* she said *"but not a sexually transmitted disease they recognised. They gave me medicine for the pain and done a whole load of tests. Many of them had to go to the States. In the end they operated and took all my insides out. I can't have no more kids. But then they said that might not be the end of it and every couple of months they take blood tests."*

"Oh God Dilly, I'm so sorry," I interrupted, at a loss to know what to say, shocked by the problems she faced and marvelling at how she usually stayed so cheerful.

"When Karl found out what he done to me, I thought he was going to kill himself. He had to have tests too. Man he was out a control. I had to send the kids to go live with my sister." Dilly eyes were dilated, her head still shaking in disbelief. *"Then he starts smoking ganja again. I'd managed to stop him when Pearl came along and he stayed clean for ten years or more. Now he come home from work, lie on de bed, curtains drawn and smoke that weed until he's out of it. When he's okay, which ain't very often, I plead with him to stop but he says he can't go on unless he kills the*

133

pain in his head." She looked at me, her eyes brimming with distress. *"Now...now, as if that ain't bad enough I find out he's dealing. Big time! Not just a few packets to the older kids.. Big time!"* She paused letting this piece of startling news sink in. *"When they catch him - and they always do - it's for sure they'll lock him away in Casemates and throw away the key."*

I could think of nothing to say and if it weren't for the fact she was still curled up like a ball in the chair, I would have given her a hug.

"I tried to talk sense into that man. Tell him to stop this dealing right now and all he says is that he's in too deep. He knows too much. He says if he tried to stop - they'd kill him." She was rocking to and fro and sighing heavily. *"So Mr teacher Jack, you tell me what I should do!"*

"Lord Dilly," I sighed, flabbergasted and feeling totally helpless. *"Do you really think his life would be in danger, if he told them he had to think of his family, of his kids, and needed to stop. Would they, whoever they are, really kill him? I find that very hard to believe."* I was out of my league; I had no experience of how crime really worked, no clue whether or not his involvement was so serious that his life was at risk.

Dilly stopped rocking, put her feet on the floor and fixed me with her brown, fathomless eyes. *"Well,"* she paused. *"Someone killed the police commissioner. Why? Was it politics or was it Mr Big in the drug world showing just how big he is - and warning the police to back off?"*

"Oh Dilly,' I sighed, *"you make it sound like Chicago in the prohibition era, not beautiful Bermuda! Is the drug*

business really so big here in Bermuda. Is it really such a problem?" I continued, slightly incredulous.

"Casemates is full of dealers." She replied. *"But they're all little guys, no one important has ever been caught. There is somebody so big with all the right connections to organise it all and scare everyone shitless to keep their mouths shut!"* She slumped back in the chair, eyes on the ceiling looking lost and frightened.

I was feeling quite helpless and very naive, I had no advice to offer. It was catch twenty-two. Karl had obviously been drawn in when at his most vulnerable, now apparently powerless to withdraw because of the threats; and yet he couldn't go to the police. They'd lock him up, as Dilly said. Unless, I thought, unless he was willing to provide evidence to the police of the people he was involved with. I put it to Dilly but could have guessed her reaction.

"Dilly would Karl go to the police and tell them his story. Don't you think they'd let him off any charges if he helped them catch the man at the top."

"Huh!" Dilly snorted, *"Everybody here is cousin to everybody else. He couldn't say nuffin, he's got to live here. There's nowhere to hide."*

"Well if that's the case why don't the police know what's going on?" I asked. *"If Bermuda is so small and everyone is related, why don't they know, they must have secret informers."* Dilly looked at me scornfully.

"Because they're all white, they don't know what really goes on!' she almost sneered.

"But I've seen lots of black policemen," I objected.

"Yes, but they're from Barbados or Trinidad - nobody will talk to them. There's only a few Bermudians."

I decided it was time to change the direction this conversation was heading and asked if she would like to explain the meetings I seen her holding with the hotel workers. She thought for a while, sipped her drink and then told me how hotel workers were poorly paid and often badly treated by management. Their union leaders were fighting among themselves and some were trying to get the workers to join the *Black Beret* movement. She was horrified by this and was encouraging the workers not to listen. She was preaching that joining the violent *Black Berets* was not the way forward. She wanted everyone to contribute to a strike fund and when it was large enough, to threaten the bosses with strike action - not violence.

"Dilly when I came here, I thought I had died and arrived in paradise," I said wistfully *"you are beginning to make it sound like any other place in the world with your tales of crime, drugs and strikes!"*

"It is paradise," she said quickly *"I wouldn't want to live anywhere else... but it's not quite perfect. My problem with Karl is a personal, one that could have happened anywhere,"* she said philosophically. I stared at her but decided she meant it. *"If the hotel workers who are almost all black - make a really strong stand, that problem can be solved and paradise will become a small step closer to being perfect."* She almost but not quite allowed herself a smile. *"But first we have to get some money so that the families don't suffer and we can put some pressure on."*

"Sorry to sound so ignorant," I said *" but what is the Back Beret movement? I haven't seen anyone wearing black berets."* I was puzzled.

"Have you heard of the Black Panthers in the States?" she asked.

"You mean Eldridge Cleaver and the anti-white business?" Some-where in the depths of my memory I made the connection, remembering too, how he had fled from the US after a wide variety of crimes against innocent white people, especially women.

"Well a local guy called John Hilton Bassett started the Berets here a couple of years ago, based on Panther principles – 'freedom by any means necessary, even if that means killing.' He's spent some time in Cuba and wants a revolution here." She emptied her glass. *"Well his Beret movement has attracted some people who ought to know better - and a lot of scum,"* she added bitterly. *"They've even started a 'liberation school' for young kids. Parents send them thinking they're learning about their African roots but really it is to indoctrinate them to hate whites."* She sighed heavily and looked despairingly at me. *"That's not what I want for my kids."* I was shocked, unable to find anything sensible to add. The silence hung between us like a thick cloud, Dilly's outburst had blown me away.

"But the majority don't want this - surely. Surely most people just want to live together and just get on with their lives?" I said hopefully.

"Of course," she almost snapped. *"But look at history, it's always the majority who get run over by the powerful few."*

137

I suddenly thought of the recent murder that had shaken the community, well had certainly shaken all the white people I had met. *"Do you think the Black Berets killed the police commissioner?"* I asked.

"Of course!" she replied, *"without a shadow of doubt."* Again she caught and held my gaze, only this time there was fear in her beautiful, bottomless eyes. Snapping out of her musings, she asked me for the time.

"It's almost midnight," I replied after glancing at my watch. *"Where did the time go?"* Dilly climbed slowly to her feet:

"I must go," she said. I too was on my feet, hands thrust deep in pockets. *"Thanks for listening but please – it's just between you and me."* She stretched upwards, gently kissed my cheek and before I could react walked swiftly to the door and in a moment was gone.

*

About five o'clock the next morning I was awoken by an enormous clap of thunder, seemingly directly overhead. I jerked into wakefulness and lay watching the lightening flicker through the shutters, etching phantasmagorical shapes over the bedroom wall. After a while the rumbling thunder became continuous and I wished I had earplugs. And then the wind started and with it the rain. I'd heard of the power of tropical storms but I was not in the tropics I reminded myself. The rain lashed the shutters, almost drowning out the cries of the palms that were squealing, as if beaten by an invisible tormentor. I got up to use the bathroom and discovered there was no power. I fumbled in the dark for what seemed an age before finding a torch and later a candle and matches. The flickering light of the candle reflected in the eye of the resident green lizard clinging to the wall above the bathroom mirror. He cocked his head to one side, as I checked my watch again, it was too soon to start moving and so I returned to my bed listening to the violence and thinking about Dilly and her problems. The shutters rattled, wind whistled under the door, the whole building creaked and groaned and I understood the reason, and was grateful, for the traditional heavy stone roofs and solid construction.

It was usually light by six o'clock but not this morning and I headed off for the bathroom planning to shave by the light of a candle! The rain had eased and it seemed eerily quiet after the shrieking gale, which had penetrated every crack and cranny. Fumbling around the bathroom I discovered there was no water and with a groan remembered that electrical power was needed to work the pump. I cursed - no shave, no shower - no tea!

Feeling distinctly unwashed and uncomfortable I locked up and walked off towards school. The lane was littered with palm fronds and someone had already hauled a large branch to the side of the road. I noticed an electrical cable wrapped round it and wondered if this was the cause of my blackout. There were large puddles everywhere and tree frogs were loudly celebrating the dank and soggy atmosphere. I picked my way round a huge Buffo toad flattened by some unseen vehicle; a brightly coloured Kiskadee perched on a low overhanging branch eyeing his breakfast, anxiously waiting for me to get out of range. The humidity was such, it created an almost visible mist and drips of water from the overhead branches accompanied my every step - but despite the heat, I flinched each time one found the back of my neck.

The staffroom was deserted, which was most unusual so I made my way to the office, Evelyn was busy at her desk, her door wide open. She looked up at the sound of my footsteps. "*Ahh!*" she said. "*I forgot to tell you,*" she paused and beckoned me into her cramped office. "*When hurricanes are about you need to listen to the radio, they tell you what's happening and whether schools are open, buses running and such.*" Then as an afterthought: "*Good morning Jack, did you sleep well?*" She smiled, knowing full well that the only people in Somerset who would have slept through the storm were resting in Saint James' churchyard. I said as much and she went on to tell me that power lines were down all over the island and that the eye of the storm was overhead, which is why the weather had quietened. This meant another storm later as the trailing edge rushed by. "*They say the worst should miss us by a hundred miles or so but you can never be sure. You should go and buy a few bottles of water, if you haven't got any and buy some food that doesn't need cooking. School should be open tomorrow but listen to the news at seven o'clock.*" She turned again to her typewriter and so I bid her goodbye and strolled round towards the Piggly Wiggly. I decided to postpone the shopping and continued past the Post Office towards Mangrove Bay to check out the sea. Despite the thick cloud and lack of sun it was so very hot and the humidity as tangible as an enveloping wet blanket; in no time my shirt was soaked. It was eerily still. The sea at Mangrove Bay

140

was relatively calm but the sky a threateningly deep blue-grey colour, the storm had attacked from the south and so the bay was reasonably well protected. Most boats were pulled up on the beach, only a few larger ones left to weather the storm. A group of young black children were hammering open some of the coconuts that had fallen from the tall palms, which fringed the beach. They saw me and I was invited to help. The skill was to crack the shell without losing the milk, it was no surprise that they were better at this than me. As I squatted with the children one looked at me, his huge black eyes peering into mine. *"You teach at the white school!"* he announced with a grin.

"I teach at Saint James'," I replied.

"That's what I said," he continued, gritting his teeth, as he struck the coconut against the curb. Inwardly I groaned. Suddenly the wind noisily rustled the fronds high above our heads and I glanced up. Perched, ominously, way above, there were clusters of coconuts looking ready to fall. Without a word the children knowingly edged away. I didn't stay long and following noisy farewells I left them to their labours and strolled on in the direction of Cavello Bay, another popular harbour for small boats. With each stride the wind increased in strength and debris from the earlier storm rolled along the road towards me, like tumbleweed in an old western movie. By the time I reached Cavello the wind was howling and low, black, rain-filled clouds scudded rapidly across the sky. Despite the harbour being enclosed, with just a narrow entrance to the Great Sound, the sea was angry and lashing the causeway, which formed the northerly flank. A day-boat was perched half out of the water up on the rocks of

the causeway, its small cabin smashing against the rocks with every wave. Two men below me were struggling with a length of rope trying to prevent another boat from dragging its moorings. I scrambled along the rocks and asked if I could help. By now it was raining and the noise of the wind carried my voice away but they thrust the rope towards me and together we heaved. It was a Tug of War as we strained in unison, trying to get close enough to a tree to loop the rope around. The wind and waves were proving tough opponents and the heavy rain made the rope slippery. Several minutes passed before we managed to successfully wrap the rope around the tree trunk. The older of the pair slapped my shoulder in thanks and yelled something I couldn't catch before making his way towards the boat wedged on the rocks. In driving rain we stood looking down at the pitiful sight, the boat, someone's pride and joy, named 'Rosie,' had a hole in the bow and the side of the cabin was smashed. The two men looked at each other and shrugged their shoulders. There was nothing they could do and so they turned and ran for the shelter of a stand of wailing Casuarinas. I followed and we leaned against a garden wall protected from the gale, regaining our breath.

The older man leaned towards me, his black, weather-beaten face a few inches from my ear. *"You're a teacher,"* he shouted. *"Seen you at the School."* I nodded. *"I painted the roof,"* he continued and thrust out a huge, calloused hand; *"name of Samuel. This is my son Randy, he works with me."* Randy nodded, his eyes only just visible under a baseball cap. They had a small motorbike under the trees and after a few moments they mounted and rode off into the rain, Samuel shouting his thanks for my help.

They had no sooner disappeared from view when a Beetle came round the corner, wipers working overtime and drove passed me. It was Eloise. She reversed and wound down the window. *"What are you doing out in this lot?"* she shouted, *"You're soaked."*

"I was out for a walk and..." I started to reply but she cut me short.

"Come and dry out." She wound up the window and continued round the bend to her cottage. I took a deep breath, I had realised of course that I was close to where she lived the moment I had arrived at Cavello Bay but had not expected to see her. For a moment I thought of ignoring her invitation but only for a moment. I was soaked and despite the heat, feeling thoroughly chilly. In any case she deserved a proper explanation for my recent bizarre behaviour.

Half an hour later I was sitting in an armchair sipping coffee, dressed in a Tee shirt and an old pair of soccer shorts that Eloise had dug out of the bottom of a drawer, my clothes dripped from a line over the bath. Eloise was perched on the arm of a sofa looking at me over the rim of a large mug of steaming coffee. She had boiled the water on a small picnic Primus stove that she had bought for such emergencies and she advised me to visit Somerset Hardware store and buy one too. *"So,"* she said softly, *"How have you been?"* I shrugged, finding it difficult to look her directly in the eyes. I coughed and cleared my throat:

"Eloise, Ellie, I need to explain," I stuttered.

"No you don't," she said. *"I can appreciate that you have been through a horridly traumatic experience and it's going to take time."* She paused and her eyes strayed towards the mantelpiece where the photographs I had seen on my previous visit stood. *"I know how I felt when my mother was seriously ill and eventually died. It must be far worse to lose your wife - without warning - from one day to the next."* Her gaze returned to mine. *"We can still be friends I hope?"*

Some time later Eloise drove me home, it was still blowing hard and the windscreen wipers could hardly cope with rain. We stopped on the way at the supermarket so that I could pick up supplies. Eloise had also insisted on driving right up to the door of the hardware store, where bearded Dave, the owner, sold me a Primus stove and some paraffin and gave a lot of advice for free. Conversation in the car was impossible, due to the driving rain beating on the roof and so we wasted no time once we reached my home. I kissed her lightly on the cheek grabbed my purchases, threw open the door, slammed it shut and sprinted to the front door. Only ten strides but for the second time that day I was soaked to the skin. I stood close to the door and waved as she reversed back into the lane and slowly headed back to Cavello.

My spirits were high, I was pleased to have made peace with Eloise, she was something special, so understanding. A part of me felt sure the future held out great things for our relationship but for the moment friendship would have to suffice. However, I couldn't ignore that lurking in the back of my mind were images of Marsha!

144

Vivid memories of this challenging woman crept unbidden into my head at the most unexpected moments. She wore her prejudice like a coat of protective armour and I wondered if its reflection was a product of history or personal experience? Was there a chink in this armour that I could exploit, to ease the bitterness and permanently reveal the joyful personality I had witnessed on the Princess dance-floor?

*

It was a considerable relief to me and all of Bermuda's sixty thousand inhabitants, that the hurricane was officially downgraded to a tropical storm and slipped by during the night, without causing too much extra damage. It continued to rain intermittently, while groaning trees and noisily chattering palm leaves kept me half-awake throughout night. At seven I listened to the radio and learned that all schools and bus services would be operating normally. I still had no power, so had to make do with a lick and a promise before setting off down the littered lane to face an excited bunch of children, all with exaggerated tales to tell. I wondered if *Crazy Dream* had survived but as the phone lines were down, I couldn't call Wilber to find out.

Evelyn called a meeting before school began and explained that two of our colleagues had suffered roof damage to their homes and would not be in until workmen had secured tarpaulins to make them weather-proof, before a permanent solution was arranged. Some of us volunteered to double-up classes at different times of the day and Evelyn said she would help out as and when she could. The aftermath of the storm together with these crowded

145

arrangements led to an adrenaline-rush for most of the children and thus made for a challenging day. A day which I thoroughly enjoyed - the kids were animated, talkative and happy, as we spent much of the day working on a huge collage of the Great Storm, which we planned to go all around the room. At break I organised the children to walk around the school grounds and collect all the palm fronds and debris, if we left the job to our solitary Portuguese groundsman, it would have kept him busy for a week. Soon a huge pile was untidily heaped at the corner of the playground and children were asking if we could put a match to it and have a bonfire. Over the next few days power and normality were restored, I called Wilber and learned that *Crazy Dream* had ridden out the storm and was unharmed. Wilber suggested a sail for the following Saturday, to which I readily agreed.

*

The real downside of Bermuda, for me, was that darkness falls so early and there is so little time for outside activities after a normal day's work. By activities, I was of course thinking of sailing. Night fishing was possible and fun but getting organised to sail wasn't really on. I played a few games of tennis, under the floodlights of the Carlton Beach in the early evening with Alan, Don and Charlie, usually a Thursday but more often or not my evenings were spent reading, marking the kids work and preparing lessons. In contrast weekends were usually hectic affairs that flew by and, as my contacts grew, so did my social life.

*

On Saturday the sky was mainly overcast and the Great Sound was uncannily flat, with the sea wearing a glazed expression that allowed no reflections, the eerie sheen fooling the eye that it was coated with an oily substance. The breeze was so light the sails were gently flapping and headway was painfully slow.

"*Sometimes*," said Wilber from behind a can of orange-juice "*you have to be very patient. At other times things are so hectic you don't know what to do first.*"

"*Just like normal life.*" I responded with a grin. We chatted about this and that and eventually came round to fishing. Wilber pointed beyond Dockyard and explained how the sides of the extinct volcano that Bermuda sat on, dropped down several thousand metres some thirty miles out to sea. The area was known variously as the Argus, Plantagenet or Challenger Banks and it was here that the serious fishermen headed. He told me how the American navy had built a tower in almost two-hundred metres of water, just a mile from the edge of the bank. That was in 1960, at a cost of one and a half million dollars but that now it was considered too dangerous to use, as the welds had been damaged by ten years or more of storms. I was fascinated and quizzed him for further information. A solitary tower sticking up from the middle of the ocean, miles away and out of sight of land, it seemed bizarre.

"*I don't know too much,*" he continued, "*it was all hush-hush, underwater experiments and listening for Russian submarines. You know what the American government is like.*" He swigged his juice and continued. "*It had two enclosed levels for living accommodation and laboratories.*"

147

I hear tell that seven men spent seven days there, being buffeted by sixty foot waves, which couldn't have been much fun. Keen divers like to explore the area and it's a bit of a marker for sailors."

"*So it's the area to go for the really big fish?*" I said.

"*Certainly is,*" replied Wilber casting an experienced eye on the pennant at the top of the mast. "*Though I don't hold with catching a fish unless you are going to eat it. Big game hunting is out of fashion on land, so how can it be right to catch Marlin, Sailfish and such, just to bolster your ego.*" He sighed, "*It makes no sense.*"

Suddenly the sails filled, the boat keeled and a tangible surge of power caused *Crazy Dream* to awake. I quickly leaped up and trimmed the sails while Wilber heaved on the wheel and took full advantage of the wind; immediately spray gushed over the gunwales and whipped our faces. "*Here, take the wheel,*" he insisted. I needed no second urging and marvelled at the sudden change of conditions and the flow of adrenaline it produced. After two hours or so of exhilarating sailing, Wilber called for me to take us home. He sat and watched and did little to help, I thought that he looked tired and thoughtful.

Back on shore after we had packed stuff into the boot of his car, he slapped me on the shoulder and told me that he thought I had made great progress, was a natural sailor and was free to take the boat out on my own at any time. Obviously I was overwhelmed and thanked him profusely. We parted company and the trip back to Somerset was a blur, as I contemplated his wonderful offer.

Chapter 5

December, 1972

"You shall go to the ball! I will conjure up a gown to turn everybody's heads and supply a coach and a team of white horses - now be off and find me a pumpkin." The beautiful Fairy Godmother waved her wand and Cinderella fled joyfully into the wings. My companions perched on the edge of their seats, as only children can, shoulders hunched with concentration, wriggled in excitement.

Some weeks back Eloise mentioned that she was playing the piano for this year's pantomime at the City Hall and suggested I buy a ticket. She had convinced me that the local drama group was as good as any professional cast and that I was sure to have fun. I had given this quite a lot of thought - pantos were for children not grown men. I would never live this down with my tennis-mates when they found out and yet I felt I wanted to support Eloise.

In a flash of genius, I thought of Dilly and her three girls and asked if she would be willing to come and I would pay for the tickets, as a gesture towards her kindness for inviting me to her show. Dilly told me that she was feeling really tired but was sure the girls would love to go. And so here I was, in the stalls, with three very excited and glamorous charges.

Each of the girls was wearing a pretty, multi-coloured dress, their best outfits Pearl had confided, with large, lovingly tied, ribbons in their hair. At the interval I introduced them to Eloise, busy by the grand piano sorting out the music for the second half of the performance. She suggested that we all go down to the ice-cream parlour afterwards and complete the treat with one of their specials - the girls gushed their approval.

The second half was a great success and the show concluded to rapturous applause, two encores and a standing ovation. My young ladies whistling and hollowing, as if they were at the National Stadium supporting Bermuda's soccer team. When calm was restored, we made our way towards Eloise busy chatting to the tall, black drummer, while writing some notes on her music. Some of the other musicians struck up a conversation with Pearl and Renee, as they packed their instruments away. It didn't take more than two minutes before the girls had been identified as Dilly's kids; the short, black trumpet player not hiding his disbelief when they said that they were with me!

Outside City Hall, Eggy was sitting in his cab waiting for us. Although we had taken the ferry across the Great Sound, Dilly had asked Eggy to pick us up. When he saw us coming, he leapt out and swung a screaming little Vernee in a wide circle calling her his favourite Bermudian girl friend. Placing her carefully down, he removed his hat and shook Eloise's hand, as I introduced her. After a couple of Eggy jokes, I managed to stop his banter and explained that we wanted to take the girls for an ice cream:

"*No problem Jack,*" he smiled, slapping me on the back: "*I'll pick you up at the Flag Pole in forty minutes;*" and to the girls "*Enjoy your Knickerbocker Glories!*" He turned and climbed back into his taxi.

Before long we were swinging down Burnaby Street hand in hand singing tunes from the show and swinging little Vernee off her feet. We piled into the ice-cream parlour and the girls poured over the multi-coloured, multi-flavoured offerings and the debate began about what to choose. With a decisiveness, I supposed, inherited from their mother's genes, their orders were in, while Eloise and I floundered - eventually succumbing to Pearl's recommendations. The Parlour was busy but Renee politely persuaded a couple of teenagers to move and we all settled round a table but not before the ever-thoughtful Renee had taken their debris away and asked the boy behind the counter for a cloth before meticulously wiping the table clean. A wordless glance between Eloise and I spoke volumes.

The girls and I eventually bid Eloise goodbye at the Flag Pole on Front Street and she set off back to City Hall to collect her car, while we crowded into Eggy's taxi for the trip home. As children do, during the ride to Somerset, the girls went through the entire script for Eggy's benefit,

151

including singing some of the songs and before we knew it, he was turning into Long Bay lane and we were home.

Renee ran in through the front door shouting that we were back; Dilly appeared and they wrapped themselves around her and the tale of Cinderella began again. Gently she hushed them, gave Eggy a hug and thanked him for bringing us home - and with a cacophony of chuckles he left. *"What do you say to Uncle Jack?"* said Dilly. A chorus of *Thank you's* ensued and Pearl snuggled her hand into mine, peered intensely into my face and whispered that tonight had been the best treat of her life. And to emphasise the fact she lifted my hand to her lips and planted a kiss. I exclaimed that the pleasure had been all mine and I was honoured to take out such wonderful young ladies - which was true, they had been an absolute joy to be with. Dilly chased them off indoors and turned to me. She started to thank me again but I cut her short:

"I meant what I said, you have the most wonderful kids and I really enjoyed myself. I'm only sorry that you weren't with us."

"Sorry but I really am feeling rotten, I've had to pull out of the show for a while." I started to question but she raised a hand: *"I'll explain tomorrow, I need to go in."*

*

Sunday dawned bright and blue, the weather was cooler now but I was still comfortable in my shorts and T-shirt. Leisurely I made breakfast and armed with coffee and a plate of toast went outside and settled into the battered old chair under the Casuarinas. High above my head the wind hummed gently causing needles to fall while the ubiquitous Kiskadee squawked away, disturbing the peace.

I thought about the kids and the previous night, as I munched through the toast and marmalade. It had been fun. I remembered asking Jill if she wanted to have children after one particularly bitter exchange, when the amateur psychiatrist in me, thought perhaps she was being so obstreperous because she was overcome with frustrated maternal instincts. The reply had been short and negative and neither of us had raised the question again. I climbed out of my chair to brew another cup of coffee when Dilly came into view. Unusually for her, she was wearing a sombre-coloured coverall; a bandana wrapped round her head. I said I was making coffee and asked if she would like one too. She agreed and followed me into the kitchen, where she took over and made cups for both of us. *"I just wanted to thank you again for taking the girls to the show, they really enjoyed it, couldn't stop talking about it last night and went to sleep singing songs!"* We were under the trees again, Dilly sipping her coffee perched on a chair that I dragged outside,

"I meant what I said last night, they are great girls and they are such a credit to you." I started to tell her about Renee finding us a table and clearing up.

"That's my girl," she smiled. *"But I can't tell you how worried I am about their future."* The smile had disappeared and I noticed for the first time how drawn her face was and her sagging shoulders.

"What do you mean - their future?" I asked.

153

"Oh nothing, take no notice of me, just feeling a bit morbid." She hid behind her mug, glowering into space.

"Do you mean educationally, politically - this movement you're involved with, you think it could lead to major problems?" I asked.

"No I think they would survive all that," she rested her chin on the lip of the mug clenched in her two hands. A tear was threatening to overflow from her eyelid.

"Well what?" I persisted.

"No I don't have to worry you about this, it's my problem." She drew herself up; the sudden movement causing the tear to slip over the lid and run unchecked down her cheek. I remembered how she had unburdened herself to me some weeks back and assumed there was a connection. For a moment I considered changing the subject but a sense of needing to help overwhelmed me.

"You mean Karl's problem?" It was whispered, like words to a lover.

"Well yes and no; I don't want you to be involved," she murmured, more tears were slipping over the edge.

"Is the drug problem worse?" I asked.

"No, it's not that," suddenly she made a decision. *"What the hell, I might as well tell you, seems you'll find out soon enough."* Dilly drained her coffee, drew a deep breath: *"I've spent two days at the hospital this week discussing test results taken months ago and sent to the States - and done even more tests. They believe that I have a rare virus in my blood that they don't know how to treat. Seems a few folk in the US have been diagnosed with this virus, which breaks down your natural protection system and so you pick up all*

154

sorts of bugs and get really sick for a long time until it eventually kills you off... Thank you Karl!" she breathed.

"*What do you mean, I don't follow?*" I was shocked.

"*Passed on through unprotected sex. Told you before about Karl in Florida and me losing my insides. Well seems that wasn't the end.*" Dilly sounded remarkably calm. "*So, now you know why I'm worried for the girls. If I ain't here and with Karl acting like a zombie most of the time; who's going to look after the girls when I'm gawn?*" For the first time she looked at me; "*It's a bugger ain't it?*" I'd not heard her swear before and I was lost for words:

"*Couldn't there be some mistake, surely there is something they can give you to clear it up?*" I mumbled.

"*Doc says not, they might give me a few transfusions but he's not sure that would help, long term,*" she said.

"*Oh my God Dilly... it's crazy.*" I cried.

She fiddled with the ring on her finger, "*You know, I think I could deal with this trouble if I knew Karl was okay. He was a great father when the kids were little, he played with them all the time, took them fishing, swimming, biking. He even liked to cook. If he was like that again then I could die in peace knowing they'd be taken care of.*" Now the tears were streaming down her face, free-falling out of sunken eye-sockets. Before I could think of anything vaguely comforting to say, Karl lumbered into view from behind their house. "*Oh, there you are ... chatting up our neighbour,*" he joked. I hadn't seen him since the party all those weeks ago and had forgotten what a big man he was. He was wearing dark sunglasses, his eyes totally hidden.

155

"Girls tell me you took em all to a show last night. That was mighty civil of you man," he said

"Yeah," I stammered, *"it was great fun. Would you like a coffee?"* I asked.

"Mighty fine idea," he replied, perching on the arm of Dilly's chair. I rose and headed for the door, as I did I saw Karl reach into his pocket and pull out a huge handkerchief. *"Here girl,"* he said softly, *"your eyes are leaking."* Polite and irrelevant conversation flowed, as we sipped our coffee. The girls came and went like the tide, later they were under one of the Royal Palms re-enacting Cinderella, Renee wearing a towel over her head, I supposed as a shawl, and holding a broom. Pearl was directing operations and waving her wand in an authoritative manner. As I looked at their antics, I was filled with despair, as I considered the implications of what Dilly had told me. Their young lives revolved around their mother, like planets round the sun, like bees around their queen; how could they possibly cope if the centre of their universe was removed. I glanced at Karl, his shoulders were down, one arm was behind Dilly, his huge fingers intertwined with hairs on the back of her head.

Coffee cups drained, Dilly turned to Karl: *"I'm taking the girls to see my sister,"* she said quietly. *"I'll only be about an hour."* He grunted and slowly stood and stretched. Dilly thanked me for the coffee, collected the cups and disappeared through the door towards my kitchen. Karl and I stood staring at the girls who were totally absorbed in another world. *"Okay girls, come, we're going to see your Auntie Josie."* Dilly had reappeared at my back door.

"In a minute," called Cinderella vigorously brushing the grass.

"Now," Dilly's tone precluded any argument. Props were dropped on the floor and the three came running.

"Why are we going to Aunt Josie's?" asked Pearl.

"So that you can tell her about your trip to City Hall and all that English culture you learned." Dilly threw a smile in my direction. *"Thanks again for the coffee, see you'll later,"* and they were gone, Vernee and Pearl holding their mother's hands, Renee bounding up ahead on her imaginary hop-scotch court.

"Great girls," I said.

"Yeah,' replied Karl, *"All four of them."* We both stood and watched until they were hidden from view.

"If you're not doing anything, why don't you sit down for a bit," I suggested to Karl.

He turned towards the chair: *"Yeah, good idea - is it too early for a beer?"*

"It's never too early for a beer," I replied and turned towards the door. He called for me to stop and insisted that he fetch a couple of cans from his fridge: *"D'you like Budweiser?"* he asked. When he returned he thrust a can into my hand. The Buds were so cold, I wondered if they had been stored in the freezer.

Conversation flowed easily between us. He was full of questions, how did I like Bermuda and the School. He wanted to know about life in England. I questioned him about his childhood in Barbados and his job. He obviously loved to talk and had a great sense of humour. I couldn't help but think of Dilly comparing him to a zombie. Having exhausted the non-controversial topics, a comfortable silence fell between us and after a few moments, although I couldn't see his eyes, I felt sure they were shut, as his breathing became heavier and I decided he was obviously dozing. Dozing, like sneezing, is somewhat contagious and soon I too was oblivious to the sights and sounds surrounding us.

The toot of a car-horn roused us both; we'd been spotted by a passing taxi-driver. Karl raised an arm and punched the air. We had only been resting our eyes for a couple of minutes, I felt sure but somehow we were refreshed.

Suddenly Karl asked; *"You talk to Dilly much?"* I looked at him but his opaque shades hid his eyes and his mouth gave nothing away.

"How do you mean?" I replied, trying not to sound wary.

"About her health," he replied, *"did she mention anything about her health?"*

"She was telling me, when you came out, that she had been to the hospital this week for tests and also that she had cancelled her performances with the dance troupe this week," I replied truthfully.

"She didn't tell you what the man said, what the doctor man at the hospital said," he persisted. He answered his own question before I could say anything, much to my relief. I wasn't sure of his reaction if I filled in too many of the gaps. *"Seems like she has this real nasty virus in her blood and they don't know how to cure it."* He took off his sunglasses and I could see his eyes were brim-full of tears.

158

He wiped them with the back of hand and replaced his shades.

"She did tell me that... but I couldn't believe it. There must be a cure. Did the doctor say anything about sending her to the States?" I asked.

"Nope.... he says he talked to people there. They also looked at the test results and they say they don't have no cure neither." Karl cleared his throat: *"Dilly doesn't know but I went and talked to the doctor-man on Friday - got it from the horse's mouth."* That huge handkerchief appeared again and he loudly blew his nose; afterwards he lifted his shades and dabbed his eyes again. *"He says she will slowly get sicker and sicker until her body can't take no more."*

"Did he say how long.. how long this..?" I was fumbling for the right words.

"Nope, he wouldn't give it no time-frame." Karl shuffled uneasily in his chair and stared at the heavens. Silence, except for whispering Casuarinas and a distant Kiskadee. He fumbled in his pocket and brought out a small plastic bag. He pulled out a cigarette paper and what I presumed was cannabis and started rolling. I guess I was shocked.

"Karl, is that a good idea?" I ventured.

"Yes, it's a great idea, takes away all the pain," he replied softly, *"all the pain."*

I took a deep breath: *"It doesn't take away Dilly's pain,'* I snapped, *"and she needs you more than ever. She needs you to be in full control to give her all the support she needs."* I was pushing my luck but couldn't stop thinking of the three girls. *"Come on man, that's not the answer,"* I

159

encouraged; *"think of your daughters, they need you in one piece."* He had stopped wrapping and tears were seeping from under his shades. I kept up the attack: *"Your girls think the world of you and will need you more than ever - you have to stop. Karl, you just have to stop,"* I pleaded.

"You been talking to Dilly," he growled, *"I know you been talking."* He paused: *"You know nothing - it ain't just Dilly leaving the girls - it's me too, I'll be leaving the girls all alone."* Words were tumbling out incoherently, I could only understand because I knew of his problems. *"I'll be locked up in Casemates,"* he cried. *"Left to rot and not see my sweethearts grow up."* He was shaking uncontrollably. I felt helpless.

"All the more reason to give it up - you need a clear head if you're going to sort this out. Come on man, don't give in!"

For a moment he continued rolling but then he stopped, removed his shades and looked at me. *"You sure are a teacher - and treating me like a naughty school boy."* He almost smiled, pushed the completed cigarette into the plastic bag and back into his pocket. *"I need me another beer,"* he said, getting to his feet.

"Me too," I said, *"a whole six-pack."* I had been so tense, unsure how far to push the issue but I was blinded by the picture of Karl's three girls and an urgent need to ensure their father was in a fit state to look after them - if ever Dilly couldn't.

When he returned Karl seemed calmer, he handed me the beer, settled into the chair and took a long pull. *"What am I goin' to do, oh wise one?"*

160

What indeed I thought. *"Well, we're not medical men, nor miracle workers, so we have to leave Dilly's problem to the experts. Right?"* I spoke quietly, looking him in the eye - or more precisely his sunglasses. *"Take those shades off man, I don't know whether you're asleep or not."* Obediently he removed his shades. *"Right?"* I asked again.

"Right" he replied almost inaudibly.

"Okay, that leaves the girls - and that means you. You have to be tough enough to see this through. If you show them you can deal with the situation, they will take their lead from you - and you'll all survive." I squeezed my can too tightly and cursed as beer spilled into my lap.

"Listen Karl," I began, *"I lost my wife a couple of year's back, killed by a car. It was like a surgeon had taken his scalpel and chopped out my inside. I wanted to die too. I'm not religious and although I had friends, I had no one I could really to turn to. Life, I thought no longer had a meaning. I became irrational, a zombie, a victim to routine. You know what I'm saying? It's tough, it's the toughest time of your life when something like this happens."* I paused remembering the agonies. *"I started running again, every day after work, I went running against the clock. Time became everything, a few seconds off each day – the pain in my muscles hiding the pain in my heart."* I drained the beer-can, Karl was looking at his hands, rotating his wedding ring. I continued: *"Well running, routine - somehow it helped me cope, got me through. And then time kicks in... and bit by bit the healing process begins."* I looked at Karl but he still hadn't moved, he was still fiddling with his wedding ring.

"Running eh? I should start running?" He was now intently scraping dirt away from under his fingernails. *"Yeh, running away from the police!"*

"Why do you need to run away from the police Karl?" I knew the answer but I still asked the question. *"What have you done? Smoking a little weed won't land you in big troubles."* He didn't reply but turned his attention to the other hand.

I persisted: *"If you don't explain, I can't help."* Hypocrite, I thought to myself, how could I possibly help. *"Have you been dealing? Is that the problem Karl? Are you Mr Big in Bermuda's drug trade?"*

"Mr Big!" he snorted. His gaze left his hands and he turned slowly to face me. *"No, I ain't no Mr Big. Anyway it's better you don't know too much, could be dangerous."*

"Okay, but tell me this, have you been dealing? Is that why you are afraid the police will be after you and will put you in Casemates and leave you there to rot?" I asked.

"Well you know how it is man, I shared a joint with the blokes I work with. And then me and Dilly had a real bad problem. It seemed there weren't no answer and I started smoking more regular. It started to cost me money." Karl slid forward on his chair, rested his elbows on his knees and gazed at the grass between his feet. *"Then the guy who supplied me asked me to make a few deliveries for a discount on the stuff he sold me. Then he started giving it me free, in exchange for more deliveries. Didn't take too much of my time, didn't seem to be no risks, so before long I was looking after Somerset for the man."* He shifted and held his head in his hands, elbows still planted firmly on his knees. *"Oh*

162

man, then Dilly found a stash among my fishing tackle. Oh man! Oh man, did she hit the roof. She punched me, she got the broom and hit me over the head; all the time screaming at me and crying her eyes out. I thought she had gone mad." He rubbed his massive hands all over his face as if trying to wash away the memory and grunted loudly. *"Man - she was so mad – raging bull mad. Then she burnt all the stuff on the barbecue when I weren't looking. Ten-thousand dollars worth of good stuff barbecued - oh shit! I tried telling my man what had happened, you know what he do? He pulled a gun from his pocket, held it to my head - here."* He made the shape of a gun with his fingers and held it against his temple. *"Well, he said, your goin' to have to work much harder to make up for all that lost cash. I said I would try and raise the money and pay him off. He said no, I would have to work for him - and when he called, I had better come running or there'd be a boat ride out to sea, a bullet in my head and I'd be feeding de fish. You know what man, I believe him. He's one mean son of a bitch."* Telling the tale had taken an immense effort, he flopped back in his chair and replaced his shades, breathing heavily, as if he had run the length of Long Bay Lane.

I had listened intently to Karl, all the time trying to think of a way out of the situation, a way of getting him to stop the habit, so that he would be in a fit state to bring up his kids. But as his tale progressed, I felt more and more as if I was walking into the sea and the water was piling up over my head. Talk about being out of one's depth - a frightening feeling of helplessness set in. *"What if you went to the police* and explained about this man threatening your life?" I asked naively.

Karl laughed: "*What you think? They arrest him and give me a medal?*"

"*Well, it would give them a lead.*" I blustered.

"*You haven't a clue Mr Teacher-man. He's just a soldier in an army - just a corporal. An army run by Captains, Majors and hundreds of foot soldiers and a General at the top. So he get's arrested, there's dozens more ready to take his place - and an execution squad to get rid of people like me;*" Karl sighed and began shaking his head. "*It's so well organised. When you're in, you're in – and the only way out - is in a box.*" I was at a total loss as to what to say. I couldn't help but understand his need to bury his head in the sand through drug use.

A child's shout broke my reverie and a hurricane of movement announced the arrival of little Vernee; who immediately launched herself like a missile into her father's lap, causing him to grunt, as she knocked the wind out of him.

Pearl and Renee appeared round the building holding their mother's hand, Pearl carrying a large paper bag. "*Aunt Josie's let us pick oranges off her tree,*" she called, "*they're real sweet.*" Digging her hand into the bag she produced a monster and placed it in my hand, "*the best for you,*" she said. Karl turned to Dilly and asked if he could get her drink, she declined and said she was going to get everyone a meal. I was invited but made an excuse, I felt they needed time together as a family unit and I had a great deal to think about.

The School took Christmas very seriously, classes were beautifully and imaginatively decorated; garlands hung down the corridors and a Christmas tree stood magnificently in the corner of the Hall. Carols were learned and a concert prepared. Eloise was kept extremely busy, being in charge of all the musical items. My contribution was training my class to present an excerpt from Dickens' *Christmas Carol*.

One Friday evening, a week before we were due to finish for the holiday, parents were invited to see the concert. The Hall was packed an hour before the concert was due to begin, as parents attempted to obtain seats near the front. Rehearsals hadn't been that great but children, being children, out-performed themselves that night and the concert deemed a great success. Everyone stayed afterwards for cookies and cakes, washed down with gallons of soft drinks. Nursing a large paper cup of something cold and golden I chatted to Eloise about the merits of her choir and various other performances. She asked if I was going back to England for the holiday. I told her that I was planning to stay, my only living relative in England was a sister and she was spending Christmas with her parents-in-law - and anyway I didn't need that level of expense at the moment. She told me that she would be around for part of the time but would also be away visiting relatives in Florida. We parted, with her promising to contact me when she returned.

The last week of the term was a typically messy end. Those children spending Christmas off the Island had left early and no one was in the mood to do anything serious. We had a class party early in the week and spent the remaining days finishing off bits of cake, crisps and

165

multitudes of biscuits. We were all pleased when the last afternoon came around and the children packed their bags, gathered up all the decorations and cards that they had made and headed home. Evelyn invited everyone to the staffroom for a drink and mince pies that she had made. We flopped around for about an hour drinking seasonal eggnog and then made our excuses and headed for our homes – and what we considered, a well-earned break.

Since my talk with Karl, I had spent hours thinking about the mess he was in; and eventually decided there was little, if anything, I could usefully do. It seemed an intractable situation. Perhaps, I had concluded, I could try and keep him from smoking himself stupid – that might be something constructive but that would require seeing more of him. Now that school was over I had more time, I decided to act.

The day after school finished I caught Dilly outside hanging up some washing on a line strung between two trees. She was wearing the long brown coverall again and her face looked drained. She was cheerful enough and still full of banter. I asked when Karl would be around, she replied that it was his last day at work tomorrow and he would be home for ten days over the Christmas to New Year period. As she talked, she looked at me through the flapping clothes:

"What are you planning?" she asked, staring quizzically.

"Nothing," I answered, *"well, I wondered if he would come fishing."*

"You'll have to ask him, he might, it's a long time since he went out fishing." She pegged the last pair of socks on the line and picked up the washing basket.

"How's he been?" I asked. *"Is he still smoking?"*

"He's a bit better,' she whispered, *"I still catch him smoking but he ain't acting zombie-like quite so much."* She looked at me sharply, *"Why d'you ask? Did you talk to him?"*

I shuffled and brushed an insect off my arm: *"Well, you could say the matter came up."*

She pushed me in the stomach with the washing-basket: *"Lord save us all from school-teachers!"* she grinned. *"Come round when he gets home."* I stood and watched her diminutive form as she went back inside. She walked slightly hunched, obviously in pain or discomfort. I sighed and cursed the injustices of this world. Back in the house I telephoned Charlie, one of my tennis-playing buddies, the owner of the boat in which we had been out fishing together. I asked him if there was any chance of us going out fishing during the holiday but he said he was leaving in a couple of days' time to stay with his girl friend in New Jersey – but that I was welcome to borrow the boat. After some discussion we agreed to meet the next day at Robinson's Boatyard on Ely's harbour.

Later that evening Karl, Dilly and I sat under the stars sipping our drinks and chatting quietly; the girls were indoors watching some game-show or other on the television. An occasional burst of childish laughter emanating from within. I was wearing long trousers for the first time and a long-sleeved shirt - but Dilly and Karl were

167

in full winter gear and Dilly enveloped in a blanket. Compared with a few weeks ago, it was certainly cooler, probably about seventy degrees in the day and five to ten degrees less at night. I was still very grateful for the warmer weather, compared to December in England. It seemed to me that Bermuda had two seasons, just Spring and Summer and that suited me down to the ground. I told Karl that I had the use of a friend's boat and after some encouragement from Dilly, he agreed to go out with me in two days time, during the afternoon and early evening. Dilly said that would suit her plans as she intended to take the girls Christmas shopping in Hamilton. Karl insisted that he would organise the beer, some food and the bait as his contribution.

*

At eleven the next morning I rode to Robinson's Boatyard situated on the wonderfully picturesque Ely's Harbour. Charlie was already there and showed me where he stowed his tiny one-man dinghy, which he used to get out to his boat. I stood and watched as he paddled out to his mooring, climbed aboard, tied the dinghy to the buoy and began fiddling with the engine. I was pleased to note that it started first time and gently he chugged to the dock and I clambered in. We returned to his mooring, looped a rope through the ring on the buoy and switched off the engine. For the next ten minutes or so he showed me the ropes, so to speak and explained the idiosyncrasies of the engine and told me the tank was full and that there was a five-gallon jerry-can inside one of the side lockers - for emergencies. I promised that I would fill the tank when I returned and thanked him for his generosity. Charlie replied that he was

168

glad to have someone keep an eye on his boat while he was away. He then suggested that I drive the boat around the harbour for a while to get used to it but explained that he couldn't stay long, as he was flying to Newark that evening.

It was fun puttering around the harbour, the sea was dead calm, protected by a peninsula and several islands, some boasting partly hidden, beautiful but expensive homes. The view of the land from the sea is always uplifting and different. The oleanders in the grounds of the Willowbank holiday centre were spectacular. The only things missing from this wondrous scene, I thought, were the Longtails. They were now out to sea and would not return until the breeding season came round again.

Charlie looked at me and tapped his watch, I nodded and took the boat back to the dock, where I chatted with a blue-overalled pump attendant; while Charlie moored his boat and paddled back to shore. Before going our separate ways, Charlie gave me an ignition key for the boat's engine and wished me luck. We parted, shouting season's greetings to each other, as we pulled out of the boatyard and headed in opposite directions.

*

It was a relief to me that the day of our fishing trip dawned bright and calm. I knocked on Dilly's door and the whole family then proceeded to help load our two bikes with all the multifarious items one needs for a day's fishing. The *piece-de-la resistance* being a delicately balanced cool box holding the beer and sandwiches, strapped on the pillion-seat of Karl's machine.

169

We set off noisily down Longbay Lane with the four girls waving us goodbye and shouted demands that we be sure to bring them back their supper. An hour later we were chugging out of Ely's harbour, passing Cathedral Rocks and around the narrow peninsula known as Wreck Hill. While I steered, Karl was busy sorting out the fishing lines and chopping up frozen squid, which was to be the bait.

"Do you know why this is called Wreck Hill?" I called out, making conversation.

He glanced up, first at me and then across to the lush headland: *"Cos of some Dutch ship or other that washed up on the rocks in the sixteen hundreds. Used to call it Flemish Hill. The captain survived, he was a pirate, so they banned him to Ireland Island where he built himself a new ship!"* I was impressed with his knowledge and said so. *"Always been interested in wrecks, I knows where they all are."* Karl said.

"Have you ever been down for a closer look?" I asked.

"No... never did learn to dive. Snorkelling round the Vixen, off Daniel's Head is the nearest I've been," he laughed. *"Your British navy bought this land once and planned to put a lighthouse on it - but changed their mind and built the one at Gibbs Hill instead."*

"Really," I replied, *"it would have been a good spot."* I was now guiding the boat close to the shore, following the channel we had used on the earlier fishing trip. *"Can you walk up to the top of the headland?"* I asked.

"Nah," replied Karl, wiping his squid-greasy hands on a cloth. *"Private property, nearly thirty acres of gardens*

up there, fabulous house, swimming pool, tennis courts. Once did some carpentry there - great place!"

"Who owns it," I asked *"someone rich and famous?"*

"Yeh, more money then you'll ever make out of teaching. An Australian guy who manages pop-groups, makes films, puts on Broadway plays and stuff. You know." We both gazed back at Wreck Hill, the house was hidden from view. *"Don't think he spends much time there,"* said Karl, *"which is sad,"*

We were now making our way along the Southampton shoreline and approaching the Pompano, where Evelyn had taken me to lunch that first week. The sea was an exquisite shade of turquoise with only a gentle swell. However, the steady beat of the engine drowned normal conversation and I couldn't help but contrast this to sailing *Crazy Dream*, when the only sounds were a joy to one's ears - rushing wind from the sails and sea slapping the bows. Spotting a marker buoy I turned the boat away from the shore and headed out between the reefs, now showing as splodges of dark-green paint beneath the glistening surface.

Some fifteen minutes later, after some discussion, I slowed the boat and Karl threw out an anchor. We waited until we were sure it was holding before I switched off the engine. The silence was palpable.

We busied ourselves baiting a line each and settled down on opposite sides of the boat, the bait between our feet. Once the lines were overboard, Karl opened the cool box and produced a couple of beer cans.

We were not so far out from land as the previous trip with my tennis-playing buddies - but far enough that the

171

shoreline, such that myriads of sparkling white-roofed houses and colourful shrubs, shimmered like an impressionistic painting. God, I loved this place!

We both lost our bait a couple of times before Karl pulled in a reasonably sized yellowtail. Fishing, or maybe the constant movement of the boat, had a somewhat soporific affect, resulting in a stilted conversation confined to mundanities. During a particularly quiet period when Karl appeared to be totally lost in his own thoughts, I decided the time had come to raise some of the issues that had been causing me to loose sleep. *"Karl,"* I began, *"you know the conversation we were having the other afternoon?"*

He slowly turned his gaze from the distant horizon to me, till I noticed that I was reflected in his shades; he nodded: *"How could I forget?"*

"Well, I can't stop thinking about your situation. And as hard as I think, I don't know what you should do; or what I could do to help. The only thing that is certain, is that you must stop drugging yourself. You need your wits about you, you need to be wide awake and alert." I knew that I was struggling to make sense.

"Okay, so I'm awake - what then?" He drew in his line, the bait was gone.

"Tell me how it all works," I said earnestly. *"Spell it out for me, names, places, the lot. Perhaps if we go through this together we can think of some way to..."* I really was struggling; *"to make sense of it all and think of a way forward."*

Karl looked at me, a wry smile puckering the corner of his mouth. *"I said it before, you have no idea."*

172

"You're right - I have no idea, which is why I want you to spell it out for me;" I repeated. *"The man who threatened you - what's his name?"*

"It's too risky man. You're a nice guy. You're a teacher, stick to kids they're less dangerous." He reloaded his hook with more squid and flung his line in an optimistic arc towards the reef.

"Karl," I pleaded, *"Karl if I don't know, I can't help. And,"* I stammered, *"no-one is going to know what you've told me out here in the middle of the ocean. And I'm not exactly likely to go blabbing it around the parish."*

"Listen Jack, all I know is how the supply chain works. I haven't a clue who's behind it or how other things work;" his gaze left my face and returned to his line, which he gave a couple of encouraging tugs.

"Well at least tell me that," I snapped. Karl's attention never left his line. *"You said that the man who threatened you wanted you to come running when he called. Has he called? What does he want you to do? Just make extra deliveries – or something extra?"* Although I was asking the questions, I wasn't totally convinced I wanted to hear the answers.

Karl tied his line around a small cleat and reached inside the cool box and handed me another beer and took a deep breath: "O*kay, the guy who threatened me is called de Vere. He looks after Somerset, he supplies me, I supply the customers - and I give him all the money.* Before *Dilly burnt all the stuff, he also used to give me a percentage back on all I sold. That stopped and he says he's keeping an account of* *what I would have received, to reduce my debt."* He took a long pull at his beer. *"Satisfied?"*

"Who's the chap de Vere?" I asked.

"He works at Cambridge Beaches," Karl replied.

The penny dropped, *"Oh the guy at your party, his name was Just!"*

"Yeh, that's him. Nice friendly guy. Always real friendly to Dilly." Karl was scowling at his can, *"real friendly."*

"So, you have regular customers that you supply?" I asked.

"Yeah, I ride round the village on my bike most Friday nights; folks know I'll be coming." Karl voice sounded resigned. *"No phone calls, nothing that can be traced."*

"Do you go out to Cambridge Beaches to collect it?" I asked.

Karl snorted: *"No way! I get a delivery each week into my hand."*

"Who delivers to you;" I persisted. Karl took another deep swig of his beer and drained the can.

He looked at me, as if trying to make up his mind. *"Eggy!"* he breathed.

"Eggy," I echoed; *"Eggy is in on this?"* I didn't really know why but I was surprised. Perhaps because he was such a good friend to Dilly.

"Yeh Eggy's just a delivery boy, he's a regular in and out of Cambridge Beaches, so nobody gets suspicious." Karl was drawing in his line until he swung a fish over the side: *"Blasted Bream;"* he said; unhooked it and threw it back.

174

"You thank your lucky stars that I didn't chop you up for chum;" he called out, as it splashed back into the water.

"Well who supplies Just de Vere?" I asked, emptying my beer can.

"Listen, I don't ask questions but I hear that each Parish has a man in charge and he organizes his sellers and his runners. There are nine parishes but some have more folk than others, so in the big ones, the guy has one or two deputies." Karl was concentrated on baiting his hook. *"Now you know as much as I do."*

"Sounds well organized," I sighed, attached more squid to the hook and hurled it as far away from the boat as I could. *"You know this guy, Just de Vere, said you had got to work off the debt? Has he asked you to do anything extra - something more than selling to your normal customers?"* I asked.

"Not yet," replied Karl, *"that's what I'm dreading!"*

It was growing dusk by the time we decided that we had caught enough fish for a reasonable meal and pulled up the anchor. The sun had slipped below the horizon, leaving in its wake a magnificently peppered ochre sky and purple billowing clouds. I steered our way back towards the coast and into Ely's Harbour, as Karl busied himself, expertly de-scaling and gutting the fish.

It was pitch black by the time we arrived back at Karl's house but Dilly had the barbecue ready; she had cooked potatoes and prepared a salad. Karl laid out our catch on the grill and the girls came out to inspect. *"Huh,"* snorted Pearl leaning over the fire; *"I thought you guys were going fishing! Them ain't no fish, they're just tiddlers; if*

175

you'd asked, I could have caught some fish like that off the dock."

Karl methodically placed his tongs down, turned slowly and faced his daughter, who was grinning widely. Then in a blur of movement he grabbed her and held in a headlock. *"Jack and I risked life and limb to catch these monsters; and you better be grateful;"* he shouted, turning her upside down. Pearl was squealing her head off, as her father pretended to squeeze the life out of his elder daughter.

We ate inside, clustered round the loaded dining table rubbing elbows with our neighbours. Pearl had organized the seating arrangements of course, placing herself between me and her father on one side of the table; Renee and Vernee either side of their mother on the other. Karl and I told tales about the ones that got away and as the fish got bigger the more hysterical the girls became, shouting, *'lies, all lies.'* Happy families, I thought during a lull; happy that is on the surface, happy for the girls' sake. I looked at Dilly, picking at her food, concentrating on her plate - and Karl smiling at his elder daughter but I knew the smile was hiding a desperate feeling of helplessness.

Later, lying on my bed my head whirled, as I recounted all the things Karl had told me and I contemplated what the future might hold. No matter which way I looked at it, I could find no route out of the complex maze in which he was trapped.

*

The following day I rode my bike into Hamilton and toured the shops seeking suitable gifts for Dilly's family. Trimmingham's store was a wonderland of fabulous treasures and though most of the items were outside of my budget, it was a great place for ideas. I moved on to A. & E. Smith's and ended up in Baxter's Bookstore. I was engrossed in reading the advertising blurb on the back page of *The Odessa File* when someone jogged my elbow; we both apologised and I looked up - it was Marsha!

"*What have you found;*" she challenged, after we had greeted each other.

"*Frederick Forsyth's latest;*" I replied. "*Did you read The Day of the Jackal?*" I asked.

"*No, far too exciting for me.*" She laughed.

"*Anyway;*" I said "*never mind books, how are you and where have you been?*"

"*Thank you, I'm fine. Busy of course; I've just come from Chambers now; how about you,*" she replied.

"*Oh, I'm fine; school's finished so I'm foot-loose and fancy-free, so to speak. Just trying to find gifts for Dilly's girls,*" I replied.

"*Ah, how are they all, haven't seen Dilly for a while.*" Marsha asked.

"*Actually Dilly is not well but this isn't the place… do you have time for a coffee or something to eat?*" I asked.

"*Dilly's not well; sorry to hear that,*" she hesitated and looked at me quizzically. "*Well, yes, a coffee and a sandwich or something would be good. I came in here to buy a couple of magazines; I'm flying to Jamaica tomorrow to spend Christmas with my mother. I won't be a minute;*" She headed for the magazine rack while I paid the fare to Forsyth's Odessa.

Seated in the *Horse and Buggy* on Queen Street, we were soon tucking into a fancy sandwich and sipping something long and cool. Marsha looked very business-like, dressed in a smart black blazer and skirt, her jet-black hair pulled tightly back from her face; gold studs in her ears with a matching cross and chain around her neck. Although we were physically close I could sense a barrier and the distance that she laid down between us.

"So, you're off to Jamaica," I said.

"Yes, I'd be in trouble if I didn't go. My mother lives on her own but my brothers will be there for Christmas dinner - there'll be a houseful." She sipped and peered round the room over the top of her glass.

"How many brothers do you have?" I asked, suddenly wanting to know more about this intriguing woman.

"I have three brothers, all older than me; all married with children - I've lost count of how many nieces and nephews I have," she laughed.

"So you'll have a full suitcase, no doubt," I said.

"Good Lord no, I'll do my shopping in Kingston, when I arrive, it's much cheaper," she exclaimed, returning her attention to her sandwich. *"This is good!"*

"And your brothers, what do they do?" I asked curiously.

"One teacher, one doctor and one layabout who plays in a band," she replied. *"And guess who's the happiest?"*

"The teacher, of course," I joked.

"Huh, in Kingston? He's more of a social worker - no, my layabout kid brother - the musician; doesn't have a

178

care in the world... where did we go wrong?" Marsha finished her sandwich and picked at the trimmings with her fork: *"You said that Dilly is not well?"*

I told Marsha the saga of Dilly's problems, leaving out Karl's involvement. She was concerned and like me worried for the girls.

"You never did tell me how it is that you know Dilly?" I said.

Marsha methodically placed her fork on the plate before glancing towards me. *"Didn't I?'* she said absently. *"Well she has a little project going on that she wanted some advice about."*

"Oh you mean her attempts to solve the hotel-workers problems with management - but keeping the Black Berets out of it," I said quietly.

She looked incredulous: *"You know about that?"*

"Yes, she explained all that to me; in fact I took her to one of her meetings at Cambridge Beaches." I said.

"Good Lord, she must trust you! I didn't think even her husband knew about it." Marsha was looking straight at me, her head slightly on one side, a different expression creeping into her eyes.

"I'm not sure whether he does or not, she didn't say." I volunteered. The waiter came to clear the table and we ordered coffee.

"I'm so sorry to hear that she's sick, she's such a great person;" Marsha held her chin in her hand; *"I'll go and see her as soon as I come back."*

179

"Perhaps we could have a meal together.. when you're back.. or I could take you sailing," I said spontaneously but not very confidently.

She fastened her eyes on the top button of my shirt: *"Jack, you seem to be a nice guy and I've enjoyed lunch but I'm not dating... okay?"*

"You mean you're not dating because I'm white!" I said stiffly.

"No man, I mean I'm not dating;" she said emphatically; *"I have too much going on in my life at the moment without complicating it any more."*

"I don't see how going out to dinner or coming for a sail would complicate your life," I said somewhat huffily.

She looked me square in the eyes, *"Jack...drop it...okay?"*

Marsha went off to the Ladies room; the waiter brought the coffee and I paid the bill. When she returned I asked her where she lived and she replied that she rented a small apartment in Pembroke, some twenty minutes walk away from the centre of Hamilton. I asked for her telephone number but she politely declined, saying she was rarely there. Conversation was somewhat stilted after this and it wasn't long before I gathered up my purchases and we headed for the door. Outside she shook my hand rather formally; then as if her conscience had pricked her, leaned across and pecked me on the cheek, thanked me again for lunch, turned and headed up the street, the clatter of her heels soon lost in the midday traffic. I stood and watched her go, unsure of my feelings, until she disappeared among the mingling masses.

Christmas Eve, I delivered parcels for Dilly, Karl and the girls; Pearl handed me a small carefully wrapped box; with strict instructions not to open it until tomorrow. Later, in the evening, I went round to Don Jeffer's apartment for a party, he lived near the church in Somerset and so I decided to walk. Don was one of my tennis-playing friends who taught Physical Education at a nearby school. Alan and his girl friend Mildred were there but most of the others were new to me, many were colleagues of Don's. It was a lively affair and wasn't long before the volume on the record-player soared and folk were disco dancing and twisting around his small lounge.

I was taking a breather outside on the balcony, overlooking the field belonging to Sandy's' Secondary School when Don came out with a tall, well-built man. *"Hey Jack,"* he said, *"meet Stephen."* We shook hands. *"Stephen this is Jack, another Phys.Ed. teacher."* We exchanged pleasantries and Don made an excuse and went back indoors.

"Are you a teacher too," I asked.

"No, I'm a policeman," he replied and I remembered Don's reference to his policeman friend, when we were discussing the murder of the Police-Commissioner. Stephen told me that he lived in Somerset but worked at Headquarters in Hamilton. I told him about our tennis games and asked if he played. He replied that he had not played for some years but was interested. This gave me the excuse to ask him for his telephone number. Thinking of Karl's predicament, this might be a useful person to know, I thought. He gave me the number and I promised to call him when we had a date lined up to play.

181

I left the party about one o'clock, when only smooching couples were left, propping each other up as they swayed to softer rhythms and the modified volume. It was pitch black and the irregularly spaced street lamps only cast tiny pools of light and I soon wished that I had taken a torch, it was pitch dark down Long Bay Lane and I feared stepping on one of those very large Buffo toads that I occasionally saw squashed along the lane. The tree-frogs were in good voice, though it was considerably cooler and I was glad of the sweater that I had taken.

Christmas morning I woke about nine o'clock and over breakfast unwrapped the present that Pearl had given me the night before. It was a beautifully turned cedar-wood bowl, and according to the sticker on the base, carved by a local Somerset man. I had a couple of other gifts to unwrap, one given to me by Evelyn, the other from one of the parents. Their shape gave them away, obviously bottles of wine. As I sat peeling the orange Pearl had given me some days' earlier, it occurred to me that this was the first morning in my life that I was on my own on a Christmas morning. A dark cloak began to settle on my shoulders, as I thought of Jill and Christmases, usually spent with her parents. My own parents had died within a few years of each other while I was at college, they had never met Jill. I had a much older sister, who was always busy with her own life, as a mother and a partner in an estate-agent business. There was a card from her, which I had kept to open this morning. Inside there was a long letter and a shorter one from her daughter, my fourteen-year-old niece. These cheered me up no end and soon I was in the shower singing and in a more festive frame of mind.

Alan and Mildred had invited me some weeks ago to join them for Christmas Dinner and so I dressed myself up, gathered up the small gifts I had bought for my hosts and set off on my bike towards their home in Warwick. I had been there before, of course, after our fishing trip and so had little difficulty finding their tiny cottage and it wasn't long before I was on their small balcony hugging a traditional Bermuda Christmas special: a glass of Eggnog, its surface coated with spicy grated nutmeg.

While Alan was busy in the kitchen, Mildred sidled up and tucked an arm through mine. *"I'm really sorry,"* she purred; *"I invited this really lively girl from our office, to keep you company. She accepted and then a week or so later said her boyfriend was visiting from England, could she bring him... I couldn't very well say no, could I?"*

I laughed: *"So your match-making plans were foiled. Serves you right for being devious."*

"Nothing devious about that, I was just rounding up the numbers, now we are odd." She frowned.

"No comment," I grinned, *"would you like me to leave, to even the numbers up?"* Mildred punched me and returned to the kitchen.

The other guests eventually arrived and Mildred was indeed correct, her colleague, Susie, was very lively and her boyfriend, Jake, proved to be quite a wag. So we were a very jolly bunch, laughing and joking our way through a magnificent, traditional, turkey dinner; which we all agreed was delicious.

"Christmas pudding," Alan announced later, *"is not really a Canadian thing, so we have to make do with fruit salad, when anyone has any room."* We groaned at the thought of more food; by then we were lounging in armchairs, still sipping glasses of a superb wine that Mildred said she had obtained through the sommelier at Carlton Beach - *'legally - and paid for,'* she had quickly added.

About eight o'clock, Susie and Jake left but Alan insisted that I not rush away - and later I was easily persuaded to stay the night and sleep on the sofa. Mildred found me a pillow and blanket, apologising that they only had one-bedroom. I told her that it was not a problem and that being well fed and watered, I could have slept on the floor. And so Christmas Day came to a close with me tucked up on the sofa, pillow over my ears to drown the vigorous huffing and puffing emanating through the thin bedroom walls.

Boxing Day breakfast was served late and casually, in fact Mildred and I had almost finished before an exhausted-looking Alan appeared. *"How about some tennis today,"* he suggested, yawning.

I looked at him sharply, relieved to note that he was joking. *"Seriously, do you have any plans;"* I asked.

"Just a walk along Warwick Long Beach, I should think. What do you say Mil?"

"Sounds a bit strenuous, I'd say," she replied, unimpressed. But so it was, the three of us walked down the hill to the beach and strolled from the Mermaid Holiday Cottages to picturesque Jobson's Cove - and back again. It was a bright sunny day, the stretch of beach and its turquoise

184

sea straight out of a tourist brochure, though no one was in the water. We all knew that only tourists swim before May 24th and that was a long way off. Once we were back at the cottage, Mildred produced the remains of the turkey and some fresh bread and we pigged ourselves once again, before all three of us dropped off to sleep in our armchairs.

About seven o'clock I said that I really must leave. I told them that I had the use of Charlie's boat and asked if they fancied a ride out in the next day or two. Mildred thanked me but said she would be back to work the following day and Alan made excuses. As I was leaving, Mildred asked me what I was planning to do New Year's Eve. I told her that I had no plans and she told me there was a private party at the Carlton Beach and she could probably smuggle me in - I thanked them profusely for a wonderful couple of days and left.

*

"Tell me about Boxing Day;" said Dilly from the depths of a battered brown armchair, its arms wide enough to comfortably rest a cup and saucer or, as in this case, a glass.

"What do you mean?" I replied, from the superior height of a dining-chair, drawn-up alongside her.

"Well you Brits talk about the day after Christmas as Boxing Day. I don't see no folks going off fighting each other - why Boxing Day?" Dilly screwed the top off a small jar and shook two huge capsules into the palm of her hand.

"God Dilly, you're always asking awkward questions!" I joked, racking my brain for an answer. A raft of laughter emanated from the bedroom where the three girls and Karl were watching television.

185

"Well, today is the day after Boxing Day; come on, share this very British secret." Dilly placed one of capsules on her tongue, took a substantial swig from her glass and pulled a face, as she tried to swallow.

"Is that rum you are using to wash down that pill?" I asked innocently.

"You know damn well it's coke; stop trying to change the subject - or don't you know the answer?"

"I'm trying to think - I'm not even sure there is just one answer; I remember my mother telling me it was the day you gave people who provide you with some service or other, a tip - you know like the postman, the milkman, you give them a Christmas-box, a present." I was struggling.

"What do you mean milkman? And no postman do anything for me!" she was still trying to swallow the second pill, *"And why wait 'til after Christmas to give a present?"*

"I don't know Dilly; I guess people like that would be back at work on December 26ᵗʰ - Boxing Day!" I emphasised the latter, pulling a face. *"And, and the milkman and the postman deliver to your door. It's not like here where you go to the post-office to collect your mail - and to the supermarket to buy your milk."*

"Seems daft to me." The capsule was at last swallowed and she could talk distinctly again. *"Why Boxing?"*

"Well, the tradition is so old, people have forgotten its origins. I remember something about keeping a moneybox all year round and putting coins in it – and then at Christmas breaking it open. Then again some people think

186

there were actually boxing matches on the 26th, when men would fight each other for money. Satisfied?"

"Nope!" replied Dilly; *"I always said you Brits were a daft lot and should have stayed at home; not come messing with sensible folk, just getting on peacefully with their lives."* She spat this out, giving me a sly smile. The verbal jousting was of course a cover-up; Dilly looked terrible, her former smooth, coffee-coloured complexion was yellow and her skin, drawn tightly over her high cheekbones. She looked so frail, she almost disappeared into the huge armchair.

"What did the doctor say?" I almost whispered.

She snorted: *"That old fool don't say nuffin, just give me these damn great pills."* She held up the jar. *"How's a body meant to swallow things like this without choking to death."* She laughed: *"perhaps that's the idea, choke to death and ease the pain!"* She chuckled.

My heart sank. *"Do you want some more coke?"* I asked looking at her glass, desperately wishing there was something I could do to ease her obvious discomfort.

"No, I'm okay." She responded with a sigh.

"Do you want to put your feet up?" I said spotting a small padded stool in the corner of the room.

"No - and stop fussing, you're worse than my husband. He don't give me no peace neither!" she emptied her glass and I rose to my feet, my attention drawn to several old photographs hanging on the wall. I wandered across and bent down to examine them; the room was quite dark and the photographs were faded.

"Who's in the pictures Dilly?" I asked, *"the photos look really old."*

187

"They ain't so old," she replied, *"just* faded in the sunlight." She hadn't moved. *"Which one are you looking at?"*

"The one with a lady sitting in a wicker chair and two girls standing each side of her - all of them dressed up. And a toddler sitting on the ground," I called out.

"The woman sitting down is Eliza, my grandmother, that's my mother on the grass." She replied.

"What was your mother's name?" I asked.

"Pearl, same as my Pearl; only I don't remember her, she died when I was three." I glanced at Dilly but her eyes were closed. *"I was brought up by her sister, the one on the left - as you look at it. Her name was Myrah. She dead too, now."*

I stared at the photo, the sepia effect adding to the damage caused by the sun. The woman, Eliza, was sitting bolt upright in the chair, wearing a huge, brimmed hat, which cast a shadow across her jet-black features; a face dominated by a strong jaw-line. I looked at the children, all neatly dressed in clothes that looked totally unsuitable for Bermuda's climate. Not a smile to be seen.

I moved on to another photograph, almost identical except there were four children in the picture. I asked: *"And the one on the right, with a lady, no hat and four children?"*

"That would be Aunt Myrah, my sister and me and Myrah's two children, my cousins;" offered Dilly. I peered at the photograph, trying to decide which one was Dilly. Once again everyone was a dressed up but this time there were broad smiles on all the faces; the children all quite

similar in age, though Dilly and her sister lighter skinned than the cousins.

"Josie's older than you isn't she? I asked.

*"By two years and one month - and don't she let me know it! "*laughed Dilly.

"Did you have a happy childhood?" I asked, moving on to another photograph.

"Sure, just one big, happy family. Four sisters who fought most of the time!" she chuckled. *"No, it was okay; Aunt Myrah was nice enough, considering the circumstances."*

"Circumstances?" I repeated quizzically.

"Well, suddenly having two more mouths to feed; you know." Dilly was sounding tired, I thought. I quickly looked at the other photographs and returned to my chair.

"I should go and leave you to rest," I said.

"No, don't go, I ain't tired, I'm enjoying our conversation. Karl ain't much of one for talking. He's an all-action man, you know what I mean?" She chortled.

"Those photographs," I said.

"Yes."

"Did you know that there isn't a single man on any of them?" I said accusingly

"Is that right," laughed Dilly, *"I wonder why that is. Must all be out fishing."*

"What about Myrah's husband?" I continued; *"What did he do?"*

"Charles, William," she said thoughtfully. *"Charles, William Foley was a very skilled engineer who worked for your Royal Navy down at Dockyard. Worked there all his*

189

life. He used to help me with my homework...treated me like his own daughter." She paused, a faraway look in her eyes. *"He gave me away when I married Karl. Nice man, a real father, even though he weren't,"* her words clearly indicated the love she felt. *"He died after Myrah; I guess Pearl was about seven, so three years ago. I miss him...Now there was someone who liked to talk,"* again she laughed, obviously remembering happy times.

"You say Myrah's husband treated you like a daughter. What about your father? There isn't a picture of your father, what about him?" I asked. There was a long pause and I looked down at Dilly; she turned her head slowly and she looked me straight in the eye.

"God, Jack Cross you ask some awkward questions!" she complained.

I laughed, *"Sorry Dilly, I'm not looking to let any skeletons out of the cupboard. I guess that was thoughtless, excuse me - forget that I asked that one."* Dilly said nothing, her eyes were focussed on a distant mirror, hanging close to the door leading towards the bedrooms.

"So long ago, I guess they would be skeletons by now," she mused. *"Anyway, I seem to have got into the habit of sharing my deepest secrets with you Jack Cross."* She turned to look at me with a sly smile and continued. *"When my mother left school she stayed at home and helped look after the younger children. Then, when she was sixteen she went to work for a white Bermudian family, living in a big house in Southampton, near Whale Bay. She lived there until she got pregnant with Josie and then she went home again. When Josie was just a few months old, she went back*

190

to work again, leaving Josie with my grandmother - until she got pregnant with me." Dilly was speaking softly and paused for breath. *"She stayed at home then - until she… died."*

I was busy calculating; *"but she must have been very young,"* I interjected.

"Twenty-two," replied Dilly in a monotone. *"Told her mother she was going to the beach by Cavello… they found her body floating in the Great Sound, next day."*

"Oh my God!" I whispered.

"Never did find out what happened; my guess is she couldn't see no future!"

Dilly answered my un-asked question: *"So, no, there ain't a photograph of my father because I don't know who he is - or was. Wouldn't need to be much of a detective, however, to work it out. My mother lived at the big house, with the big, wealthy owner and his wife, who have two sons a bit older than my mother; there are no other white men at the house! So take your pick – any one of the three could be my father."*

I was sorry that I had raised the question and said so.

"Not a problem Jack, not any more. I worried about it when I was a teenager and hated being a lighter colour than all my friends. I started asking questions, even went, a few times and stood at the end of their drive looking and wondering. Remember once there was an old man with white hair and a beard and we stood and looked at each other but we were too far apart to speak – not that I would have known what to say." Dilly paused and drew a deep breath. *"He waved and I ran away. Anyway, I read in the paper that he had died soon after that - and that his wife*

went to live with her son in California - and the house was sold."

"*What about the other son?*" I asked.

"*The article said he was a priest working in Africa and couldn't come to the funeral,*" she replied. There was a sudden flurry of movement and almost silently five-year-old Vernee appeared and stood looking down at her mother. Dilly reached out and they clasped hands. Nothing was said.

*

Over the next two days, I saw a new side to Bermuda; the temperature sank to less than sixty degrees and it poured with rain. It was thoroughly wretched and there was nothing I could do, except read - and think about Jill and Dilly. I sat at a window and watched the rain dripping off the roof, large, glistening globules, which reminded me of tears, tears shed for these two women, which only added to the depression.

During one lengthy break on the second day, when the sun threatened to shine, I went and checked Charlie's boat at Ely's Harbour. The boat was fine but I got drenched on my return; had to take a shower and change my clothes. Once dressed, I picked up the *Odessa File*, ready to resume from where I had left off the night before. I was suddenly aware that the piece of paper I was using as a marker, was in fact the piece on which Don's policeman friend had written his telephone number. I looked at it: *Stephen Henderson* and a Sandys' number. This got me thinking in a different direction: how to rescue Karl from his dilemma.

What would be gained if I told Stephen Henderson that Just de Vere supplied Karl, using Eggy as a delivery

192

boy? Would he organise a trace to find out who supplied de Vere, and then on to find out who was at the top? I soon concluded the answer would be no. From what Karl had said there was a long chain of command and the big chiefs were, no doubt, well hidden and protected. I then wondered if the police knew who all the minor players were but were ignoring these, as they drew a net round the major players. I remembered the suggestions that the Police Commissioner may have been killed because they were getting too close. It would be really interesting to know. I began to wonder how much Stephen knew - and how much he might be persuaded to divulge. I lay on my bed considering how I could achieve this.

After some while I had a brain wave and looked at my watch; it was four pm, worth a try. I picked up the phone and dialled Stephen's number, almost immediately he answered. After explaining who I was, exchanging pleasantries and telling him that my call had nothing to do with tennis; I came to the point and asked if there was a chance that we could meet, as I needed his professional advice. He said that he was on nights and was about to leave for Hamilton; he would be catching up on his sleep the following morning but he could meet me in the afternoon. I suggested that we met at his place and he gave me his address, which was on a side street, off Beacon Hill Road. I jotted it down and we agreed to meet at two pm. Wishing him a quiet shift, I lay back down on the bed and worked out my strategy, before delving again into Frederick Forsyth's intriguing novel.

*

The weather on the 31st could not have been more different from the previous few days. The sun shone, the humidity soared and the sky was totally cloudless. I needed to be outside and so I donned running shoes and shorts and set off to jog down to Long Bay Beach. The road was still wet under the oleanders but I was glad of the shade. At Skeeter's Corner I turned up Greenfield Lane and along the West Side, the sea was almost the same shade of blue as the sky. I stopped, settled on a boulder and gazed out to sea, overcome with a sense of gratitude and wellbeing. There were no boats out and no sea birds - just the ocean. I was near the home of Laura Miles-Smith but knew I was too late to catch her swimming. Despite the small size of the place I had not set eyes on Laura since her party back in October. I wondered how she was - and what she did with herself.

After a while, I clambered to my feet, performed a few stretching exercises and continued my jog along West Side before turning homewards down Rushy Lane. At a quarter to two I was already showered, changed and aboard my bike and heading towards Beacon Hill Road. It wasn't far and Stephen's directions were clear and so I had no trouble finding his tiny apartment, built on the side of a much larger home. He made me welcome and offered me a beer, which I gratefully accepted. He chose to drink fruit-juice, explaining that he would soon be going on duty. We were seated on his tiny but very private patio, it was totally festooned with colourful climbers and potted plants. He told me that he rented the apartment cheaply because the owners, who lived next door, felt his presence made for more security. I asked how he had chosen to come to Bermuda

194

and learned that after police training he had served with the Metropolitan police in London for two years before deciding to spread his wings. I asked him how the job compared to London and he had laughed and said there wasn't any comparison. He thought that there were too many policemen from anywhere but Bermuda and what the Island needed more than anything else was a Bermudian police force, staffed by Bermudians. Foreign policemen just evoked resentment, no matter how hard they tried to be sensitive to local needs. I was already on my second beer before Stephen said: *"You mentioned that you were looking for some professional advice."*

"Well, yes - if you don't mind;" I began. *"I am well aware that secondary schools here invite outsiders in to speak about the problems of drug use; do you know if that includes policemen?"*

"It does indeed," responded Stephen; *"we have a couple of guys who do little else but try and get the message across in schools, youth clubs and the like."*

"Does this mean drug-taking is a major problem here in Bermuda?" I asked innocently; *"I've only been here since last August."*

"Oh yes, huge;" Stephen replied; *"mostly cannabis, marijuana, hashish, ganja, call it what you will."*

"You'd think that on a small island like this it would be easy to control," I went on. *"Only one airport - and so far away from other islands and the USA!"* Stephen laughed:

"You have no idea. Crooked airport officials turning blind eyes to certain cargo but happy to catch some poor

tourist with just a few grams in his pocket. Crooked staff on the visiting liners leaving behind the odd suitcase or two. Not to mention fast ocean-going speedboats bringing it in by the ton. It's a major, major problem for us but making some people here millions of dollars every year." Stephen sounded frustrated.

"*Millions;*" I said incredulously.

"*Probably tens of millions, we don't really know,*" Stephen said.

"*But that sounds like there must be a highly sophisticated set-up, behind it all,*" I continued, "*people with influence and power?*"

"*I'm sure of it,*" rasped Stephen.

"*Is that why I've heard people say that the Police Commissioner was killed, assassinated - because he was close to revealing the person or persons at the top?*" I was fishing.

"*It's just one of the many rumours; some say it's more likely to be the Black Berets trying to take-over. Have you heard about them?*" he asked.

"*Yes, my neighbour told me all about their activities.*" I replied. I gazed out across the street, the houses opposite were masked by palmettos.

"*So, if you've got a supremo at the top organising all the imports, he must have a huge network of people selling it on, dozens of tiddlers doing his dirty work.*" I was thinking of de Vere, Eggy and Karl.

"*And each one taking their cut,*" snapped Stephen, emptying his glass.

"Well, that's all very interesting," I said, "but sad that such a fabulous place is polluted with so much crime."

"It's the main reason for crime here," said Stephen, "robberies of all sort, just to feed the habit."

"Well Stephen, I really came here to ask you whether the police had a drug education programme - and you've confirmed this... but what do you think about them coming into primary schools and talking to the younger children. Kids of eight to eleven are more likely to listen. Wouldn't surprise me if most of the teenagers the policemen speak to in Secondary schools are already users?" I said.

"Yes, we know that's true by the number of young men who sit on their bikes outside schools at the beginning and end of the day, selling small amounts to the students," Stephen replied.

"Do you prosecute these dealers?" I asked.

"Sometimes, every now and then we have a blitz but we spend a lot of time trying to discover who supplies the dealers." He laughed; "But because everyone here is related to each other, no one spills the beans, it's really, really frustrating."

"How would I go about asking your team if they would come and talk to my class?" I asked.

"Leave it with me, I'll talk to them about it and let you know what they say," Stephen responded.

"Okay, thanks Stephen. If they are interested in coming I will talk to my boss and get her approval." The conversation moved on and eventually I asked him what he did to keep fit and he explained he liked to jog. It wasn't long before we had made a date to jog together, once his stint

197

of nights were over. *"Sorry to hear that you are on night-shift tonight - New Year's Eve;"* I commiserated.

"Oh, I don't mind;" he replied*; "except for picking up the odd drunk, I don't expect there will be much trouble. Do you have plans?"* he asked.

"Well yes;" I answered; *"I'm supposed to meeting a couple of friends at the Carlton Beach."*

"May see you there then;" replied Stephen. *"I expect we will do the rounds of the major hotels."* We shook hands and I made way home. It was already growing dusk and the sky had taken on a magnificent pale-golden glow, prior to the sun dropping into the sea.

*

It was pitch-black by the time I began my walk up towards the church and the bus stop. I had decided earlier that it was probably not a good idea to be out on my bike, with its dim headlights, on New Year's Eve. Once free of the overhanging oleanders the mind-blowing quantity of stars lit my way. I stopped and peered upwards; it was amazingly clear and I couldn't help but feel a totally insignificant dot in this confusing universe. I had been reading how earlier in December, the *Mars-3 Lander* had successfully reached its destination but how elation had quickly turned to despair when it sent home a frustratingly small quantity of data and then failed. What a complex universe we inhabited, on one hand humankind pushing the boundaries with no expense spared - on the other, Dilly dying from an unknown disease, and her family in jeopardy.

I was somewhat surprised when the bus arrived at the scheduled time and I climbed aboard the vintage, pastel-

198

pink, people-purveyor and sank into a well-worn seat. The bus was about half-full, a mix of excited teenagers and older folk peering out, unseeing, through the dusty windows into the darkness. The bus groaned and complained its way up Scaur Hill before dropping down to Ely's harbour and on towards my South Shore destination. The elderly, jolly bus-driver seemed to know the names of all the older folk and when he stopped at ill-lit bus stops to let them off; he jovially wished each a Happy New Year, as they disappeared into the inky darkness.

"You have a good evening and a Happy New Year;" he sang out to me as I dismounted at the end of the drive leading down to the Carlton Beach Hotel. I responded, clambered out and then stood waiting for my eyes to adjust to the darkness, as the bus chugged off towards Hamilton. The drive down to the hotel was quite steep but there were token lamps to light my way and a procession of taxis both up and down illuminated my path.

The foyer of the hotel was abuzz with guests, many of the men in tuxedos and their be-jewelled partners dressed in long evening gowns. I was wearing my one and only charcoal-grey suit, a white shirt and college tie. It was the first time I had worn the suit since my arrival and I felt rather uncomfortable and over-dressed. I made my way slowly towards the bar and settled on the one and only vacant stool and gazed at the reflections in the huge mirror, behind the shelves of bottles at the rear of the bar. The room was a kaleidoscope of colour and awash with the noise of people enjoying themselves. I was half way through a beer and busy people watching, when Alan arrived and threw an arm around my shoulder.

"*You made it then?*" he said.

"*Yes, I came on the bus,*" I replied.

"*Good idea, you can spend the night with us, Mildred has organised a taxi to take us home at two o'clock.*" As he spoke, Alan was gesticulating at the barman, who eventually placed a glass of beer in front of him with a knowing nod.

"*What's the order of events?*" I asked.

"*Well,*" said Alan looking around; "*Susie's boyfriend Jake will join us. I told him we'd be in the bar. But Mil and Susie are officially working but they hope to come and eat with us about nine.*" He was still scouring the crowded bar. "*Oh, there he is.*" Alan waved an arm and Jake pushed his way through the crowd to join us. Gradually the bar thinned out as the partygoers headed for the main dining room and the evening's entertainment. At this point we took our glasses and settled into comfortable armchairs in the corner. "*Mil and Susie will come and collect us here and take us to eat;*" Alan winked, "*after the hotel guests have had a head start.*"

For the next half an hour we sat chatting and enjoying Jake's tales and jokes. He told us that he worked in local government, I said he was wasted and that he should be on the stage. At a quarter to nine I needed to find a toilet before going off to eat and left the guys in the bar. On my return, as I approached the reception area, I suddenly stopped: Eggy had just entered the main door and was being met by the burley, uniformed doorman, who had been busy talking to the girl at the desk. Eggy was carrying a box

200

decorated with Christmas wrapping paper, tied up with ribbon. He handed it to the doorman, who, being much taller than Eggy was leaning down to place his ear by Eggy's mouth. They both turned towards the door and I eased forward to see the doorman escort Eggy to his taxi. He waved him off, turned and returned to the foyer. Looking neither left nor right he headed down one of the corridors and without thinking, I followed him. We went through two swing doors and into an area restricted to guests. I felt like a sleuth, peering round corners, trying to keep up but staying out of sight. Eventually the doorman approached a bank of lockers and fumbled in his pocket for a key. He looked up and down the corridor, opened the first locker; placed the box inside, locked up and headed rapidly back towards me. I turned, heart pounding, and opened the first door I found and scuttled inside. It was pitch back and I knocked over a bucket; the sound as it rolled away seemed loud enough to wake the dead. I cursed, hand wrapped round the knob and counted to twenty. Gingerly I eased the door open and peered round - no one. I stepped into the corridor, still no one. I sped towards the lockers and peered at the name on the first locker: it read: *Jobo Crane*.

When I got back to the bar Mildred and Susie were already there; Mildred threw her arms around me; gave me a hug and a peck on the cheek.

"Wait here, while I go and prepare the way;" she said mysteriously and exited the bar. A few minutes later she returned and led us into the crowded, noisy dining room. We all stood and gazed around, while Mildred spoke to a harassed-looking man, whom I supposed to be either a

201

manager or the Maître d'. There was a long buffet running down one side of the room and a row of white-hatted chefs standing behind a bewildering array of dishes. In one corner a glittering Christmas tree, its crowning star almost reaching the ceiling. The latter strewn with balloons, baubles and streamers. In another corner a three-piece band played but were almost drowned out by the hubbub of laughter and conversation. In front of the band was a small wooden square for dancing. The man with Mildred came and shook hands with us and led us to a table set slightly apart from the other guests. *"Reserved for senior management,"* laughed Mildred instructing each person where they should sit. Two more men arrived and three women, who seated themselves and began introductions, one of the men, the older of the two, Mr Williams, was introduced as Mildred's boss. A waiter placed opened bottles of red and white wine on the table, before Mr Williams rose to his feet and invited us to visit the buffet.

The next two hours flew by as we emptied bottles and made numerous visits to the buffet. At intervals Mildred circulated round the guests, stopping to chat and share a joke.

"What exactly is Mildred's job and who is Mr Williams?" I hissed at Alan.

"Mildred's Head of keeping guests happy." he laughed, the red wine already taking affect. *"Mr Williams is an under-manager."*

After the plates had been taken away, Mr Williams and some of the others drifted away. Magnanimously, earlier, Mr Williams very pointedly told Mildred and Susie to stay with their guests and he would send for them if he needed them. They almost curtsied! He was hardly out of sight before Mildred dragged an unwilling Alan off to the dance area; the small space already full, causing waiters to begin moving tables further away. When they eventually returned, Alan sank back wearily on his chair but Mildred grabbed my hand and pulled me off towards the whirling dancers.

Later while we were all recovering from the exertions I told Mildred that I had been talking to the doorman when I first arrived: *"I didn't catch his name, did he say Jona... Jomo?" I asked.*

"You mean Jobo," she replied, *"nasty piece of work, he's already on an official warning for roughing up one of the guests."*

"Really," I said but not at all surprised.

As the hands of the clock neared midnight, everyone was on their feet and dancing between the tables; the band was in full swing and on full volume. It wasn't long before a Conga started and everyone grabbed the hips of the person in front. The multi-coloured snake wove its way drunkenly around the room and eventually down the corridor and around the foyer area - ending outside on the terrace, just as a set of rockets whistled into the sky signalling the imminent approach of the New Year. People rushed indoors to reclaim their loved-ones; while the master of ceremonies, microphone in hand, encouraged his audience into a count down. A large clock had been placed, somewhat incongruously, in a prominent position above the band and as the minute hand clicked onto the twelve there was a great shout from all assembled and 1973 was heralded in.

Chapter 6

January, 1973

The morning of January 1st dawned bright - which was more than I felt, as I rolled off the sofa and into the bathroom. Frilly, female under-garments were hanging on a line over the bath and so I decided against a shower. A quick wash and I struggled back into my suit trousers, noticing a cup of cold tea on a coffee table alongside the sofa. I was wondering how long it had been there when Alan appeared and leaned against a door-jamb, he wore only shorts, unshaved, hair akimbo, drinking from a mug.

"What's the matter," he said laconically, *"you don't like cold tea?"*

I picked up the mug, *"How long has it been there?"* I asked.

"Well Mil had to be in work for eight o'clock, so she would have put it there well over an hour ago I'd say, would you rather have a hot one?" he asked unconvincingly,

sinking on to the sofa alongside me. I shook my head and sipped from the mug, grateful for anything that would ease my evil-tasting mouth.

After breakfast Alan ran me home in Mildred's battered Ford Escort, for which I was most grateful. I gave him a quick tour of my cottage and then he left. January or not, it was warm and so I donned my shorts clambered into the hammock outside and lazily read and dozed the morning away.

The afternoon clouded up and the temperature dropped and I was soon back into long trousers. Realizing that I had left my book in the hammock I went outside to collect it and spotted Dilly, muffled up in a large, black sweater, hanging up washing. I called out to her and she wandered towards me:

"Wow, you look better today," I said enthusiastically.

Yeah; I feel great today," she said with a smile.

"Happy New Year," I said unthinkingly, kissing her cheek. She gave me a strange look. *"I really hope that it's going to be very special."* I added giving her a hug.

"Yes, thanks, same to you. Did you celebrate in style last night?" she asked.

I explained that I had been at the Carlton Beach with friends and she nodded. *"What about you?"* I asked.

"We had a quiet night, Josie came round for a while."

"Is Karl around?" I enquired.

"Nope, he's taken the girls to a friend's house." She tucked a strand of hair that had come loose back under her bright pink turban. *"I don't know what you said to him but*

he's been more his old self lately," she lightly punched my arm and locked her fathomless, brown eyes on mine.

"That's good," I said, shifting my gaze, shuffling uncomfortably. *"I guess, like me, he's back to work tomorrow?"* I said changing the subject. Dilly nodded. At her invitation I went into her kitchen and she made coffee. The room was dominated by a long, solid, wooden table made from a single slice of cedar, lightly varnished but with the occasional knot-hole, through which tiny fingers could make unwanted food mysteriously disappear. We perched on chairs at either end, facing each other, armed with large, steaming mugs. A comfortable silence endured as we sipped. Eventually, I felt compelled to speak. *"Did Karl make the table;"* I said running my hand over the sensual surface.

There was a hint of a nod from across the room but Dilly said: *"Marsha phoned this morning."* I swear Dilly looked for a reaction. I didn't cooperate, it wasn't forthcoming. *"She back from Jamaica... glad to be back!... coming to see me tomorrow evening,"* she continued. I explained how I had spoken with Marsha before Christmas and that she had told me that she intended to visit, when she returned. Dilly nodded knowingly.

"Don't say nuffin but I've been wondering if she will help me organise the folk I've been talking to... and take over from me," Dilly paused; *"if I get too sick."*

"How are things going? I asked, ignoring the implication; *"are they listening to you."*

"Some," she replied. *"We have a bank account set up and a few fund-raising things planned."* Dilly peered into

her mug: *"Marsha's a lawyer; she'd be very useful, she'd know what to do."* I couldn't help but agree, thinking back to her bitter response to my question when we had first met, concerning what type of law she practised: *Helping poor oppressed black people get justice.*

*

The next day, was a Tuesday but the first day back at school. It was good to be back in the classroom and there was an atmosphere of *bon-amitié* between members of staff and the children, all refreshed and stimulated by the two-week break. Evelyn was in good spirits and ran a lively assembly straight after the mid-morning break. Eloise, poised and elegant, at the piano eliciting a great volume of sound from the children, the quality of which, caused staff to look at one another with raised eyebrows.

Eloise was standing by the door as we filed out but there was only time, as our eyes met, for a hasty greeting. The rest of the afternoon was filled coaching soccer skills to enthusiastic seven-year olds. As the children joyfully chased around, the sound of the piano and youthful voices emanated from the Hall, causing me to think about the pianist and what this new year, if anything, would hold for us both.

That evening, about eight o'clock, there was a knock on the door and Karl called out, as he poked his head inside. I had a lap full of maths' exercise books and they slipped to the floor as I stood to greet him. *"Hi Jack;"* he called, *"can I disturb you?"* I invited him in and proffered a chair. *"Dilly's got a visitor; I'd rather be out of the way,"* he said. No doubt this would be Marsha but I said nothing. We chatted about this and that, he sounded cheerful enough but I could

208

tell from the heavy expression in his eyes, something was bothering him.

I fetched a couple of beer-cans from the fridge and handed one to Karl. *"Dilly looks much better;"* I said *"and seems happier."*

"The new pills seem to be helping," replied Karl.

"Are you off the weed?" I asked pointedly.

"Most of the time," he cleared his throat and took a swallow.

"Is that why Dilly is happier?" I asked.

"Maybe." Karl said quietly, eyes focussed on my solitary Birdsey print on the wall.

"Maybe?" I echoed.

"Change the subject Mr Schoolteacher!" hissed Karl. *"I ain't in no mood for the inquisition - sure you ain't got Spanish ancestors?"* He laughed at his own joke.

"Are you still making deliveries?" I persisted. Karl didn't answer but quickly drained his beer and balanced the can on the arm of his chair. *"Have you been threatened again?"* I continued. Karl looked at me and rolled his eyes.

"Damn you Jack; you a mind-reader or something?"

"You have been threatened," I stated.

"Not exactly, I was coming home from work on the bus tonight when this guy, never seen him before, gets on in Southampton and on a near-empty bus sits right down alongside me. As we get towards the next stop he pushes a piece of paper in my hand and gets off." I noticed that Karl was sweating.

"What did it say?" I asked, puzzled. Karl pulled a crumpled piece of paper out of his pocket and passed it to

me: '*Wednesday 8 pm; Pitman's boat rentals - or else,*' I read.

"*That's tomorrow;*" I thought aloud, "*doesn't say who's it's from.*" I turned the paper over - there was nothing on the back. "*Do you think it's from de Vere?*" I looked at Karl.

"*From Mr Just de Vere - I guess so,*" he sounded resigned. "*Pitman's is only just round the corner from where he works.*"

"*I wonder what he wants you to do?*" I said quietly, my mind racing.

"*I don't know but for the sake of Dilly and the kids I have to play along,*" he whispered, almost to himself.

"*Listen,*" I said forcibly, tapping his knee. "*Promise me that you'll call in here on your way back and tell me what happened.*"

"*You don't want to be involved,*" he said getting to his feet.

"*Stop,*" I said, "*we've been through all that. Promise me you'll call in. If you don't - I'll come looking for you.*"

"*Okay,*" said Karl, "*don't worry, I'll drop by.*" A slamming car door and the sound of an engine fading into the distance brought Karl upright.

"*Sounds like Dilly's friend's gone. I need to go.*" Karl moved slowly towards the door and looked over his shoulder; "*Thanks for the beer,*" he said and merged into the blackness.

Later that night, lying on my bed, unable to sleep because of the myriads of thoughts spinning around, I drew back the curtain and gazed at the stars. I thought about Karl and his forthcoming appointment and whether or not I should secrete myself at Pitman's wharf and spy on the proceedings. I thought about Dilly, her illness and her mission to help the lowly paid workers without them resorting to violence. Eloise entered my head and my disappointment at not yet having had a proper conversation with her about her holiday and future plans. Then Marsha stole into my thoughts; her striking, exotic beauty raising all manner of questions. Gradually, even she had to give way, as vivid pictures of Jilly came to the surface and the whole macabre tragedy re-spooled itself, like a horror movie.

I tossed and turned trying to clear my head and concentrated on the stars clearly visible around the Casuarinas trees. Startled, I suddenly became aware of a dark shadow creeping towards my window and eased up on one elbow to watch, my pulse in overdrive. As the dark shape drew closer, I slipped off the bed and headed for the door. The key seemed to make an earth-shattering click as it turned over and I feared squealing door-hinges would give me away. I slipped outside onto the porch and peered around the corner of the building. I could just make out a tall, thin figure staring in through my bedroom window. I pulled back, considering my options - and then remembered the conversation with Laura Miles-Smith. This was probably the man she called Jimmy, a bit of a simpleton.

I peered round the corner again, he was still there but facing away from me. Barefoot and on tiptoes I made my way behind him in a wide arc; he was back at the window again. I was within five yards when he suddenly spun round.

211

"Is that you Jimmy?" I hissed. He jumped a mile and made to run off but I stepped in front of him and grabbed his arm. I was expecting a struggle but he went limp. *"We haven't met Jimmy, my name's Jack."* I said firmly.

"Hello Mr Jack," he said indistinctly but politely.

"Does your father know you're wandering about?" I asked. He didn't answer. *"Would you like a coke?"* I couldn't decipher his reply but he came willingly, as I guided him towards the front door. Once inside I led him to a seat and then fetched a coke from the kitchen and sat down opposite him. Jimmy was taller than me but as thin as a rake. He was wearing a black tracksuit but the pants only reached halfway down his shins and there were flip-flops on his feet. His hair had been cut very short, probably by his father, I thought, noticing a few uneven tufts. He was gazing at the floor, quietly talking to himself and mopping away spittle from his lips with a large handkerchief. *"Jimmy,"* I said. He looked up and I saw that he was clean-shaven and except for a slightly loose jaw, quite good-looking. I guessed he would be about thirty. *"Jimmy, it's not good to go looking in people's windows, especially at night."*

He mumbled *"Sorry,"* and gazed again at the floor wringing his hands - hands with long elegant, pianist's fingers but with a workman's calloused palms.

I tried to gain his attention again: *"Jimmy, I hear that you like to build boats,"* I said. The reaction was amazing, he sat bolt upright, his face broke into a wreath of smiles and he gabbled away so fast I could only catch the occasional word. He waved his arms expansively and the coke bottle went flying - not that he noticed, even when I retrieved it.

212

Obviously I had pressed the right button! I reached out, held his arm and asked him to speak slowly; he must have been used to this instruction because like an automaton he moved into low gear and the words came out slowly and deliberately. In simple monosyllabic terms he told me about the current project he was working on with his father and I asked if I could come and have a look. He seemed delighted and so I promised to call by to see this very special boat they were constructing. I stood and held out my hand, slowly he unwound to his feet and grasped my fingers and I led him to the door and outside. *"Okay Jimmy,"* I said, *"time to go home - and remember no more looking through windows - okay."*

"Okay Mr Jack," he said, *"you come and see boat"* and faded into the night.

I didn't arrive home Wednesday night until it was almost dark. It had drizzled during the afternoon and so I held the soccer practice in the Hall, which was never very satisfactory. Afterwards I had shopped at the supermarket and visited Lopes Liquor store for some beer. I cooked myself some pasta and watched Karl Davidson reading the local news on the black and white, second-hand television that I had recently acquired; all the time watching the clock and thinking of Karl and his imminent rendezvous. Eight o'clock came round, after which my eyes hardly left the clock, willing the hands to move faster. About eight-thirty I pulled on a sweater and went outside and sat on the porch, so that I could see when Karl arrived back. I was probably there for fifteen minutes before I heard the sound of an engine and soon the single weak beam of a headlight lit up

213

the palm trees. Karl switched off the engine, as he left the road and bounced over the grass towards his home. I threw open my door and waved, hoping he would see my silhouette.

A few moments elapsed before I spotted his dark, hunched form heading towards me. I moved inside and he followed. *"This is so stupid and dangerous,"* he spat. *"What if someone followed me? Then you're in trouble too. I should go."*

"Oh sit down," I commanded. *"Stop being so melodramatic!"* He gave me a look, which spoke volumes about my ignorance of the world's wickedness. I collected a couple of beers from the fridge and we settled in the two armchairs, knees almost touching. I studied his face and despite the cool ride, beads of perspiration had gathered on his brow and were caught up in his bushy moustache. *"Well?"* I demanded, *"was it de Vere?"*

He nodded: *"And his minder,"* he added.

"Tell me exactly what happened," I said quietly, *"every little detail, second by second."* Karl took a long, hard pull at his beer-can, wiped his lips with the back of his hand and deliberately placed the can on the floor alongside his chair.

"Okay, so I get to the wharf at eight o'clock and there's a bunch of kids under the light just chatting and messing about. I sit on my bike in the shadows; then this car comes onto the wharf and turns round. The driver speaks to the kids and they drift away."

"What sort of car?" I ask, *"what make."*

214

Karl thinks for a minute; *"Triumph Herald, you know a convertible sort. Only the cover was up."*

"And?" I asked.

"Well, the driver, he gets out, lifts the seat and tells me to get in the back. They only have two doors. De Vere was sitting in the passenger seat. The driver starts to get back in but De Vere tells him to take a walk. So he slams the door, walks to the end of the wharf and lights a fag." Karl reached down for his beer and emptied the can. *"There's so little space in the back of them cars, so I'm all hunched up."* I said nothing but gazed into his face willingly him to continue.

"He say something like, can't remember his exact words. He say, the time has come for me to start paying off my debt and he wants me to go and help when they collect a new shipment on Saturday the thirteenth."

A week on Saturday, I calculate, ten days time.

"He tell me not to make any plans that I'll be gone from two in the afternoon Saturday until about two the next morning," Karl sighed.

"Where do you fetch the shipment from?" I asked.

"Out at sea; he tell me to be at Dockyard at one-thirty on the Saturday - and to tell everyone I'm going fishing with pals from work - and to tell my wife not to be worried and I'll see her at breakfast. God - no way she'll believe me!" he frowned, holding his head in his hands.

"Did he threaten you?" I asked.

"Nope, not in words, just patted his pocket where I could see the shape of a pistol; and he say - he know he can rely on me."

215

"My God Karl; how far out to sea, if you will be away for twelve hours?" I said puzzled.

"Maybe it's so long cos it's not just the collection but stacking the stuff away somewhere when we get back," he replied, squeezing the life out of the beer can in his hand.

"Ah, you're probably right, they may need to hide the stuff when everyone else is in bed," I said. *"He didn't say anything about the boat you're going out on?"*

"Nope that's it; you know as much as me. I gotta be at Dockyard on the thirteenth, standing where the ferry come in - and someone will fetch me to the boat," Karl climbed to his feet.

"I've never taken the ferry to Dockyard Karl," I said, *"where does it come in?"*

"Don't even think about it," Karl said curtly.

"No, no, of course not," I bumbled, *"just curious ... where does it dock?"*

"On a jetty just past the Cut Bridge, the last bridge before the Dockyard. But stay away," Karl commanded. Although he sounded authoritative, his face was creased with worry. I held his arm at the door and confidently told him that things would work out. Though in my heart of hearts I feared the worst.

*

Thursday it drizzled all day, the sort of fine rain that lulls you into a sense of confidence that you can get from A to B, without getting wet but in fact soaks you to the skin. I set off on foot to school earlier than usual, ended up running and then had to go looking for a towel to dry myself and a Tee-shirt to change into. Adjacent to the Hall cum Gym was a tiny room that was allocated for me to change my clothes and store the more valuable sports' equipment. I dried my hair and hung up my shirt. I met Evelyn as I emerged and apologised for looking so scruffy and explained I had misread the weather. She dismissed my apology and launched into a diatribe about a problem she was having with the parents of one of the children and would I keep an eye out for any signs that he was being beaten. As she headed back towards her office, Eloise entered the Hall carrying a music case and looking as elegant as ever. *"How do you do it?"* I asked with a grin.

"Do what?" she asked.

"Manage to look like you stepped out of Vogue, when I look like drowned rat!" I complained.

"By having four wheels and an umbrella of course," she smiled. *"And thank-you for the compliment."*

"Did you have a good holiday?" I went on. *"We should have a coffee or something, so that we can have a good old chat."*

"Okay, good idea, what about the Somerset Squire about four o'clock? I'll be coming back from Boaz Island School about then," she said with a smile.

"Sounds great, I'll see you there - oh, unless it's raining," I added.

"True, maybe it's better if I come and pick you up here about the same time - whatever the weather," she said.

The rain was absolutely beating down as we sat on the covered terrace of the Country Squire sipping cappuccinos. Eloise pointed out neighbouring Kings Island, hardly visible through a curtain of raindrops relentlessly

217

dripping from the edge of the gutter. It was a dismal, un-Bermudian scene.

"Except for the hurricane," I said, *"This is the first full day of rain we have had since I arrived."*

"Lucky you," snorted Eloise, *"but it's good for the water-tanks."*

"So how was your holiday?" I asked. Eloise then told me that she had spent most of the two-week break in and around Miami, visiting relatives and friends but was quick to change the subject, asking instead what I had been doing. I filled her in, omitting any reference to Karl and his problems. The conversation switched to the Dramatic Society, the recent pantomime and the fact she was attending a meeting later that evening to discuss the next production. As she was speaking, I found myself studying her deep brown eyes, her full lips, high cheekbones, infectious mannerisms - and not totally concentrating on what she was actually saying. It must have become apparent for suddenly she seemed embarrassed and asked if I had heard what she had been telling me. I apologised and lied, I couldn't tell her what I had actually been debating - but the spectre of Jilly and thoughts of how to take this relationship forward were cavorting like mad gymnasts in my head. We finished our coffees and she repeated that she was going into Hamilton for the Drama Society meeting and needed to shower and change. We kissed farewell and for a fleeting moment I held her close before quickly stepping back and making a joke. The rain had stopped and the road was steaming, matching my emotions. I walked to the car park and held the door as she climbed behind the wheel. Eloise offered to run me

218

home but I insisted that I was happy to walk, despite not wanting this moment to end. *"What about a movie Saturday night?"* I suddenly gushed, my mind racing; *"Maggie Smith's starring in Travels With My Aunt - or the Bond film Diamonds Are For Ever is still showing?"* I knew this because the films had been discussed in the staffroom; with Evelyn waxing lyrical about the wonderful Maggie Smith.

It clearly registered that Eloise didn't even hesitate, *"Sounds a great idea;"* she replied. *"I haven't seen either, we could have a bite to eat first in Hamilton, if you like - my treat!"* And so we parted with Eloise promising to pick me up at six-o'clock Saturday evening. I watched and waved, as she wheeled out of the car-park and turned up East Shore Road, while I strolled alongside Mangrove Bay, doing my best to avoid the huge drips exploding at my feet from the lofty Royal Palms; my spirits soaring up there with the coconuts.

*

I met Charlie at Robinson's boatyard the next evening, which was a Friday, to return the *Next Best Thing*'s ignition-key. When I arrived he had the small boat tied to the dock and I climbed aboard. Charlie handed me an oar and we paddled back to the mooring-buoy, and tied up. He disappeared inside the tiny cabin to reappear a moment later and with a flourish produced a couple of bottles of beer - to celebrate the end of the week, as he put it. He pulled two foldaway chairs from inside the cabin and we sat, chatted and watched the sun sink towards the horizon. I quizzed him about *The Best Thing*; seeing that we were aboard the *Next Best Thing*. He laughed and said that she lived in a small

219

town in New Jersey and was a nurse in a local hospital. Apparently they had met when she and some of her colleagues visited Bermuda for a holiday a couple of years earlier – and yes, Charlene, the girl friend, did know about the second love of his life.

"*Don't you just love this place;*" Charlie said wistfully. I nodded my agreement, my mouth full of beer. "*Sometimes, when it gets too hot in the apartment I sleep out here on the boat; you know, just on a blanket under the stars… magic.*"

"*It's so calm in this harbour, it's just so well protected,*" I commented glancing round; "*I guess you just get gently lulled to sleep by the tide – like a baby in one of those swinging hammock things.*" He nodded and silently we both gazed at the surrounding shore dotted with colourful foliage and pastel-coloured houses, while *Next Best Thing* bobbed gently and swung to and fro on the incoming tide.

"*It is idyllic;*" I said thoughtfully, "*but I'm told that there is a dark under-belly.*"

"*You mean the petty crime, I suppose,*" Charlie replied looking at me.

"*Not just petty, I'm told,*" I answered. "*Are drugs a problem at your school, you know, with the older students?*"

"*Well yes and no, we have a very strict Bermudian Head who won't stand any nonsense in that direction, so if kids do take drugs, they certainly don't do it during the school day. He'd get their mothers in - and most of our kids are scared stiff of their mothers - certainly more scared of them than they are of their teachers!*" Charlie laughed.

220

"Well if they don't have drugs at school how do you know any students use them?" I asked.

"Cos, there's always a dealer or two sitting on their bikes, with the engines running, at the end of every day and a gaggle of kids furtively waiting to collect, if the coast is clear. My colleagues and I take turns to chase them off," Charlie said, with an air of annoyance.

"Don't you ever tell the police?" I asked, puzzled.

"No, they're not really interested in these guys; they want the big boys who make the big money. In any case our Head doesn't want the kids getting a police record while they're still in school. He'd rather we deal with the problem ourselves," Charlie explained.

I was tempted to tell Charlie about Karl - without using any names. But in the end decided against it. "So you think drugs are a major problem here - and the cause of most crime?" I asked.

"Yes, it's a massive problem but let's put it into perspective - no worse than anywhere else! Seems worse because Bermuda is such a small place," said Charlie. "Anyway, why so serious - it's Friday for God's sake and it's been a hard week!"

After another couple of beers, we paddled back to the dock, where I stood and watched while Charlie tied up his precious boat. The sun had set and the western sky was aglow, painting billowing cumulus clouds an array of pinks and reds. We bid each other farewell and like a couple of easy-riders gunned out onto the main road and sped off in opposite directions - the weekend had started.

*

221

Saturday dawned bright but with a hint of rain in the air; definitely sweater weather but I still wore my shorts. About ten o'clock I wandered along the lane and down a couple of unfamiliar side roads. Outside a meticulously maintained bungalow I came across the flock of elegant *Bird-of Paradise* flowers that I had seen previously; they stood proud and tall, reminding me of a flock of flamingos. I had brought my camera and spent some minutes trying to capture their striking, exotic beauty before strolling on. Around the corner I came across a long, low, pale green bungalow, festooned with bougainvillea. In the grounds, dotted with citrus trees, were a number of boats at various stages of construction; each resting on a wooden cradle to keep them off the ground. I climbed over the low wall and strolled towards the nearest boat. There was a shed in the corner, away from the house and I was aware of someone moving about inside, softly singing. I called out.

A short, square man with a thick, white beard and a shock of matching hair poked his head around the shed door; the white hair starkly contrasting with his jet-black, weathered face. This face fell into a broad smile and he hobbled awkwardly but quickly towards me, thrusting out a hand. I took it and he pumped it vigorously up and down, squeezing my hand. I noticed that in his other, he held an ancient-looking pipe. *"Ah, Mr Cross, the new neighbour,"* he said loudly in a wonderfully musical Bermudian lilt. *"Welcome,"* he continued effusively, *"welcome; I hope that you are enjoying life in paradise - and they are treating you well down at that school?"* he chuckled.

222

When at last he released my hand, I stepped back studying his face and judging him to be in his early seventies. *"You obviously know who I am; but I'm sorry I don't know your name."*

"No, I should be sorry, I should have come and introduced myself to you months ago," he fumbled in his baggy, grey trousers and pulled out a tin of tobacco and began deliberately to stuff his pipe. *"Well folks call me Papa Pete, so you should do the same. Don't hold with all this formal stuff. I'm going to call you Jack,"* he chuckled again.

"Well Papa Pete," I said grinning, *"I've already learned that everyone in Sandy's parish seems to know everyone else - and all their business. So I'm not really surprised that you know all about me."*

"Well it's such a small place, there's nowhere to hide - anyway, why would you want to. Most of us are related you know - distant aunts, uncles and cousins - one big, happy family - that's Bermuda!" This really amused him and he slapped his thigh, laughing loudly.

"I'm not sure you mean that," I smiled. But he just kept chuckling, as he struggled to light his pipe, screwing up his face and sucking vigorously on the stem. Once he had it going; he took a huge breath, sucked, disappeared in a cloud of smoke and coughed, as if he was on his last legs, bending low as he did so. I reached out and slapped his back and eventually he came up for air, straightened, pulled a large purple handkerchief from his pocket and wiped his streaming eyes - even after this near-death experience, Papa Pete emerged still chuckling!

Once he had regained his composure Papa Pete asked me how I liked my little bungalow and I replied that it was very cosy and suited my needs very well. He asked about the water supply and whether the pump was behaving itself. *"You sound as if you know the property well?"* I said.

"Should do," he answered, *"built it with my own hands,"* he waved his large, calloused palms at me.

"Really?" I replied, surprised.

"I really did, Jolene and me lived there from day-one of our marriage, until with three children, it was too small and so when my Daddy died we moved in here - the house where I was born. And no doubt the one where I will die!" He was still chuckling.

"So you sold the house?" I asked.

"No, it still belongs to me. When it came empty last year, that nice Miss Evelyn came and asked me if I would rent it to the School, so that's what I done!"

"So," I said with a surprised grin, *"then you're my landlord and I come to you if I have any problems?"*

"Sure do," he replied and for some reason this set him off in another paroxysm of laughter.

"And you live here with your wife and children?" I asked.

The chuckling ceased and his face became grave: *"The good Lord got jealous and took my sweet Jolene to keep him company some five years ago;"* he stopped and gazed at the sky; *"no five and a half years ago,"* he sighed heavily and I expressed my condolences.

"And your children?" I continued.

224

"*Noah; he the eldest, he captain of a ferry boat and lives in Southampton;*" there was an edge of pride in Papa Pete's voice. "*He got a wife and three kids. Samuel's a qualified electrician; work with your neighbour Karl most of the time. He married, lives round by Sandys' Boat Club, he got just one son.*" Papa Pete was sucking vigorously on his pipe and was wreathed in smoke. "*And then there's my Jimmy. They say a man should not have a favourite child but I make no bones about it, Jimmy is my pride and joy. Loveliest boy you'd ever meet.*" Papa Pete puffed a perfect smoke ring and we both watched it dissipate; "*he special!*"

"*I've met Jimmy,*" I said, a little unsurely.

"*Know you have; he told me.*" Papa Pete looked at me pointedly. "*You have to understand that he was born in your house and lived there until he was eight or nine. He just likes to check up it ain't gone away or something.*"

"*It's not a problem;*" I reassured him.

"*I know he sometimes goes out when I'm still asleep but he means no harm and I can't just lock him up.*" Papa Pete's voice was cracking. "*You know he's a better craftsman than me. Come and look at this boat;*" Papa Pete caught my arm and walked me to one of the boats. "*Look at this; all cedar. Look at this planking, look: it's perfect, each one shaped and fitted... just perfect. That's Jimmy's work!*" Papa Pete said proudly.

"*It's the same when we are out on the water; I showed him what to do just once and he never makes a mistake. He handles a boat as good as anyone I know! He can take an engine to pieces and put it back together again.. just perfect.*" Papa Pete's sigh reminded me of the turtle I'd

225

heard coming up for air. *"And yet;"* he sighed yet again but with exasperation; *"some people say he's simple!"* I didn't know what to say. *"My Jimmy ain't simple - just different!"* Papa Pete said vehemently. *"Look he just coming down de lane."* He waved to his son but Jimmy was oblivious, two large Piggly Wiggly bags clutched to his chest; his eyes locked on the ground watching carefully where he placed his feet. *"He meets my daughter in law at the same time each Saturday morning; she fills the shopping trolley and he brings the stuff home. Good system!"* Papa Pete said; *"Saves my legs and gets him out for a bit."* We both watched as Jimmy trailed deliberately up the drive to the house and in through the back door. *"He'll put the stuff in the fridge and then come and find me;"* said Papa Pete, *"routine – routine's the answer. If he's going to survive when I've gone, it will be because of routine."* I glanced at Papa Pete recognising the worry of what would happen to his dependent child when his own time was up.

Papa Pete was just showing me one of the other boats he was constructing when Jimmy came out. We both looked up and his father called out. Jimmy walked towards us and his face lit up when he saw me. *"Shake hands with Mr Jack;"* Papa Pete instructed. Jimmy obeyed; his hand barely gripping mine but muttering my name.

"I've been looking at your handiwork Jimmy;" I said. *"Been looking at your boat."* As in my house, he again became animated and dragged me off for a closer look. He was gabbling and his father told him to slow down and to speak properly. Like an automaton, he responded and I was

shown the finer points of fitting planking together on a Bermudian dinghy.

It was difficult to drag myself away from my newfound friends. I was impressed by Papa Pete and the rapport that he had painstakingly constructed between himself and his son. I was equally amazed by the skills he had taught Jimmy and although he made light of it; I imagined it represented uncountable hours of repetitive instruction. I did eventually get away with a promise of returning to see the progress on Jimmy's boat - and to be present when it was launched; sometime in the summer.

Karl was busy clipping the hedge when I returned, the three girls buzzing busily round him like acolytes. Pearl in charge of the wheelbarrow, Renee active with a large broom and tiny Vernee following behind her two older sisters, armed with a dustpan and brush. I stopped for a brief moment to observe this fragment of family life before becoming overwhelmed with concern for them all. With a deep breath I chased away the agonising thoughts, replaced the scowl with a cheery grin and barged in on their efforts.

"Lots of willing helpers I see Karl!" I called out from a distance.

They all looked up; Pearl was the first to respond, *"Hello Mr Jack, do you need your hedge cutting while Dad's in the mood and we all have the tools."* It was Pearl's idea of a joke, as there wasn't a hedge around my property!

"Have to keep it trimmed this time of year, or the missus moans the flowers won't bloom;" Karl said, mopping his brow. Renee was gazing at me, one-leggedly leaning on her broom, exactly in the pose as the one adopted by her

227

mother when I first set eyes on her. For the first time I realized that she was more like her mother than either Pearl or Vernee. After several minutes of banter, I left them to finish; their activity reminding me that I ought to get my mower out and cut the grass.

*

Promptly at six o'clock Eloise gently bounced her green Beetle onto the grass outside my bungalow, I was sitting on the porch waiting. It was a chilly evening and so I was glad of my long trousers and bulky sweater. I clambered in and we set off for the island-nation's capital some thirty minutes drive away. Eloise was very animated and the conversation flowed and in no time we were parked and heading for the *Horse and Buggy* on Queen Street.

The pub-restaurant was quietly humming but we had no trouble finding a table amid the beamed, mock-Tudor décor. I picked up the menu and read aloud: '*Bermuda Hospitality with old English Charm!*'

"*That means their speciality is fish and chips*;" laughed Eloise; "*local fish. You know we've only got forty-five minutes;*" Eloise announced; "*so no dallying!*" We both plumped for the fish and chip supper and a couple of beers but by the time the meals arrived we were running out of time and had to gulp them down. Eloise hastily paid the waiter and we dashed outside and ran up Queen Street, hand in hand like a couple of giggling teenagers, heading for the Rosebank Theatre in Bermudiana Road. Soon we were comfortably ensconced towards the back of the theatre and in time to catch the trailers of the forthcoming films. We had opted to see *Travels With My Aunt* and it wasn't long before

228

my arm was around Eloise, her head resting on my shoulder and we were chuckling at Maggie Smith's wonderful portrayal.

"*What a great film;*" said Eloise as we were driving home. "*Great fun!*"

"*Did you ever read the novel?*" I asked.

"*No;*" replied Eloise, her eyes glued to the road and doing her best to avoid the youngsters racing passed her on their bikes. "*I'd never heard of it before. A well-known author?*" she asked.

"*Yes, Graham Greene;*" I replied. "*Not that I've read it;*" I admitted.

Having successfully negotiated all the bikers, Eloise pulled into Long Bay Lane and drew up outside my bungalow. "*Will you come in for a coffee ... or something,*" I asked. Hoping the *something* did not sound as obvious to her, as to my thumping emotions.

"*Thanks but no. It's been a lovely evening ... let's just leave it at that,*" she said quietly squeezing my hand.

"*Or tea, or a glass of wine;*" I hoped I didn't sound as if I was pleading.

"*No, I appreciate the offer.. but I could do with catching up on some sleep.*" She leaned across and pecked my cheek. "*We must do that again some time,*" she laughed; "*but allow more time to eat properly.*"

Reluctantly I opened the door and slid out. "*See you at school then;*" I said flatly, trying to keep the disappointment out of my voice.

"*I'll be in on Tuesday ... till then;*" she whispered, and I closed the door quietly. I stood in the pitch-blackness watching, until the taillights disappeared, my emotions again in turmoil. Could I have been more insistent, I asked myself. Should I have explained how I was really feeling about her? Was I sure how I was feeling about her? I gazed heavenwards; there were no stars, just total darkness, no streetlights just a faint glimmer from two of the windows in Dilly's home. I fumbled my way towards the front door like a blind man, hands reaching out feeling for the edge of the porch. This wasn't how I pictured the day ending!

Later, lying on my bed, I replayed the evening; spooling the events in slow motion, frame by frame, as if it were a film; savouring the pictures of my desirable companion, smiling again at her amusing anecdotes. I mentally kicked myself for my stupid behaviour; our relationship had begun in such a wonderful and meaningful way and then I had wrecked it with my stupidity and guilt.

Guilt? My thoughts turned to Jill and I realized that I had not given her one thought in the last twenty-four hours - and certainly not this evening. I cursed myself and all the mixed-up feelings whirling round my brain. Would I ever get over this, I wondered; ashamed of the self-pity wrapping its arms around me like an old-fashioned London fog, engulfing my every sensation. After tossing and turning fitfully for some time, I eventually switched on the light and worked on the crossword in the Gazette until my eyes shut of their own volition and I slept.

*

Monday came and went; and much to my frustration I didn't have a chance to speak to Eloise when she visited on Tuesday. She had waved when I was taking a class out on to the field while she was welcoming another into the Hall. Later I saw her leave promptly at three o'clock with the children clustered around her Beetle, as she edged her way out on to the road. Later that evening I tried phoning but did not get a reply, which set my mind racing, wishing I knew more about her - and I experienced another restless night.

When I arrived home on Thursday about five o'clock, Dilly came round, knocked on the open door and called out. I was pulling on a clean T-shirt in the bathroom and shouted out for her to come in. When I entered the lounge she was already seated on the sofa. I peered at her face, except for the scowl sullying her good looks, I thought she looked well - and said so.

"Karl tells me he's going fishing Saturday afternoon and may not be back until the early hours - and that I shouldn't wait up," she blurted.

"What's wrong with that?" I replied, settling in a chair in front of her. *"I thought you'd be glad he was doing something different."*

"Are you going?" she asked, fixing me with a steely gaze.

"No, I'm not going," I answered.

"Did he ask you?" she continued, fidgeting with her hands.

"No, he didn't ask me," I replied.

"I don't believe him... he's up to something, he can't lie to me." Dilly forced her wringing hands into her lap. *"He says he's going with some men from work."* She snorted; *"Why has he never done that before - he doesn't particularly like the men he works with?"*

231

"Can't help you Dilly," I said, hoping that I sounded convincing.

"He's been acting strange this last week, fussing round me and that... like he was trying to sum up courage to tell me he was up to something." Dilly peered intently at the ceiling, as if she was looking for spiders and cobwebs. *"I bet it's the drugs,"* she hissed.

"If he says he going fishing, why don't you just believe him," I said, ignoring her comment about drugs, *"And stop worrying."*

"I bet it's that De-Vere," she said quietly. *"Just De-Vere - I bet he's got something to do with this."*

"What are you talking about," I said alarmed. *"What's De-Vere got to with anything?"*

"Cos he's a crook, that's what," her voice cracking with anger.

"What makes you say that, I met him at your party, he seemed a nice chap," I said.

"He can't be trusted. After my last meeting at Cambridge Beaches I found out that he told the Manager and I'm not allowed down there any more."

"How did you find that out?" I questioned.

"I have my informants... my spies. They all hate him. And I know he distributes drugs... I also know he supplies my Karl!" Her voice took on a snarling tone and her petite face screwed up with distaste.

"He supplies Karl," I repeated, hoping that I sounded shocked.

"And others... I've seen him." Dilly continued.

"Does Karl know that you know?" I asked.

"*Course not,*" Dilly said abruptly, "*He'd only deny it.*" Dilly got to her feet, "*I must go, he'll be home in a few minutes.*" She started towards the door and I rose too and rested a comforting hand on her shoulder.

"*I bet he's just going fishing,*" I said, trying to sound reassuring.

"*I think I'll follow him up to Dockyard and see exactly who he meets with. Yes that's what I'll do,*" she whispered.

"*Dilly,*" I interrupted. She ignored me.

"*Yes, I'll leave the girls with my sister and play detective,*" she pulled away.

"*Dilly, you can't do that,*" I cried.

"*How can I help him; if I don't know what's going on.*" Her back was towards me but here was a sob in her voice.

I pulled Dilly's arm, hadn't I expressed the same sentiment to Karl? "*Sit down again;*" I insisted. She flopped back into the sofa hugging her knees. "*What good would it do for you to creep off to Dockyard and watch him get on a boat and sail off out of sight - no doubt everyone will have fishing gear whether they intend to use it or not,*" I was trying not to sound as exasperated as I felt.

Dilly fell silent. I settled alongside her and she leaned into me, the tension ebbing away. "*I have to do something,*" she whispered. Slowly she turned and looked me in the eyes, pleading. "*Take me up there on your bike, just so I can see who he meets, I would recognise some of the guys he works with... please.*"

233

Don telephoned later that evening to say he was meeting policeman Stephen Henderson, Friday at seven in the evening, at the Country Squire for a beer and did I want to join them; I readily agreed and wondered whether or not I should raise the subject of Karl's rendezvous.

At the appointed time on Friday I rode my bike round to Mangrove Bay, it was already dark after a cloud-filled day. We had a convivial evening and being joined by a couple of other acquaintances there was no opportunity to sound Henderson out for advice. About ten o'clock we parted company and on the spur of the moment I decided to ride round East Shore Road to see if Eloise was at home. I pulled up outside her bungalow and from the light thrown from the kitchen window I could see another car was parked next to her Beetle, it was in deep shadow and I couldn't identify the make, though I could see it had a soft top. This threw me - and so I wheeled round, rode up and over Scott's Hill and fell into bed feeling annoyed and confused. I decided that I needed to know more about this woman, a lot more, before I could make a decision to move this relationship on to something more tangible and meaningful. With such thoughts tearing round my brain like a grand-prix racing-car, it was no wonder sleep would not come.

"This just won't do," I said out aloud - sat up and flicked a switch, squinting despite the dim glow emitted from the table-lamp and gazed around the gloomy, shadow-filled room. My eyes fell on the exercise-book wedged under the lamp. At my previous school I once had an elderly colleague, probably the most scholarly individual I have ever worked with - and incidentally an inspirational teacher; who

confided that he had never shown interest in promotion because compiling rotas for playground duty, dinner duty and detention-supervision, as well as wrestling with timetables, missing orders and conjuring up substitute-teachers at a moment's notice, would interfere with his *raison d'être*. When I quizzed him as to what this was; he peered over his half-glasses, deliberately placed the Times' crossword he was sailing through, in his lap and snorted – *'living my dear boy - living!'*

I later learned that this unmarried, eccentric gent had kept a diary ever since he was ten years' old and had accumulated over sixty exercise books filled with both the trivia and the momentous. Meticulously recorded were facts such as what he had for lunch on Monday the fifth of November nineteen twenty-eight - and his thoughts about the first meeting of the United Nations held in London on January tenth, nineteen forty-six at Westminster Central Hall. *"My life is totally documented;"* he had chuckled.

Because of this conversation I too decided to keep a diary but I soon grew bored with all the mundane happenings that seemed to fill my life and my resolve soon evaporated. However, I had recently decided to try again - after all, life in Bermuda was different and something I should be able to write about. Unlike my eccentric colleague, however, I left out all the trivia and concentrated on the people I met, the places I visited and snippets gleaned from the local newspaper. I was using the book that I had purchased upon my arrival where I had jotted down my first impressions - and the diary entries had only begun some two weeks earlier. I eased the book from under the lamp and read what I had written. Typically male, I supposed, there was no mention of Eloise, or Marsha, or my feelings or emotions - just facts! Even references to Karl and Dilly's respective problems were dealt with in a simplistic code - a reminder to me but could not be used in evidence! I picked up a pen and caught up on the last few days in an attempt to concentrate my mind on the more recent and escape the past. Now what happened Wednesday, I pondered? Ah yes that was the day I packed my excited soccer team and a couple of reserves on to a service bus and we set off down the Island for a friendly game at Charlie's school, in Southampton. It had been my suggestion that we organize a mini-tournament over the next few weeks between schools in the western section of the Island and this was the first match. It was an exciting game with fortunes swinging first one way and then the other but to my delight captain Graham Simons scrambled home the winner just before Charlie blew his whistle to end the game. We gathered the boys together afterwards and while they downed gallons of soft drinks, that Charlie had provided, we told them how much we admired their skill and sportsmanship - and insisted they all shake hands before we gathered up our belongings and made our way to the bus stop. That thought was soon précised into two short sentences!

Sucking the end of the pen, my thoughts turned to Dilly and her emotional request to secretly observe Karl's *fishing-trip* departure. He had said that he had to be on the jetty by Cut Bridge at one-thirty, where a boat would pick him up. I wondered how easy it would be for us to get up close, without drawing attention to ourselves. Although I had not admitted as much to Dilly, I too was very anxious to know who was involved. Perhaps I should go tomorrow morning and scout out the area - though ideally, I thought, we should be on a boat. The idea of asking Charlie if I could borrow *Next Best Thing* crossed my mind? I tried to think this through, if they sailed off miles out to sea to rendezvous with the delivery vessel, what could I possibly do? Just follow and watch from afar. In any case I had no experience of nocturnal navigating in open waters - and I had no idea how Charlie's boat could cope if the weather got rough. Better, I eventually decided, to watch them go - and perhaps return!

*

About nine the next morning I rode out towards Dockyard, it was dry but cold and I was muffled up in a heavy sweater and anorak. This part of Bermuda was composed of a string of tiny islands linked by a series of bridges – Watford Bridge, Grey's Bridge and The Cut Bridge, the latter crossing a gap called Cockburn's Cut. Wilber had told me on one of our sailing expeditions that it was named for Vice Admiral Sir George Cockburn, the Commander in Chief at the time and dug by the Royal Engineers as a defensive ditch about 1817. Later they decided it wasn't necessary and filled it in again! A decade or so later it was excavated again and the first-ever concrete bridge in Bermuda built over it - which the locals refused to cross, deeming such 'porridge' would never take their weight. Wilber had laughed and told me how unfounded their fears were, as it was the same bridge used today.

I parked my bike at the junction of Pender Road and Freeport Drive, where the jetty protruded out as part of the harbour defences of the South Basin and wandered around seeking suitable cover. I eventually decided a clear view of the jetty might be possible from behind some trees to the side of a row of houses, known as Prince Alfred Terrace. Satisfied this was the best solution but filled with apprehension I headed back home.

*

I heard the engine of Karl's bike when he left about a quarter to one. Five minutes later Dilly appeared, pulling a large black anorak over her head, as she eased through the door. *"Are you sure you want to go through with this?"* I asked.

"Of course," she replied sharply, fiddling with the dark blue turban she wore on her head. I cruised carefully through the village, over Watford Bridge and along Malabar Road; Dilly had both arms around my waist and in my mirror I could see that she had covered most of her face with a silk scarf. I rode slowly over the Cut Bridge so that we could see the jetty, overtook a parked car and kept going until we well clear and then stopped.

"I saw three men, did you?" I asked.

"Yes, three," said Dilly. *"One was Karl - but no boat."*

I explained that I was going to turn round and park close to Prince Alfred Terrace, so that we could make our way behind the trees. The parked car was still there, as no one else was about, I concluded it must belong to one of the men on the jetty.

238

"*Do you recognise the car?*" I shouted over my shoulder. I could feel Dilly swivel round but she said nothing. Once out of sight of the jetty I stopped, switched off the engine and propped the bike on its stand. I pulled the hood of my anorak over my head, while Dilly tied her scarf over the lower part of her face and we climbed a low bank and slid behind the first tree, looking, I'm sure, to any passer-by like a pair of would-be villains. "*Did you recognise the car?*" I asked again.

"*Not really,*" Dilly replied "*but it looked familiar, convertibles look different with their soft-tops up.*" Although we could see the jetty, we were too far away and without a word Dilly slipped from tree to tree and I followed, until we could go no further. I fumbled about in the huge pocket of my anorak and pulled out a small pair of binoculars and handed them to Dilly. She looked up and briefly smiled: "*Good thinking;*" she mouthed. Not that we would be heard due to the sea crashing on the rocks and wind whistling in the pines. She focussed the binoculars on the threesome, while I unzipped the front of my anorak to reveal my Nikon F with a 300 mm lens attached. Dilly turned, saw the camera and momentarily grinned: "*You really are well prepared!*" she said. "*I don't know who's with Karl, they have their backs to me,*" she continued. I asked for the binoculars and peered at the three men; Karl and another man had small rucksacks. Suddenly one of the men turned round - I felt sure it was Just De Vere. I'd only seen him once but I felt certain it was he, his tall, confident manner, suave, good looks caused him to stand out. He was wearing a baseball cap and was hunched into an expensive-looking jacket, the rucksack hanging off one shoulder. Karl was standing well apart, as I supposed he would be, in the circumstances. I said nothing to Dilly.

She asked for the binoculars and peered again at the threesome. I focussed my camera and waited in the hope de Vere would turn again. Eventually he did and I fired off a barrage of shots. Dilly gasped and may have cursed: *"I was right, I told you."* She turned towards me: *"It's De-Vere, it's him."* Before I could comment a sleek game-fishing boat, with a tuna-tower edged into view and we watched, Dilly through the binoculars, me through my lens, as a crew-member threw a rope, which the unidentified man caught and held while Karl and De-Vere climbed aboard. Dilly kept muttering and I kept shooting. After a few moments the man on the jetty hurled the rope back and the boat reversed away. My final shot was of the stern, where I read *Bermuda Folly* and underneath *Hamilton, Bermuda.*

"Looked like there were two men on board," said Dilly, as we watched the powerful engines drive the boat into the central channel and towards the open sea. The remaining man had already reached the road and was heading for the parked car.

"Stay here;" I said to Dilly and walked quickly to the edge of the trees, I wanted a picture of the car. The man turned as he opened the car door to get in and I felt confident I had a good picture of him and the number plate.

"Did you get a picture of his face?" Dilly had silently sidled up behind me. I told her that I thought I had. In mutual silence and with a sense of anti-climax we wandered

back to where I had left my bike. We clambered aboard and I kicked it into life.

Back in Long Bay Lane I freewheeled over the grass to the side of my house where Dilly slowly dismounted. She gazed into the distance with unseeing eyes, as I lifted the bike on to its stand. I looked down at the diminutive, lonely figure and realised that she was shivering. I put a protective arm around her shoulders: *"Come in, I'll make some coffee;"* I said.

She didn't move. *"I have to go and fetch the girls, I promised Josie I'd be quick."* Dilly seemed to shake herself out of the trance, gave my hand a quick squeeze and was gone.

Once inside and clutching a mug of coffee, I pondered on the morning's events. I was suddenly struck by the thought that perhaps Karl's life was in danger. Perhaps they intended to throw him overboard and report an accident - or was the crook De-Vere getting Karl even more involved, deeper into a hole that he couldn't escape from? It wasn't long before the familiar sense of being out of my depth swept over me and I dropped on to the sofa, almost spilling the steaming coffee. I don't know how long I sat contemplating the many and varied scenarios playing out in my mind. The coffee was long since consumed and gradually I became aware of the distant sound of Dilly's girls playing outside. Assuming the villains were collecting a new drug shipment and the fishing trip wasn't just a ploy to get rid of Karl; what would they do with it? Did they have a secret central store? Or was the plan to distribute the stuff as

241

soon as they came ashore. Either option seemed feasible to my naive, criminally inexperienced mind.

I needed to get out, take my mind off Karl and his problems, there seemed nothing I could usefully do to help him. I phoned Eloise but either she chose not to answer or she was out. My heart grew heavier. I phoned Don but he wasn't answering either. It was raining again and already dark but I was growing desperate for company and contemplating a soggy ride round to the Country Squire. My gloomy thoughts were interrupted by a knock on the door, which opened before I could reach the handle. Pearl peered quizzically round the door, her huge eyes blinking as they adjusted to the light. *"Hey Mr Jack - Momma says we got more food than we can eat and why don't you come and join us for supper."* Before I could answer she continued: *"be ready in ten minutes!"* And she was gone.

I smiled, wondering about Dilly's propensity to read minds; before heading for the bathroom for a quick wash. I donned a clean shirt, grabbed a bottle of Portuguese *Vinho Verde* from the fridge; flung a sweater round my shoulders and ran through the murk. The glow from a curtained window cast a warm, inviting path across the grass, guiding me towards my neighbour's modest home. At the door I paused, drove all negative thoughts about Karl and Dilly from my mind, fixed a smile on my face and with a loud knock, pushed open the door.

*

Later that night I lay fully clothed on my bed reading but listening for Karl's return. I had in fact dropped off to sleep, when a slight sound caused me to wake with a start. I

242

peered through the mesh, could see nothing but caught the squeaking sound of a bike being lifted on to its stand. In an instant I was through the door and heading round the back of the neighbouring bungalow. I could just make out Karl's bulky figure, he was fighting with the anorak he was trying to pull over his head. I whispered his name and he visibly jumped and turned towards me. I hissed my name and asked if he was all right. He just grunted, folding the anorak into a bundle before wedging it under the seat of the bike. I held his arm and again asked if he was okay. *"Let's talk;"* I said, *" come to my place and I'll make some coffee."*

"I need to sleep;" he mumbled, *"I don't need coffee."*

I glanced at my watch and was amazed to see that it was after three o'clock; obviously I slept much longer than I had previously thought. *"Just five minutes,"* I hissed, *"I need to know!"* Reluctantly and without a word he followed me into my place and flopped on the sofa. He looked terrible, with great bags under his eyes, a smudged grease mark, like a scar, across one cheek. I then noticed he was holding a piece of blood-stained rag wrapped round his hand. *"Looks like you should wash that;"* I nodded at his hand. He grunted and rose wearily to his feet and I led him to the kitchen and turned on the tap. He had a jagged cut between his left thumb and index finger, it was deep. I went to the bathroom and returned with some antiseptic cream, bandages and plasters. *"Here, let me see,"* I said reaching for his hand. *"This needs hospital treatment;"* I said.

"Tomorrow;" was the laconic reply.

It took some minutes to stem the blood flow. *"What happened?"* I asked, wrapping a tight bandage round his palm.

"A warning," he mumbled; *"said they'd cut my hand off next time, if I didn't cooperate more willingly."*

I shuddered, as I checked that my handiwork would hold, before ushering him into the living room and onto the sofa, where I placed a beer in his good hand. Karl closed his eyes, his face frozen into a permanent frown. *"Right,"* I began, *"so you were picked up by a boat at Dockyard; how many of you?"* I had no intention of telling Karl that Dilly and I had witnessed his departure.

"You don't need to know," he said wearily.

"Don't start that again, who was with you? Was it De-Vere himself?"

Karl nodded.

"Who else?" I demanded

"A Portuguese guy they called Reno. He the guy who stuck the knife in my hand."

"Why did he do that?" I asked.

"Just De-Vere told him. He said I needed to be taught a lesson."

"Who else was there?" I continued.

"A guy called Earl Boon; he was at Dockyard but didn't come with us - he was driving De Vere's car, brought him to the boat and after he took him home." Karl took a long swig of his beer and wiped his lips with the back of his bandaged hand.

"Who was on the boat?" I persisted.

244

"Two guys, Sven - don't know his other name. And the skipper called Serge Thomas."

"So tell me what happened, where did you go;" I was anxious to get the full story.

"We went out near the Challenger Banks and met up with a large, powerful, real-expensive motorboat; we drew up alongside and they threw several large plastic bags on to our deck and some real heavy boxes then we sailed back again." Karl said dispassionately.

"Hold on," I said. *"The Challenger banks, isn't that where Argus Tower is - and where folk go game-fishing?"* I remembered Wilber Marshall telling me about the area on one of our cruises.

"That's right, about thirty or so miles south-west from here;" said Karl. *"The skipper had lines out to make it look as if we were fishing."*

"And where was the other boat from?" I enquired.

"Grand Turk... Turks & Caicos Islands... least that's what it said on the stern." Karl clambered slowly to his feet, *"I have to go to bed; I'm bushed."*

"Wait;" I said, on my feet, hand on his arm. *"What happened when you came back?"* Karl yawned; *"We put the stuff inside an old boat moored in Red Hole, you know, off Harbour Road. This bloke Boon met us there and after it was locked away he took De-Vere home in a car... and the skipper took me back to Dockyard so I could pick up my bike."*

"Did you get the name of this old boat at Red Hole?" I asked.

"Yeah... said Georgie Girl on the stern – though somewhere else I saw the name Bermuda Belle;" Karl replied.

"What about the other boat, where do you think the fishing boat is moored?" I asked. Karl looked at me as if I was mad:

"No idea," he hissed and made for the door.

"Perhaps we can talk more tomorrow," I said.

"Not in front of Dilly, we don't;" he said and disappeared into the night, grudgingly whispering his thanks for the beer and for dealing with his hand.

I flopped back on to my bed, where I lay mulling over what Karl had said, trying to make sense of it all. At one stage I turned on the light and wrote down the names of the men Karl had mentioned before slipping into a dreamless sleep.

*

Sunday dawned bright and sunny, though in reality dawn was long gone by the time I roused myself. I did some washing and made a token gesture at cleaning up. Through the wide-open front door I could hear the girls playing outside, one of them, probably Vernee, the youngest, was quietly singing. I peered around the door jamb, they had scratched out a hop-scotch pattern in the dirt and Renee was hopping from square to square, while her older sister offered advice. I called out: *"Hi Girls, is your Dad about."*

Vernee stopped singing, turned languidly in my direction and in a loud whisper said: *"He's still sleeping."*

Pearl elaborated: *"He was out fishing all yesterday, Momma says he's bushed!"* I nodded and left them to their

246

games. Later I saw Dilly hanging out washing and asked after Karl; without stopping pegging out one of Karl's shirts, she explained he had gone to the hospital to get his hand fixed.

"What happened?" I asked innocently.

"He said he cut it guttin' fish!" she gave me a very straight look, devoid of expression.

"Coffee?" I asked, nodding towards my place.

"Yeah... but I already got some warming;" she gathered up her basket, headed indoors and I followed. Seated opposite across the solid table, we peered at each other over the rims of giant-sized mugs of steaming coffee. Dilly huddled inside a large polo-necked sweater, her hair hidden under a turban.

Eventually, I broke the silence: *"Did Karl tell you anything?"* I asked.

Dilly shook her head: *"Nope, he said he had a good day's fishing, stayed and had some beers with his mates... even put some fish in the fridge and said he would barbecue them tonight."* She shook her head, as if in disbelief. I contemplated telling Dilly about the early morning conversation with Karl but in the end decided she looked too frail and changed the subject. Then the girls descended and I took my leave.

Later that afternoon, on the spur of the moment, I rode my bike towards town, stopping at intervals along Harbour Road to take in the view. Although mid-January, it was pleasantly warm, the Great Sound was a wonderful turquoise blue and the flowering hedges and gardens still had the power to take my breath away. I reached Red Hole, where Karl had said the drugs had been stored, parked my bike and studied the boats through my binoculars.

Red Hole was a small bay next to where Wilber moored his pride and joy, *Crazy Dream*. At this time of year there were only about twenty boats moored in the bay. I decided that the one Karl had described was probably the largest one, which had two masts and was moored away from the others. Its bow was facing me, meaning I could not read the name but it was certainly old, its peeling paint producing an air of neglect - it didn't look as if it had been anywhere for some time. I leaned on the wall and peered through the binoculars but there was no sign of movement, I felt sure no one was aboard. Over the wall there was a six feet drop on to rocks and I contemplated leaving my clothes there and swimming the two or three hundred yards to the boat. But commonsense prevailed and I decided to see if I could get any nearer. I rode slowly along Harbour Road but except for a small exposed area where boats were pulled up onto some rough ground, private houses prevented me getting any nearer. If I wanted to get aboard, I needed to do so by boat. I returned to my vantage point, sat on the wall and for a further ten minutes trained my binoculars on the twin-masted schooner. I wondered if *Georgie Girl* was just somewhere obscure to store the drugs or headquarters of the whole drug operation.

The sun was disappearing fast by the time I arrived home. I was surprised to see Pearl lying comfortably on my hammock. When she heard me approaching she leapt guiltily to the floor and skipped towards me. *"Sorry Mr Jack,*

I've never sat in a hammock before, I wondered what it was like." Pearl balanced on one leg.

"Not a problem Pearl, you're welcome; what did you think?" I asked, pulling my bike up on its stand.

"I think it's a great place to think, just lying there, swinging from side to side, looking up at the tree tops and all the clouds rushing by. It helps you concentrate," Pearl's brow was furrowed.

"Penny for your thoughts," I said.

"What do you mean?" Pearl's face was still screwed up.

"I mean what were you thinking about on the hammock, you look very serious." I said.

"I was thinking... I was thinking... that my Dad's left-handed." she paused.

"So, I don't understand," I replied, puzzled. *"what's that got to do with anything?"*

"So if he cut himself guttin' the fish, as he said... why did he cut his left hand?" Without another word Pearl turned and skipped away calling her sisters.

Riding back to Somerset earlier I had made a decision, I was going to talk to Stephen Henderson, the policeman that I'd met. I felt sure that he could point me in the right direction. Doing nothing wouldn't solve anything and every day that passed Karl would be getting more and more involved. I made the telephone call.

Later that evening, seated comfortably in his tiny apartment I told Stephen the tale of how an acquaintance, through being an occasional user, had been sucked in by drug dealers, his family threatened, a knife stuck in his hand

249

and how he was at his wit's end but too scared to inform the police. Stephen wanted to know why, if the guy was so scared, he had told me? I explained that his wife had found out and been so distraught, she had talked to me. I went on to explain how the wife and I had watched him being picked up by a boat and taken out to a rendezvous near the Challenger Banks and how the stuff was stored on a boat in the harbour, close to Hamilton.

I was trying not to give too much away but Stephen was skilfully prying. *"Basically, this is a great guy, with a great family who has dug himself into a hole and needs help - he's certainly not a criminal."*

"He's broken the law," said Stephen laconically, *"so he's a criminal."*

"An accidental one," I responded. *"Anyway, I came here to ask you for advice, how can we help this man and his family so that he doesn't get deeper into trouble. He's a good guy!"* I realised that it sounded as if I was pleading.

"Well," said Stephen inspecting his nails: *"I'll give it some thought, I'll have a few words with colleagues who deal with this sort of thing. If you find out any more about your friend's involvement, let me know. Especially if he starts dropping names."* Up to this point I had denied knowing the names of Karl's tormentors. I agreed and rose to my feet, shaking Stephen's hand and saying how pleased I was to be able to share the dilemma that was bothering me. *"Is this friend a local, a Bermudian?'* asked Stephen as we reached the door.

"If you don't mind, I'd rather not say at this point. The guy is so scared and convinced that, if he tells the

250

police, he or his wife and kids will just disappear into the ocean." I said.

"I'm sure he's being too melodramatic, probably watched too many crime movies," said Stephen with a laugh. *"Anyway you keep me posted and I'll talk with my colleagues to see if we can help this friend of yours."*

As I rode home I felt as if some of the weight Karl had loaded on my shoulders was somewhat lifted and I convinced myself that I had done the right thing.

*

A series of events the following week left me reeling and with a head full of confused questions. The week had started quietly enough with normal classes on Monday and an after-school soccer match at home against the Heron Bay School; which we had lost, much to the boys' disappointment. In the evening I saw Dilly briefly and she told me that she was meeting Marsha at the Southampton Princess on Tuesday evening, to introduce her to the hotel staff. Poor Dilly looked drawn and bent; obviously in pain; her attempt at being her usual cheerful self, tugging at my heart strings.

Wednesday was a fabulous day, the sun was bright, the humidity unseasonably low, so at every opportunity I took the students outside. At the end of the day I decided to go for a run, so went home, changed and began by loping down Long Bay Lane towards the entrance to the Canadian Naval base. I continued following the road and passed the entrance to Cambridge Beaches Cottage Colony. Feeling a need to catch my breath I slowed to a walk and wandered down towards the secluded wharf. As I drew nearer I noticed two cars, this was not unusual for this was a popular fishing spot for the locals but then I realised that one was a Beetle, like Eloise's. A few strides nearer and there she was - talking to a tall, well built man, smartly dressed in a blazer, shorts and matching knee-length socks. His back was towards me. I could see from Eloise's face, they were engaged in an intense conversation, I drew back partially hidden by overhanging oleanders. Eloise turned, so that they both faced out to sea and my imagination lurched into overdrive, as I watched this tall stranger slide a massive hand around her shoulder and down her back, to rest possessively on her shapely backside. Then in a flash he planted a peck on her cheek, clambered into his car and started towards me. I dived behind the trunk of a tree until he was out of sight. Eloise was still gazing out to sea, as I trotted towards her. I called her name. She turned sharply, an expression at first of surprise and then, I thought, genuine pleasure, when she realised it was me. *"What are you doing here?"* she asked, reaching out a hand and grasping my arm.

"It was such a great day, I decided to go for a jog," I responded. *"Anyway, I could ask you the same question - or am I sabotaging a secret rendezvous?"*

"I can't deny it," she said mischievously, still holding my arm. *"I did have a rendezvous, with a tall, handsome man who just drove away - you must have seen his car!"*

"The topless Triumph Herald convertible?" I said knowingly.

"Was it?" she replied, *"well certainly topless, as you suggestively put it!"*

"None of my business with whom you have secret assignations," the same jovial tone masked my more confused thoughts.

"My rendezvous was with one of the managers from Cambridge Beaches. I have become the proud part-owner of a boat and I have been trying to negotiate the rental of one of their moorings," said Eloise with a smile.

"Wow, a boat-owner," I exclaimed. *"Now you'll never have any money!"*

"Part-owner I said, so half the costs," she responded with a tinkling laugh, shaking her hair away from her face.

"What sort is it?" I asked. *"A motorboat?"*

"I don't know what sort it is, but yes, a motorboat, similar to so many others you see around here." She laughed.

I didn't buy this, I knew she was very genned-up on boats - she would know exactly what make it was, what size engine and all its capabilities. *"Well what colour is it?"* I joked. *"And where is it?"*

"Colour? Wait and see," was the response: *"it's up at Dockyard having its bottom scraped, if you'll excuse the expression."* Eloise glanced at her watch, *"Nice as it is to chat, I must fly, I have a piano lesson to give."*

It was my turn to receive a peck on the cheek and then she was gone and I was left to contemplate the stunning, glistening bay of glassy water, edged with oleanders delightfully drooping their lower boughs to kiss the turquoise sea. The jaw-dropping beauty of the scene before me was marred by the vivid memory of the large male hand intimately cupping Eloise's butt. The hand of Just de Vere!

253

I wasn't really so concerned about the truth of Eloise's story of the need for a mooring - I was devastated by her connection to De Vere, realising that he was the owner of the same car that I had seen parked outside her bungalow a couple days earlier!

*

The departure of the students on Friday afternoon came as a welcome blessing and after I gently pushed the last reluctant child out through the door, I slumped onto the nearest chair, breathing a sigh of relief, until, that was, my unseeing gaze rested on a pile of unmarked English books, the sight soliciting yet another heavy sigh. Pulling myself together, I clambered out of the child-sized chair, settled at my desk and opened the top exercise book.

*

It was dark by the time I arrived home and as I lifted the bike onto its stand someone called out. It was Dilly's older sister Josie. She told me that Dilly was unwell and had been in bed all day. She had fed the girls but she had to go and get a meal for her own family, would I mind keeping an eye on Dilly until Karl came home - he was due any moment. Of course I agreed and we went into the kitchen where the three girls were sitting around the table picking at something healthy that Josie had prepared. She kissed each one on the cheek, told them to be good and left; I sat at the head of the table and made a joke. It fell on deaf ears. *"You're in Dad's chair,"* said little Vernee, with a frown.

"I promise to move, when he comes," I reassured her and asked if their mother was asleep. Pearl rose to her feet, said she would go and see and tiptoed out of the kitchen.

She returned immediately and said her Mom was awake and I should go and see her. Without another word she slid her had into mine and led me to a bedroom. Dilly was propped up on several cushions; she waved a weak arm at the chair alongside her bed and told Pearl to go and finish her supper. I was shocked at Dilly's condition, her cheeks were hollowed with pain, her breathing irregular and noisy. I tried to jolly her along but it was hard going. Eventually, short of things to tell her, I asked if she had met with Marsha. She had, she said and the introduction to the hotel staff had gone well. It was obviously an effort to speak and so I cut her short and said I would go and see if the girls were all right. Karl was in the kitchen and the girls were taking their turn to give him a wet kiss and a hug. Pearl explained why I was there: "*Mr Jack is baby-sitting,*" she said with distain! I soon made an excuse to leave, promising I would look in again in the morning to see how Dilly was.

*

I had just finished eating a couple of slices of toast and marmalade on Saturday morning when the phone rang. It was Wilberforce Marshall, I was surprised for it was weeks since we had last spoken. After apologising for calling me early and for the short notice, he asked if I was free to join him and his wife for dinner that evening. "*Quite informal,*" he insisted, "*just a few friends.*" I readily agreed and a time was fixed. I was really pleased at the invitation, as I was not looking forward to a quiet night in, on my own and mentally noted that I would need to scoot down to the Piggly Wiggly for some chocolates and flowers for Madge. I also decided that I would order a taxi, rather than risking the

255

ride home in the dark with a particularly poor headlamp! My deliberations were interrupted by a knock at the door, it was Pearl asking if I would like to join her Dad for a coffee? I followed her out into the bright sunshine, a cool breeze rattling the palm leaves high over my head, mimicking the sound of an incoming tide.

Karl was slouched over the picnic table, resting his chin in his massive hands, peering unseeingly at little Vernee, she was swinging a skipping rope and quietly counting to herself. I called out and dropped onto the bench opposite him. I studied his face, which was lined with worry and weariness. His hand was still heavily bandaged.

"Doesn't look like you slept much last night," I said.

He nodded agreement. *"Dilly had a bad night, soaked with fever, had to change the bedclothes at some ungodly hour."* Pearl pushed her way through the mesh outer door, using an elbow to prevent it banging, she carried a tray and we both followed her progress to the table, as she concentrated on keeping the coffee pot and milk jug upright, picking her way, barefoot down the sandy path. Without a word she set the tray on the table and carefully placed a cup and saucer in front of her father and filled it to the brim with coffee. Karl reached out and squeezed her arm in a gesture of unspoken gratitude. She pushed a cup and saucer towards me and partially filled the cup:

"Please help yourself to milk," she said and wandered off towards her younger sister.

"Have you heard from De Vere again?" I asked. Karl shook his head. *"You would tell me?"* I continued. Karl didn't answer but glared at me, as if I was mad. We chatted

about this and that before he excused himself and went indoors to check if Dilly had awoken. He returned some moments later and said that she was up and having a shower. I excused myself, thanked him for the coffee and made my way down to the supermarket seeking flowers and chocolate to present to Madge later that evening.

*

A car horn gave a solitary, mournful toot at ten minutes past six; it was Eggy. I had phoned him earlier and he agreed to come and pick me up at six o'clock. Ten minutes late wasn't bad by laid-back Bermuda standards, I thought. He greeted me like a long lost friend and we set off down the island for foreign parts - Smith's parish. *"So, where in the lovely parish of Smith's do you wish to go?"* asked Eggy, trilby at a jaunty angle, elbow out of the window, a cigarette wedged in the corner of his mouth.

"First left after Devil's Hole," I replied, *"the house looks out onto Harrington Sound."*

"Ah the Sound, named after the delightful Lucy, Duchess of Bedford;" said Eggy in his best English accent. I ignored him, he was in his show-off, local-history mode. *"And did you know that Smith's is named after another of your countrymen - Sir Thomas Smith, one of the original nine investors in these glorious Somers' Isles?"* Eggy went on in a similar vein for the next half an hour, until we reached Devil's Hole, when he stopped chattering and concentrated on finding the right turn. Satisfied he had found the correct one, he drove carefully up a narrow, potholed road and pulled up outside a pair of wrought-iron gates, leading onto a well-lit drive and a sprawling beige-

257

coloured bungalow. As I clambered out Eggy went to the gate and rang a bell, somewhere within a dog barked. I waited and Eggy nimbly got back into the driving seat. *"What time do you want me to pick you up?"* he enquired.

"Wait a moment and I'll find out," I replied.

A voice called: *"Is that you Jack?"* it was Madge. She unlocked the gates and let me in, calling out to Eggy: *"Can you come back about eleven?"* I thanked Eggy and he shouted for us to have a nice evening and eased his taxi into a ten-point turn. Madge locked the gate before possessively tucking her arm into mine and led me towards a flight of steps leading up to the front door, continually gushing about not having seen me for ages.

Inside the ornately decorated hall, full of carved, Bermuda Cedar furniture, I presented her with the flowers and chocolates that I had brought. She hugged me, told me I was a naughty boy and pushed me into the lounge, calling out:

"Wilber, everybody - it's Jack. And look at these exquisite orchids he has brought, I must find a vase." It took a moment for my eyes to adjust to the softly lit room. In the corner was a full-sized bar and behind were shelves reaching to the ceiling, decorated with bottles of every shape and hue. Wilber was busy with a cocktail shaker. Two people were perched on bar stools, one looking very uncomfortable, due to his huge but squat size, it was the man Lewis Lane, whom I'd met on Wilber's boat - and the other, I was delighted to see, was Marsha!

"Welcome," said Wilber boisterously, *"come and have a drink; you've met Lewis and Marsha before!"* I

leaned over the bar and shook Wilber's hand, then turned and did the same with Lane. His hand was clammy, somehow I wasn't surprised. Marsha put out a hand which I grasped, leaning towards her and planting a kiss somewhere behind her ear, carefully avoiding the huge dangling earring, while being rewarded with an exquisite burst of Jasmin scented perfume.

"Pull up a stool," said Wilber planting an ice-cold beer in front of me. *"Did I do right?"* he said with a cheeky grin. I reassured him that he had indeed 'done good.' Madge reappeared, a vase of orchids in one hand, an empty glass in the other.

"Wilber I'm ready for a refill," she said, placing the glass on the bar and the vase on a nearby cedar chest. She wrapped an arm around my waist: *"So what have you been doing since we last saw you,"* she asked. *"And what have you been teaching your little charges?"*

"Well, if I'm honest I haven't been doing much - and yet the weeks just disappear." I replied. *"And as to what I'm teaching my little charges: well, this week was a mixture of backward somersaults, Venn diagrams, calculating areas of rectilinear shapes and journalistic writing."*

"Oh," said Madge, *"I wish I went to your school. There were no handsome young male teachers in my school - just nuns! How about your school Marsha?"*

Eventually the banter ceased when Madge went to *check on the cooking.* And I was able to ask Lewis Lane what business he was in. He replied that he had an import/export business in Miami, as well as an interest in a shipping company and some real estate. Naturally there

259

were all sorts of licences and permits to be negotiated, he explained and Marsha, being a lawyer, helped out at the Bermuda end.

The doorbell rang and Wilber excused himself and headed for the door. A few moments later he ushered two more dinner guests into the room and introduced them as neighbours from the next house. It transpired they were Canadian, the man was exceptionally tall and thin, looking uncomfortable in an oversized, pink blazer. His handshake slithered in and out of my grasp like an elusive viper. In contrast his wife was half his height, equally as thin but with handshake designed to let you know she meant business. He was an insurance broker, I learned, while she worked in a bank. Conversation swirled around until it became an intense discussion about currency fluctuations. I used the opportunity to ease Marsha away from the bar and onto a deeply cushioned sofa.

"You look as beautiful and elegant as ever;" I said - in my head, looking into her amazing, shimmering brown pools that doubled as eyes. I think the brilliantly original words that actually came out were more like: *"So what have you been doing with yourself, since we last met?"*

It wasn't long before Madge appeared at the door waving her boxing-sized, oven gloves and summoned us to the table. Dinner was delicious and we all agreed Madge had done a wonderful job. She then let slip that she had a gourmet-angel she could call on - and that this angel had done all the preparation during the morning, leaving Madge to put everything in the oven at the appointed time. We didn't believe her but she giggled and insisted it was true.

Later, ensconced on the comfortable sofa, nursing an oversized cut glass brandy goblet, that Wilber had pushed into my hand; he asked me why I hadn't taken *Crazy Dream* out for a sail since his offer. I made excuses and he repeated that I didn't have to ask, just go, when I had the time. He would not be using the boat without me, so if he hadn't asked me to crew, then it was free! He then disappeared to return with a key on a long ribbon threaded through several champagne corks. *"This is a spare key for the cabin door,"* he said. *"You keep it."*

I was quite overwhelmed by his generosity and determined to take advantage of his offer as soon as I had a day to spare and the weather was right. Later, wedged on the sofa between Marsha and Madge, the latter, drumming her pink-varnished fingernails on my naked knee, while she dominated the conversation, her every phrase filled with sexual innuendo. My defence mechanism was to laugh, I noticed Marsha stared coyly into her glass. As she launched into another risqué anecdote a horn blew outside.

"Good lord!" I said glaring at my watch, *"Must be my taxi, it's 11.15, how can that be?"*

"I ought to go too," said Marsha. *"Lewis has someone picking him up at midnight but that's too late for me."* Madge made discouraging noises, urging us both to stay, but I interrupted, said I must go and offered to share the taxi with Marsha and take her home first.

We bid our farewells and both Madge and Wilber took us to the gate. Eggy leapt out of his taxi, flung open the door, at the same time doffing his battered trilby to our hosts with an exaggerated bow. Once underway, Marsha gave

261

Eggy instructions how to find her apartment and we settled back both tired after a surfeit of food and alcohol - I was grateful that Eggy was quiet and not doing his tourist guide bit. In the back streets of Pembroke Eggy expertly found a large house, which Marsha said was divided into three apartments. I walked her to the door, mentally noting the street name and house number. *"You heard Wilber offer me the use of his boat, would you come out with me one Saturday soon, if the weather holds?"* I asked.

"I'd love to," she replied. *"I love being out on the water."*

"Well I'd need you telephone number so that I can contact you," I continued.

Marsha fumbled in her handbag, eventually finding a business card. She scribbled her home phone number on the back and handed it over. *"There's an answer-phone if I'm not in. I can always call you back."* She then inserted a key into the lock before turning and offering her cheek. *"Good night Jack, it was a fun evening."* I agreed, laying my hand on her arm as I pecked her cheek. Without another word she suddenly spun on her heel and disappeared into the darkened hall.

We were well into Warwick parish when Eggy spoke: *"Mr Jack, if you don't mind me asking, how you know that Mr Wilberforce Marshall?"*

"I met him at Miss Miles-Smith's house and I sometimes crew for him on his boat." I replied, surprised that Eggy knew Wilber's first name.

"Ah yes," said Eggy knowingly...*Crazy Dream."*

*

262

Sunday morning dawned cloudy, bright and humid. I snatched a quick breakfast and hurried off to Carlton Beach - I was meeting the guys for tennis. After an hour we were soaked and exhausted and not one of us needed encouragement to quit, head for the terrace, flop into the cushioned bamboo chairs and order beers.

After some thirty minutes Don, Alan and Charlie made excuses and headed off. I had no plans for the day and so decided to have a bite of lunch but beforehand needed to freshen up and so made my way inside the hotel and towards the bathroom. Crossing the Reception area I noticed a couple of taxis parked at the door - Eggy was leaning on the bonnet of his car in deep discussion with Jobo Crane, the doorman - the same man I had previously seen secreting a package into his locker. I saw the doorman was holding a similar package again! Suddenly my heart was in my mouth for there was another person involved in the discussion. I had not previously seen her, she had been hidden by Crane's massive bulk. It was Eloise! I found an empty chair facing the doorway, picked up a newspaper and surreptitiously studied the trio but particularly Eloise. What was she doing here? How was she involved? I couldn't help but notice how svelte she looked in tight blue jeans and a white turtle-necked blouse, her hair meticulously piled up on the top of her head. Eggy was doing all the talking, the others intent on his frowning face. From time to time he glanced furtively around, peering over the top of his dark glasses, ensuring no-one was in hearing distance. A waiter approached me and asked if I would like to order. I made an excuse and he wandered away. During those few seconds the trio had

263

dispersed, Crane was in sight, walking purposefully down a corridor away from Reception, no doubt to stash his package but I couldn't see the other two. I went outside, Eggy's taxi was heading for the hill leading up to the main road, there was no sign of Eloise. I presumed she was with Eggy in the taxi. I was just about to go back inside when someone called my name - and there emerging from behind a palm tree was Eloise and beyond, her parked Volkswagen Beetle. She gave me a hug and demanded to know what I was doing here before instantly complaining that I was *"all wet."* I explained about the tennis and the fact that I was about to have some lunch. *"On your own,"* she teased, *"that doesn't sound good."* It wasn't long before she had agreed to join me and I continued my mission to freshen up. When I returned to the terrace, Eloise had found a quiet, corner table with an entrancing view out to sea and the nearby line of reefs. I paused for a moment to study her, wondering what her exact connection was to Just de Vere, Eggy and Jobo Crane? The waiter approached her, she looked up and I saw her in profile. I found myself swallowing hard, she looked so innocent and happy, laughing with the waiter - no matter how she was involved, or whatever she had done, I could almost find it within me to forgive her.

We chit-chatted our way through lunch and soon were sprawled back in the comfortable chairs enjoying coffee. I had received no specific reason from Eloise why she was at the Carlton Beach Hotel today, she had brushed aside my questions - and had just laughed when I suggested she was stalking me! I had even asked point blank if she knew Eggy but she denied that she knew anyone of that

264

name, stating that she rarely used taxis. I was feeling uncomfortable and not sure where to lead the conversation.

"I have an idea," she suddenly said. *"You know I have part use of a boat?"* I nodded. *"Well I have managed to sort out the mooring business at Cambridge Beaches with that de Vere man but I could do with some help getting the boat over there. What do you say about helping me this afternoon? Might involve getting in the water, are you up for that?"* Her voice bubbled with enthusiasm.

"I thought the swimming season started after May 24th - it's still only January!" I joked.

"Yes but that's for us nesh Bermudians! Not for big strong Brits used to hard winters!" She was grinning.

"Now I know you were stalking me," I replied. *"You just want me to do your dirty work!"* We split the bill and clambered into the Beetle, Eloise gunned the poor creature up the steep drive and out on to the main road, where she turned towards Somerset.

"Where are we going?" I queried. *"Where is this boat?"*

" Still at Dockyard," she shouted, *"they put her in the water on Friday. Would you be willing to drive my car back to Mangrove Bay Wharf, you know where you saw me discussing the mooring? Then I will meet you there and you can help me. Apparently the chain is on the sea bed and it needs a buoy... it also needs a man!"* She was grinning like the proverbial Cheshire cat. *"I know you like to free dive!"*

It wasn't long before we rolled into the old naval Dockyard and were soon among a mass of boats of every colour, size and state of repair. Eloise brought her car to a halt in the shade cast by a huge hull, precariously cradled at the water's edge. Being a Sunday there were few people about, just one or two elderly folk taking a stroll through the once thriving naval base. Eloise excitedly pointed to a boat some twenty yards off shore. *"There she is, nice lines don't you think?"* I was quite taken aback, for it was much larger than I expected, a hundred times grander than Charlie's and really streamlined. It was freshly painted in light and dark blue and obviously designed for long range sailing in the open sea.

"So which half is yours?" I asked. Eloise was bent low, poking about under the half-sanded hull of the cradled boat.

"Stop being clever and come and help!" she called out, tugging a tiny wooden boat, no more than a box really, from under a tarpaulin. We carried this box down a slipway to the water's edge, together with a short paddle she had found. *"Right,"* she said pushing the boat into the water, *"I'll go and see if it will start and see you at the Wharf. I'll show you round later."* She settled into the box, knees up under her chin and I gave her a push, which put her into a spin. *"You did that on purpose,"* she cried fighting the water with the battered paddle. *"Catch hold of the rope, the idea is that you pull it back once I'm aboard."* I picked up the filthy, sodden rope and let it out as she slowly made her way towards her new possession. As she drew nearer, the boat swung round and I could read its name written in fresh new paint across its stern - *Marlborough Country*.

"What a stupid name for a boat, especially such a grand boat," I thought – and then remembered, with a start

that Marlborough was the name of my Headmistress's dead husband? Eloise was nimbly climbing up the ladder connecting a small swimming platform to the deck and I watched as she flung a leg over the rail and stood on the deck. *"I've tied the dinghy to the ladder for the moment, just till I know it will start, don't try pulling."* With that she disappeared and a full five minutes elapsed before a throaty roar indicated she had succeeded in starting the powerful inboard engine. The roar dropped to an almost silent throb and Eloise appeared again: *"That's all right then! I'll just undo the dinghy;"* she leaned down over the ladder, untied the rope and tossed it into the excuse for a dinghy. *"Haul away,"* she cried *"and please, will you put it back under the tarpaulin where I found it."* As I busied myself retrieving the dinghy, I could see Eloise was busy unfastening the ropes that attached the boat to the mooring buoys fore and aft and a few moments later she was heading out of the harbour waving gaily in my direction.

Mangrove Bay Wharf was deserted when I arrived, I reversed the Beetle and sat on a capstan admiring the sun flickering through the stately palms across the water and wondering if the oleanders, dipping their branches into the water, had been planted or were the result of seed being washed up on the shore. Either way, it was a stunning bay and the reflections of the multi-coloured plants on the shimmering water gave the sense of one huge impressionistic painting.

The sun's rays glinting on a windscreen caught my eye and sure enough Eloise was inching her way towards me and it wasn't long before her new boat was tied to the wharf

267

and I was invited aboard. She was justifiably proud of her new possession and led me down below were there were two good-sized, well-equipped cabins, a small galley, while under the bow was a further cabin with a couple of sleeping spaces. The cockpit was a maze of high tech switches and gadgets and I joked about her sailing to Miami next time she needed to visit. Following the quick tour around her new boat, Eloise produced a scrap of paper indicating that a plastic bottle some thirty yards out from the wharf was where her mooring would be. The bottle, she said, was tied to a chain resting on the seabed and nearby was a second length of chain, which needed fastening to a buoy – hence the need to me to go diving. A part of the boat's inventory was a substantial rubber raft, which we lowered into the water and while Eloise paddled out to the bobbing bottle, I stripped off to my y-fronts, climbed down the steps at the stern and gingerly lowered myself into the water. About an hour later we had *Marlborough Country* securely moored and we were seated comfortably on the deck enjoying cans of luke-warm Coca-Cola. I was wrapped in a towel drying out.

"I'm really grateful for your help," Eloise was repeating, patting my hand. *"I was desperate to get the boat to its new home and close enough so that I can use it."*

"So who is your partner, who owns the other half?" I asked. *"Why wouldn't he or she risk life and limb dragging heavy chains off the seabed?"*

Eloise grinned: *"Sorry, I was being selfish, they won't be here until next month and I wanted to use it! My friend lives in Florida and wants a boat to use when he visits here, which he does several times a year.*"

"*Must have plenty of money,*" I commented.

"*He does - it was his idea. Really it's his boat but he wants me to look after it!*" she admitted.

"*They always say it is better to have a friend that owns a boat, rather than own one yourself. Boats are holes you pour money into!*" I said philosophically! "*By the way, who gave the boat its name?*"

"*I did,*" replied Eloise, giving me a very straight look!

"*I know that you are dead against people smoking, so why advertise cigarettes?*" I said, crushing the empty coke can.

"*The cigarettes are spelled differently; M a r l b o r o,*" she said, spelling out each letter and grinning widely.

"*Maybe,*" I agreed, "*but how many people would notice the difference? They would all think... fags! So why Marlborough, which ever way you spell it?*"

Eloise's looked thoughtful as she gazed down at my feet. Slowly, she tilted her striking face until her eyes met mine. "*It was my father's name,*" she said quietly "*and the sea was his home, his country. He was a bit like,*" she struggled for a metaphor. "*He was like a penguin, awkward on the land, I don't mean walking or anything... just uncomfortable... but get him on the water and he was absolutely in his element.*" Eloise was gazing unseeingly across the bay and I watched as a single tear oozed over an eyelid and slide rapidly down her cheek.

269

"*Marlborough, is an uncommon name,*" I said quietly. "*Is he the same Marlborough who was married to Evelyn Harding, our illustrious headmistress?*"

"*One and the same,*" Eloise replied in a flat monotone. "*But that's my problem, not yours.*" She clambered to her feet: "*Right let's get things straightened out here, then we can go.*"

"*Wait!*" I caught her hand. "*Please sit down and finish the story. I need to know.*"

Eloise reluctantly sank back onto the seat: "*Nothing to tell. My mother died when I was fourteen. My father brought me up on his own and we were inseparable, until I went to College in the States. Sometime during the four years I was away he met... her... and eventually they married.*" Eloise paused and drew breath: "*He still used to take me fishing and whatnot and it was plain to see that she resented every minute he spent with me. This made me mad and one day we had a real big row, ending with me walking out... and two days later my Dad disappeared, presumed drowned and I am burdened with guilt knowing he died thinking that I hated him. How could I hate him? He meant everything to me!*" Eloise was quietly sobbing and I moved and wrapped a comforting arm around her shoulders.

"*He knew you didn't hate him, even if you said you did.*" I whispered. "*He would know it was just something said in the heat of the moment, not really meant. You don't have to worry about that, we all say things we don't mean to the one's we love most! Believe me, the scars eventually heal*" Eloise raised her head, kissed me quickly on the lips, leapt to her feet and busied herself clearing up. Soon we

270

were paddling the small dinghy back to shore, having ensured the boat was securely moored and the cabin door locked.

On the beach we stood side by side admiring our handiwork. *"Lovely boat,"* I said. *"You'll have lots of fun with Marlborough Country."*

"Yes, " responded Eloise, *"Of that I'm sure."* Eloise decided she didn't want to risk leaving the dinghy on the beach and so we strapped it onto the roof of the Beetle, where it overhung, mushroom-like.

"You'll have to drive slowly," I said, *"or the Beetle will take off!"* Eloise took me home and we parted with a promise that she would take me out for a spin *"one day soon!"*

That night as I struggled to sleep my mind kept returning to Eloise's unexpected appearance at the hotel and the fun time we had later; her obvious love for her father and dislike of Evelyn Harding.   On the surface she was a loveable, sensitive woman, so why did she tell me an outright lie about not knowing Eggy?

*

I couldn't believe that a whole weekend had elapsed without me catching sight of either Dilly or Karl, so Monday after school, I knocked on their door and Pearl appeared. *"How's you Mom?"* I asked.   Before Pearl could say anything, Dilly called out from the kitchen inviting me in. She was standing at the kitchen table, hands covered in flour, while the two younger girls were shaping cake mixture and scraping it onto a baking tin, their faces screwed up in concentration. Dilly's hair was scraped back from her face, emphasising her fine, though gaunt features.

"As you can see, I'm okay again:" she flashed me a smile. *"And you, how's you - and where's you been man?"* Pearl offered to make me coffee and Dilly jokingly scolded her about me being English and therefore wanting tea not coffee!

I was halfway through a mug of tea when the door was flung open and the huge figure of Karl filled the doorway. The children shouted their welcome and the two younger ones rushed to throw their arms around him, leaving floury fingerprints on his working jeans. I stood and he wrung my hand. *"No welcome from you Miss Pearl?"* he said in a slightly offended tone.

She was buried in a book but she put it aside and reached up her cheek for a kiss. *"You had a good day Daddy?"* she murmured. After several minutes I excused myself saying I had only popped in to check up how Dilly was, after Friday's scare. Again she repeated that she was fine and walked me to the door. Outside she whispered: *"We need to talk, perhaps tomorrow."* I nodded and we parted. As I fumbled my way through the darkness, I couldn't help but feel amazed how Dilly's health was so up and down. On Friday I had feared for the worst, today she looked so much better. And what did she want to talk about?

*

I didn't see Dilly the next day as she had suggested; when I arrived home from school, the girls told me their mother was in bed again. Later I saw Karl and he confirmed Dilly was unwell and unable to keep any food down.

Imagine my surprise when on Wednesday, as darkness was falling, she was collecting washing from the line strung between two trees. I parked my bike and went to talk to her. She shrugged off my enquiries about her health and immediately began whispering that Karl was not acting normally and he must be 'up to something.' She urged me to try and find out, saying she would be out the following evening at the Bermudiana Hotel with Marsha.

So Thursday evening, when I thought the girls would be in bed I gently knocked on Karl's door. I hissed at him that I needed to speak to him and suggested he join me on my porch, so as not to disturb the girls. At first he objected but in the end he came, armed with two cans of beer. *"Dilly's worried about you again,"* I said. *"She says you are - up to something, to use her words!"*

"God...that woman reads my mind," hissed Karl, frustration edging his tone. *"She was in no fit state to go out tonight... but no matter what I said, she still went!"* He took a long swig from the beer can.

"So what do they want you to do?" I fished.

"Go to that store boat in Red Hole to do some work." He muttered.

"What kind of work," I quizzed.

"He didn't tell me. But he did say...just be there, or your wife won't be home when you next come home from work... bastards!" he spat.

"When?" I asked, ignoring the worrying threat. *"When do you have to go to Red Hole?"*

273

"Tomorrow, Friday. I gotta stand on the quay at Albouy's Point and someone will pick me up. You know Albouy's in Hamilton? Said Karl.

"Yes, I know Albouy's Point," I replied. We were sitting in the dark, serenaded by the monotonous whistling of a million tree frogs. *"What time is your appointment?"* I continued.

"Straight after work - at five thirty." I couldn't see Karl's face but I could imagine how screwed up he was by the outline of his hunched body. Before I could add anything more he opened his heart about how worried he was about Dilly and how he felt she was gradually slipping away. I did my best to reassure him but he was not in the mood to be reassured and with a muttered farewell he stumbled off towards his front door. I was chilly, despite the heavy sweater and made my way inside for an early night and many questions to wrestle with.

Besides grappling with the issues Karl's predicament raised, I had a less serious one to resolve. Earlier in the week I had telephoned Wilber Marshall and asked if I could take *Crazy Dream* out at the weekend. He had said he was delighted and reminded me that I had no need to ask. My issue was whom I should ask to crew? My first thought was to ask Eloise but my nagging concerns about her connections with Just de Vere and her lies about Eggy had me worried. A counter-argument was to use the opportunity to confront her with my fears but that might be difficult without spilling the beans about the connection to Karl. In the end I decided to ask Marsha and left a message on her answering machine, suggesting she call me early on Saturday and we could set off about eleven o'clock. In fact she called me before I left for school early on Friday morning, expressing her delight and I explained we should meet at Foot of the Lane. She offered to bring a picnic lunch, I gratefully accepted and said I would bring drinks.

Friday's lessons had gone particularly well, the children were keen and the day just flew. I left early, collected my camera and binoculars and set off towards the capital. I wasn't really sure why, I just felt an urge to watch what happened and perhaps get some photographs of the people arriving at *Georgie Girl*, the boat where Karl was being forced to work.

I made my way along Harbour Road admiring how the sinking sun was illuminating the city, across the bay. Finding a suitable spot I stopped and sat on the wall. I pulled the binoculars from the rucksack, rested elbows on knees and focussed on an old boat, which I assumed was Georgie Girl, though I couldn't see a name. I could clearly see a motorboat tied alongside but no sign of movement anywhere. I glanced at my wristwatch, it was only five o'clock, too soon for Karl to be arriving. A police car drove slowly by, travelling towards the city from Somerset. I decided to try and get a bit closer, so jumped off the wall and astride my bike. I moved about fifty yards and stopped where I thought I might have a clearer view. I clambered onto the wall again but before I could raise the binoculars to my eyes, I became aware that a police car had pulled up behind my bike, possibly the same one that had trawled by in the other direction a few moments earlier. I watched as two policemen climbed out, the driver was a huge white guy with massive thighs bursting out of his uniform navy shorts. He looked a real thug, who would have been more at home on the other side of the law. His dark sunglasses failed to hide the vicious scowl, his belly indicating far too many free beers. The young policeman who climbed out of the passenger seat was, in contrast, jet black, athletic and all smiles.

"Good afternoon sir," he called out. *"Are you bird-watching? Too soon for Longtails!"* I didn't have time to respond before he continued: *"Just need to check your papers please sir. There's been a bit of trouble at one of the residences along here. Just a formality. Have you seen anything suspicious?"* I jumped down off the wall and started fumbling in my shirt pocket, hoping I had remembered to bring my license and bike papers, mumbling that I had seen nothing abnormal. The policeman indicated that I should move towards the car, the thug was behind me. I glanced round to see he was fiddling with the fastener on my saddlebag. *"Your papers please sir!"* the young policeman said, displaying a perfect set of gleaming white teeth. I handed them over: *"So Mr Cross, Mr Jack Cross, Longbay Lane."* He leaned through the window of the car and picked up a microphone. He repeated my name, license number plate and we waited. I shuffled about, feeling very uncomfortable, the thug was still rifling about in my saddlebag. *"That's fine Sir, everything in order. Sorry to have bothered you but you know how it is, have to check everyone in the area, when there's a problem."* He saw me looking anxiously at the other man. *"It's okay sir, my*

276

colleague is just checking to see if you have any of the items reported stolen - just a formality."

At that moment the thug turned towards us and held up a brown paper package about the size of a paperback book. *"Is this what I think it is sir,"* he glared through his dark glasses but the hint of a smile played round his mouth.

"I've no idea what it is," I blustered. *"Nothing to do with me!"*

"Well then, let's have a little look. Not a birthday present for one of your friends?" He asked, as he laid the packet on the saddle of my bike and took out a small penknife from his pocket. After slowly and carefully opening the blade, he meticulously sliced through the paper to display a neat cardboard box. With a snarling glance at me, he lifted the lid. It was full of white powder. *"Nasty!"* he growled. *"Heroin...do you know what this stuff does to people? Get in the car, you have a lot of questions to answer."* The next few moments were a blur of movement, as they snapped on handcuffs and forced me into the back of the police car, while all the time I was protesting my innocence. One of them asked for the bike's key and said a police van would pick my bike up later, as evidence. As we headed towards town, I was in turmoil; this was a set up by the thug but why? As we drove toward Hamilton I had plenty of time to think. Karl had only talked about cannabis never heroin. Surely he hadn't lied or perhaps he didn't know what stuff he helped collect? I felt sure it had been planted by the driver sitting in front of me. The man whose huge bulk was blocking out any view to the front, he must have put the package in my bag.

277

Before I knew it, we were pulling up at what I later discovered was the Prospect Police Headquarters. I was bundled out of the car and into a reception area. Three scruffy black men were sprawled on some benches and an elderly policeman behind a high counter was peering at a logbook.

"*What have we here?*" he said gazing at the two men who had brought me in.

"*Routine check Sarge and we found an interesting package in the bag on his bike,*" said the thug, placing the package on the counter. The Sergeant grunted.

"*Name?*" he asked. The young policeman handed over my papers and the sergeant began to meticulously copy details into his book. My head was still spinning when some ten minutes later I was led down a dismal corridor and pushed into a cell. The policeman, whom I thought looked more like he belonged to the Mafia, rather than law and order, unlocked the handcuffs and thrust me away from the door.

"*The Inspector will be along later for a chat,*" he grinned; "*mean-while you can make some new friends.*" He laughed and disappeared from sight. It was only then that I realised that I was sharing a cell with three other men. Two appeared to be sleeping, the third looked resigned to the fact that he was locked up, whereas I was furious. So furious, I knew I was not thinking rationally. How could this have happened? Why? If the thug said he found the heroin in my bag, it would be just his word against mine, who was going to believe me? I found myself clutching the bars, staring out into the dimly lit corridor. I automatically looked at my

278

wrist, wondering what the time was, before remembering that my watch, wallet, binoculars and camera had been taken from me.

"Sit down man, you're making the place look untidy!" I heard one of the men say. *"Come on sit down, fretting don't help! Not good for the blood pressure."* I turned round to look at the speaker; he was aged about sixty, unshaven, straggly grey hair but quite tidily dressed in baggy trousers and Hawaiian style shirt, the other two men were curled up on benches.

"Come and sit here," said the old man, patting the bench, *"you need to save your energy."*

With a huge exhalation of breath, I flopped alongside the man. *"How long do they keep you here?"* I asked. *"How long have you been here?"*

"I think introductions come first - before the questions," said my new companion patiently. *"My name is Jeremiah, and who might you be?"*

"Jack," I responded without enthusiasm; *"Jack Cross."*

"Well Jack Cross, I can hear you are an Englishman, I must presume a tourist who decided to rob a bank," he chuckled. *"Not a good idea!"*

"It's ridiculous," I said. *" Crazy! I haven't done anything wrong. I've been set up!"*

The old man held up his hand: *"Shush, not too loud, better not to wake the sleeping beauties… they can be a bit difficult when they're awake. So you're innocent of the crime - it's what we all say - but nobody listens."* I glanced at our two sleeping companions, one was quietly snoring, the

279

other twitching in his sleep - doubtless fighting with his conscience.

"So which hotel are you staying in?" asked Jeremiah, making conversation. I explained that I was a resident and teaching in Somerset. Jeremiah nodded wisely and waxed lyrically about Somerset but I was not in the mood and flopped forward, head in hands.

"I need to telephone someone and explain what's happened," I said suddenly, jumping to my feet.

Jeremiah tugged on my arm: *"Sit down man, they'll let you call after you've been interviewed - not before!"* I allowed myself to be pulled back on to the bench.

"Have you been interviewed yet?" I enquired.

"Oh yes, I've been interviewed," he chuckled. *"They'll send me home soon. One big mistake, just like you said - they'll send the chauffer soon."*

There was no window in the cell, which looked like something out of the Victorian era, except for the single fluorescent strip lamp in the middle of the ceiling and on the wall a battered old air-conditioning unit rattling inefficiently, as if in its last throes. The grubby, graffitied walls, once white, contributed to the utterly depressing scene. Jeremiah droned on but I was not listening. Eventually tired of inaction, I went to the bars and shouted. Jeremiah shushed me and told me I was wasting my time, while casting glances at the recumbent figures. However my shouts did produce a reaction and the young black policeman who had arrested me wandered down the corridor.

"How can I help?" he said politely.

"*I need to make a telephone call.*" I almost shouted. Before I could say more he interrupted and said that he and his colleague had almost completed their report, after which the Inspector would need to read it and then discuss it with me. I demanded to know how long this would take and was told about half an hour. At this Jeremiah laughed out loud and burst into a paroxysm of coughing. I continued to protest but to no avail, the policeman walked away, while I continued to shout after him, *that this was just not good enough.*

After several circuits of the tiny cell I sat again alongside Jeremiah. One of the other men was now sitting up, eyes wide open but for all intents and purposes looking as if he was still asleep.

Exasperated, I asked Jeremiah how long it was since he was interviewed. "*I really don't know*," he replied. "*Time is like the sea, it just keeps rolling by! Don't worry about it, sit back and imagine you are lying on Horseshoe beach listening to the waves;*" he shut his eyes, pulled up his feet and gently rocked.

The other man was now on his feet and pacing around the tiny cell like a caged tiger. Suddenly he stopped leaned against the bars and stared at me, as if it was the first time he realised that I was there. He caught my eye, walked towards me and squeezed himself next to me on the bench. I tried to ease away but dozing Jeremiah was on the edge, his toes no doubt being washed by the gently lapping tide.

The man suddenly placed his hand on my naked knee and started caressing my thigh. I firmly grasped his hand and lifted it away. As soon as I released his hand it was back again trying to slide under my shorts. I stood and walked towards the bars only to find he was also on his feet, an indescribably lewd expression contorting his drug-worn features. He slowly advanced towards me until suddenly, without warning one hand went for my throat the other for my groin. His nails were digging into my throat and I was gasping for breath, as I struggled to free myself. I had just managed to prise his hand from my throat when without warning he head butted me and an explosion of shooting stars and excruciating pain caused me to drop to my knees, momentarily blinded. I heard a laugh, as I struggled to sit up. He was gazing down at me, his eyes full of hatred: *"White trash!"* he spat. The other man was now on his feet, dancing around the tiny cell like a boxer circling his imaginary quarry. I looked round, shaking the blood and tears from my eyes. Jeremiah was still on the bench, eyes shut, rocking backwards and forwards. Fortunately I guessed what was coming and as the dancing man lashed out at me with his foot, I was ready for him, grabbed it and pulled. He fell backwards cracked his head on the bench, and lay moaning. The other man moved behind me and before I could see what he was doing he kicked me in the kidneys, hissing obscenities and knocking all the breath out me. I rolled across the floor and as he moved in aiming a kick at my head I managed to grab his foot and twisted. He fought with the air to maintain his balance but I pulled even harder and he fell back, cracking his head on the wall before slumping to the floor unconscious. I struggled to my feet wiping the mess from my face, shouting for help. I glanced at Jeremiah but his eyes were tight shut, he was still at the

282

beach, soaking his toes and listening to the waves caressing the shore.

The young policeman appeared again, took one look at my face, the moaning men on the floor and unlocked the door. He led me into an empty cell and insisted I sit while he fetched a first-aid kit. After a few moments he returned with a bowl of water that he placed on the bench alongside me. Thrusting a sponge into my hand he told me to clean myself up. *"What happened?"* he asked, almost kindly, after I had removed the worst of the blood.

"Those two set about me without provocation or warning," I replied.

"Now why would they do that, I wonder," he said.

"Because I stopped one of them sticking his hand up my shorts and reaching for my balls," I hissed.

"Ah... that sounds like our Abraham," he said quietly. *"Not cooperating would really upset our Abraham."*

I lost track of time but it was probably about two hours later when I was collected, taken to the office where the duty inspector sat behind an impressive cedar desk, littered with files and loose papers. His eyes didn't leave the document he was reading, as the young policeman wheeled me into the gloomy room. We stood before his desk, like naughty school children before the headmaster, awaiting our punishment. *"All right constable, you can go,"* the inspector suddenly said, without looking up. The young policeman muttered a polite *"Sir"* and left.

"So Mr Cross, you were caught with 400 grams of heroin in the saddlebag of your bike. What were you planning to do with it?" He said sternly.

283

"I knew nothing about it until your men stopped me on Harbour Road, saying there had been a robbery in the area and they wanted to check my papers and look in my saddle bag for stolen items." I replied, desperately trying to keep my composure, when all the time I wanted to scream at him that I had been framed.

"Don't waste my time Mr Cross - the truth if you don't mind." His beady eyes pierced mine and he stuck out his jaw in a belligerent manner. *"The truth."*

"The truth, the truth is that your man planted the heroin in my bag, I'm positive it was not there when I set out from home." My voice was louder, despite my efforts at control.

"You've been reading too many cheap detective novels, policemen don't go round implicating innocent people. And by the way, why have you got sticking plaster all across your face?" he asked, as if noticing for the first time.

"I was put in a cell with three other men and two of them attacked me - for no reason at all!" I could feel myself shaking.

"Did you provoke them?" he said showing more interest in the report before him than my answer.

"Yes I provoked one of them by stopping him sexually abusing me!" I was almost shouting.

The inspector grunted, running his finger round the inside of his collar: *"You'll soon get used to that after a few days in Casemates! You told my officer that you are a teacher."*

"Yes, I'm a teacher. A teacher in Somerset. I try to protect children from drugs and alcohol by telling them about all the problems. I don't use them or deal in them. It's ridiculous, it's against everything I stand for! I even asked one of your officers if he would come and talk to the children......Stephen Henderson...ask him, he'll tell you."

"Then how did this heroin get into your bag?" He was staring at me again, his mouth clamped shut.

"I really don't know, I'm positive the package was not there when I left home, I put my binoculars in the bag, I would have seen it - I can only think your officer wanted to cause trouble." I was shaking again with frustration, but choosing my words carefully, I didn't want to antagonise this man.

"Why would anyone want to get you into trouble Mr Cross?" said the inspector, his eyes back to the report. *"Who would want to have you locked up for a good many years?"*

"I have no idea," I replied. *"I've only been here since last August, I hardly know anyone."*

"Well Mr Cross, we'll have to keep you here for the night while we make further enquiries. Is there any one you would like to call?" I slumped and rested my hands on the desk.

"You're going to keep me locked up? It's just so ridiculous," again I was shaking with pent up frustration. *"Yes, I would like to make a call, I was supposed to be taking a friend out sailing tomorrow."*

"So you have a sailing boat do you Mr Cross?" asked the inspector tearing his eyes from the report.

285

"No, it belongs to a friend, Wilber Marshall, he lets me use it." I replied.

The inspector suddenly sat bolt upright, as if he had been poked with a pin, he started to speak but thought better of it: *"There is a phone at reception that you can use, one call, that's all."* He pressed a buzzer and the young black policeman who had patched me up came in. *"Mr Cross is going to make a call, after which he will be our guest, see that he is made comfortable for the night."* He began shuffling papers again and I was ushered out into the lobby.

"Do you know the number Mr Cross?" asked the policeman, indicating a phone hanging on the wall.

"No, it's in my wallet," I replied. The policeman went over to the desk sergeant and after a few moments returned with my wallet. I found Marsha's business card and rang the number she had written on the back. I hadn't expected her to pick up and she didn't, my heart sank. I tried again and her answering machine cut in with Marsha's lilting voice suggesting leaving a message. I don't know what I actually said but no doubt something about being unable to take her sailing because I was locked up.

I was led back down the same dim corridor and down another before being ushered into a cell containing a chair and single bed pushed up against a wall with a folded sheet and a towel laid out on the pillow.

"Someone will bring you something to eat in the next hour or so, and there's a latrine just round the corner there. Good night Mr Cross, I'm going off duty now." The young policeman clanged the door shut and turned the key.

As he started to move away I called out: *"Constable, what's your name? We've seen such a lot of each other today and I'd like to know your name."*

"Simmons," he called over his shoulder, *"one of the thousands of Simmons on this island."* He laughed.

"And your colleague," I called after him.

"Truelove," he chuckled, " *Constable Truelove."* I could still hear him chuckling to himself, as he disappeared from sight.

I dropped onto the bed, head in hands and wondered whether or not I should have called Wilber Marshall instead of Marsha. I presumed Wilber had connections but Marsha was a lawyer I argued. I supposed that I could ask her to contact him, I just had to be patient and see what she recommended. A sense of helplessness was spreading through my whole being that was hard to dispel.

I have no idea how long I sat there lamenting my situation; when my musings were disturbed by an elderly policeman carrying a tray holding a plate of chicken and rice together with a glass of water. I asked him what time it was and learned it was seven o'clock. Half an hour later he returned to retrieve the tray - time was dragging, my head hurting, frustration building.

It was probably about nine o'clock when I became aware of voices in the corridor, I was stretched out on the bed dozing but when I heard the key in the lock I swung my feet to the floor. My heart thumped as Marsha stepped into the cell, the policeman locked the door behind her. I leapt up and hugged her, thanking her profusely for coming, my spirits lifted at the sight of a familiar face - a beautiful familiar face.

She told me to sit and pulled up a chair. *"I have read the report,"* she said, peering into her handbag; *"so I know what the charge is likely to be. I'm afraid it doesn't look good. What an earth were you thinking about?"* Before I could utter an indignant response, she looked at me for the first time. *"My God, what happened to your nose?"* She leaned towards me for a closer look before getting to her feet and calling out. The elderly policeman opened the door at the end of the corridor. *"Get me a bowl of water, a cloth and a first aid kit;"* she ordered. The policeman muttered and disappeared. *"Tell me what happened, it looks terrible."*

I had finished explaining about the attack, when the policeman returned and unlocked the cell door. Marsha took the bowl from him indicating the first-aid kit should be placed on the bed. *"Someone should have called the doctor to look at this,"* she said authoritively, the policeman's response was a non-committal grunt, as he exited, relocking the door. Marsha eased off the blood-soaked plaster and began bathing my face with the cloth. I examined her face a few inches from mine, her lips were pursed with concentration, a pained expression causing a frown. I looked into her eyes; for a second she caught and held my gaze and I realised they were moist! She cares, I thought, she really cares!

Having cleaned my nose and forehead she smeared a salve before cutting pieces of plaster and expertly covering my wounds. *"Looks like you have done this kind of thing before,"* I whispered. She grunted but said nothing. *"You*

288

don't really think I was peddling heroin?" I said quietly. *"I've been framed - probably by a Constable named Truelove or by someone who put him up to it."*

"Why would he do that?" she asked checking her handiwork and placing the roll of tape and scissors back in the first-aid bag. *"Why would this Constable Truelove want you locked up?"* she repeated.

"Well obviously I've never met him before - so it has to be someone else who's paid him to get me in trouble," I said.

"Yes, okay but why?" she said.

I shrugged my shoulders helplessly; *"That's what I need to find out,"* I said determinedly.

Before she left, Marsha apologised saying that she could not meet with a judge until Monday morning to organise bail. *"It's a ploy the police often use,"* she said, *"arrest someone on a Friday and they are locked up until Monday."*

*

I slept fitfully Saturday night, occasionally awoken by shouting as drunks or petty criminals were pushed protesting into cells in the adjacent corridor. Breakfast came and went, delivered by a young policeman I had not seen before. From time to time I stalked up and down the tiny room like the proverbial caged animal, my head spinning, as I tried to work out who was behind my arrest. Obviously it had to do with Karl but why had I been targeted? Who knew Karl had shared his problems with me? He wouldn't tell anyone - and I certainly hadn't. Perhaps the policemen had seen me spying on Georgie Girl, though that wasn't very

289

likely. I supposed I was going to have to share this information with Marsha, which was awkward seeing she was Dilly's friend. I tried doing a few push-ups in the hope the physical exertion might clear my mind. It didn't help and breathing heavily I flopped back on the bed and began to work through minute by minute the events of the last few weeks leading up to yesterday afternoon.

Later, the same young policeman brought me a cup of coffee and Saturday's Royal Gazette. The paper didn't take long to read and the crossword even less to complete. Time was really dragging, frustration again began to build. More push-ups and a determined but failed attempt to sleep. Lunch appeared - an unappetising plate of chicken and chips, accompanied by an apple and a glass of water. I barely looked up at the noise of the cell door being unlocked, assuming my gaoler was collecting my lunch tray. Then behind him I saw the figure of Marsha. The policeman took the tray and locked us in. I hugged her and was slow to let go. She looked really concerned, as she asked how I was and the state of my nose. I made a joke and we laughed, as she sat on the chair and I settled on the bed. *"I've brought you some reading matter,"* she said digging into her bag and producing a couple of magazines and a Sunday Times. I thanked her profusely and complained about time dragging.

"We should have been out sailing in the Sound today," I frowned. She nodded, her thick black hair swirling around her shoulders. *"I've never seen you with your hair down,"* I said. She ignored my comment and told me that perhaps it was as well we didn't go sailing, as the weather was grey and dull.

"Have you had any more thoughts about who would want to get you into trouble?" asked Marsha.

"None," I replied, *"I'm baffled!"* I was about to launch into the saga of Karl's involvement with drugs but thought better of it. *"I'm certain that package of heroin was not in my saddlebag when I left home because I stuffed my binoculars in the bag and would have seen it. So that leaves the policeman who said he found the package. The other policeman, Simmons, made me go towards the police car with my back towards Truelove. He opened my bag supposedly looking for loot from a nearby house-breaking... but I told you all this before."*

Marsha suddenly reached out across the narrow space between us and grasped my hand: *"I've been checking,"* she whispered. *"No burglaries or thefts of any sort were reported Friday night, nor Saturday, in Paget nor near the Harbour Road area."*

I squeezed her hand. *"That proves it,"* I said excitedly. *"I told you it was a set up!"*

"But..." interrupted Marsha, *"it's still your word against theirs and there's two of them."* My shoulders slumped. *"We're back to the question of who wanted to get you arrested?"* said Marsha. *"You must have upset someone really badly for them to go to all this trouble?"* She was still holding my hand. *"By the way, what were you doing on Harbour Road?"* She dropped my hand. *"Who were you planning to meet?"*

"I wasn't planning to meet anyone," I blustered. *"I just went for a ride... to check Crazy Dream was okay before*

our trip." I crossed my fingers hoping against eternal damnation, as the lie slipped glibly from my lips.

"*How would these policemen know where to find you? How could they know you would be out on your bike? Do you think they followed you from Somerset?*" she surmised.

I shook my head but then a light suddenly dawned, a distant memory sparked by Marsha's comment. "*You know, I may have been!*" I said frowning.

"*Been what?*" questioned Marsha.

"*Followed! There was a police car outside the Hitching Post super-market on Middle Road as I rode past. I didn't see who was in it but it could have been those two.*" I was puzzled.

"*Sounds too much of a coincidence to me,*" said Marsha.

"*You're right,*" I agreed. "*Unless whoever wanted me arrested wasn't in a hurry and told the two policemen to keep an eye out and wait for the right moment.*" I wasn't convinced with my own theory and sighed deeply.

After a further half hour Marsha excused herself, saying she would return Monday morning, as soon as she had obtained the permission to have me released on bail. We hugged and she called out down the corridor to be let out. As she followed the policeman down the gloomy corridor, she called out: "*I'll see you in the morning Mr Cross, sleep well.*" I didn't sleep well but tossed and turned on the narrow bed, alternating between nightmares and brief periods of unconsciousness.

*

I was already awake and propped, hunched on the bed reading one of the magazines, that Marsha had brought, when breakfast arrived – another new face! The young, grinning black policeman, in answer to my question, said he was from Barbados. We got no further than that, as an angry shout from the desk-sergeant summoned him away.

Marsha arrived just after ten o'clock; apologising she was late, complaining that the judge had been busy and she had to wait to see him. Formalities were quite soon completed and my belongings were returned. I asked about my bike and the policeman who had brought me breakfast was ordered to show me where it was. Marsha and I followed him outside and into the bright sunlight of perfect Bermuda day. *"What about a coffee somewhere?"* I asked, the sun hurting my eyes.

"Sorry but I'm already late for an appointment and I'm tied up all day." She replied, pulling a face.

"Oh my God!" I said, a sudden thought hitting me. *"It never entered my head, I'm supposed to be in school! Mrs H. will be having a fit!"* I hugged Marsha again and thanked her profusely for all her help and she promised to telephone later that evening. And so we parted, Marsha towards a waiting taxi, while I sped off down the hill and towards Somerset and a hatful of explanations.

Riding back along Harbour Road I pondered on what I would say to Mrs Harding. A string of explanations were formulated, each more preposterous than the former, until at last I decided it had to be the truth. Presumably at some stage I would be summoned to court and then everyone would know anyway, so better the truth.

293

Mrs Harding stared in disbelief as I sat opposite in her tiny office: *"I swear Mrs Harding I knew absolutely nothing about the package being in my saddlebag. I was out for a ride to take photographs and relax after a tough week. I stopped to admire the view of Hamilton and this police car pulled up and said there had been a robbery and they needed to search my bag - and there was the package! I suppose it is someone's idea of a sick joke."* I babbled on for some moments while Mrs Harding sat immobile and speechless, peering into my eyes. *"I was only allowed one call and I spoke to a lawyer but forgot to ask her to inform you - I'm really sorry!"*

At last she broke her silence. *"It seems to me Mr Cross that missing a morning of teaching is the least of your worries."* She said nothing more on the matter but suggested I go to my class and take over the reins from one of my colleagues who was reluctantly baby-sitting when she needed to be marking books.

I left school early that afternoon, needing to get home to shower and change the clothes I'd worn for the last two days. Later, feeling a new man I slumped on the porch chair with a mug of tea. I'd hardly taken a sip when Dilly appeared and wandered over.

"Ain't seen you for a couple of days," she said with a straight face. *"Oh my God, what happened to you?"*

"Ran into a door," I lied. *"Would you like some tea? Or a cup of coffee?"* I rose to my feet and kissed her cheek.

"Sit back down," she said putting a hand on my arm: *"My that looks sore - And no, I'm good."* She looked

haggard again I thought, as she perched on the edge of my chair. *"You had a good weekend?"*

"No, not particularly;" I said, thinking that was the understatement of the year.

"You had visitors on Saturday," Dilly said looking down at me. *"They let themselves into your place through the front door."* I started and placed the mug of tea on the floor.

"You're joking!" I was incredulous. *"What sort of visitors? I didn't see any sign of anyone having been inside - the door wasn't forced!"*

"Well, they had no uniforms but I could smell, they was police."

"Are you sure?" I questioned, though upon reflection, I wasn't surprised.

"Yup, I'm sure. Have you been a bad boy?" she asked. Without stopping to consider the consequences it all came pouring out and as the tale expanded, Dilly's eyes grew wider, her frown deeper, her mouth inched wider, as her jaw dropped towards the floor. She slid from the arm of the chair onto my knee, reached out and held my hand. She weighed nothing. I expounded my theory of being framed, she was silent but pursed her lips and ground her teeth, her eyes narrowing to slits until they resembled an angry tiger out for blood.

When there was no more to relate, she squeezed my hand and shuffled to her feet. Stretching upright, she turned, arms akimbo and gazed at me - she still hadn't said a word. I was waiting for a reaction, an opinion, something. *"Finish your tea, I need to think!*" she broke off the intense gaze, spun on her heel and headed for her front door.

I wasn't surprised when Karl rapped on my door later that evening, opened it and called out. He could only have been home from work a few minutes but no doubt Dilly had been talking. I pulled a couple of beers from the fridge and offered him one, as I flopped in a chair.

Karl paced round the room, his beer unopened: *"I told you not to get involved... I told you... I told you,"* he hissed.

"Who could know?" I responded *"and anyway I haven't done anything except listen to what you had to say."*

"You must have said something to someone," he said accusingly, *"even if you didn't mean to."*

"I haven't said a word," I protested, thinking of Dilly but saying nothing.

Eventually Karl stopped pacing, sank onto the couch and opened his beer. *"Tell me what happened, Dilly only gave me a part of the picture."*

I recounted my experiences from the moment I stopped on Harbour Road until Marsha produced the bail documents. Like his wife before him, Karl said nothing but his face spoke volumes. No sooner had I finished when Karl clambered to his feet, placed the empty beer can on the table and said:

"I was sent round to fetch you to come and eat - Dilly's been cooking!" It would have been pointless to argue, so I followed him out into the dusk, across the patch of grass that separated our doors and into the bright kitchen where the girls were seated around the table. I was warmly welcomed

296

and regaled with tales of the school day, their warmth and enthusiasm lifting my spirits helping to dim the memories of the distressing weekend.

*

Tuesday morning dawned chilly and damp, the combination of cold and high humidity distinctly unpleasant. I arrived at school early, I had a pile of books to mark but as I passed Mrs Harding's door she looked up and called me in.

"Obviously you are aware that the charges against you are extremely serious," she began; *"and no doubt considered even worse due to your position as a teacher, a role model for the children in your care. I spoke with the Director of Education and he would like to see you. I've made arrangements for someone else to teach your class. So go to the Education Department and ask for the Director, he said he would be available until ten-thirty."* Her tone was harsh, her face flushed with mistrust.

I began to object, realised it was useless and sank onto a chair head in hands. *"Surely you believe me."* I pleaded. *"I've been set up... framed but can't for the life of me imagine why or by whom!"* I was close to tears.

"Mr Cross," interrupted Mrs Harding, I noted with alarm, she no longer used my first name. *"I haven't known you long enough to make a judgement whether you are capable of the crime or not."* I glanced up at her face, it was as if I was looking at a different person from the woman who had met me at the airport. Her eyes were ice-pools, her expression damning. *"I suggest that you get off quickly to Hamilton,"* she said in flat monotone. *"The sooner you see the Director, the sooner your future will be decided."*

297

I left the Headmistress's office close to despair, it hadn't occurred to me that I could lose my job; surely I was innocent until proved guilty?

*

The ride to Hamilton was long and tedious, twenty miles per hour when you are travelling towards your destiny would test anyone's patience. I only had a rough idea where the Education Department offices were and had to ask before I eventually found them. I told the girl at reception my name and from her reaction it was obvious I was expected.

I had met the Director at the interview in London and remembered being surprised that he undertook the job of conducting interviews himself. He seemed a tough character and had brought me back to earth when I was gazing at a tourist poster of Bermuda's beaches and turquoise sea during a lull in the questioning. *"When you're in the classroom you could be anywhere,"* he had boomed in a hard north-country accent that I couldn't place. *"I need teachers who care about kids - not sunning themselves on the beach."*

I found my way to the inner sanctum where a secretary told me to take a seat outside the Director's room. I sat, despondent, again feeling like a naughty child waiting to see the headmaster and fearing the worst. I only had to wait about five minutes before a bell rang and the secretary nodded for me to go in.

*

Lying on my bed that night I continually replayed the meeting over in my head - it had probably lasted no more than five minutes! When I entered the room the Director remained seated behind a massive cedar desk, astonishing because it was totally uncluttered. I had expected the man to be hidden behind skyscrapers of documents but no; the desk was clear except for a single report consisting of half dozen pages. I wondered where he kept the skyscrapers?

I was told to sit and in the hard no-nonsense voice that I remembered, he waved the report at me and said that because I was the subject of a police enquiry, he had no alternative but to suspend me until the matter had been to court and a verdict reached. He ended by saying that we would meet again after the matter had been concluded. He wished me Good Day and that was that. I had tried to explain but he had no interest, just held up his hand repeated Good Day and had pointed towards the door.

Chapter 7

February, 1973

The following days slithered slowly by; the wet, windy weather matching my dismal mood. I'm sure if the police had not been holding my passport, I would have fled. The lack of the daily routine of work and the joyful company of the kids left an emptiness I cannot properly describe - my raison - d'etre deserted me.

I scrawled pages of notes and lists of names in an attempt to clarify my thinking and discover who might be responsible. The catalogue of names included everyone I had met since I arrived in Bermuda. I was confident the problem was due to my involvement with Karl and his drug problem - there could be no other explanation. My lists became almost illegible, as I drew lines connecting one name with another where I believed there could be a connection. The waste-basket overflowed with discarded theories. During the day, Dilly occasionally popped in bringing tea, coffee or cake. In the evenings Karl would drop by, share a beer and speculate.

I didn't go out in the daytime, for I was reluctant to meet students or their parents and quizzed why I wasn't at school. A couple of times, after dark, I jogged around the lanes for exercise and attempting to clear my mind but the miserable weather limited the outings.

Eloise called wanting to know why I wasn't at school? I asked what explanation Mrs Harding had put out. Apparently, if asked, she had said: I had important personal matters to attend to! I agreed this was the case, not wishing to elaborate. The conversation ended with Eloise suggesting that I join her for a trip on her boat on Saturday, the weather was going to change, she had said.

*

Eloise was right, Saturday dawned bright and sunny, such a relief after the squally, cool days that had kept me confined. I rode my bike around to the dock to find Eloise was already aboard her boat. She greeted me warmly and once I was aboard, set me to work releasing the boat from its buoys. In no time at all she was picking her way between reefs, under Watford Bridge and heading towards the open ocean. *"I thought I would take you to Saint Georges,"* she shouted against the wind, a nautical cap stuck on her head, hair streaming out behind. The roar of the powerful engine and the force of the wind restricted conversation to brief shouted comments, even though I stood alongside her where she grasped the wheel. As we passed Spanish Point I sank back on the luxuriously padded seat and admired the passing coast. The sea was relatively calm but still the boat rocked and rolled its way towards the eastern end of the Island. While I could see the value of this enormous power for getting one from A to B in the shortest time possible, give me a sailing boat any time, I couldn't help but think.

After passing Fort St Catherine at the extreme eastern end of the Island, we passed through Town Cut, the narrow passage leading into St George's Harbour. Eloise deftly moored the boat at Ordnance Island, a large dock connected to the mainland by a bridge. We walked towards King's Square, stopping for me to examine the full-size replica of the Deliverance, the seventeenth century ship, which Eloise told me allowed the shipwrecked mariners to continue their voyage to Virginia. The bridge led us into the charming quadrangle flanked by 17th century buildings and the elegant Town Hall; the Square was deserted, so different from how it would be in a couple of month's time, when crowds from the visiting cruise liners would be queuing up to have their photographs taken in front of the cannons and the ancient stocks.

We found a waterside restaurant, sat outside and ordered drinks and lunch, only two other tables were occupied. *"So what's this personal business that's keeping you from school?"* Eloise questioned with a laugh, *"or shouldn't I ask?"* She was peering at me over the top of a large Rum and Coke decorated with slices of lemon and a floral cocktail stick. While Eloise had been engaged guiding us towards St. Georges I had been contemplating how I would explain my absence from school, for it was obvious that she would eventually ask. I had once again decided that the truth was the easier option and so I explained what had happened leading up to my suspension - but without any of my theories of what may have precipitated the disaster. As I spelled out the details I watched her carefully, aware of her connection to DeVere and even possible involvement. Her reactions of horror and concern seemed genuine, I thought, as she reached out and grasped my hand. Why would someone do this? Who could be responsible? The expected questions flowed and I repeated how I was totally bewildered and had no answers. The waitress appeared with a tray of food and the questions ceased. As soon as the waitress had disappeared back inside the restaurant Eloise resumed her inquisition until she probably grew tired of my constant response of having no idea of the cause or the perpetrators.

It was almost dusk by the time we had the boat safely secured to its moorings. Eloise invited me back to her home for a *simple supper*, which I gratefully accepted - I was sick of my own company. She showered while I pulled the cork from a bottle of Shiraz and while she cooked, I showered. After a day on the sea my skin felt crinkly and encrusted in salt. We ate from trays wedged in the comfortable armchairs and it wasn't long before I was again pulling another cork.

After a lull in the conversation she said: *"You must have your suspicions about the cause of the police stopping you, there has to be a reason. And who would want to cause you such harm?"*

I suppose it was too many glasses of red wine and weariness but my guard was down and I found myself saying: *"Well I do have a friend who has run into a really nasty situation with a group of drug pushers. I've been trying to help."* I drained my glass. *"It could be that someone thinks I know more than I really do!"*

"How have you been trying to help?" asked Eloise.

"Listening mostly," I replied.

"Has he given you any names?" she continued.

"Yes," I responded: " *your friend Just DeVere."* I was watching carefully for a reaction.

"He's not my friend," she said quickly. I suddenly realised that I had said too much and quickly changed the subject. *"Wait,"* she interrupted sharply. *"I repeat, he is not my friend. He was just the man I had to see about the mooring."*

"Okay," I said, throwing up my hands in defence. *"I'm sorry. I was going to ask if you have any plans for the Half Term break? It's only a week away."*

"Not sure yet," she said getting to her feet. *"I may have to go down to Miami again, though I'd rather not."*

"What's the attraction in Florida?" I asked, aware that I was slurring my words but she had already left and was in her bedroom. When she returned, Eloise was wearing a very short and flimsy nightdress; she dropped onto my knee, wrapped her arms around my neck and kissed me long and hard signifying an end to conversation.

*

I woke with a start the next morning, not recognising the room nor the bed I was in. Remembrance hit me, which explained why I was naked. Eloise appeared at the door carrying a steaming mug of tea, she was fully dressed.

"Come on sleepyhead, it's almost lunchtime and I have to go out." She placed the mug on the bedside table and kissed the top of my head. *"You're quite the loverboy aren't you?"* she purred and returned to the kitchen. Of course it wasn't lunchtime but heading towards it. After toast and more tea we both left, Eloise saying she had a lunch appointment with a girlfriend in town and that we should go out in the boat again: *"Perhaps next weekend?"* she suggested.

*

Both Dilly and Karl came round that afternoon - at different times. Dilly told me she had been talking to Marsha and that she had asked her to find a good barrister to represent me, if a trial was planned. I thanked her and optimistically said that I hoped it wouldn't come to that. As she sat in one of my armchairs I studied her face as she spoke. Gaunt was hardly the word, her cheek bones appeared to be almost through the skin, I felt sure she had lost more weight - and yet her eyes still gleamed with fire and determination; especially when she told me she had a meeting with the staff at the Southampton Princess planned for Wednesday afternoon.

Karl did little but complain about Dilly wasting all her much needed energy trying to put the world to rights, rather than looking after herself. He point-blank refused to discuss anything about his own problems, saying that I knew too much and he was the cause of my being arrested. I was actually quite pleased when he eventually shifted himself out of my chair and went home!

*

Tuesday night I drove to the Carlton Beach Hotel to play tennis with the guys. We didn't start until six o'clock but we had a great session under the lights, as there were no tourists pushing us for the court and the temperature was perfect for vigorous exercise.

Afterwards we settled on the terrace and once we all had beers and the waiter had gone Don Jeffers turned to me and said: *"Okay Jack, spill the beans. What's the problem?"*

"What beans, what do you mean?" I replied.

"We know you have a problem," said Alan earnestly, *"perhaps we can help."*

"We have contacts," added Charlie.

"How do you know I have... a problem?" I blustered.

"Your team should have played us at West End, if you remember." said Don. *" When you didn't show up I phoned Mrs H and was told you were away and there would be no match! I wasn't best pleased! So I made a few enquiries and found out you'd been suspended. Never heard of that happening before, so made more enquiries and my contact at the Education Department told me you'd been busted for possession! I said what a load of rubbish."* The others all murmured in agreement: *"Total rubbish."*

If they already knew this, I thought, then there is no point in keeping it to myself and so once again it all came pouring out. My tale was greeted with gasps, oaths and general horror, as well as reassurances that all would come right in the end. When the hubbub quietened Don turned to me and said: *"So you think the copper planted the stuff while the other one checked your licence?"*

"Yep, I was told to go to the car with one copper while he radioed in the details; my back was towards the other while he was poking about in my saddlebag." I responded. *"But it's his word against mine!"*

"Do you know his name?" Don continued.

"Truelove," I spat out, *"PC Truelove, how could I forget?"*

Don looked thoughtful and drained his glass. *"I'll ask around and call you,"* he said. I thanked him and soon after, we bid our farewells and headed off into the cool, starlit Bermuda night.

*

The next morning I was doing some washing when Wilber Marshall telephoned to enquire how Sunday's sailing had gone? I made excuses about the weather but wondering why he had called at a time I should have been at work. He ought to have known that, I mused. Suddenly he said: *"I hear that you have met Police Inspector Williams."*

I was puzzled. *"Williams?"* I questioned.

"Yes, he was the Inspector on duty at Prospect Friday night. Rees Williams, a Welsh chap." I really didn't know what to say and cast about for a suitable reply. *"He told me you had been charged with possession of heroin and wondered if you had been using my boat for smuggling the stuff - afraid I laughed at him?"*

"Mr Marshall, Wilber," I began. *"It's all a terrible mistake, a deliberate plot to implicate me..."* I paused for breath when he interrupted:

"I know he told me everything, sounds like you were set up."

"That's true," I said vehemently *"but it's two policemen's word against mine."*

"Try not worry too much," continued Wilber, *"I'm sure a good lawyer will get you off the hook, I'll see what I can do."* I thanked him profusely for his support and after some pleasantries and an urging to take *Crazy Dream* out any time I wished, we hung up. Later, as I rinsed my socks, I pondered on the fact that while he had talked about getting me off the hook, he hadn't asked a single question about what happened or demanded any kind of explanation - he just assumed I was innocent!

About four in the afternoon Dilly appeared and I offered her a choice of coffee or tea. *"Since you been here,"* she said with a grin, *"I've acquired a taste for English tea - never used to drink the stuff before!"* I suggested we sat out on the porch and so we settled down with our mugs surrounded by the gently whispering Casuarinas.

"Is it today you are due to meet staff at the Princess?" I asked.

"Bin there, done that" she responded, her voice bright and positive.

"Already," I said surprised.

"Uh uh, caught them all for half an hour after lunch, it was long enough." She sipped her tea, little finger cocked like an English aristocrat.

"And?" I questioned.

"Them Black Beret folk been putting pressure on and they had a strike planned but they promised to talk about it again, I can't ask more. Anyway I ain't got the energy to do battle for much longer." I looked at her sharply, it was the

first time I had ever heard her admit she was weakening. *"I was at the hospital again yesterday - they gave me some blood, man did that perk me up."* I was shocked and said so. *"I said, I don't want no white fella's blood. I hope you keep the donations separate. I was joking of course but man o man did I get a talking to from this great big black mama in a blue uniform,"* Dilly laughed. *"I got a real lecture about how blood is blood and we all be the same on the inside - I had to hide my tears in the sheet I was laughing so much."* Her body shook with silent laughter at the thought.

"You're such a tease Dilly Simons," I scowled, *"a shameful tease."*

The sudden appearance of Dilly's three uniformed girls emerging from, under the Casuarinas, school bags over their shoulders, drew our attention and Dilly called out to them. They came over to the porch and dropped onto the floor, the two younger ones grasping their mother's legs.

After a few moments: *"Momma I'm hungry,"* said the youngest.

"I know chile, let's go see what we can find," Dilly slowly climbed to her feet; *"Thanks for the tea Jack, I'd better go and feed these starving kids. Don't know what you teachers do to our kids to make them get so hungry."*
Before they had reached the front door Karl arrived, bouncing across the grass on his bike. As he lifted the machine onto its stand the girls raced over shouting and wrapping themselves around him. He feigned annoyance gently swotting at them like pesky flies. Dilly waited at the door, leaning on the jamb, as slowly the foursome made their way towards her.

The following day was unseasonably warm so I went up the lane opposite and onto the Westside, close to where I first met Laura Miles-Smith. I had only seen her a couple of times since the party some months earlier, each time in the grocery store. On each occasion she had tried to persuade me to join her Bridge group, but I vehemently pleaded overwork. I had brought a towel and was wearing my swim trunks under my shorts. Bermudians don't normally swim in mid February, but for me, used to British summers, I thought it would be quite warm enough for a dip. I found the spot where Laura had come ashore and launched myself out into the ocean. The water was cool and initially took my breath away but soon I acclimatised and front-crawled my way up and down the coast, enjoying the workout.

I hadn't been home long when Marsha telephoned. She had spoken to a barrister and between them they had been making enquiries that might help my case. She wanted me know that she hadn't been idle. I thanked her and was really surprised when she suggested dinner the following evening; nothing posh, perhaps the Horse and Buggy, where we had eaten previously.

The conversation and forthcoming date raised my spirits and when Dilly invited me to eat with the family that evening I had no hesitation in accepting. If it went on like this, I thought, I would forget how to cook.

*

Friday evening I carefully shaved, showered and put on my best shirt and sweater, checking in the mirror before leaving that I'd done a good job with the razor. I was really looking forward to seeing Marsha again and ashamed, in retrospect, that any thoughts of Jilly or Eloise never entered my head. It was dusk when I set off towards Hamilton on my bike, the ride taking all my concentration to avoid potholes and stray dogs. I was first to arrive at the Horse & Buggy and persuaded the waiter to find a cosy table tucked into a corner. I ordered a beer and settled into a chair where I could see the door. I didn't have to wait long before I saw Marsha arrive. I watched her for a moment before attracting her attention; she looked stunning, thick black hair piled up on top of her head, trademark huge circular earrings, and white blouse hidden under a fluffy blue sweater. Her face lit up when she saw me and we briefly hugged before settling down opposite one another. *"What can I get you to drink?"* I asked. *"Sorry, I've already started."*

"I'd like an ice-cold glass of something bubbly," she smiled. *"And you should have one as well, so hurry and finish your beer."* I looked at her but her face was impassive, as she glanced around the room avoiding my eyes. A few moments later my beer was finished and two glasses of champagne stood before us, the fizzing bubbles shimmering like crystals. Once again her eyes were sliding around the room, as if waiting for the right moment, gradually like birds they landed and stared into mine. *"Well Mr Cross, Mr Jack Cross, I have news,"* her fingers slid around the slender stem of the glass.

"News to celebrate?" I asked. *"Big promotion perhaps?"*

Marsha nodded: *"News to celebrate,"* she said emphatically and paused dramatically: *"The case against you has been dropped and the two policemen suspended pending an inquiry.*" I looked at her incredulously and the sense of relief was palpable, as the weight of the world lifted from my shoulders and my head sailed up to the ceiling. Fumbling for words I flew around the table and awkwardly hugged Marsha's shoulders, as she remained seated.

"*Oh Marsha,*" I gushed, once back in my seat, composure gradually taking over. "*I can't begin to thank you enough. You have no idea how screwed up I've been, how...*" She leaned across the table and gently laid her fingers across my lips silencing my outburst.

"*I think I can,*" she whispered. "*But it's behind you... it's over.*" There were tears in my eyes as Marsha raised her glass: "*To justice and to you Jack Cross!*" she said.

"*To us,*" I croaked.

During the meal Marsha explained that someone from the prosecutor's office had called her to say that charges would not be pressed but had refused to explain why. Later she made a few phone calls and discovered the two policemen had been suspended. We both put forward our various theories at length before Marsha drained her glass, suggested a second - and a change of subject. The rest of the evening flew, no doubt due to my now buoyant spirits and Marsha's wit and skill as a raconteur. As the restaurant emptied we looked at each other and decided it was time for us to move also. Outside I said firmly that I would walk her home, I wasn't taking no for an answer. We strolled through the quiet streets laughing and joking about nothing and everything until suddenly we were standing outside Marsha's front door. I thanked her profusely for her news and companionship; it had been a great evening and I clasped my

312

arms around her. Her lips found mine and the kiss was deep and passionate. *"I'm not inviting you in,"* she murmured into my ear.

"Not even for a coffee?" I suggested.

"Not even for a coffee," she echoed. *"Because if you come in, I know you won't leave until morning."* Her voice was breathy and laboured.

"Would that be such a terrible thing?" I whispered, nibbling her ear.

"Sorry Jack, I'm not ready for this. Try and understand." She pulled apart and searched her handbag for the door key. Once it was in the lock she turned and embraced me again. *"I'm so, so pleased your ordeal is over,"* she breathed, kissed me again and disappeared.

The ride back to Somerset was tricky, few street lamps and poor headlamps meant life and limb were at risk and I had no wish to cause myself harm now that, once again, life was worth living.

*

I was awoken early by the sun streaming in through the window. I leapt out of bed, wide awake, with a feeling of unrestricted joy, now that Damocles' sword, that had been hovering threateningly over my head, had been removed. It was Saturday, I needed to do something different. I quickly made tea and filled a bowl with cereals all the time weighing up my options. Eventually I decided to take up Wilber's offer and take Crazy Dream out into the Great Sound, the wonderful stretch of water that is almost enclosed by fish-hooked shaped Bermuda.

I speedily packed a rucksack with necessities, sandwiches and beer, jumped on my bike and headed off towards the metropolis. Along Harbour Road, the wind streaming in my face I sang at the top of my voice. I sang especially loudly as I passed the spot where the two policemen had stopped me, there was nothing that could dampen my spirits! I was soon aboard Wilber's wonderful boat and unlocking the cabin with the key he had entrusted to me. I checked around that everything was in order before starting up the motor and releasing the buoys. I was ultra careful guiding Crazy Dream through the maze of moored boats, having no wish to ruin the wonderful opportunity I had been afforded. Once out into clear water, I hoisted the jib and switched off the engine. There was a gentle breeze but progress was very slow. I contemplated raising the main sail but the thought of handling all that canvas single-handed, in the relatively confined area of the Inner Sound caused the hairs on the back of my neck to stand up.

It seemed to take an age but eventually I was clear of the small islands that lie scattered like diamonds in the Sound and level with Darrel Island. As I glanced at this unimposing island I remembered Wilber telling me how in 1936, Imperial Airways had built a terminal there and used as a staging post for trans-Atlantic Flying Boats. Looking at it now, it was hard to believe. Once clear of Grace Island I took a deep breath and set about raising the main sail. I was so glad that I did for it was like changing gear in a sports' car as Crazy Dream leapt into life sending spray glistening into the clear morning air.

I tacked my way across the Great Sound towards Watford Bridge before going about and returning towards the area known as The Little Sound, home to the little used American Naval Base. In the lee of the land I dropped anchor and lowered the sails, before leaning back on the comfortable seats perusing the wonderful landscape of green, dotted with white roofs - and eating the sandwiches. Gently bobbing on the tide my thoughts returned to Karl and his problems and I determined to cast a closer eye over the boat used to store the contraband: Georgie Girl. Red Hole was, after all, quite close to where Crazy Dream was usually moored.

After draining the can of beer, I started the engine and wound my way back towards Hamilton, running parallel to the Harbour Road. Eventually I arrived at Red Hole, slowed the engine and shaded my eyes, as I gazed around seeking out Georgie Girl.

There were several boats moored around me but only one of any size and it looked in need of TLC, so I decided it must be the one. I eased Crazy Dream a little nearer until I could read the name fading across the stern. It certainly looked neglected - and deserted. I began assessing what information I might find if I went aboard but after some soul searching decided to leave that for another day. Instead, I retrieved my camera from the rucksack and took a few photographs of Georgie Girl. It was only then I noticed two men on another boat some distance away. I focussed my telephoto lens on them and discovered one of the men was staring straight back at me through a pair of binoculars. I quickly took a couple of shots of them before busying myself stowing sails, hoping that if they were crooks, they would not think I was snooping. Once everything was shipshape I eased my way out of the cove and back towards the mooring. I glanced in the direction of the two men and was alarmed to see that one of them still had binoculars trained on me.

In the evening I telephoned Wilber and told him that I had taken Crazy Dream out for a sail and how much I had enjoyed myself. He seemed genuinely pleased and at the end of the conversation asked if I would consider going out with him the very next day. I didn't hesitate and we arranged to meet at the usual place.

*

Wilber was his usual jovial self when he arrived, without Madge but armed with a huge hamper, which he said she had prepared. For the second time in twenty-four hours I eased Crazy Dream away from its mooring and through the myriad of small islands. It was another fabulous day, with the sun beaming from a cloudless sky and low humidity. Once away from obstructions, Wilber took the wheel while I raised the sails. The motor was cut, the main sheet pulled tight and Crazy Dream heeled gently and cut through the water like a knife. I settled alongside Wilber and listened as he enthused about life in general but the sea in particular. He told of how he would like nothing better than to sell up and become a maritime vagrant, pulling in at any old port when he needed supplies. But Madge, he groaned, would not countenance such dreams! *"Talking of sailing to faraway places,"* he said. *"I had a technician on the boat last week. The radio has been defunct for some time but because, for the last couple of years, I've only pottered about in the*

316

Sound, I had done nothing about it. Anyway, I've ordered a new system, which he will fit as soon as it arrives from the States. You should be there when he's finished and explains how to use it ... so that you know too."

"*So you're hankering for a long trip again, are you?*" I asked.

"*One can dream*," he replied. "*Anyway, you might want to go a bit further, so it's sensible to be prepared.*"

At the end of a long tack heading back towards Hamilton, Wilber asked me to take down the sails. He then manoeuvred Crazy Dream between the small islands until he found a sheltered spot where I was instructed to drop the anchor. Wilber settled down on the seat and asked me to bring the hamper, which I placed at his feet. He rummaged through putting neatly packed packages on the table, all the time complaining that Madge had prepared far too much stuff and did she think we were away for the week?

Eventually we tucked into tasty chicken sandwiches, accompanied by cans of beer, followed by individual homemade apple pies and a thermos of coffee. I asked Wilber to thank Madge for all her efforts but he only grunted something about the maid having done all the work! Placing his coffee mug on the table, Wilber turned and caught my eye: "*Well Young man*," he said in a fatherly way. " *It occurs to me that you have had a rather trying time lately!*"

It was obvious what he meant. "*You can say that again*," I retorted. "*You cannot believe the weight that was lifted off my shoulders when I heard the case had been dropped. Was that anything to do with you?*" I asked.

317

"*I admit I had a long chat to that police inspector I mentioned to you, Rees Williams. But I don't think I had any influence, other facts must have come to light.*" Wilber poured himself more coffee.

"*I'm told the two policeman who arrested me have been suspended,*" I said.

"*Really,*" replied Wilber, "*I didn't know that.*" He looked thoughtful. "*Difficult times for the police, well all of us really, since poor George Duckett's death last year. What exactly happened, how did they come to arrest you?*" Wilber asked.

I gave him the details and he listened carefully, without interruption. When I finished he asked the question that I had asked myself so many times. "*So who would want to get you into trouble and why?*" he asked quietly. "*Surely you haven't been here long enough to make any enemies.*"

I resorted to the same theory I had espoused to Eloise: "*I have a Bermudian friend who, inadvertently, has got himself mixed up with a gang of drug dealers. He has told me of his problems but all I have done is listen and try to persuade him to go to the police. I can only suppose someone has seen me with this man and thinks I know more than I do.*"

"*How much has he told you?*" enquired Wilber. "*Has he given you any names or other details?*" A sudden loud creak from the mast reverberated in my head like an alarm and I made an excuse to check the anchor. My mind was whirling; I was saying too much, being too open. I should be on my guard. Wilber's quiet fatherly manner was inspiring

318

confidence but in reality, I thought, I know nothing about the man.

I returned to the seat. *"Sorry, you were saying?"*

"I asked if this friend gave you any details of the operation or the names of anyone connected?" He said examining his sandwich.

"No, he has said very little." I lied. *"He has a very sick wife, she brought the matter to my attention because she feared that she may die and with her husband in jail, there would be no one to look after the children. As I said, I have listened and told him to report the matter to the police… but he fears for his life and just does as he is told."*

"What is he told to do?" continued Wilber.

I don't really know. I think he makes deliveries to people who use the drugs and collect the money. A very minor player I think." I explained.

"Well it sounds as if this is not a good friend to have and for your own wellbeing you should stay well away from him." I looked at Wilber sharply, was this advice or a threat? His face gave nothing away.

Wilber said nothing more about the business, as we enjoyed the last leg back to the mooring. I cleared everything up, paddled Wilber back to shore and stowed the hamper in the boot of his car. He thanked me profusely for *taking him out*, saying he could no longer manage on his own and if it wasn't for me he would be deprived of the chance to get out on the water, which he said: cleared his mind and raised his spirits. I was busy saying that it was me who should be thanking him, when I noticed a man lurking behind some distant palms who seemed to be taking

319

more than a normal interest in our activities. I tried to keep the conversation going, as I manoeuvred around to get a clearer view – and then my heart sank, as I recognised the swarthy, unshaven face and the grubby navy T-shirt, with Miami emblazoned across the chest. It was the man with the binoculars, whom I seen the previous day.

I waved Wilber off and busied myself packing things into the saddlebag of my bike, all the time keeping a watchful eye on the man. He was still behind the trees but looking my way. I picked up my, rucksack and wandered towards the water, pretending to be taking an interest in Crazy Dream, gently swinging with the tide. I walked along the beach towards him but keeping my gaze out to sea. The next time I looked, he had disappeared; I speeded up towards the spot where I had last seen him and arrived in time to see him swinging a leg over the crossbar of an old bicycle and pulling out on to the road. I rushed back to my bike and kicked it into life and set off to follow my scruffy looking observer.

It wasn't long until he came into view and I had to stop for fear of getting too close. I continued this stop/start procedure until he suddenly turned right. I glanced at the sign, which read: Pomander Road. He wasn't exactly in a hurry and away from the traffic I was having to stay further and further back. We soon returned to the busier Harbour Road when he suddenly pulled onto a piece of rough ground, dismounted and was soon hidden by a number of boats, propped on trailers. At this point I ditched my bike and started walking until I could take cover behind one of the boats. I realised that we were not far from where Georgie

Girl was moored and I watched as the man placed a bag, of what I took to be groceries, in a tiny rowing boat. After glancing furtively around, he pushed the boat into the water and set off paddling towards the old lady. I stayed until he was safely aboard and certain that no one had come out to greet him. There was nothing else I could do and so I retraced my steps and continued my journey home, confident that the man was living aboard, no doubt guarding the illicit store. But had he recognised me, I kept asking myself. I had certainly never set eyes on him before but it's for sure he now knew of my connection to Wilber and Crazy Dream.

*

Monday morning I awoke early before remembering that it was the Half Term holiday and I could have a lie-in. Typically, though, I was wide-awake and so got up and made tea. As I sat sipping, I considered what I would do. With everything that had been going on, I hadn't given the holiday a thought and had no plans. Later, when the clock showed the reasonable hour of nine o'clock, I telephoned Eloise but she was either not at home or didn't pick up. I remembered she had said something of perhaps going to Miami. For a moment I wondered what her connection to Miami was, she had never explained.

After kicking my heels for a while wondering how to spend the day, I eventually decided to take the ferry to Hamilton and set off towards Cavello Bay, where I could catch the ferry. The ferry-stop was close to Eloise's home, her car was parked outside and so I knocked on the front door. There was no reply, I left my bike in her garden and

321

wandered over to the dock, where a couple of elderly Bermudians were waiting and we exchanged pleasantries.

It wasn't long before the ancient ferry puttered into view around the point and manoeuvred carefully up against the dock. Two crewmen heaved a gangplank across the gap, shouting greetings and in a few moments we were throbbing our way across the Great Sound.

Once in the city, I wandered past the birdcage, located in the middle of a busy junction, where a policeman leisurely directed the traffic. It was easy to see where it got its name, for it resembled a Victorian birdcage, with a raised podium, vertical bars and a roof to protect the duty officer from the searing summer sun. However, I remember Wilber telling me it was not called the birdcage because of its looks but because it was designed by one Geoffrey Bird, a well known Hamilton businessman. I continued up Queen Street before turning right into busy Reid Street, where I dropped off a couple of films to be developed at Stuarts' photo shop. It wasn't long before I found myself in another camera store, called Masters' and discussing Nikon camera lenses with an enthusiastic salesman. Eventually I fought off the urge to buy a new lens and went in search of lunch before catching the ferry home.

*

Tuesday I phoned the Education Department and asked for an appointment to see the Director and a time was fixed for Wednesday morning. I was in his office for less than ten minutes, during which time I said the charge had been dropped, he said he already knew - and there was no reason why I should not return to work. He grudgingly added that he was delighted at the news, told me my salary would not be affected by my absence, wished me well and nodded towards the door. A man of few words, I thought!

During the afternoon Dilly joined me for tea under the Casuarinas. I talked her into the hammock and dragged up an old cedar chair alongside. As she swayed gently, sipping her tea I couldn't help but notice how weak she looked. Her wonderful coffee coloured skin had lost its sheen and dark circles surrounded her eyes. She told me that she was going to the opening of a new hotel the next day: The Grotto Bay, which had been built out towards the airport. Apparently her dance troupe was performing, though she would not be taking part.

We talked of my sailing trips and she asked when I was going to take her sailing but when I suggested taking her out on Crazy Dream, she stopped me and said she wanted to go out on a Sunfish, I was surprised for it is little more than a board with a sail. She then went on to say there was an old Sunfish in the shed at the back of her house and she would ask Karl to find it and now the girls could swim, perhaps I would teach them how to sail?

*

Thursday I was back in school, Mrs Harding called me to her office first thing and explained that she had told the staff that I had urgent personal business to attend to and I should say as little as possible. She had wrung my hand and said how delighted she was that there was no charge to answer. Back in the classroom I was happy that the kids were pleased to see me though they were full of direct questions, which I ducked and dived. Colleagues also asked awkward questions but I slithered my way through and soon the matter was dropped.

*

On Sunday afternoon I met Marsha at the Botanical Gardens where we strolled round admiring the beautiful plants. After an hour or so we climbed onto my motorbike and set off for Spittle Pond, a nature reserve alongside the southern shore. It transpired that Marsha had never been before and so I relished showing off my botanic knowledge and pointing out olivewood, prickly pear, pittosporum, palmettos, Mexican pepper and of course Bermuda cedar. We followed the trail and clambered up to the top of some rocks that afforded a breathtaking view out to sea. Having soaked up the scene for a few moments we dropped down a little and I pointed out some initials carved in the rocks. *"RP, 1543,"* read Marsha; *"What's that all about?"*

"Thought to be done by Portuguese sailors who were probably shipwrecked here." I explained.

"Wow, so long ago but I suppose not a bad place to be shipwrecked! Plenty of food, though water may have been harder to find," she said. I held her hand as we walked back to the bike and somehow, I thought to myself, it felt right!

Later, I dropped Marsha at her front door, where she apologised for not inviting me in, pleading piles of documents to prepare for Monday morning. I didn't protest, I didn't want to push it and I too had essays to mark. We agreed to meet again the following Sunday and I suggested that I take her out on Crazy Dream, if the weather was kind. To which she readily agreed.

324

The following week just evaporated, as I caught up to speed at school and spent several early evenings entertaining Dilly & Karl's kids, as Dilly was unwell. One evening Karl called a taxi and took Dilly to the Emergency Room at the hospital. For a while the girls and I played cricket under the Casuarinas. At some point I mentioned the Sunfish to Pearl, telling her that her mother had said there was an old boat in the shed and I asked if she was interested in learning to sail. Needless to say, the three of them were excited at the thought and went delving into their father's shed, unsure of what they were looking for. A joyous shout announced it had been found and the three girls ceremoniously lugged it out onto the grass in front of the house, where the three of us closely inspected the hull and its fittings. It was a thirteen feet by four feet, piece of fibreglass, with a shallow footwell and daggerboard. *"Seems to be okay,"* proclaimed the smallest of the trio, Vernee.

"No it ain't," came the prompt reply from Renee, the middle child. *"There's bits missing."*

"I think we can fix it, without too much trouble," I said.

"Anyone seen the sail?" asked Renee.

"Nope," said Vernee, she was carefully balancing on one leg, a well-sucked thumb in her mouth. *"I ain't never seen no sail."*

"This boat's never been out of the shed in my lifetime," announced Renee, accusingly. *"Maybe it don't have no sail."*

Pearl disappeared back into the shed: *"Mr Jack come and help me look,"* she pleaded. *"It has to be here*

325

somewhere. Man have you ever seen so much junk?" She sounded just like her mother.

"It's sure to be in a bag," I volunteered and ducked into the small shed. As my eyes adjusted to the light I realised that it was archetypical of most sheds: chock a bloc with items that should have been thrown away but kept because one day there would be an urgent need for exactly that piece of chain, that length of rope, that block of wood, sheet of plastic, bolt - you name it, it's here somewhere.

We were almost at the point of giving up when Pearl pointed at the roof and there wedged between the rafters was an old sack. I heaved it out, covering us all in dust and debris. I took it outside and tipped it up. Out fell the aluminium mast with the sail wrapped around it. The girls all cheered.

The next hour slipped by as we fitted the Sunfish together, like a jigsaw puzzle. Pearl found her father's screwdrivers and I set too, tightening all the screws.

Eventually we all stood back and admired the craft, the Lateen sail barely moving. *"It just needs a couple cleats and a new sheet - and she'll be ready to go"* I announced; *"I'll pick them up at the hardware store tomorrow."*

"What's cleats?" asked the smallest child. I pointed one out and explained what it was for.

"Why do we need a sheet?" asked Renee, *"we ain't going to sleep in it."* I explained the meaning of sheet and she clucked and frowned with annoyance: *"If it's a piece of rope, why not call it piece of rope?"*

"And then can we see if it floats?" asked Vernee.

326

"*We sure will,*" I said "*perhaps on Saturday.*" The girls cheered.

We had just returned the Sunfish to the shed when a taxi pulled up and hooted. The girls sped across the grass as Karl helped their mother climb out of the rear seat. They were full of questions, wanting to know how she felt. Eggy clambered out of the driving seat and waved to me, as he wrapped an arm around Pearl's shoulder announcing that their mother would be just fine.

When things had calmed down and Eggy had left, Karl joined me on my porch. He thrust a can of beer in my hand and explained that Dilly had been so sick and unable to eat, he had decided to take her to the hospital. Of course, she told him she wouldn't go but he had insisted. I reminded him that he had told me all this earlier and in fact it was I who had called Eggy. Apparently, at the hospital, they had given Dilly a shot to stop the vomiting and arranged for her to see the specialist in a couple of days' time. I commiserated and squeezed his arm - we both felt so helpless. "*How were the girls?*" he asked.

"*A delight,*" I replied. "*Hope you don't mind but we raided your shed!*"

Karl gave me a quizzical look and I explained about the Sunfish. He grunted: "*Dilly and me spent hours and hours on that thing - before the kids. Then it got put in the shed and forgot!*"

"*Dilly asked me if I'd teach them to sail. Do you mind?*" I asked.

"Naw, that would be great," he didn't sound too enthusiastic, probably because this was something he would really like to do himself.

"It needs a few spare parts but if it's okay with you, I'll fix it up."

"Go ahead," Karl replied, with that most Bermudian of expressions.

*

I didn't see Karl again until Friday evening when, about nine o'clock, he dropped round explaining that the girls and Dilly were sound asleep. He settled back on my battered sofa and closed his eyes, his huge hands enveloping the customary can of beer. I looked at him but didn't speak, he looked exhausted. After what seemed like an age and my can was empty, he spoke: *"That sod De Vere's bin bugging me again,"* his voice a resigned monotone, his eyes still tightly shut. I cursed and demanded more detail. *"Same as before, got to fetch another load of shit!"* he spat.

"You can't do this Karl," I said. *"Dilly needs you... the kids. Tell him you can't."*

"I did," Karl hissed, *"and he took out a knife and poked it in my neck, saying if I didn't do I was told, my wife would be even sicker!"*

"The bugger, the absolute swine," I swore, angry and frustrated. *"When are you supposed to go?"* I asked.

"Tomorrow...at seven... same place," he replied, he sounded desperate.

Shortly after ten o'clock, Karl dragged himself out of the sofa and made his way home. We had agreed that I would look after the kids and keep an eye on Dilly while he

328

was away. It was the only practical thing I could think of to help. Once he had gone, I went through the motions of preparing for bed but my mind was whirling, bursting with anger at the unfairness of it all. I contemplated calling the police. I remembered that Stephen Henderson had promised to get back to me – but he hadn't, perhaps I should call him. I looked at my watch, it was after eleven and I decided it was too late to call him at home.

*

A loud noise caused by three sets of fists hammering on my door woke me next morning. I pulled on my shorts and drowsily opened the door.

"*Look what we got!*" the three girls shouted. I rubbed my eyes as they stood aside revealing a small boat trolley. "*Aunt Josie's lent it to us,*" said Pearl, "*so we can get the boat to the beach.*"

"*Fantastic,*" I said, not very enthusiastically. "*You'll have to give me half-an-hour to get ready.*"

"*Okay,*" said Pearl, "*we'll be back.*" It sounded like a threat!

An hour later we must have made a jolly sight as we took it turns to tow the Sunfish down Longbay Lane towards the beach. Before we left I had spoken to Dilly, she was up and said she was feeling better and might join us at the beach a little later.

Once at the beach we fixed the mast and dagger board in place and fastened the sail. Earlier in the week I had fitted new cleats and a new sheet and now with Vernee, the youngest, sitting in the boat I began explaining the rudiments of sailing. They were keen students and it wasn't long before we pulled the boat into the water and I took each out in turn to take the helm and sail us around the shoreline, keeping to the shallows. It was a perfect day, with flat water and just enough wind to fill the small sail. Despite being February, the sun was hot, even if the water was considered chilly by my Bermudian companions, who squealed when splashed.

The girls suddenly spotted their mother strolling slowly towards us along the beach and two of them rushed off to meet her. Pearl asked if she could go out on her own, to *"show momma what I can do."* I argued and we compromised with me sitting on the bow, my feet in the water while Pearl expertly tacked out and back.

Once we had pulled the Sunfish out of the gently lapping waves, Pearl ran excitedly up to her mother: *"Did you see momma...did you see? I can sail, Mr Jack's a great teacher."*

Dilly gave her daughter a squeeze and settled on a towel she had brought with her. From her bag she took out a tennis ball: *"Here Pearl, give Mr Jack a rest. Go and play catch for a bit."* The girls ran further down the beach where Pearl organised her sisters into position for a catching game. I sat alongside Dilly asking if the walk to the beach had not been too far. She shook her head, pulled the shawl she was wearing tighter round her shoulders and said: *"You know Karl's gone again."* She gave me a knowing look.

I nodded. *"He told me last night when you were already asleep."* I admitted.

*"When he left this morning, he was crying like a baby
- he told me you knew ... and said you would take care of the
girls."* She choked back a sob.

"They're bastards," I hissed, *"heartless bastards...
How can people behave like this... it's inhuman... without
them this place would be paradise?"* I was so angry, I was
struggling to find the right words.

Dilly was running her hands through the pink sand
and letting it run through her fingers: *"You're right it is
paradise,"* she mused. *"Look at this sand, it's unique... pink
coral sand... pink sand in paradise. Sadly not everyone
understands that. There's a hard core of people who'd
rather make trouble, they even make a living by causing
trouble - we're plagued with these parasites! Bermuda is a
land of pink sand and parasites."*

"You're being too hard Dilly," I said. *"The parasites,
as you call them, are a tiny minority. Most people here are
normal and law abiding and love this place as much as you
do,"* I said earnestly squeezing her hand.

"I suppose you're right," she agreed and suddenly
brightened: *"You know I haven't sailed that piece of junk
since Pearl was a baby. Think I'll just give it a try."* I gave
her my hand and she struggled to her feet.

*"Do you think that's a good idea? The water is not
very warm."* I warned.

"It's fine," she replied, *"I don't intend getting wet!"* I
pushed the boat into the water and Dilly settled herself
aboard and grasped the tiller with one hand and the sheet
with the other. The wind caught the sail, she tightened the
sheet and the little boat leapt away from the shore.

331

A sudden shout from Pearl to her sisters brought them running: *"Look, look Momma's sailing. Wow watch her go!"* The four of us stood shielding our eyes from the glare, as the tiny boat whistled across the bay towards Cambridge Beaches Hotel.

"Is she ever coming back?" asked a worried Vernee. I shovelled her up into my arms so that she could see better.

"Yes, she's coming back," I said reassuringly. *"She'll turn round in a minute."* And so she did. After another couple of sailing lessons for the two older girls, we loaded the Sunfish onto the trailer, folded the sail and set off for home. The girls sang and skipped, as I pulled the trailer under the floral arch of sagging oleanders that grew in profusion each side of the narrow lane. The girls were high with excitement and proud of their newly acquired skill and demanded to know when I would take them again. Provisional promises were made, all the time Dilly insisting the girls should reduce their enthusiastic demands. Back under the Casuarinas, Dilly slept most of the afternoon away in my hammock, while the girls watched television in a darkened bedroom.

When evening came and the tree frogs were in full chorus Dilly put the children to bed and joined me on the porch. I found a stool, a couple of cushions, a blanket and ensured she was comfortable. I was admonished for making a fuss but the tone of her voice showed how much she appreciated my actions.

We hadn't mentioned Karl all day, yet for both of us he had never left our thoughts and even now, as we sat in the darkness, I knew we were both anxious and wondering where he was and if he was safe. Eventually Dilly voiced our concerns and I tried to reassure her that he would be fine but she wasn't convinced. I told her that if I had known earlier about Karl being forced to go today, I would have contacted the police and told them where they could find the men and pick them up.

"I'm sure this will all end badly," Dilly sighed, *"and the police will have to be told."*

"I'm sure it's Karl's only chance... to come clean. He may be charged but in the end it will best... for all of you." In the shadows I could see her nod in agreement.

As the clock ticked round to ten-thirty Dilly climbed slowly to her feet and said that although she wouldn't be able to sleep, she was going to bed. I gave her a reassuring hug and walked her to the front door. I knew that I too wouldn't sleep but decided to lie on my bed, read and listen out for the returning Karl.

At midnight I looked at my watch, he was still not back. The next thing I knew the Bermuda cockerel, the Kiskadee, had woken me with its raucous squawking from a favourite perch on a neighbouring tree - my watch read half past seven. I got out of bed and crept outside, Karl's bike was propped on its stand, so, he had returned safely but I had not heard him. I made tea and remembered that I had promised to take Marsha out sailing today. I was in a dilemma - desperately wanting to know what happened last night but knowing I had to be in Hamilton by nine-thirty. Eventually I salved my conscience by deciding that if Karl had returned late, he would not be out of bed until midday.

*

By nine o'clock I was aboard Crazy Dream and checking everything was shipshape. When I was confident everything was as it should be I started the engine and began unfastening the mooring ropes. Soon I was picking my way through the moored boats; the water in the sheltered bay was like a millpond, full of quivering reflections, the early morning sun warm on my back.

I made my way across to the quay on Front Street and was delighted to see that Marsha was already standing there, a large bag at her feet, I waved and concentrated on not making a fool of myself, as I brought the boat alongside the dock. When I was close enough, Marsha leapt nimbly aboard and retrieved the bag. I hadn't needed to tie up and Marsha joked how slickly it had all been done. As I turned the bow out towards the Great Sound, she came towards me, looking very nautical: in long shorts, a blue and white striped shirt and crowned with a white baseball cap. She offered her cheek for a kiss and I told her how wonderful she looked. The compliment was ignored and she asked what she could do. I told her there was nothing at the moment, until we were clear of the shore and then she could help raise the sail. She nodded and went towards the cabin to stow her bag.

There was a reasonable breeze and it wasn't long before the sails were up and we were racing across the Great Sound, filling the air with fine spray. After a couple of tacks, I eased the sheet and suggested Marsha took the wheel, which she did enthusiastically. I found my camera and took several shots of her smiling like the Cheshire Cat, jet black hair streaming out from under her cap.

When my stomach reminded me it was a long time since breakfast, I eased Crazy Dream towards the tiny islands where we had swum that day with Wilber. Marsha lowered the sails and I switched the engine on and carefully picked our way to a centrally sheltered spot and dropped anchor. Marsha had brought a sumptuous array of sandwiches and fruit to which I added a bottle of ice-cold wine. Settled on the thick cushions, we chatted and enjoyed the delicious picnic. Could life ever get any better, I asked myself, looking over the rim of my glass at the gorgeous, intelligent woman in front of me. My mind strayed back to our initial meeting and the icy cold reception I had received and I thanked my lucky stars that her attitude had changed. However, I had already determined that I was not going to push this relationship, it would be up to her if she wanted to move it to the next level. When we had finished and cleared up, I asked if she wished to swim but Marsha declined, saying she hadn't brought a costume and anyway it was too chilly for a girl from Jamaica!

Marsha asked me if I had seen Dilly lately and how she was. I explained that she had had a bad week, though had seemed better the previous day. I explained about the sailing and how Dilly had joined us down to the beach. Marsha congratulated me on *'being so nice to the girls'* and continued: *"The last time I spoke with Dilly I had the feeling that things were not right between her and Karl."*

"Oh no, they're fine," I said.

"Well, she seemed really angry with him but wouldn't say why but did say he was putting the whole family's wellbeing at stake by his behaviour."

I looked away thinking what a relief it would be to share Karl's problem with someone like Marsha. *"You know something, don't you!"* she said, looking me in the eye.

She was so sensible, I thought and might well have ideas and certainly had contacts who might help, I decided to spill the beans. *"It's complicated,"* I began. *"Let me fill your wine glass."* And so under a wondrous blue Bermudian sky, sitting aboard this fabulous yacht, sheltered by several palm covered coral-coated islands I began the story. *"This place really is paradise. I thought I'd died and gone to heaven when I came here,"* I gushed. *"But it seems - and you probably know this more than me. There is a dark underbelly and even innocent people can inadvertently get caught up. Dilly talked of parasites feeding off this pink-sanded paradise. Karl has got caught up by these parasites and they're sucking the blood out of him."*

Over the next hour I told Marsha the story from the very beginning, up to Karl's enforced labour of last night. Marsha hardly interrupted during the telling but the moment I finished she was full of questions. Most of which I couldn't answer. *"I have tried to persuade Karl to go and explain everything to the police.* "I explained. *" I really believe that if he gave them all the names of those involved so that they could round up the whole bunch of crooks, his actions would be taken into account and he wouldn't go to prison."* I said vehemently, waving my arms about.

"It's not that simple," said Marsha quietly. *"The scale of the drug problem here is such that there has to be many people of influence at the top. No doubt the people that Karl deals with are pawns in this chess game. This*

means there may well be fearful repercussions for him - and Dilly."

"*Isn't there anything we can do?*" I pleaded.

"*I'll think about it,*" said Marsha,"*... and thank you for telling me.*"

Marsha reached for a sweater and pulled it over her head: "*It's cooling off,*" she said. It was true, the sun was sinking, it was time to return the yacht to her mooring.

I carefully guided Crazy Dream through the narrow channel between the islands and towards Hamilton. As we approached Red Hole, I pointed out Georgie Girl to Marsha, explaining that this was the vessel where the drugs were stored. Marsha said that she could see someone moving about on the deck, so I hastily went about and headed back into the main channel, I had no wish for any of the villains to think I was keeping an eye on them.

At the Front Street quay Marsha helped me secure the boat, so that she could disembark. She gave me a hug and kissed me on the lips, saying how much she had enjoyed being with me and hoped I would invite her to go sailing again. I promised that I would. She clambered up on to the quay and looked down at me: "*I'll call you in the week, perhaps we could go and have a drink one evening?*"

"*Great,*" I replied, "*I look forward to that.*" She unfastened the mooring rope, tossed it aboard and stood at the waters edge waving. I blew a kiss and eased away from the dock and towards Foot of the Lane and Crazy Dream's mooring. I was elated from our day together and conscious of an overpowering urge to get to know this lady better.

Once Crazy Dream was safely moored I paddled ashore, loaded my gear on to the bike and set off for Somerset. I did a detour around Pomander Road so that I could follow the water's edge and pass close by to Georgie Girl, where I stopped and stared. There was a small motorboat tied up alongside, so there was definitely someone aboard, confirming in my own mind that the boat was always guarded.

Later that evening, after a welcome shower, I knocked on my neighbours' door, Karl answered, stepped out and shut the door behind him: *"Dilly's sleeping in front of the TV,"* he said.

"How is she today?" I asked.

"She been good, though pretty tired." He replied.

"Fancy a beer?" I asked. *"I've been sailing all day and have a mammoth thirst."* Karl nodded and followed me across to my porch, where he sank into one of the large, old chairs. Later, armed with cans of beer and serenaded by the ubiquitous tree frogs, we chatted for a while, mostly about Dilly. It struck me that Karl was strangely quiet, no doubt worried about his wife's condition, I thought. I tried to reassure him but he didn't respond.

"Well," I said, *" how did you get on yesterday, I didn't hear you come home?"*

Karl sighed: *"Not good,"* he muttered. *"Not good at all."*

"So did you follow the same procedure," I enquired. *"You know… sail out to sea, collect the stuff and then back to Georgie Girl."* Karl nodded. *"So why wasn't it good, what happened?"* I asked.

"I got into an argument with that bastard De Vere," he hissed. *"When we was nearly back I tried to tell him how sick Dilly is... and how I need to be with my kids... and I wasn't goin' to do his dirty work any more. One of the guys was gutting fish. De Vere nodded to this guy and he tried to stab my hand, like he did last time. Man this huge knife he uses just missed and stuck into the wood and he couldn't pull it out."* Karl paused to draw breath, he was shaking. *"I was so pissed off that he coulda taken off my hand; I punched him. He fell, hit his head.. I don't know if he dead or alive. Then De Vere pulled a gun, so I dived over the side, he couldn't see me in the dark. Luckily we weren't far from the shore, so I ran to my bike and rushed home."* Karl held his head in his hands. *"No knowing what these bastards will do now,"* he murmured. *"I'm real scared!"* I was at a loss for words, the situation had escalated dramatically - it wasn't just Karl that was scared. When I eventually got to bed, sleep did not come easily.

*

For a Monday, the school day just flew by, and at four o'clock I was at my desk hunched over a pile of essays deep in concentration, when the door opened. It was Eloise, I scrambled to my feet and gave her a hug. *"I saw you earlier,* I began *"or should I say, I heard you!"*

  "Sorry about that," she laughed, *"one of the classes was being particularly obstreperous, so you may well have heard me! It's amazing what a week away from school does for the behaviour of some children!"* I agreed and asked what she had been up to during the holiday. *"I'm really sorry,"* she began, *"I did try to call before I left but you*

339

weren't home. I've been to see an elderly Aunt who lives near Miami, she hasn't been very well. I think I mentioned that I might go. Anyway, a cheap flight came up, so I decided I should go. She may not be with us for much longer." I commiserated. *"Well, I'm really here to try and make amends,"* she said. *"If this weather holds, will you come out on the boat with me on Saturday, and bring your mask and snorkel I want to show you something. Then in the evening I'll cook you supper?"* I thanked her and said I would enjoy that and explained about taking Crazy Dream out sailing a couple of times in the holiday. I didn't mention Marsha!

That night, as I lay in bed my mind was whirling. I was not happy with the way I was seeing two women at the same time and was trying to rationalise. Eloise was rather special but did I trust her? Her connection to Just De Vere and the memory of his hand encasing her butt, her hatred of her dead father's widow, our boss, raised all kinds of questions. I just didn't know enough about her to make a rational decision. And then there was Marsha, if anything my feelings for her ran stronger but she was clearly holding back. Then, before I could come to any sensible conclusions about the way forward, the thought of Karl fleeing from an armed De Vere filled my head. He obviously wouldn't let this drop. Would De Vere or one of his minions creep round one night and shoot Karl? It was a relief when all these characters merged into a nonsensical dream and I slept.

*

Tuesday the 27th February is a day I shall remember for the rest of my life - for all the wrong reasons. It started

340

smoothly enough, waking early, strolling to work to the sound of Kiskadees and rustling palm leaves. All the children were in a positive mood and the day just evaporated. There was no after-school soccer on Tuesdays and so I drifted home somewhat earlier than usual. Dilly was hanging out washing when I arrived, I called out to her dropped my bag on the porch and wandered over to where she was busy pegging out a pair of Karl's jeans. I asked how she was and though she looked tired and drawn, she said she felt fine but then she would. *"Girls not home yet?"* I asked.

"No," replied Dilly unconcerned. *"I guess they've stopped on the way to play, you know kids."* She hardly had the words out of her mouth when the two younger ones came charging over the rise and under the Casuarinas shouting for their mother, obviously distressed. They both shouted at once making no sense. Dilly wrapped an arm around each urging them to be calm and it all came spilling out. We learned that as the three of them were starting to walk home a car had pulled up and a man had opened the door and started talking to them. He had tried to show Pearl something on a piece of paper and when she leaned in across the passenger seat to see what it was, he had grabbed her and, pulled her into the car and driven off. Hearing this my heart sank and I feared the worst. Renee, the second child, explained how she had rushed back to school, found a teacher and explained what had happened. At this, Dilly dived into the house and phoned the school. It took some time but eventually the Headteacher confirmed Renee's story but apologised that was all she could do, because no one else had seen it happen and she had wondered if Pearl had gone

off with a relative. The Headteacher asked if she should call the police but Dilly said that she would take care of that. On the surface Dilly was calm but underneath she must have been distraught. We sat Renee down on a kitchen chair and Dilly gave her a drink and a banana, then we both pulled up a seat and sat facing her. *"Now,"* said Dilly, *"let's start again. How far away from school were you?"*

Both Dilly and I continued the questioning but we learned nothing new, except the man was white. Neither the man nor the car was familiar. Dilly sent the pair out to play and collapsed into my arms sobbing: *"This is Karl's fault,"* she hissed, cursing his stupidity.

"Why Karl's fault," I asked innocently, unsure how much she knew.

" He fell out with De Vere and ran away," her tears were soaking my shirt.

"He told you?" I said.

"Yes, he told me, he was in such a state when he got home the other night. He had no option but to tell me. And you know too?" she demanded.

"Yes, he told me too," I whispered into her hair. *"When do you think he will be home?"*

"Soon, I guess, he'll be here soon." The sobbing had stopped but she was a dead weight in my arms. I lowered her into a chair.

"We should call the police," she said, her voice hoarse and thin *"Every moment we wait, the trail goes cold."* Dilly began to stand but fell back into the chair exhausted.

"*Let's wait for Karl,*" I said. "*He needs to agree and tell the police everything - to ensure that not just Pearl but all of you are kept safe.*"

"*But,*" Dilly objected…"*Pearl!*"

I made way home, where I washed my face and stared into the mirror, wracking my brain. This had to be De Vere's work - revenge for Karl's rebellious actions. What did they plan to do with Pearl, surely not kill her? No, it must be a display of power, a threat, to ensure Karl towed the line. But I couldn't be sure, I had no idea how these people's minds worked when their actions were so incomprehensible. My mind ticked over to considering where this man would have taken Pearl. The more I thought about it, the more certain I was that I knew.

Outside I packed a torch into my bike's saddlebag, pulled on a dark sweater and sat astride my bike, waiting. After some ten minutes Karl had still not arrived and I was growing impatient. Renee suddenly appeared shouting that Momma wanted me. I clambered off the bike and headed towards the door, remembering with a start that I was due to be playing tennis with the guys later that evening. I would need to phone and tell them I wasn't coming, as soon as I'd spoken to Dilly.

Dilly was slumped on a chair, the phone still in her hand. "*Karl's at the hospital,*" she said, her voice a dull monotone. "*He's been knocked off his bike.*" Renee interrupted wanting to know about her father - Dilly hushed her. "*He just called to say he's okay, nothing broken but shaken up and lots of gravel-rash…someone deliberately ran into him... he's called Eggy to pick him up.*" I grasped Dilly's hand and squeezed.

"*Listen, I think I know where Pearl might be, so I'm going to call the police and arrange for them to meet me there... don't worry, I'll find her!*"

I rushed back to my house with Dilly's voice ringing in my ears: to take care and not do anything heroic. I let myself in and searched for my tennis partners' telephone numbers. Don's was the first that I found; I dialled and waited, impatiently hopping from one foot to the next.

"*Jeffers,*" answered Don, his deep voice reflecting his powerful physique.

"*Don, it's Jack,*" I began. "*Listen I have a problem, you know I told you about my neighbour's little predicament, well it's escalated and someone has abducted his daughter and put him in hospital. I think I know where she might be but I need some physical back up - how are you fixed.*"

"*Raring for a scrap,*" he replied instantly.

"*Can you call the others and meet me in Pomander Road as soon as possible, I'm just setting off from Somerset now.*" I said breathlessly.

"*Leave it to me,*" he replied, "*see you in twenty minutes or so!*" I put the phone down, dashed outside and kicked my bike into life. As I raced at full throttle down Middle Road towards Hamilton my mind was racing too. I was certain the 'white' man Renee described was the man I had seen on Georgie Girl – and that's where I was heading.

*

It was almost dark as I swerved into Pomander Road, switched off my lights and engine and freewheeled behind

344

the parked boats, dimly silhouetted against the dusky night sky. Leaning on the stern of one of the boats I peered out to where I thought Georgie Girl would be, I could just pick out her outline with a couple of lights showing through portholes. I could also see a small motorboat tied alongside in the same spot as before. To get to Georgie Girl we too would need a boat. I began searching inside the parked yachts and underneath, probing the darkness with my torch, being as discrete as possible. I was in luck, pulled up on the beach was an old wooden rowing boat, which I decided looked watertight. The fact that it was secured to a bush with a long length of fairly new rope augured well. I busied myself untying the rope from the bush when I heard an unlit car coast alongside my bike. It was Alan, driving girlfriend Mildred's car. I briefed him of the latest events and said we needed to be as quiet as possible and get aboard Georgie Girl. He took one look at the rowing boat and said he had a paddle in the car, which we could use and crept away to fetch it. There wasn't an oar with the boat but after searching around I came across a piece of plank, which would have to do. Alan returned and as quietly as we could, we began sliding the boat towards the water's edge. I could hear a generator throbbing aboard Georgie Girl, which was good, as it would drown any noise we might make. Don arrived, saying that he had been unable to get hold of Charlie and between us, we soon had the boat in the water. I sat feeling around to check if it was leaking, not feeling any quantity of water I motioned for Don to climb aboard. *"There's room for me, if I stand,"* said Alan, as he stepped into the boat and crouched precariously between us, a hand on my shoulder. Don began paddling with the oar, while I used the plank that I had found. Keeping a straight line was difficult but after several minutes we were alongside the small motorboat and could just make out a ladder hooked over the side of the larger vessel. I tied the painter to the motorboat and we listened - nothing but the rhythmic pulsing of the generator. I scrambled over the motorboat and up the ladder, closely followed by Alan. We stood silently inside the wheelhouse waiting for Don to emerge over the side. A single porthole was casting a faint glow across the deck; we crept towards it, cautiously feeling our way. Crouching beneath the porthole, I eased my head towards the light source an inch at a time and tried to look in but the glass was salt encrusted; it was difficult to see clearly. I could just make out a distorted image of a man standing in the middle of the room; he was looking at a dark figure lying on a bed. His back was towards me and so I risked a quick rub of the glass with a couple of fingers. I gradually eased my eyes towards the porthole again - now I could see that the figure on the bed - it was indeed Pearl. I pulled back and let out a sigh of relief. *"She's in there,"* I hissed. *"Pearl's in there... looks like she's tied up."*

"The door must be this way," whispered Don and ducked under an arch, we followed. On the left was a small galley with a dim light burning which cast a beam on a door opposite, the door into the cabin where Pearl was being held.

I gave Alan my torch. *"Check there's no one else here,"* I mouthed and as he slid silently away, I put my ear to the door.

346

"So my darling, you and I are going to be great friends," I heard the villain say, with an ugly laugh. *"We have a lot of time to kill and I know a great way to spend it. How old you my dear... not that it really matters."* Again the threatening cackle.

Suddenly Pearl screamed: *"Keep away from me you dirty old man, I'll tear your eyes out."*

"With your hands tied behind your back, I don't think so!" he sniggered. Pearl screamed again. *"Oh...try and kick me would you, you need to be taught a lesson. I'll enjoy spanking your backside."* Another desperate scream.

Alan noiselessly appeared: *"There's another character sleeping in a cabin,"* he whispered. *"Looks like he's been drinking, fallen asleep with a rum bottle by his bed."*

"We need to act," I said quietly. *"Don get ready to hit him, as he comes out - like the shark,"* I added! *"Alan stand by, in case we wake sleeping beauty."* I took a deep breath, rattled the door handle and stepped back into the shadows. Nothing. I tried again. This time I heard a tirade of oaths and the door opened.

"Don't you know I'm busy..." the man began, peering into the darkness. *"Where are you? What d'you want?"* He stepped out into the corridor. Don slid silently forward gave the villain a hefty karate chop to the back of his neck and the scrawny man collapsed into a silent heap.

I dived into the room where Pearl was crouched on a bed, cowering silently against the wall. *"It's okay Pearl, it's me,"* I whispered. *"You're safe now."*

"Mr Jack," she cried and collapsed in tears.

"Do you know," I asked, holding her close, *"is there just one other man here, did you see anyone else?"*

"Just this man and the drunk," she whimpered, pointing a toe towards the prostrate figure, face down on the floor.

"Turn over," I said, *"let me untie your hands."* She rolled on her side and I cut through the cord with my pocket-knife. She rolled back again and into my arms silently sobbing.

Alan had secured our victim's hands behind his back, he was still unconscious. Don dragged him into the cabin. *"Let's deal with the other one,"* he said, *"Come an Alan."* I ordered Pearl to stay on the bed and followed.

We crept down a set of steps and Alan gingerly opened a cabin door. The man was lying on his back, snoring, a dim light glowed by the side of his bed. I nodded and the three of us leapt and pinned him to the grubby mattress. He bellowed and kicked ferociously but Don soon had his hands tied behind his back and lashed to his feet.

"We need a gag," I said and ripped a couple of strips from the bed sheet. *"Okay, we'll lock him in here,* I said, *"Let's go."* As we left I turned the key and dropped it in mop-bucket standing on the floor. When we got back to Pearl, the man on the floor was groaning, Alan fastened a gag around the man's mouth. It wasn't really necessary but somehow or other, it seemed to finish things off!

I held out a hand, *"Come on Pearl, we need to get you home."* I turned to the guys, *"When I get home, I'm going to make an anonymous call to the police and tell them they need to pay a visit to Georgie Girl. I'm really, really grateful for your help."* I slapped each on the shoulder. Pearl whispered her thanks and Don, quickly followed by Alan, and gave her a hug.

It took two trips in the small boat to get the four of us ashore. We secured the boat as we had found it and congratulated each other on a job well done. *"We were lucky,"* I said, *"they were nasty pieces of work."* Alan offered to take Pearl home in the car and so after bidding Don farewell, I jumped on my bike and followed Alan towards Somerset. I knew there were a couple of public phone boxes en-route. I stopped at one and called the emergency number and was put through to the police.

"How can I help you?" the woman's voice was calmness personified.

"Do you have a pencil?" I said. She seemed surprised.

"Your name please sir." She responded.

"Write this down," I said, she interrupted again asking for my name.

"Georgie Girl, it's the name of a boat moored at Red Hole. Tell Sergeant Henderson to get down there as soon as possible, there's two dangerous men and a load of drugs on board." I was trying to disguise my voice.

"Your name please sir," she repeated.

"Did you get that? Tell Sergeant Henderson... Georgie Girl... Red Hole... quick," the operator was still asking for my name when I hung up. I hoped she would pass on my message or two men could starve!

*

349

What a joyful reunion ensued, when I knocked on Dilly's door and pushed Pearl into the room. Tears, laughter, the whole gamut of emotions assailed us all. Pearl was enveloped in turn by her parents demanding to know if she had been harmed. Except for bruises around her wrists and ankles, I felt sure there was nothing serious - I dreaded what might have happened if we had arrived any later - but I kept that to myself! I introduced Alan to Karl, who had one arm in a sling and a large piece of plaster covering half his forehead. He gave Alan a one-handed bear hug, while Dilly wrung his hand and thanked him profusely but after a few moments, he made his excuses and left.

I departed shortly after, saying I needed a shower. Karl said he needed to know what happened and that he would come round in half-an-hour or so. It was in fact quite late when Karl did eventually show up, he looked a mess, baggy eyes, giving away how many tears had been shed. He grabbed and squeezed the breath out of me, more tears fell as he wept - gratitude, anger and pain sweeping over him in equal amounts. Gradually he calmed and sank heavily into one of my chairs. *"Dilly told me all that happened up to the time you left saying you might know where Pearl was and you were going to call the police."* He said. *"Why didn't the police bring Pearl, home?"*

"I didn't call the police," I replied, *"I just called a couple of mates…. I figure that it's up to you to call the police…for everyone's sake."* I looked at him pointedly.

"Pearl told me that she been kept on a boat, was that Georgie Girl?" Karl asked, ignoring my comment. I nodded.

"The description little Renee gave us reminded me of the guy I'd seen on the boat recently. It seemed a pretty obvious place to take her. So obvious, that at one time I wondered if it might have been a trap. Fortunately the low-life holding Pearl weren't too bright and we had no trouble overpowering them."

"Don't you believe it," interrupted Karl. *"The guy who took Pearl was the guy who stuck the knife in my hand... the guy I knocked out the other night... he's totally mental?"*

After I had described all that took place, including my anonymous call to the police, I asked what had happened to him. Karl told how a van had followed him for some way along Middle Road and then somewhere near a golf course, called Belmont, had pulled out and tried to squeeze him up against a wall, ending up with him being thrown over the wall and his bike totally mangled. He admitted that Madam Luck had been with him because a row of bushes had eased his fall and probably why he had no broken bones.

"Okay," I said, *"so what happens now? De Vere or whoever, has tried to kill you and put Pearl's life at risk. You can't sit back and wait to see what happens next, you have to do something. And that something, logically ...is to tell the police what is going on...you owe it to Dilly?"* I pleaded.

"I thought you'd told the police" Karl began, *"and so all evening I've been expecting them to come knocking on my door. Now you say you've made an anonymous call... so what will happen now?"* He lay back and stared at the ceiling. I followed his gaze, clinging to the lampshade was a small, bright green lizard, patiently waiting for an

351

unsuspecting insect. *"They will pick up the two guys on the boat,"* Karl continued, *"one or both will give them De Vere's name, and he'll get picked up. And that's where it will end because De Vere won't talk. So what I'm saying man, maybe I will be off the hook, no need to tell the police."* Karl looked appealing at me, *"You don't look convinced?"*

"Don't you think if De Vere is arrested, he would tell them you were involved - just out of spite, he'd think you had organised Pearl's release, so why should you get off?" I suggested.

"Maybe he'd think, I'd talk too much."

"But you said, you don't know anything about the organisation above De Vere?" I argued.

Karl looked glum: *"I don't."* We sat in silence for a few moments, battling with the dilemma.

"Listen," I eventually said. *"I know this British policeman who lives here in Somerset but works at the headquarters, at Prospect. Would you talk to him and see what he advises."*

Karl thought about it but eventually shook his head: *"Tell you what man, if De Vere gets arrested, I'll talk to your policeman... till then I'm saying nothing."*

"But if De Vere isn't arrested, he'll come looking for you because of what happened tonight!" I almost shouted, I was exasperated at Karl's stubbornness. *"Talk to this policeman... it's the lesser evil."*

I chipped away for another half an hour before Karl finally capitulated and agreed to meet Henderson at my house as soon as possible. It was late and once Karl had left I fell into bed, the emotional trauma of Pearl's abduction had left me mentally and physically exhausted

*

I had trouble getting hold of Stephen Henderson the next day, he was out on a case, I was told. I left messages for him to call me back but he didn't. In the evening I watched the news read by the perennial Canadian newsreader, a homely, elderly man called Wilf Davidson but nothing was said about any police activity and I wondered if the two men had been found? When the news finished I tried calling Stephen Henderson's home again. This time he replied, apologising that he had only just arrived home. I told him I had news about the drug issue that we had discussed, that there had been developments and asked if we could meet. The following day, Thursday, was not possible: he said, could it wait until Friday? I agreed and arranged for him to come to my house about seven in the evening.

Marsha telephoned later that evening saying that she had spoken Dilly and learned of Pearl's ordeal. She was utterly horrified and wanted to know more about the part I had played. I said it wasn't something to discuss over the phone, so she suggested meeting the next day. She was going to be at the Princess Hotel, halfway between where I lived and Hamilton. She had a business dinner there but should be free about nine o'clock. Before we hung up I cautiously asked if she could find out if the police had raided Georgie Girl, the boat where Pearl had been held, or arrested anyone? But please, I pleaded, don't say anything about the abduction or my involvement. This stimulated a rash of questions but I begged her to wait until tomorrow, when I would explain everything.

Chapter 8
March, 1973

After school on Thursday I went round to see Dilly, she had spent the afternoon at the hospital and had received another blood transfusion. She was almost literally skipping around her kitchen, claiming the blood must have belonged to an athlete or even the Big Dipper himself. *"What are you talking about woman?"* I asked.

"The Big Dipper, you know, Wilt Chamberlain? ...L.A. Lakers?.. Basketball? ...Where's you bin... you ignorant Englishman?" she laughed and poured tea from a fancy teapot that I had bought her several weeks ago.

"I know all about Wilt Chamberlain," I said, *"just didn't know his nickname. Anyway... why the Big Dipper?"*

"Man... he was seven feet one or two inches tall... so he had to dip his head to get through doors, everyone knows that!" I said nothing, drank my tea and pulled faces at her.

Before I had finished the girls arrived from school. *"You're early,"* I said, as Pearl dumped herself in my lap throwing an arm around my neck.

"Eggy's picking them up from school," said Dilly giving me a knowing look. *"Just to be on the safe side."*

I swallowed hard, remembering that Eggy was in on the drug scene. I cursed myself for not remembering to ask Karl what his friend thought of the extra demands and made a mental note to ask if he could be trusted. *"How are you bruises?"* I asked, taking Pearl's hand.

"They're okay, stopped hurting," she said, slipped off my knee and disappeared into a bedroom.

"Is she really okay?" I said to Dilly.

"She's being strong," replied Dilly. *" We had a long chat about it, underneath she's still real scared… that man… that man was capable of…"* She stopped, not trusting herself to voice her thoughts. *" Oh Jack. It could have been so much worse… he'd started… touching her."* She gulped, hiding a deep sob. *" Ten years old…. He's sick. I'm sorry you didn't kill him."*

*

Later that evening I took my bike and rode to the Princess Hotel, perched on the top of a hill with fabulous views over the Great Sound and Hamilton to the north and the open ocean to the south. I parked my bike and wandered into the lobby, I was early. I made my way to a bar and settled down on a thickly padded armchair among the rich and famous. A waiter appeared from nowhere and I ordered a beer. A few moments later, he returned with the beer and a bowl of assorted nuts and asking for my room number. It was about nine fifteen when I spotted Marsha entering the bar, she was wearing a smart business suit, a purple coloured chiffon scarf tied round her neck. She saw me almost immediately and waved: *"Sorry I'm late,"* she gushed. *"I've had to desert them."*

"Them?" I asked, hugging her and planting a kiss behind her ear.

"Lewis Lane… you know, you met him… and a couple of his business acquaintances."

"It's great to see you," I said, *"you look fantastic."*

"Stop it Jack Cross, I've had a very long day, my feet are killing me and I could drop off to sleep in this very chair." So saying she dropped into the deep armchair and stretched out her endless legs. The waiter appeared and she order fizzy water. *"I've drunk enough expensive wine for one night,"* she said, raising her eyebrows. *"Now tell me about what happened. All Dilly said was that Pearl was taken… abducted…and that you rescued her?"*

"That's it in a nutshell but not just me," I began. *"But tell me… were you able to find out if that boat I told you about was searched or anyone arrested?"*

"Why is that so important? But yes I found out – though that Brit Henderson put me on the spot demanding to know how I knew about the boat and who told me."

"You didn't say anything?" I asked.

"Of course not." She responded sharply.

"Well, did he?" I was desperate to know if I had a murder charge hanging over my head.

"Yes," said Marsha. *"He said they found two men bound and gagged. They were taken to the police station,*

357

quizzed and let go, pending further investigation. They told him they lived on the boat and were going to return there." I sighed with relief, as Marsha leaned forward and took my hand: "*Now tell me what happened to you and Pearl.*"

I recounted all that happened in an as matter-of-fact manner as I could muster. But gasps of astonishment and horror betrayed her emotions, as she held my hand and squeezed. "*Poor Pearl... you're sure she wasn't harmed?*"

"*We were just in time,*" I said, "*I don't think she was physically harmed... though maybe mentally scarred.*"

"*And to think those men are on the loose. Do you think they recognised you? Oh Jack, your life's in danger.*" Her eyes were moist.

"*You'll have to tell the police... you need protection.*"

I told her that Stephen Henderson was meeting Karl and me tomorrow night but for Marsha, that wasn't sufficient, she said we needed a police presence all the time.

It was almost eleven o'clock by the time we parted; we both had work tomorrow and needed to be up early. Riding back to Somerset, with the warm breeze in my face, I felt uneasy and knew I was in danger. I felt certain the villains would know where Karl lived but surely they had no idea I was a neighbour. I was still pondering the problem, as I freewheeled onto the grass outside my house and quietly parked the bike on its stand. Once inside I checked all the windows, they would be easy to force open. I decided to make it difficult and tied string to the handles of each, from which I suspended empty beer cans, which would rattle against the window, if anyone tried to open them. I turned my attention to the doors, front and rear and again with

358

string and cans constructed simple booby-traps. It was well after midnight before I fell into bed but not before placing a baseball bat that I had once brought from school, under the bed, within easy reach.

*

The buzzing alarm at six o'clock startled me into wakefulness, I'm alive I thought, no one had tried to get in. Just as well, for I had slept so soundly, I wasn't convinced that I would have even heard an intruder.

I saw Eloise briefly at school, as I took my class to the hall for their music lesson and we agreed to meet at Mangrove Bay Wharf at ten o'clock on Saturday morning, the forecast she added was for a bright, sunny day. I had football practice when school ended, after which I strolled home admiring the purple and white Morning Glory flowers growing in profusion at the side of the road and a neighbour's tree loaded with delicious looking limes. The girls were playing French-cricket outside their house when I arrived and I was persuaded to join in but after a while I made excuses and went inside and tidied up, making sure to hide my booby-traps behind the curtains.

It was almost seven-fifteen when Stephen Henderson knocked on my door, he apologised, explaining that he had trouble locating the house. I settled him into a chair with a beer and began to explain why I had asked him to come. *"I have persuaded my friend to talk to you about his problem and to ask for your advice."* I said. *"I really believe that his life is in danger and probably that of his family too."*

"He should have come to the station," replied Henderson.

"Yes, you and I know that, but he is very apprehensive," I added. *"I don't want to say any more, I want him to give you his perspective."* I had primed Karl to come at seven-thirty, I glanced at my watch. *"He'll be here soon,"* I said.

"You asked me about getting someone to come to school and talk to the kids about drugs," Henderson said, *"it's been agreed in principle but I haven't been able to get anyone to commit to a date yet,"* he continued. *"I didn't want you to think that I had forgotten."* I nodded and thanked him.

There was a knock on the door and Karl let himself in. I introduced him to Henderson and he lowered himself gingerly into a chair.

"Looks like you've been in the wars, did you come off your bike?" asked Henderson, looking closely at the sling and plaster on Karl's head.

"Could say that," said Karl.

"It's part of the reason why Karl wants to talk to you," I interrupted, *"someone purposely tried to run him over. Go on, tell him Karl."*

With a great deal of prodding on my part, Karl eventually spelled out his problem, how he been more or less blackmailed into making deliveries, with threats to his wife and children. How he twice had been attacked with a knife and the last time how a man had pulled a gun on him and he had to swim for his life. And then, he said, waving his damaged arm, a couple of days ago someone had tried to run him over. So far he hadn't mentioned Pearl - that would mean explaining about my involvement.

360

Henderson listened intently, his face expressionless. When Karl came to the end of his story, Henderson pulled a small notebook from his shirt pocket. *"I'll need the names,"* he said.

Karl looked at me and I nodded. He took a deep breath: *"De Vere is the guy in charge, he works at Cambridge Beaches."* Karl listed some of the other names and Henderson dutifully wrote them down in his book. *"Then there's the two guys on the boat at Red Hole. One's Earl Boon?"*

"Never heard of him," said Henderson.

"Reno, " continued Karl, *"a Portuguese guy, don't know his other name, he also seems to live on the boat."*

"Ah ...my old friend Reno Alvarez," Henderson said. *"Until the other night I hadn't seen him for a while. Nasty piece of work. Fancies himself with a knife. Once told me he'd been part of knife throwing act in a circus."*

"He's the one that stuck a knife in my hand, I had to get it fixed at the hospital," Karl complained.

Henderson nodded. *" Sounds like my old friend. Lucky it was only your hand."*

"I think Karl and his family are in danger," I said. *"Is there anything you can do about that? Some kind of protection?"*

"I'll speak to my boss," said Henderson getting to his feet. *"In the meantime keep quiet about this, I won't see my boss until Monday and then I'll call you. He might want to see you, Karl, to help set up some kind of sting. See how many we can catch in the net at one go."* He grinned, thanked me for the beer and made for the door.

After Henderson had gone, Karl and I discussed possible outcomes. I wasn't convinced Henderson had been the right person to speak to and it would be a further two or three days before he saw his boss. *"You didn't mention Eggy,"* I said when we had exhausted discussing Henderson.

"Eggy's a friend," replied Karl defensively.

"But can he be trusted?" I asked.

"Of course, he's a friend, I trust him."

"Why is he involved?" I asked.

"Same reason as me… to protect his family." Karl said. *"Listen, he has a boy and the boy got into drugs, Eggy threatened De Vere he'd go to the police and De Vere said that he'd tell the police the boy was dealing. They'd got photographs of him under the influence and pictures that looked like he was dealing. They offered Eggy the photos if he'd do a little delivery work… and so he does because he knows they kept the negatives!"*

"Doesn't sound very convincing," I said.

"You ain't got kids," snarled Karl. *"Most parents I know would do anything for their kids… especially to keep them out of prison!"* Not knowing all the facts, I dropped the matter, hoping that Karl's trust in his friend was justified. A few minutes later, we parted both promising to be on our guard. Karl explained that tomorrow he was borrowing his sister-in-law's Alsatian dog - I told him I would be out most of the day boating with a friend.

*

Saturday March 3rd, 1973 is etched on my mind as the most terrifying day of my life – a day when I almost lost both my life and my sanity. That date is a landmark, all my experiences before and after are measured from that fateful Saturday. It began so beautifully, an unseasonably warm, sunny morning. A happy, cheerful ride to Mangrove Bay Wharf, a hug and a kiss from Eloise and a gentle calm cruise into the ocean straight out from Ireland Island, the most westerly tip of Bermuda. I was impressed how Eloise picked her way between the reefs and she looked so at home behind the wheel of her powerful craft. Once we were out of the sight of land Eloise slowed the vessel and began looking around, she consulted a chart and then her instruments and eventually proclaimed: "*We are here, can you drop the anchor.*" I hurried to the bow and unfastened the anchor chain. Once she was satisfied we were secure she said: "*There's a wonderful reef here I'd love you to see, get your mask and snorkel.*"

I pulled my shirt over my head and stripped off my shorts, I had bathing trunks underneath. Eloise was perched on the top of the ladder at the stern pulling on a pair of flippers, bronzed and athletic in a one piece costume. When she saw I was following she dropped into the sea, the azure water piling over her head. She emerged spluttering and pulled on a mask, laughing: "*I think the word is invigorating,*" she yelled.

"*You mean cold,*" I said, dipping in a toe before squeezing my feet into a pair of flippers.

"*It's fine once you're in,*" she smiled. "*Come on... be brave.*"

I took a deep breath and dropped into the water and emerged feigning agony: "*It's perishing,*" I complained.

"You'll soon adjust," said Eloise, *"get your mask on. I'm going to show you a wonderful new world."* With that, Eloise struck off with a powerful stroke away from the boat. Having adjusted my goggles, I followed. After a few moments we glided over a wonderful shallow reef, covered with different varieties of coral, around which a multitude of fish darted and danced.

On one side, the reef dropped vertically out of sight and for what seemed like an age, we dived down the side of the reef, exploring the wide variety of marine life. Treading water gently at the surface, Eloise asked if I had ever seen anything like it - I had to admit that I hadn't. My previous snorkelling expeditions had been confined to the sandy-bottomed bay nearest to my home. We set off again down the side of the reef where I spotted a vivid green Moray Eel poking his head out of a crevasse in the rocks. A shoal of barracuda sailed ominously by, intent on a mission, judging by the collective gleam in their eyes. Suddenly Eloise was signalling to me and I kicked my way to her side. She pointed to a pair of tiny sea horses before kicking to the surface where she pulled the snorkel from her mouth: *"I've been making a collection of photographs of marine life,"* she spluttered. *" I haven't got a good photo of sea horses. Will you wait here while I fetch my camera? Keep an eye on them, don't let them get away."* Grinning, she bit into her snorkel and kicked powerfully towards the boat. I gently trod water, watching her go. The boat was swinging gently on its mooring some thirty yards away. I watched Eloise climb aboard before diving down again to see if I could relocate the Sea Horses. Of course they had moved and I had trouble finding them. I was probably about six feet down, examining the reef wall when I was suddenly aware of a great rushing noise and then a disturbance of the water. I turned to see a huge shadow and my heart fluttered, I don't know what I was expecting but it was a boat. I clung to the reef as a pair of propellers churned viciously just above my head. The moment it passed I shot up to the surface with a sense of bewilderment. Where had the boat come from? I was convinced there were no other boats in our vicinity. I pushed the mask on to the top of my head and peered after the speeding boat, cursing at someone's stupidity. Across the stern I thought I could read Marlborough Country, I spun round - there were no other vessels in the area. It had to be Eloise - what was she thinking about. As I watched, the sleek vessel turned sharply and came towards me at great speed. I waved furiously and shouted - it was still heading straight for me. Convinced it wasn't going to stop, I grabbed at my mask and pulled it down over my eyes, scrabbling to get the snorkel in my mouth - all the time watching the boat heading straight for me. Surely it would slow? I waited as long as I dared not wanting to believe what seemed to be happening. I grabbed a huge breath and threw myself into a surface dive and kicked as hard as I could. By how much those death-dealing propellers missed me, I shall never know. Two or three yards down I grabbed hold of the reef until I could hold my breath no longer. Hand over hand I inched my way upwards until I could poke my snorkel out of the water and take a breath. Eloise and her boat were almost out of sight, I watched until all I could see was a plume of glistening spray. My heart was still pumping madly, while my muscles seemed to have collapsed to quivering, useless jelly. I was shaking, as if with a fever and my legs could not even tread water, I kept sinking. Making a great effort, I pulled the snorkel from my mouth and flipped onto my back and floated, attempting to bring some semblance of normal rhythm to my breathing. My mind was in turmoil - Eloise had just tried to kill me!

It seemed I had been right not to completely trust her, she must be in league with De Vere. Despite the disbelief, which had rapidly turned to anger, I was in a real predicament! I was miles off shore, couldn't see land and was unsure of the direction in which to swim. For the first time in my life I was facing death straight in the eye. Either a slow lingering death brought on by exhaustion, or a quick agonising death at the hands of a shark. I shuddered and then shouted a string of oaths as loud as I could, cursing Eloise to hell. But there was no one to hear - I could not have been more alone.

*

Lying on my back trying desperately to bring some sense of order to my thoughts. It crossed my mind that the furthest I had ever swum was probably about two or three hundred yards! I looked at my watch, it was twelve-forty-five, I looked at the sun, it was no longer overhead but slightly sinking. That gives me a rough direction of west, I thought. But how could I be sure? I could quite easily start swimming in the wrong direction!

I remembered once experimenting with the children how to find directions with a watch, I racked my brains trying to remember how it went. I have to point the hour-hand at the sun, or was it the minute hand? Hour-hand, I decided and then south is halfway between that and the figure twelve. I fiddled about for some time before deciding which direction was south, the direction I would need to swim. It seemed to tie in from where I had calculated west would be from the sinking sun. With no landmarks, swimming in a straight line was going to be impossible, a wave of fear and apprehension swept over me. I was suddenly overwhelmed by the silence; it was tangible, nothing but the occasional slap of a wavelet against my chest. I wedged the mask on top of my head and slowly kicked in the direction I had decided was south. If I had miscalculated I would be heading away from Bermuda and out into the open ocean. I tried to shut my mind to the possibilities and concentrated on achieving a steady breathing pattern. After a while I decided that I would stop every ten minutes and check the direction on my watch.

After twenty minutes I stopped, gently treading water and checked, if I was heading in the right direction, surely I should eventually hear motorboats returning from fishing - but at the moment only silence. The thought suddenly struck me about what might be swimming below? My head was filled with hallucinations of Great Whites with gaping jaws appearing unseen from below. I remembered the modest sized shark we had caught when out fishing - and tried to drive the thought from my head that it must have older and bigger siblings.

*

Thirty minutes later I turned on to by back and rested, the wind must have got up for small waves were now slapping into my face and the temperature seemed to have dropped. I started to consider my chances of survival; still astounded that Eloise could be such a cold-blooded killer. If she was part of the gang that was prepared to do this to me, there was no hope for Karl and his family! I rolled over, checked my watch and set out again until my legs and arms ached. I kept glancing at my watch, willing the minutes to pass, so that I could rest again. How could ten minutes possibly be so long, perhaps my watch had stopped? After eight minutes I gave up and rolled on to my back, despite all the effort I was cold. I started talking to myself, urging muscles to respond and not let me down. In a lucid moment I remembered reading Hemmingway's story of Santiago to the class. *The Old Man and the Sea* was one of my favourite's, which I almost knew off by heart. The children had been spellbound, as I told the story of the battle between the old man and the great fish and how the old man's body weakened and how he talked to his hands, willing them not to let him down. Now here I was, telling my legs not to cramp, my arms not to tire, my will not to weaken. I hoped that somehow, giving these instructions out loud would make them more effective.

Before setting out again, I peered round but there was nothing to see, just vast emptiness. I checked the direction using the watch and set out again heaving one tired arm over the other in something resembling the front crawl. My weary legs hardly moved, if I kicked too hard my calves protested and threatened to cramp. I knew if that happened I was in trouble.

I didn't believe there was a God; the idea was too far-fetched for my practical nature but quite unbidden, on every second stroke I found myself saying a line from the 'Lord's Prayer,' over and over again.

Despite looking at my watch at such regular intervals, the amazing thing was that I had no idea of time and absolutely no concept of how long I had been swimming. For what seemed like the thousandth *'Thy will be done,'* I was suddenly aware of a rhythmic throb of a marine engine - or was it just my imagination? I stopped and peered around - nothing! I listened carefully, trying to judge the direction. Gradually the sound ceased, though I was heartened, for the noise seemed to have come from the general direction in which I was swimming. My legs had totally given up and trailed behind paraplegic-like. My stroke had slowed and I constantly feared cramp. For a while I tried swimming on my back, kicking my useless legs, not using my arms but progress was minimal.

It was so frustrating, watching the minute's pass by and no means of telling if I had made any progress. Unwittingly, I started to review my life, cursing that I had ever come to this so-called 'sceptred-isle' set in a turquoise sea! I began feeling sorry for myself, a state guaranteed to sap one's energy. After some moments, again out loud, I began lecturing myself, telling myself to stop whinging, be thankful that the bloody woman had not succeeded in cutting my head off and to get on and swim. I checked my watch, looked at the sun and set off again.

I hadn't been going long when the throbbing of a boat engine caused me to stop and bob up and down in the water trying to see. This time the engine noise seemed much nearer. I tried shouting but soon realised I wasting my breath. I lay on my back and waved my mask and snorkel just in case someone was looking my way. Soon the engine faded into the distance but I was cheered, I may well be nearing the channel into the Great Sound used by boats returning from a day's game fishing. After going through the direction-finding routine, I pulled on my mask and once again launched into a front crawl. However, it didn't last long, my legs screamed objection and gave up the ghost. I lay on my back and floated.

I began to wonder which direction I would drift, if I just lay and floated? Would it be towards my precious Bermuda or out into the vast ocean, further debris to add to the Sargasso Sea. Once again my head was filled with questions and I began to wonder what I would say or do to Eloise, if I ever got out of this situation!

*

Fearing that I may indeed be drifting further away from land, I rolled over for the thousandth's time, pulled the mask over my eyes and began a gentle breaststroke. I don't know how long I swam, my mind was fuzzy and my limbs barely going through the motions. I was awoken from this stupor by shouting and the sight of a tuna-towered fishing boat drawing closer. I heard someone shout: *"He's alive!"* There were four men in the boat and I was soon hauled over the side, wrapped in a large towel and handed a mug containing rum. Shivering uncontrollably, I took a slug and thanked my rescuers.

Immediately I was regaled with questions of how I came to be swimming so far from the shore. Before answering, I staggered to my feet and gazed round, the tip of Ireland Island was still some distance away. My head was spinning, I couldn't tell the truth or these men would immediately call the police. I wanted to handle this my way. *"I was out on a Sunfish, when the rudder broke and I drifted out to sea. So I decided to swim back."* I lied.

The men looked at each other and pulled faces. *"Sounds a bit rash mate!"* said one of them.

"Yeh, I know. It was further than I calculated." I said. Eventually the fishing boat pulled in at Robinson's boatyard in Ely's Harbour, where one of the men offered to run me home. I took him up on the offer and inside ten minutes I was home. Before he left, I asked the man to write down his telephone number, so that I could get he and his friends together at some time and thank them properly. After he left, I dived under the shower where I tried to wash away the salt, anger and frustration before collapsing on my bed exhausted.

A couple of hours later, I awoke, grateful to have survived but still furious - and the longer I lay and considered Eloise's heartless actions the more angry I became. Eventually I eased my weary bones from the bed determined to go straight round to Eloise's house, demand an explanation before marching her off to the police station.

It took me a long time to walk from my home to Mangrove Bay Wharf, where I had left my bike. Not surprisingly, my body was seriously objecting to even more exercise. Eloise's boat was not there but her VW Beetle was, which left me puzzled. Where could she be? I didn't rush around to her cottage because I knew she was unlikely to be home but not knowing what else to do, I pottered round to Cavello and parked outside her house. I tried the door and peered through the windows, as I thought, no sign of her. I rode my bike towards the beach and sat looking out to sea, considering all possibilities. With dusk approaching, I decided to go home and try again tomorrow.

*

I didn't wake until well after nine the next morning, I had been totally exhausted, mentally and physically. I was relieved it was Sunday, another day to recover - perhaps? I rode round to Mangrove Bay Wharf and was baffled to discover Marlborough Country at its mooring and Eloise's car gone.

"*Right*," I thought, drew a deep breath and headed off towards Cavello and Eloise's home. I leaned my bike against a wall and strode purposefully towards her front door, noting that the Beetle was parked in its usual place. I hammered on the door. No response. I turned the handle - locked. I peered through the windows but could see nothing. I scrambled around the back and side of the low single-storied cottage and looked through each of the windows, she was obviously not at home. I felt a deep sense of anti-climax, I needed an explanation. I wasn't going to get one. There was nothing for it but to go home and try again later.

*

Karl was in the garden, playing cricket with the girls when I rode up onto the grass outside my home. There was an ancient, longhaired Alsatian tied to a tree; panting, ears pricked watching my every move. Karl called out and Pearl begged me to join in. Reluctantly, I agreed and before long we were involved in a highly competitive test match. Eventually when Pearl's side won, we flopped on the grass under the Casuarinas and Dilly brought out glasses of juice for everyone. While the girls were talking to their mother, Karl whispered asking if I was all right, saying I looked bushed. I nodded and changed the subject. *"I see you've got the dog,"* I said. *"What's his name?"*

"Yes, he's called, Caine... he's old but at least he'll bark if anyone tries to get in during the night." He then asked if I thought we would hear again from Stephen Henderson, the policeman? I replied that probably not until Tuesday.

At five o'clock I telephone Eloise's number but there was no reply. I then tried again, on the hour, until nine o'clock but either she wasn't home or not picking up. The adrenaline was flowing; I strode up and down the small living room anger gnawing away at my insides. Eventually I couldn't bear doing nothing and so grabbing the keys, I dived outside to my bike and rode round to Cavello. It was pitch black, few streetlights and my pathetic headlamp beam made the trip dangerous. I coasted towards Eloise's cottage, the Beetle was still parked but there were no lights from the windows and no curtains drawn. I now knew why she hadn't picked up the telephone. I moved away from the house and parked in the shadows of some palm trees. By ten-thirty, she still hadn't come home, so I reluctantly kicked the engine into life and rode home, feeling extremely disgruntled and puzzled as to her whereabouts.

I was at school early the next morning and after I had prepared my classroom for the first lessons, I headed downstairs to the staffroom. Mrs Harding was chatting with a couple of my colleagues. *"Ah Jack,"* she said. *"I'm afraid there will be no music for your class today... or this week. Miss Shaw... Eloise... is away... a death in the family."* Mrs Harding turned and headed back to her office. I was speechless - a death in the family, I thought; if Eloise had had her way, it would have been my death.

After exchanging a few words with my colleagues I made my way to the office. *"I'm really sorry to hear about Eloise's problem, did she say who had died... a close family member?"* I asked.

"An Aunt, I believe, in Florida," replied Mrs Harding.

"Did she call you herself?" I asked innocently.

"No, a man called, said he was a close friend why do you ask?"

"No particular reason," I said, *"the children will be disappointed, they enjoy their music."* I left and re-climbed the stairs to my classroom, my head full of questions. What was going on? Did Eloise think she'd killed me and had run away? Perhaps she was waiting to hear whether my body had been found, or I was reported missing, before she felt it safe to return. Bewilderment seemed to be my usual state of mind lately. Then the thought struck me, that if she learned I was still alive, she may never return?

I found it very difficult to concentrate during the school day, I went through the motions but I knew the kids had been short-changed. As soon as school finished I went home, sat inside and tried to sort out my thoughts. I didn't

374

have much time because the phone rang - it was Stephen Henderson. When I answered there was a long pause before he asked who was speaking. I assured him it was me. He apologised and asked if I could arrange for him to speak to Karl about eight o'clock that night. I told him that I thought that would be okay and if it wasn't, I would call him back.

I went in search of Karl but Dilly told me he wasn't home yet, it was almost dusk. We chatted for several moments but I could see she was busy preparing a meal and the girls were seated around the kitchen table pouring over their homework, so I didn't linger. I asked Dilly to tell Karl to come and see me after he had eaten and mouthed the word police - she nodded.

Stephen Henderson arrived dead on eight o'clock, as promised. I thought he seemed agitated and was, at first, reluctant to sit down. I pushed a can of beer into his hand and invited him to sit. *"Did you speak to your boss?"* I asked. *"Have any decisions been made?"*

"Yes, I spoke to the Chief Inspector," he replied. *"Perhaps we can wait until your friend arrives and then I'll explain."*

"Right, he shouldn't be long," I said.

Henderson swigged his beer: *"Did you have a good weekend?"* he asked. *"Do anything special?"*

I looked at him, weighing up whether or not I should tell him of my ordeal and how this business had moved up yet another notch. I cleared my throat: *"I went boating with a friend on Saturday,"* I stated flatly.

"Oh, good day to be on the water, I imagine," he replied. *"With anyone I know,"* he continued.

"Probably not," I answered, *"a colleague from work."* Nothing more was said due to a knock on the door and Karl calling out and pushing it open.

After shaking hands with us both, Karl dropped into a chair with a heavy sigh. *"Well,"* he said, turning towards Henderson, *"Are you gonna arrest me?"*

"No, we are not going to arrest you," Henderson replied seriously. *"The Chief Inspector would like you to continue what you are doing... helping the dealers. He wants to know who De Vere reports to, he needs to get further up the chain. Find out who is really responsible, he's not so interested in the tiddlers!"*

Karl grunted in disbelief. *"Help them!"* he snorted, *"They've already tried to kill me twice."*

"Karl needs protection from this lot," I interrupted. *"They're not going to forget he knocked one of their mob out cold and then had to swim for his life."*

"I did explain all this to the Chief Inspector," said Henderson, emptying his beer. *"He thought you would be able to think of some way of getting back into their good books... in return for all charges against you being dropped!"* He glanced at Karl and then at me.

"So no protection for Karl nor his family?" I said in disbelief. Henderson shook his head.

"That's akin to blackmail!" I snorted.

"Not blackmail," Henderson replied quietly, *"a chance for a criminal to get back on the right side of the law."* He nodded at Karl. *"I can assure you we will be keeping a very close eye on this man De Vere... and remember I am at the end of the telephone line and ready to*

come to your aid if needed." He stood. *"Well if you'll excuse me, I'm on duty and need to get back. Let me know if I can be of further assistance."* Henderson made his way to the door but neither of us moved. I stared at Karl, who was holding his head in his hands. When I looked towards the door, Henderson had gone.

We must have talked for another hour after Henderson had left. We wondered if his response would have been different if we had told him about Pearl's abduction - or the attempt on my life. Though I had not yet even mentioned the latter to Karl. We went round in circles but could think of no logical way forward to placate De Vere and get back to the status quo. *"It was stupid not to mention Pearl,"* Karl eventually said.

"I agree," I replied. *"That's my fault, I didn't want to explain about my involvement in her rescue. If I come clean, I feel sure the police would lay on some kind of protection for Dilly and the kids."*

"What will you do?" asked Karl. *"Call Henderson again."*

"Yes, I suppose so," I responded but then had an idea. *"When I was at the Police Headquarters I met a senior officer, I wonder if he is Henderson's boss? I think I'll go and talk to him. Things might happen faster."* Karl nodded and got to his feet, squeezed my arm in a wordless gesture of thanks and left.

I was collecting up the beer cans when the telephone rang - it was Don, my tennis partner. He wanted to know if there had been any developments concerning Pearl's abduction. I replied that not much had happened and the two men had been released before the drugs were found, by which time the two men had disappeared, he cursed in disbelief. Before our conversation ended I asked him if he was interested in going sailing on Saturday? He said he would love to, so I suggested he call the other guys and we'd make a party of it. After sorting out all the arrangements he hung up and I went to bed, only to dream again of swimming for my life, chased by several huge sharks and awakening at regular intervals in a cold sweat.

*

Between lessons, the following morning I crept into the empty staffroom and telephoned the police headquarters at Prospect, on the outskirts of Hamilton and asked for Inspector Williams. He wasn't available but I made an appointment to see him at five o'clock. As I stepped out into the corridor, Mrs Harding came out of her office. I greeted her and asked if she had any news of Eloise? *"No, nothing more since Sunday's phone call,"* she said.

"Does Miss Shaw have any relatives in Bermuda, do you know," I asked.

"Not to my knowledge" she replied, glancing down at the papers in her hand. *"Why do you ask?"*

"Well I saw her briefly on Saturday, she said nothing about leaving the Island, I just thought it a little odd."

"I'm sorry, you know as much as I do," replied Mrs Harding and set off down the corridor towards the classrooms.

"Curiousier and Curiousier," I thought and headed back to my room.

*

A few moments after five o'clock, I was shown into Inspector Williams' office at the police headquarters. I couldn't help feeling apprehensive after the trauma of my earlier visit. The Inspector rose from behind his desk and thrust out a hand. He enquired after my health, told me the enquiry concerning the two policemen was continuing and for the moment they were suspended from duty. He then wanted to know how he could help.

"*It concerns a Bermudian friend of mine, who has been blackmailed by threats to his family, by a group of thugs.*" I began. "*When I was here before, I told you that the only reason I could think of, for my being framed, was because of this friendship...do you remember?*" Whether he did or not the Inspector nodded. "*These drug dealers made further demands and my friend objected and got into an argument and was attacked with a knife. He managed to knock the man out but when another man pulled a gun he had to swim for his life - all this happened on a boat.*" I explained. "*Their response was to abduct his ten year old daughter.*" I let this sink before continuing: "*Fortunately, I had an idea where they might be holding her and managed to free her. Then my friend had another near escape, when they knocked him off his bike and tried to run him over. Again he was fortunate not to be seriously hurt.*" I decided to say nothing about Eloise's attempt to eliminate me. "*I really believe that this man and his family are in real danger and need police protection until the thugs have all been rounded up.*"

The inspector spoke for the first time: "*Why hasn't your friend come himself and explained?*" he asked.

"Initially he was scared and felt that if he came to see you that word would get out and the situation would be made worse." I began. *"But a few days ago we spoke to one of your men, who told us that his Chief Inspector wanted my friend to continue helping the thugs, while they observed and gathered information. But... that no protection for the family would be provided. At that stage the policeman didn't know about the child's abduction, so I decided I would come and explain the situation to you."*

"Who did you speak to? What was the policeman's name?" asked the Inspector.

"Henderson," I replied, *"Stephen Henderson... I'd met him socially and initially asked for his advice."*

The Inspector nodded: *"Henderson... I know him but he doesn't report to me."*

"My friend's wife is very sick, they have three small daughters and since they grabbed the eldest, he is terrified of what might happen... he really needs your help and protection," I appealed.

He nodded again: *"Right... I'll have a word with Henderson's superior officer and find out what he is aiming to do in this case and I'll certainly tell him about the child's abduction... I'll need to know more about that. I'll pass you on to one of my colleagues in a moment and he'll take your statement."*

It was dark by the time I left the police headquarters and headed for home. I was feeling much better, Inspector Williams had been very supportive and except for Eloise's involvement, he had possession of all the facts, including how we rescued Pearl from Georgie Girl and how the two

380

men we had tied up were now on the loose and probably seeking revenge. Surely now he would organise someone to keep an eye on Karl and Dilly.

*

About ten o'clock the next morning when I was in full flow to my class, trying to inspire them into some meaningful creative writing, Mrs Harding came into my classroom with a slip of paper. She explained that someone had called from the police headquarters and wanted me to call back. She gave me a very straight look.

I thanked her: *"No doubt to do with the two policemen who were suspended for trying to frame me,"* I said. She nodded and said that I should use the phone in her office while she would stay with my class. I explained what we were trying to do and left.

It was Inspector Rees Williams and a very short call. He said he needed to talk to me urgently and would come to Somerset. He then asked where and when we could meet - somewhere discreet, away from prying eyes. After a moment's thought, I suggested Sandy's parish church, Saint James, during my lunch break.

*

At twelve fifteen I parked my bike at the gate and walked up the long, straight path towards the church. The glistening spire etched against an azure sky, the white painted gravestones standing out against the background of the turquoise sea. I was wondering what had happened to precipitate this urgent meeting with the Inspector. I didn't have long to wait, for when I reached the welcome shadow of the church, I heard a car stop at the gate and Inspector

Williams came striding towards me. He was wearing khaki shorts and knee-length socks, a wide-brimmed hat pulled down over his sunglasses and carrying a small briefcase. We strolled round the back of the church where there was a weatherworn seat. We sat and he opened the briefcase and took out several sheets of paper. *"Your statement,"* he said, *"I have some questions. Firstly, tell me how you met Stephen Henderson?"* I thought for a while.

"Through a fellow teacher, Don Jeffers. I met him at Don's house here in Somerset."

"And when did you first contact him about your friend's problem?"

"Not sure about the date but when my friend, Karl, would not talk to the police for fear of repercussions, I asked Stephen for advice. He said he'd talk to his boss."

"And...?" asked the Inspector.

"Well, he didn't get back to me. He had asked me to try and gather names from Karl... but I didn't get back to him either."

"Go on," encouraged Inspector Williams.

Well it was after things started to get nasty I persuaded Karl to tell Henderson what was going on. So I invited him to my house and Karl, told him." I explained.

"And Henderson said he would talk to his Chief Inspector... is that right?" asked Williams.

"Yes... and then the next time we saw him he said that his Chief wanted Karl to keep working for the gang. But he was already in fear of his life and told Henderson that. Henderson's response was that he was sure Karl could find a way, in return for all charges being dropped."

382

The Inspector grunted. *"I spoke to Henderson's superior officer. He told me that Henderson had not said a word to him about your friend. He knew absolutely nothing about it! And nothing about this boat, which you say is where this gang keeps their drugs."*

I was puzzled and then it dawned. *"So Henderson's in with this gang then? Is that what you think?"*

"Possibly," replied the Inspector. My heart sank, who could you trust, first the two policemen, then Eloise, now Henderson? Inspector Williams took a blank sheet of paper and a pen from his briefcase: *"Right,"* he began, *"Let's go all through this again... right from the beginning."* When he was satisfied that I had nothing more to give, he closed his briefcase, focussed on the glittering panorama in front of us and sighed. *"Why aren't people just satisfied to live here?"* he said. *"Why don't they understand how fortunate they are?"* He clambered to his feet and thrust out a hand. *"I'll organise someone to keep an eye on your friend's home, though I can't do much about your friend when he's at work. Just tell him to take as many precautions as possible - and do contact me directly, if you have any further concerns."*

"What about Henderson?" I asked.

"I think we'll let him dig himself into a deeper hole before we deal with him. It would be interesting to know where he fits into the chain of command." He turned to leave.

"One other question, if I may?" I said.

"How do you know Wilberforce Marshall?" I asked.

"Oh, your yacht-owning friend," said the Inspector. *"Purely socially. His wife and mine used to serve on the*

383

same charity committee and at times both he and I got dragged in to help...why do you ask?"

"I just wondered if he could be trusted?" I said.

The Inspector laughed, cynically: *"Trust nobody is my motto, then you are never disappointed."*

*

I was quite late home on Wednesday due to after-school soccer and then a trip to the Piggly-Wiggly super-market to refill my empty fridge. After I had stacked things away, I went round to see Dilly, she was on her own, sitting at the kitchen table peeling potatoes. She looked exhausted, so I offered to put the kettle on and make tea. The girls, apparently, were with her sister. As we sipped our tea, she asked if I had heard anything from the young policeman, Karl had told her about. I shook my head, deciding there was no need to worry her with what I had learned from Inspector Williams. I did tell her that I had spoken with someone else at Police Headquarters and had been reassured a policeman would be keeping an eye out for her and her family.

I told her that I was taking friends out sailing on Crazy Dream on Saturday and tried to persuade her to come. She declined but suggested I ask Karl, saying that he needed a break from worrying about her and the kids but after he arrived home and I put the idea to him, he cried off, saying he needed to spend time with the family, though I'm sure he was thinking more about the two villains seeking revenge.

Later that evening I made two telephone calls, the first to Wilber Marshall and asked permission to take Crazy Dream out sailing on Saturday. In his usual manner, he began by saying that I had no need to ask but then remembered that his wife would be out all day and asked if he could come too. I explained that I had half suggested to some friends they might like to come but I could easily put them off. He wouldn't hear of it and so we arranged to meet me at the usual place but not before he had insisted on bringing all we would need for lunch. My second call was to Marsha and I invited her to join us on Saturday as well. She sighed and said that Lewis Lane and Darren Davies were in town, staying at The Hamilton Princess and she was busy with them all day Saturday, including dinner in the evening. I expressed my disappointment and she promised to call me Sunday morning, saying that perhaps we could get together later in the evening.

*

During the next two days my class was as keen as ever and a joy to be with and so time just evaporated and the horrors of my ordeal eased a little. Before we knew it, the bell rang signifying the end of the week, some students cheered, others groaned. Friday afternoon was spent on art projects and so there was lots of clearing up to do before they could escape. Eventually all was to my satisfaction, chairs were on desks and I was at the door shaking hands and wishing each child a great weekend. And as we went through this friendly ritual, none of us knew that a most dreadful plot was working towards its climax and that Saturday March 10th. 1973 would go down in history as Bermuda's darkest day!

*

Streaky grey, blue clouds tinged with red fleeting across the sky, greeted me as I left my cottage Saturday morning. As I drove towards Hamilton on my trusty bike, the wispy clouds reminded me of a woman's chiffon scarf waving in the breeze, The trip along Middle Road was relatively quiet, a pair of buses, a water truck and a couple of taxis were all I encountered. On Harbour Road I checked the Great Sound, it was fairly smooth, though an occasional white horse indicated a breeze, it looked a great day for sailing. By the time I reached the Foot Of The Lane and pulled under the trees, Don was already there. I'd brought a box of beer, strapped to the pillion seat and bottles of wine in the panniers. Don helped me load these into the dinghy, together with a box of Coke, that he had brought. I pointed out Crazy Dream to Don, the sleek yacht was gently swinging on her moorings. He whistled between clenched teeth: "*Wow, Jack! What a beauty!*" he exclaimed. I could only agree. We paddled out towards Crazy Dream and clambered aboard. I unlocked the cabin and while Don stashed the drinks in the galley and explored, I paddled back to shore. Wilber Marshall pulled his car under the trees at the same time as Charlie and Alan arrived together on Charlie's bike. I introduced Wilber to my two friends and we helped him unload three iceboxes from the boot of his car. "*Lunch!*" he had announced. It took several trips in the minuscule dinghy to get everyone and the food aboard but soon it was done and 'my crew' were busy untying buoys. The motor kicked into life and I picked our way through the multitude of tethered boats.

Once clear of the moored boats, I handed over the wheel to Wilber and called to the others to help raise the sail. I glanced across towards Red Hole, Georgie Girl's stern was towards us but there was no sign of life - I couldn't avoid an involuntary shudder. Wilber cut the engine, the huge main sail billowed, the boat heeled and we zoomed across the Great Sound, it was utterly exhilarating and the horrifying thoughts of Pearl's captivity soon faded.

For the next couple of hours we tacked back and forth across the enclosed waters of the Great Sound, with Don and I taking turns at the helm, it transpired that Don was an experienced sailor, though as he explained 'a little rusty.' Eventually Wilber announced that his stomach was rumbling, it was time to eat. He then sailed Crazy Dream close to Somerset Bridge, where Don dropped the anchor and Alan busied himself in the galley organising lunch. We were a jolly crowd and much entertained by Wilber, who was full of amusing anecdotes and in his element surrounded by attentive listeners.

As lunch drew to a close, Wilber asked if anyone had any deadlines with regard to getting home. No one had. Alan said Mildred was working late, the rest of us were free agents. Hearing this, Wilber suggested we sailed out of the Great Sound, down the South Shore and into the open ocean, we all agreed this was a good idea.

Rounding Ireland Island, close to the scene of my ordeal, I couldn't help but shiver and thank my lucky stars. I'd had several sleepless nights since that terrifying event, dreaming about what might have been. Once out in the open sea the movement of the ocean changed to a distinctive swell. Wilber ordered the sheets drawn tight and as he faced into the wind, Crazy Dream heeled so that the water was close to the rail and we literally zoomed through the waves. Wilber called for me to take the helm to get a feel the power of a sail filled with wind. The others were laughing and hanging out over the side, their backsides often dipping into the foaming waves.

With the sun sinking towards the horizon, Wilber asked me to head towards home. The sheets were eased and we made our way back towards the mouth of the Great Sound in a more genteel fashion, my buddies settled comfortably in the padded seats downing cans of beer. Once in the Great Sound and approaching Hamilton, Wilber announced to everyone how much he had enjoyed the day and said he would like to buy everyone supper. He apologised that he had an appointment for dinner at the Princess but if we tied up at Albuoy's Point adjacent to Front Street, we could eat nearby. He would go to his appointment and that we could meet up afterwards and sail back to Foot of The Lane. We thanked him, though Alan declined, saying he was happy to take a taxi home. And so it was, Crazy Dream was secured to the quay, Alan hailed a taxi and together with Wilber, we walked across the street to the nearest restaurant. Inside he shook hands with the head-waiter and told him to charge our meals to his account before wishing us well, saying he'd be back about ten-thirty.

The meal was a lively affair, the food was good, accompanied by much laughter and story-telling. Suddenly we realised that we were the only customers left in the restaurant and so bid our farewells to the staff and spilled out onto the pavement. We strolled across Front Street and made our way towards Crazy Dream, where we settled down with cans of beer to wait for Wilber. I became aware of the silhouette of a large motorboat that must have arrived while we were in the restaurant and had tied up some fifty yards or so away from us. I could just make out the figure of a man standing on the deck, while another one was standing on the quay, the glow of a cigarette occasionally lighting up his face. Front Street was deserted.

Some ten minutes later we heard a group of people coming towards us, voices were raised, as if in a minor argument. I stared and as the group passed under a dim street lamp I realised that one man was forcibly holding the arm of a woman behind her back pushing her ahead. As they hit another patch of light I realised, with a horrifying start, that the woman was Marsha and she was being frogmarched by the huge man who had once come sailing with us... Colin something or other, the bodyguard of Marsha's boss. As the group neared the large motorboat I could see that Wilber Marshall was with them and that his arm was being held by the other man who had come sailing that day: Darren Davies. The final member of the group was indeed Lewis Lane. I called quietly to the other guys to come and look and pointed out that Wilber was being forced on board, as well as a woman that I knew.

"*That guy on the quay is wielding a gun,*" whispered Don. "*What the hell's going on?*"

"*We need to do something,*" I said.

"I'll go across the road to a restaurant and phone the police," hissed Charlie, leaping up onto the quay before strolling calmly away, so as not to draw attention to himself.

The two men I had seen earlier, presumably crew, stepped up onto the quay, lit cigarettes, continually glancing up and down, as if waiting for someone, there was no sign of the others, they were presumably below deck. I tried to think what we could do if the police did not arrive before the boat left. If it hadn't been for the fact Don had seen one of the crewmen waving a gun, I would have suggested we immediately confront them, even though outnumbered. Perhaps we would need to do that anyway. I spotted Charlie crossing the grass towards us and held my breath as he flitted from tree to tree trying to keep out of sight. He was behind the trunk of the last tree that stood between him and our boat, when I watched him freeze. The reason soon became apparent: two men ran silently down Front Street, across the quay and leapt onto the boat. The two crewmen said not a word but stubbed out their cigarettes and while one went aboard, the other untied the rope holding the bow to a bollard and then, as the engine started, calmly headed for the stern and repeated the process. Nimbly, rope in hand, the crewman stepped onto the boat and as it quietly pulled away from the quay, a million-volt shock reduced me to rubble, for across the stern was the name of the boat: Marlborough Country, Eloise's boat!

The sight of the boat disappearing into the night brought me back to earth and spurred me into action, I instructed Charlie to undo the mooring ropes while I kicked the engine into life. *"Don,"* I called. *"Turn off all our lights... then get up to the bow, keep an eye on them...and make sure I don't run into anything."* I was almost motoring blind, though occasionally, Marlborough Country was silhouetted against the lights of the distant houses across the Sound.

"They seem to be heading for the other side," Don called.

There were plenty of quiet quays and jetties across there, I thought. Perhaps they had a car waiting at one of them. Fortunately the powerful motorboat was cruising quite slowly across the Sound and I had no trouble keeping, what I hoped, was a safe distance behind. There was no other activity on the water, I just wished a police-boat would appear out of the darkness demanding to know why we had no lights showing - but no such luck!

A few moments later Don called out that the other boat was slowing and we were getting a bit too close, I throttled back peering into the darkness. *"My God,"* I hissed to Charlie, who was standing by my side, *"They're heading for Red Hole!"* And sure enough, minutes later, we could just make out that Marlborough Country had pulled alongside Georgie Girl and there was a lot of movement. It was frustrating not to be able to see clearly what was going on but I couldn't get too near or they would smell a rat. There were several boats moored close by, I called out to Don and asked him to try and grab a mooring buoy so that I could switch off the engine. After much scrabbling about he succeeded in wrapping a rope round one of them and I switched off. Silence, except lapping wavelets. We huddled together and discussed out options. *"We need to know if they have Wilber and the girl aboard Georgie Girl and what they plan to do with them,"* I said, as calmly as possible. The thought of Marsha in the hands of those scumbags was causing me great distress. I asked Charlie exactly what he had said to the police. He explained that he had told them that he had seen a man and woman being forced to board a boat and the location. Unfortunately he didn't know the name of the boat when he called but the operator said she would inform a patrol car in the area and they would take a look. I nodded.

"I think there are usually police-boats about, so hopefully they passed the message on to them," I said, though I was not optimistic. Little did I know at that moment, every available policeman on the Island was busy elsewhere with other things on their mind. I fretted, agonising over the best course of action. *"The guy definitely had a gun,"* said Don, interrupting my thoughts. *"We have nothing!"*

"You're right," I replied. *"Though I do remember seeing a flare gun somewhere."* Charlie said he would try and find it, at least it would be something.

"Don," I said, *"There's nothing for it, I'll have to go for a swim. See if I can find out what they are planning."*

"Is that wise?" questioned Don. *"They haven't switched the engine off, probably not staying long."*

"Maybe it's keeping the generators going," I said, pulling off my shirt and kicking off my trainers.

"Good luck," said Don. *"We'll cause a fuss with the flare gun, if things get awkward."*

392

I slipped silently over the side and struck off towards the pool of light cast by Georgie Girl, adrenaline deadening the water's chill.

I was soon clinging to the anchor chain holding Georgie Girl in place and listened. Silence. I remembered that Eloise's boat, like Crazy Dream, had a small swimming platform at the stern, to allow easy access. I took a deep breath, let go of the chain and swam slowly round to the rear and clung to the short ladder. I shook my head clearing the water from my ears and listened. Satisfied all was quiet I pulled myself onto the platform and inch-by-inch clawed my way up the ladder leading to the deck. At the top, I cautiously peered over the gunwale. Two men were seated with their backs to me, smoking. It was the two men I had seen earlier and assumed were crew. They were muttering to one another but it was difficult to catch what they were saying. Eventually I caught a few snatches: "*Should be a calm trip to the Tower*," said one, who was then ribbed about getting seasick. And then "*D'you think they'll throw that lot down below to the sharks when we get out to the Challenger Banks?*"

"*'Spect so*," was the reply "*but not until we've had some fun with the girl, I hope!*" I peered at the outline of the speaker and was convinced he was the scoundrel who had held Pearl, I recognised the voice.

Soundlessly I slipped back into the water and swam back towards Crazy Dream. Putting the yacht between me and Marlborough Country I called Don's name in a loud whisper. He appeared immediately.

"Listen", I said. *"They're heading for the Tower at Challenger Banks. Drop Charlie off to tell the police then follow me. I'll try and slow them up."* Before he could object I took a breath, turned and swam back towards Marlborough Country.

As I struggled back onto the swimming platform there was sudden movement and quiet laughter. I peeped over the stern-rail just as the crewmen got to their feet, moved to the side and helped each of the five men aboard. I carefully descended rung by rung and crouched low on the swimming step.

"Right captain," it was Lewis Lane's voice. *"Let's not waste another moment... to the Tower."* The engine kicked into life and for a moment I considered staying where I was but realised I'd soon be spotted but the open deck also meant nowhere to hide. The only hope was to get into the cabins were I presumed Wilber and Marsha were being held.

Marlborough Country, Eloise's pride and joy, which I had last seen in daylight, as it cruised away over the horizon, leaving me to drown, was now ploughing gently across the Great Sound. It was pitch dark and although I peered I could see no sign of Crazy Dream. I needed to free Marsha and Wilber and then perhaps the three of us could cause a delay to enable Don and, or the police, to come to our rescue. I climbed the steps, peering into the darkness, watching for a chance to dash across the open deck and down the stairs to the cabins, judging from the conversation and clink of bottles, the passengers were gathered at the front of the boat. Taking a deep breath I scrambled over the stern-rail and sprinted across the deck into the stairwell - and straight into the open arms of the larger of the two crewmen. He swore and shouted, as we fell intertwined down the steep stairs leading down to the cabins. In the dim glow of a bulkhead lamp I could see the gun in his hand but before either of us could react my head hit the bottom step with a sickening thump, shooting stars filled my brain and I passed out.

*

I awoke some time later, with a sharp pain shooting across my forehead and something wet and warm trickling down the side of my face. Instinctively I went to wipe it away, only to discover I couldn't move, my hands were tied behind my back, everything hurt and throbbed. My feet too were tied and there was tape across my mouth. The powerful throb of the engine reminded me of my actions and I cursed myself for being so naive. It was pitch black in the cabin but after a great deal of effort I struggled to an upright position and leaned back against the cabin wall. For several minutes I heaved trying to free my hands, sweat ran down my face but to no avail, someone had done a good job. I tried twisting my feet in an attempt to loosen the bonds but again they were immovable. I sank back against the wall, dejected.

Suddenly a muffled female voice caused me to jump and I realised I was not alone. I grunted Marsha's name but the tape made the sound totally unintelligible. The female mumbling continued and I struggled to my feet, shuffling towards the sound. My shins caught the edge of a bed, I turned and sat, whispering loudly through the gag that Marsha should move her face towards my hands and I would remove the tape. Nothing understandable came out but my wriggling fingers soon encountered a face, which after several false starts managed to position the tape in line with my fingers, I gripped and Marsha snatched her face away, groaned and whispered grateful thanks.

I was dumfounded because although only two words were uttered I knew that this was not Marsha… but Eloise!

"Let me do the same for you," she said, her voice hoarse and shaking. *"My hands are tied behind my back, so I'm rolling over."* After a few moments the tape was successfully removed from my mouth and I turned to sit on the side of the bed, my mind whirling.

"My name's Eloise, who are you and what are you doing here?" said the voice from the darkness,

"It's Jack," I replied. *"And why did you try to drown me!"*

There was a strangled cry of disbelief, followed by gasps and sobs, *"Oh Jack, Jack, thank God, Thank God,"* she gushed. *"I thought you were dead, oh God Jack!"*

"I want to know why you deserted me…just left me to drown," I began again, trying hard to keep the furious emotion under control.

"I didn't," sobbed Eloise. *"I went back to fetch my camera but there was a man in the cabin, he used a drug… chloroform or something, to knock me out…and I've been kept a prisoner ever since."*

"A prisoner on your own boat…why?" I demanded, considering the likelihood of what she had just told me.

"It's a long story," she was still sobbing.

"Okay," I interrupted. *"let's see if we can get these damn knots undone first, then you can explain."* We moved

396

and sat back to back on the bed while I fumbled with the knots of the rope holding her wrists together. After several minutes I swore with frustration, I was getting nowhere. *"We need a knife or scissors,"* I snarled.

"The galley's the only place you might find a knife," said Eloise.

"I'd never be able to get up the stairs, with my feet tied together," I sighed.

"Why don't you have a go at the string around my feet, I've been working on the knots for hours, I'm sure they're getting looser," suggested Eloise.

I slid down the bed and once again began fumbling. *"So, this long story you mentioned, why don't you begin while I work on these knots."*

"It's hard to know where to begin," said Eloise, gulping back the tears. *"My father… you must believe this, my father, whatever his faults is at heart an honourable man."*

"Your father is an honourable man?" I interrupted. *"You told me he was drowned at sea… his widow told me he was drowned at sea?"*

"His life was in danger…my life was in danger…he had to disappear for everyone's sake," Eloise said, her voice quivering with emotion.

"I don't understand," I said.

"He was a game-fisherman, he took tourists out to catch the biggest fish he could find. He was good at his job but the money was poor, he was always hard-up and borrowing from his friends. One day a friend asked him to take him out to the Challenger Banks, but it turned out it

*wasn't to fish but to collect a large consignment of drugs.
He was well paid and it became a habit. Then a rival gang
decided to put Dad's boss out of business, it got nasty his
Boss disappeared presumed dead, another key player was
found with his throat cut and after Dad was beaten up and
threats made against me and his wife, he decided to
disappear. He couldn't bring himself to tell his wife, our
esteemed boss, the truth and so he just left."* Eloise paused
but I urged her to continue. *"Well somehow or other he
made it down to the Turks & Caicos and tried to start a new
life. At holiday times I would go and stay with him but on
one occasion I was followed and he was threatened that if he
didn't start delivering drugs for them I would die. It's more
complicated than that but anyway he agreed to transport
drugs from the Turks to Bermuda waters on condition they
would leave me and his wife alone."*

"So why are you a prisoner?" I questioned.

*"Well Dad stopped delivering because the local
authorities starting getting suspicious and he was worried
they were on to him. He also wanted to use it as an excuse
to stop working for the crooks. The big boss in Miami was
furious."*

"You mean Lewis Lane?" I asked.

"Yes, how do you know about him?" asked a puzzled
Eloise.

"I've met him," I said. *"He's on this boat...anyway go
on with your story"*

Eloise groaned. *"He's wicked,"* she said. *"Once
again they threatened Dad. They said they would kill me*

398

and to prove they are serious they are taking me to meet him out at the Argus Tower."

I groaned and flopped back on the bed: *"I can't undo the knots, it's a knife job, I'll have to try and climb the stairs to the galley."*

"Wait," said Eloise. *"I don't know what it is but something else big is going on, for the last couple of days everyone has been nervous, lots of whispering. They kept me prisoner for some days on an old boat, it seemed to be stuffed with guns; boxes of them."*

"Guns, why guns?" I wondered. *"I can also tell you Eloise,"* I said, *"that there are two other people on board being held prisoner... and two men jumped aboard the boat just as it was leaving Albuoy's Point, it seemed the others were waiting for them."*

Before we could say anything more we noticed a change in the engine note and felt the bow of the boat drop back into the water, as the boat slowed.

"What now?" I mused aloud.

"Oh Jack, I'm so afraid, especially for you - and I don't even know why you're here."

"Well that too is a long story," I echoed.

"We must get you untied or you'll have no chance." Eloise shifted round on the bed. *"You know there are tiny cabinets set into the wall around the top of the bed. I can't remember what I put in them, except books and magazines. You try your side of the bed."*

I scrambled to the head of the bed swung round and started running my fingers over the wall. A click signified that Eloise had succeeded in opening a cupboard her side.

"As I thought, books and magazines here," she said. I continued running my fingers over the panelling until I too found a knob and pulled. My hands were too big and too tightly bound to feel inside. I explained this to Eloise and she shuffled across the bed and I listened as she rummaged blindly inside the tiny cabinet. *"Eureka!"* she suddenly exclaimed. *"Damn, why didn't I think of this before - nail scissors."* She had found a pair of tiny nail scissors and a file inside a leatherette case.

"Don't drop it," I said. *"We'll never find it again."*

"Sit on the edge of the bed," ordered Eloise. *"I've got the scissors open, you feel gently for them and try to use it like a knife but be careful they have sharp points."*

It seemed to take an age before I had the blade between the skin of my wrist and the string but not before I had punctured the skin several times. Eloise held the blade still and I gently sawed.

"Come on" urged Eloise, *"the boat has stopped, they'll be down here in a moment."*

Sweat was pouring off me from the effort of keeping the blade in place, while the tension wreaked havoc on my nervous system. I heaved and pulled my arms, trying to prise them apart when suddenly the rope broke. *"Give me the scissors,"* I said to Eloise, feeling for her hands in the dark. Just as we heard voices outside the door I grabbed them, wrapped my fist around them and fell to the floor.

The two crewmen came inside and switched on the light. They took one look at my lifeless body half under the bed and turned their attention to Eloise. They heaved her onto her feet and then carried her through the door and up the stairs.

The moment they were out of sight I sliced through the binding around my ankles and dived through the door and turned the knob of the other cabin. It opened to reveal Marsha and Wilber lying side by side on a bed. Both were tied hand and foot with tape across their mouths, Marsha's eyes were wide with wonder as she realised it was me. Quickly I rolled her on to her side and began sawing through the string around her wrists. In no time it was through. *"Keep them together, as if still tied,"* I ordered, heard voices and dived back into the other cabin and lay down on the floor.

A few moments later the two crewmen shuffled noisily down the stairs and into the other cabin, where they obviously cut the string on Wilber's feet and forced him to climb the stairs. The larger of the two men then returned to the cabin were he scooped up Marsha and carried her up to the deck. A few moments later they returned and began kicking me in the ribs ordering me to my feet. Gingerly I did as I was bid and wedged tightly between them shuffled painfully up the stairs, pretending my feet were still tied.

It was really dark out on the deck but in the starlight I could just make out a group of people; I supposed Lewis Lane and his cronies, while Wilber, Marsha, Eloise and I were squeezed between the two crewmen. Lewis Lane was holding court.

"So Mr Shaw, as you can see, we have brought someone to see you," he said.

"Dad!" sobbed Eloise pushing past the crewman.

One of the group stepped forward quickly and threw his arms around her. *"You'd better not have harmed her,"* he snarled.

"I'm okay Dad...really," said Eloise.

"She is totally unharmed Mr Shaw...this time," said Lane, his voice full of menace. *"Whether she and your 'widow' stay unharmed is entirely up to you. You keep your mouth shut...you keep working for me... you keep making the deliveries. Step out of line again and her pretty face may not be so pretty. Remember I know where you live!"* Lane turned to the others: *"Start getting aboard the other boat, while I deal with this lot."* I glanced round and noticed for the first time a huge vessel close by, it must have been the one Eloise's father had sailed up from either Florida or the Turks & Caicos Islands. I glanced around the ocean but it was too dark to see anything, I wondered where Don was and whether the police were on their way.

Lewis Lane moved towards me and pushed his face close to mine: *"Why are you here, Mr Marshall's crewman?"* he snarled and then smiled. *"You were, as they say, in the wrong place at the wrong time."* He moved towards Marsha. *"I'm really sorry Miss Rawlins, things could have been very different, I've enjoyed working with you.. You're a smart cookie."* He tried to kiss her cheek but Marsha leaned away from him. *"And Wilber...Wilber Marshall, you pompous little ass. You could have made a fortune if you had played your cards right."* At that moment I heard the sound of an engine, I presumed the boat transferring the others to the larger vessel. Lane heard it too. *"You cheated me out of several million dollars, with your*

402

prissy, holier than thou actions." With each word he poked Wilber in the stomach with a sharp finger. *"Millions!"* he shouted in Wilber's ear. *"And in the end you're nothing more than...shark meat...stupid man!"*

Lane turned his back and walked to the gunwale, checking whether the small lifeboat they were using had returned. Wilber turned his head towards me and hissed: *"You and Marsha jump in the sea when I make a fuss, make for the tower."* I leaned towards Marsha: *"Be ready to jump in the sea,"* I whispered. *"Swim to the tower."*

"Shut up," yelled one of the crewmen waving his pistol at me. Lane turned and walked back in our direction, the sound of the lifeboat just audible as it made its way back.

"Right Mr Shaw, you will take this boat...and your daughter back to your base and await my next instructions. We'll just dispose of the rubbish and then we'll be on our way. Reno, come here." The guy turned to keep his gun trained on the three of us and backed up to his boss. *"Right Reno...blow their brains out!"*

"No" screamed Eloise, *"No... Dad... don't let him do it."*

"Reno... do it," shouted Lane.

"Wait," said Wilber. *"There's no need to kill these young people,"* he was shuffling forward an inch at a time towards Reno. *"Lane, these young people are no threat to you...let them live."*

I touched Marsha's hand and hissed: *"Get ready to jump."*

"Lane be reasonable, be a human being for once," urged Wilber gasping with the strain of it all.

"Reno...shoot the old fool!" yelled Lane.

By the time Reno pulled the trigger and the crashing sound of the gun echoed across the empty sea Wilber was almost touching him, which gave Marsha and me half a second to turn and throw ourselves over the side. The last sound I heard was Eloise screaming *"Nooooooooo,"* before the sea-water closed over my head shutting out everything.

I swam as far as I could under water before easing up and filling my gasping lungs. The air was filled with shots as Reno fired blindly in the hope of hitting one or both of us. And then suddenly it was eerily quiet and I saw the two crewmen lift, what I supposed was Wilber's body and drop it overboard. I could not see Marsha anywhere and worried that she still had her feet tied together. I made my way towards the strange, ghostly silhouette of this extraordinary building in the middle of the ocean, that towered upwards outlining a series of buildings balanced on four legs arising almost two-hundred feet from the depths.

"This is so bizarre," I said, thinking aloud. *"This huge building stuck in the middle of nowhere!"* I circled the first leg I came to, seeking a ladder, all the time calling out Marsha's name in a loud whisper.

The sound of the lifeboat engine signified Lewis Lane had left Marlborough Country and I bobbed about, treading water, waiting to see who would leave first. Perhaps, if Lane left first, Eloise and her father might start looking for us. I could but hope.

It wasn't long before the sound of powerful engines from both boats carried towards me on the cool night air. I began to cross my fingers in hope and with surprise realised I was still gripping Eloise's nail scissors in my fist. I was not actually sure which boat left first, I think they set off together but it was only a few moments before their throbbing motors had evaporated and I was left with just the slapping noise of waves against the legs of the tower. A sense of dejection swept over me and with it exhaustion. I rolled over on to my back and floated. Every few moments I bellowed out Marsha's name but my voice seemed to lack power and I felt sure not carrying any distance.

"*Here. Jack, I'm here.*" It was Marsha calling from one of the other legs. I bellowed back, rolled over and began swimming towards the sound. After my first two or three strokes I saw the first shark's fin slice through the water towards the spot where Wilber body had been dropped - and then a second fin and the water heaved and swirled. I put my head down and swam with all my strength. Marsha was hanging from the lower rung of a ladder.

"*Thank God,*" I gasped and awkwardly hugged her. "*Ease up a step and I'll cut the rope round your ankles,*" I ordered. It wasn't easy but eventually her feet were free and she started off up the ladder, with me one rung behind, grateful to be away from the voracious creatures no doubt reducing poor Wilber to nothing. I closed my eyes trying to shut out the terrifying scene playing out in my head.

It wasn't long before we reached a platform and I was able to hug Marsha properly and hold her with my head buried in her hair, while she sobbed uncontrollably. When her shoulders had at last stopped shaking I suggested we climb up to the next platform where there were some enclosed buildings that would provide shelter. It wasn't really cold but because we wet through both of us were shivering.

At the next level there was several buildings clad in fibreglass, I tried the door of several before finding one that opened. It was empty except for a pile of sacks and canvas in one corner. Without a word we both flopped down and wrapped our arms around each other. *"I'm exhausted,"* wept Marsha.

"Me too." I replied.

"What about Wilber?" she asked.

"I saw them throw him overboard," I said.

"Poor Wilber," she sobbed, *"he saved our lives."* I nodded silently and held her close.

It was almost light when I woke with a start. I disentangled myself from Marsha's arms and legs and went outside. The sky was a kaleidoscope of pastel pre-dawn light. And in the middle of this empty sea, in full sail was Crazy Dream heading straight for the tower, I couldn't help but shed a tear of relief, *"Good old Don,"* I thought. *"What a pal!"* I went back inside the building, knelt down and kissed Marsha on the end of her nose several times until at last she started into life.

"Get up," I murmured, *"our taxi's here."*

For what seemed an age, we stood at the rail waving and shouting, unsure whether or not we had been seen. Eventually we saw a figure at the bow waving back, we had been spotted. At this point we began the long descent down the rickety ladders towards the sea. As Crazy Dream drew nearer I saw Charlie take down the sail, while Don carefully reversed the boat towards one of the Tower's legs.

406

"I'll go first," I said, descending the last steps and dropped into the sea and turned to face Marsha. *"Come on,"* I called, *"let's get you home."* Marsha dropped off the bottom step and gasped, as the cold water hit her. *"Follow me,"* I called and began swimming towards the welcome outline of Crazy Dream; fully clothed, except for her shoes, Marsha followed.

Fortunately there were towels and blankets aboard Crazy Dream and it wasn't long before we were dry and Marsha was buried under several blankets on one of the bunks. Having ensured she was comfortable, I left her saying she should try to sleep. I wrapped a blanket round my own shoulders and returned to the deck. I took over the wheel while Don calculated the co-ordinates for home, we raised the sail and were on our way. *"So what happened?"* asked Don as soon as we under way. And where's Wilber?"

"Sadly Wilber is dead," I replied. *"He was shot but his brave actions saved our lives. I'll tell you everything when I get my head straight but I need a few moments."*

Don didn't answer. We continued in silence, alone with our thoughts. The wind was behind us, the billowing spinnaker against the blueing sky.

"There's so much I don't understand," said Don, his voice empty and resigned.

"I know," I replied. *"Why is living in paradise so complicated?"*

"I didn't know it was complicated, until you showed up," he joked.

Some time later, I asked Don to take over the wheel and went to check on Marsha. As I opened the door she rolled over and poked her face above the covers. I asked how she felt? She responded that physically she was fine but her head was still a swirling vortex. I dropped onto the bed and she reached out and took my hand. *"Well Sir Galahad,"* she whispered, *"how the hell did you know where I was... I don't understand?"*

"That was the easy bit," I replied. *"I saw them bundle you onto the boat in Hamilton. But never mind that... can you talk... do you want to explain?"*

"Yes," she whispered, squeezing my hand, *"I need to talk."*

"So you had dinner with Wilber, as well as the others," I asked.

"Yes," began Marsha. *"I had worked for the bastard Lewis Lane, most of the day preparing some documents that he and Wilber Marshall were going to sign. They had a multi-million dollar deal going on... they were due to sign the papers at a meeting in the hotel before dinner."* Marsha paused for breath, muttering, *"What a bastard, may he rot in hell!"*

"He will," I said. *"We'll make sure of that... so did they sign the papers?"*

"No," replied Marsha. *"For some reason Wilber insisted we had dinner first, saying we could deal with the formalities afterwards. Then the moment dinner was finished, he said he wasn't going to sign and started making insinuations that Lane was a crook. Lane was furious but because we were in the public dining room he had to keep quiet but he kept getting more and more purple in the face, I thought he would have a heart attack. Wilber Marshall kept*

408

going on, calm as you like. Said he started to get suspicious about the source of the money, Lane was meant to be paying for this business and that he had employed a private detective to follow Lane around in Miami. He accused him of being a drug dealer, into prostitution and gambling... and that most of his money went to funding the Black Panthers in the USA and the Black Berets in Bermuda." In the dim glow cast by the bulkhead light I could see Marsha's eyes wide open, her brow furrowed. *"When Wilber said to Lane... 'I have proof'... Lane called his minder, Colin Clark. He was eating at another table. He called Clarke told him to show Marshall his gun and to take him outside. He then grabbed my arm and told me to follow."*

"As I said," I interrupted, *"I saw you all arrive and had a fit when we saw the crewmen waving guns... so we called the police but you left before they arrived... so we followed you to Red Hole. Then I managed to get onto the boat and found out they were taking you out to the Argus Tower! I told Don to tell the police and then clambered back on board but I was seen, knocked out and shut up in the other cabin!"*

Marsha pulled herself up and leaned against the bulkhead. I pushed a pillow under her head.

"So," she said, *"you were in the other cabin?"* I nodded.

"With the other woman?"

"Correct,"

"Cosy!"

"As cosy as one can be tied hand and foot," I replied with a grin.

"Who is she anyway? Asked Marsha, "she seemed to know you."

"Amazingly she is a colleague from the school where I work - and she owned the boat - or at least she said she did. Now I think it may have belonged to Lewis Lane or her father."

"Lewis Lane was threatening her and her father, if he didn't continue drug-running. Is that right?" said Marsha wearily.

"Yes, she explained to me he was trying to get out of working for Lane but Lane's men captured her to use as a bargaining tool to keep him working." I explained.

Sounds pretty bizarre to me," said Marsha

"By the way," I said. *"What happened to Lane's minder, he wasn't around?"*

"You mean Colin Clarke, no Lane sent him back to Florida by plane because he's such a lousy sailor."

A shout from Don brought me back to the present. We were approaching the channel he called and needed to take down the spinnaker. Once that was neatly packed away, I asked Don to start the engine and set about lowering the sails. Soon we were rounding Daniel's Head and shortly afterwards motored past Dockyard and into the Great Sound. As we sailed through Two Rock Passage, Don turned to me and said, *"I'm going to stop coming out with you... far too much excitement, not good for my heart!"*

"You think you have a problem," I said, slapping him on the back.

410

By the time Crazy Dream was safely moored and we were seated astride our bikes, Marsha on my pillion hanging tight, it was midday. After an emotional farewell we motored down a busy Front Street. Nothing was said as we entered Marsha's apartment, in the living room she pointed at a cabinet and said that two Brandies might be a good idea before heading straight into the shower. By the time I had drunk mine, she was in bed. I too dived under the shower and then fell naked into the bed and into her arms. We clung to each other... and slept like babies.

*

It was late afternoon when Marsha appeared at the bedroom door with a mug of tea. She was already fully dressed. We nibbled on biscuits and cheese, before she said: *"We need to report all this to the police."*

"I know," I said. *"I've been thinking the same. It'll take all day to get the story down on paper! I'm going to call and see if I can make an appointment to see Inspector Williams."* Marsha agreed this was a good idea.

At four o'clock we were shown into Rees Williams' office, he was polite but seemed very agitated. The whole Prospect Headquarters was heaving with people. *"I'm sorry,"* he said, *"I can't give you very long, we have an emergency on."* I commiserated but warned him that we had a very long tale to tell.

"Our mutual friend Wilber Marshall," I began. Inspector Williams nodded. *"He's dead... murdered!"*

*

It was seven o'clock before we had finished our tale and it was all committed to paper. We weren't far into the tale of the day's events, when the Inspector stopped us, called for a secretary and asked us to begin again, as the grisly tale was recorded in shorthand. When we had answered all the his questions and the secretary despatched to type up the report, the Inspector again asked me to confirm times and give as much information as possible about the two men who had appeared running down Front Street. I was able to give an accurate time but as to a description, that was impossible, I told him: the two men had leapt onto the boat and then the boat had left. Marsha confirmed that she had only glimpsed the two men while at Argus Tower. I asked the Inspector why he was so interested. *"You've heard that the Governor, Sir Richard Sharples, has been shot I suppose?"* he said.

Marsha and I looked at each other incredulous. *"Is he badly hurt?"* I asked.

"Dead," said the Inspector, *"and his ADC, Captain Sayers...and the dog!"*

"My God," said Marsha, her hands flying to her mouth *"what happened?"*

"It seems the Governor and his ADC went into the grounds of Government House, after dinner, to walk the dog...and someone shot them."

"Oh my God!" cried Marsha, *"how terrible...and so soon after the Police Commissioner,"* she was on the edge of her seat: *"Do you think there's a connection?"*

"Almost certainly," said the Inspector. *"I am very interested in what you said Miss Rawlins about Wilber Marshall accusing this man Lane of funding the Black Berets."*

"That's exactly what Marshall said," agreed Marsha, *"and Lane didn't deny it."*

"Since Commissioner Duckett's murder, we have been looking very closely at the workings of the Black Berets and I believe therein lies the answer... but the politicians are not happy about this becoming public knowledge... so please don't repeat what I've said. But from what you have now told me... I am even more convinced."

"But what about the two men who came running to Lane's boat and sailed off with him? Do you think they could have been the murderers? The men who killed the Governor?" I asked, puzzled.

"Possibly," replied Inspector Rees, rising to his feet; *"though more likely the brains behind the crime... it's too soon to start speculating."*

At the door Inspector Williams turned to me and said: *"By the way, I have De Vere and three others in custody. We found just enough marijuana in de Vere's apartment to hold him, while we make more enquiries... and one of the others said enough for me to arrest your so called friend, Henderson. So he's locked up too."*

Out in the courtyard, I held Marsha in my arms. *"What do we do now?"* I murmured into her hair.

"I think we should go and see Wilber Marshall's wife... and tell her," whispered Marsha.

"But the Inspector said he would send a policeman to break the news," I said.

"I know," continued Marsha, *"but we were there. I'd like her know how brave he was. He saved our lives."*

*

Madge, Wilber's wife, threw her arms around us both when she opened the door, exclaiming how worried she was…and where was Wilber? As we walked towards the sitting room, she told us how she had called the coastguard about midnight, to say her husband hadn't returned from a sailing trip and to ask if any incidents had been reported. They of course knew nothing. Earlier that morning she had called the police but they had no news. She had tried calling me but I hadn't answered. In the end a friend drove down to Foot of the Lane and reported back that Crazy Dream was safely moored. *"That made me even more anxious!"* she had exclaimed. By now we were seated and Marsha leaned across towards Madge and took her hand:

"Mrs Marshall, Madge," she whispered, *"We have some terrible news."*

*

In retrospect Madge had been amazingly restrained. Yes, she wept, she told us what a wonderful husband and friend Wilber had been. Marsha gave her a brief outline of the circumstances, emphasising how brave Wilber had been and how he had given us the chance to escape. We explained that we had told our story to the police and they had alerted the authorities in Miami. No doubt someone would come from police headquarters to tell her officially. At one stage she insisted going to the kitchen and making tea and we heard her sobbing. But when she returned with a tray, although her eyes and cheeks were wet with tears, her emotions were under control.

Eventually we left Madge, she insisted she would be all right, and that she had many phone calls to make. We promised to visit her again later in the week but insisting that if there was anything we could do, she should telephone one or both of us.

That evening we watched the television-news: it was all about the Governor's murder and how a State of Emergency had been declared, plus the fact that a group of Scotland Yard detectives had arrived from London. Nothing was said about Wilber's death.

About nine o'clock, I said I should go. I needed to get ready for tomorrow's classes. Marsha was reluctant for me to leave: *"Saturday's events have left me feeling so... empty, so vulnerable,"* she had whispered, as I kissed her farewell. *"Please stay,"* she pleaded. I did.

*

The following week passed in a haze, not just for me but also for almost the entire population of Bermuda. Most were traumatised by what happened to their island paradise, with just a few hoping that the Governor's assassination might precipitate the start of an historic constitutional change.

After school on Tuesday I invited myself into Mrs Harding's office and quietly closed the door. I had agonised whether or not to tell her but in the end decided that the fact her husband was alive may well, eventually, come out in the press. And so I decided to tell her everything about her husband and his drug-running exploits. By the time I had finished she was in floods into tears, insisting he was dead... lost at sea, the authorities had said. When I told her that I had seen him with my own eyes and that he had fled Bermuda with his daughter, she had flopped back into her chair and buried her head in her hands, quietly sobbing. Later she went home and didn't reappear until Friday, when she summoned me to her office to question me in more detail about what had happened. From her emotional reaction it was obvious she really thought he had been drowned and the fact he had deceived her was utterly devastating.

I had spent many hours thinking about Eloise, it seems I was wrong and that she hadn't tried to kill me. From her reactions, I truly believe that she cared for me. But she had told me a string of lies, covering her tracks and the fact that her father was alive. I supposed her trips to Miami to see relatives, were in fact, trips to see her father. And now, by going off with him, she had put herself on the wrong side of the law, destined to spend the rest of her life on some remote island in the Turks & Caicos. I presumed that the Miami police would eventually arrest Lewis Lane and his associates. Would they then go looking for Eloise's father? I may never know.

I had of course told Dilly and Karl that De Vere and some of his cronies were under lock and key: they were pleased to hear this news but were horrified with the events at Government House. Dilly announcing that something like this was what she feared most and it was this fear that had driven her to try and keep people from supporting the Black Berets. She pointed an accusing finger at some of the country's leading politicians, for encouraging the ideals of the Black Berets - change at any cost, to further their own political ends. She was espousing these views as we sat on Long Bay Beach. Renee and Vernee were pottering at the water's edge, while Karl was with Pearl, racing around the bay in the Sunfish. Marsha was lying with her head resting on my thigh. Dilly next to her, knees drawn up, her arms clasped around them. *"I don't care for me,"* Dilly whispered, *"it's too late... but what will happen to my girls? What sort of future does Bermuda hold?"* At this particular moment in time, it was a question that we couldn't answer, though both Marsha and I tried to reassure Dilly that all would be fine.

"People will come to their senses, life will go on." I said.

Dilly turned and looked at each of us with a piercing gaze. Her face gaunt, her eyes blackened with pain. Somehow she managed a grin: *"You know what?"* she began." *The moment I set eyes on you two, I knew you were made for each other."* She dug Marsha in the ribs, *"Am I right girl... or not?"* Marsha had no time to answer for Karl and Pearl returned and laughingly dragged the Sunfish up onto the beach.

"Think I'll take a sail," said Dilly and painfully dragged herself to her feet. *"Karl, push this load of scrap into the water for me."*

Karl did as he was told and held the boat steady, as Dilly settled herself in the stern, waved and blew each of us a kiss. He pushed the tiny boat into the surf where she pulled on the sheet and headed slowly out into the turquoise blue yonder. Marsha, Karl, Pearl and I sat in a line on the damp sand our eyes glued to the diminishing sail heading for the distant horizon, our hearts in our mouths.

"Karl," I said quietly: *"you are so privileged to have a wife like Dilly."* But my words went unheard, tears were

rolling unchecked down his cheeks, he was out there on the tiny Sunfish, alongside his wife.

Vernee the youngest of the children suddenly looked up from her task of collecting miniature shells at the water's edge and ran towards us: *"Where's Momma?"* she shouted anxiously. As one, we all pointed towards the speck of sail. *"Is she coming back?"* Vernee cried for a second time, large, bulbous tears flowing down her cheeks.

"Of course she's coming back," said Karl, a frog in his throat, grabbing his tiny daughter and pulling her into his lap, burying her in his arms: *"Of course she's coming back!"*

POSTSCRIPT

A month after the assassination of the Governor, Sir Edward Sharples, his ADC Captain Hugh Sayers of the Welsh Guards and the Great Dane, Horsa, two Hamilton supermarket managers were ambushed, tied up, shot and killed. A ten-day amnesty was declared and one-thousand, four-hundred and forty firearms were handed in. A reward of three-hundred-thousand dollars was offered for information leading to an arrest.

In July, 1973 a new governor, Sir Edwin Leather was sworn in.

In September 1973, The Bank of Bermuda was robbed of twenty-eight-thousand dollars by an armed man, later identified as Erskine Durrant (Buck) Burrows.

.

On 18th October, 1973 Burrows was arrested and charged with the murder of Sir Edward Sharples and Captain Hugh Sayers.

In February 1975 Queen Elisabeth and Prince Philip visited Bermuda.

In 1976 Burrows was tried for the murder of Police Commissioner George Duckett, he refused to plead and remained silent throughout the trial. He was convicted and sentenced to death.

At a second trial Burrows was charged, along with Larry Tacklyn, with the murder of the Governor, Sir Edward Sharples and his ADC, Captain Hugh Sayers. Burrows confessed to the murder and again sentenced to death, Larry Tacklyn was acquitted.

At a third trial Burrows and Tacklyn were charged with the murder of the two supermarket managers, both were found guilty and sentenced to death.

Burrows and Tacklyn were hanged at Casemates Prison on the 2nd December, 1977. These were the first hangings in Bermuda since the Second World War. Burrows and Tacklyn were the last men to be executed under the British legal system, anywhere in the world.

Three days of rioting following the hangings, causing an estimated two-million dollars worth of damage.

It was not until 1982 that the first case of AIDS was identified in Bermuda.

While the above facts are true, the novel is entirely fictitious.

Printed in Great Britain
by Amazon.co.uk, Ltd.,
Marston Gate.